W9-CLH-066

# Guilty as Sin
## Cathy Gillen Thacker

# *Harlequin Books*

TORONTO • NEW YORK • LONDON
AMSTERDAM • PARIS • SYDNEY • HAMBURG
STOCKHOLM • ATHENS • TOKYO • MILAN
MADRID • WARSAW • BUDAPEST • AUCKLAND

ISBN 0-373-22300-5

GUILTY AS SIN

Dear Reader,

The verdict is in: Legal thrillers are a hit. And in response to this popular demand, we give you another of Harlequin Intrigue's ongoing "Legal Thrillers."

In this new program we'll be bringing you some of your favorite stories. Stories of secret scandals and crimes of passion. Of legal eagles who battle the system...and undeniable desire.

Look for the "Legal Thriller" flash for the best in suspense!

Sincerely,

Debra Matteucci
Senior Editor and Editorial Coordinator
Harlequin Books
300 E. 42nd Street
New York, NY 10017

# He was nearly at the edge....

One more really good push and Susan would break down Jake's guard. She had to find out what was really going on.

She leaned in closer and went for broke. "You never took that hunting knife and thought about plunging it into Miss Saint Claire's heart?"

"No, I did not," Jake responded with unnerving calm.

"You never wanted her dead?"

"No!"

"You never wished your affair had never happened?" Susan asked.

Before she could do more than utter a soft, startled gasp, Jake was out of the witness stand. He had her by the shoulders. Hands tightening on her body, he brought her against him and stared down, looking as if he wanted...

Susan wasn't sure what.

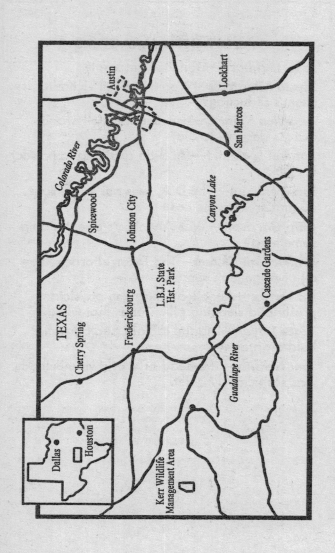

# CAST OF CHARACTERS

*Jake Lockhart*—Guilty or innocent?

*Susan Kilpatrick*—Would she fall victim to her client's seduction?

*Angelica Saint Claire*—Did the Hollywood actress deserve to die?

*Samuel Lockhart*—He'd do anything to protect his son.

*Tom Peterson*—The D.A. was out to get Jake... no matter what the cost.

*Chip Garrison*—Was Angelica's agent hiding something?

*Walter Van Cleave*—The Texas attorney knew all of Angelica's secrets.

*Dr. Torrex*—Angelica's longtime physician prescribed sleeping pills...ones that killed.

*Vince Boyer*—Did the tabloid photographer hold a grudge?

*Toni Griffith*—The head of Worldwide Pictures was suspiciously quiet.

# Prologue

His temper simmering, Jake Lockhart turned his Jeep into the Austin, Texas, motel lot and slammed to a halt in front of room number six. He saw by the white Mercedes convertible that Angelica was already there. Good. He wanted to get this over with. The sooner the better, as far as he was concerned.

She'd said she would leave the door open for him, but Jake knocked anyway. When she didn't answer, he went on in.

Lounging in the doorway of the dimly lit room, Jake scowled at what he found. The room smelled like perfumed bubble bath. A vase of fresh flowers, two glasses and a pitcher of margaritas stood on the bureau. Famed movie actress Angelica Saint-Claire lay in the center of the double bed, her tousled mane of auburn hair spread out on the pillows like a soft sexy cloud. The covers were drawn up over her breasts, and she appeared to be naked beneath them. She also appeared to be sleeping.

Jake's frown deepened. He didn't know what kind of games she was up to now, but they were coming to an end. Tonight.

He shut the door behind him and leaned against it. "Okay, Angelica." Jake crossed his arms in front of him impatiently. "I'm here. Let's get on with it."

Again she didn't move.

Jake glanced around. Angelica's expensive clothes were strewn across the cheap carpet in seductive fashion, like props on a movie set. First her shoes, near the bathroom door. Then her blazer, blouse, skirt. Stockings, bra, garter belt, panties all traced a path from bath to bed.

Angelica had never been subtle. That was part of her appeal, both before and after her movie success, but in this case the ploy was obvious and pathetic. "Look, Angelica, I'm not sleeping with you, no matter what happened in the past," Jake growled. "And if you think I am, you've got one hell of a bloodletting on your hands."

Still she didn't move.

With a sigh that was part frustration and pure anger, Jake pushed away from the door and moved toward the bed. "Enough of this, Angelica!" he said, and yanked back the bedcovers.

And that was when the real nightmare began.

# Chapter One

Susan Kilpatrick watched as Jake Lockhart assumed the witness stand. In conservative navy blue suit and tie, his starched white shirt gleaming against his suntanned skin, the handsome defendant appeared every inch the successful rancher-politician he was.

Unfortunately, Susan thought, Jake Lockhart's ruggedly handsome looks did nothing to abate the seriousness of the crime with which he had been charged. Just as his unwillingness to talk about the night in question was doing little to further his claim of innocence.

As his attorney, Susan was determined to see this changed, whether Jake wanted it or not. Judging from the scowl on his face, he wasn't going to make it easy for her. So be it. Pen in hand, Susan glanced at the notes on the legal pad in front of her. "Let's start at the beginning. How did you first meet Angelica Saint-Claire, Mr. Lockhart?"

Jake settled his six-four frame more comfortably in the chair. "We were students at the University of Texas in Austin. I was in the law school—she was an undergraduate."

"How would you characterize your relationship?"

Jake eyed Susan speculatively in a way that gave the term *hostile witness* new meaning. "We dated for several months," he allowed in a tone that said he found this whole process extremely tiresome.

"Why did you stop dating?" Susan probed, ignoring his restless impatience.

Jake shrugged. His slate gray eyes became remote. "We realized we had little in common."

Susan always knew when a defendant was hiding something from her. Realizing that what she was doing carried a hefty risk, she pressed on. "Who initiated the breakup?"

For a second, Jake Lockhart stopped evading and looked deep into her eyes. "I did," he said flatly.

"Why? Did Angelica do something to anger you?" Susan asked, watching him closely, appraising his every move.

"No." Jake compressed his lips firmly. "We just weren't suited for each other."

Susan studied Jake's dark brown hair before returning her glance to his face. "Why not?"

The chiseled, angular lines of his face grew more pronounced. "She wanted a career as an actress in Hollywood. I intended to stay here and practice law."

"But I assume there must have been some attraction," Susan persisted, trying to discover the background leading up to the crime, "or the two of you wouldn't have dated. So, what did the two of you have in common?"

"We went to some of the same parties," Jake said flatly.

Susan willed herself not to get sidetracked by the suppressed emotion seething in Jake. She wanted to get his feelings out in the open, then rein them in. "Was your relationship a romantic one?" she asked.

Jake's jaw took on a stubborn tilt. "I don't know what you mean by that," he parried lightly.

The hell he didn't, Susan thought. "Did you kiss her?"

"Yes."

So he was going to force her to get even more technical. "Did you ever stay over at her place?" Susan asked, then immediately struggled against a mental picture of Jake in bed.

"She lived in a sorority house. It wasn't permitted."

Susan consulted the notes in front of her. "Did she ever spend the night with you, then?"

Jake resented that question, too. Susan knew, however, it was one the district attorney would ask, so they might as well get it over with while she still had some control of the presentation and outcome.

"Yes, she spent the night with me."

"And did you make love with her?"

His glare was steely with resolve. "Yes."

Susan had the feeling it was taking all Jake's willpower to remain calm. Unruffled, she braced a hand on the lectern in front of her and continued, "How many times?"

"I don't know." The words were ground out.

"Once? Twice? A lot?" The room fairly crackled with electricity as she waited for him to deign to answer her.

"A lot."

Susan could buy that. What she couldn't deal with were her own conflicted feelings about Jake Lockhart. Whenever she was in the same room with him and looked into his mesmerizing slate gray eyes, listened to his soft Texas drawl, she fervently believed that he wasn't capable of the crime he was accused of. But she had learned the hard way that her instincts were seriously flawed. So she went on cold, hard, provable facts—period. Unfortunately, at the moment, the evidence—circumstantial though it might be—was all against Jake. To get him acquitted, she was going to have to blow this case wide open.

"So your relationship with Angelica Saint-Claire was a sexual one," Susan concluded coolly. Her job would be so much easier if he would just open up. She was going to have to provoke him in order to get information.

"Fourteen years ago it was," Jake stipulated carefully. "Not recently."

"Oh, I'm getting to now, Mr. Lockhart," Susan reassured him sarcastically, then gave him a smile and turned the page. "So, back to fourteen years ago. You broke up with Angelica."

"Yes."

Jake was tense again, looking as if they were headed for territory he did *not* want to discuss. Good, Susan thought. "How would you characterize the breakup?" she continued.

Given the emotional nature of her questioning, Susan half expected an explosive answer. Instead Jake just got cooler.

"Our breakup was like any other, I guess. Unfriendly."

Susan smiled, making sure her intent was as hard to define as she knew the district attorney's, Tom Peterson, would be. "And how did you feel?" she asked deferentially.

Jake narrowed his eyes at her. "Relieved."

Susan wasn't sure why, but she was relieved, too, that he hadn't been more devastated over the end of the relationship. "Why?"

"Because she expected me to party every night, and I couldn't do that."

"So you're telling the court the two of you fought while you were together," Susan said, trying to draw Jake out again.

But again he knew what her game was, and seemed determined to beat her at it. He sat up even straighter in his chair.

"I wouldn't say that," he retorted mildly.

Susan felt a prickle of annoyance. She didn't like the tables being turned on her, and now Jake was in control. "Then what would you say?" she asked.

"We hardly fought at all while we dated. When we did, it was because she was unhappy I had to study."

"And in the process neglected her?" Susan asked.

Jake shrugged, as if that were a given conclusion. "I was trying to finish law school, and after that I had to take the bar exam."

Susan was willing to bet he was just as busy with his work now, as attorney general for the state of Texas. "What about Miss Saint-Claire?" she continued. "Didn't she have to study, too?"

"By the time we started dating, fall semester of her senior year at UT, she had already made up her mind that school wasn't for her. She left a month or so after we broke up, without graduating, and went on to Hollywood."

"Were you in touch with her after she went west?"

Again Jake tensed. Susan sensed she had treaded headlong into a danger zone.

"No." Jake's answer was clipped.

"But you were aware of her move?" Susan persisted.

"We had mutual friends," he said with stoic finality. "Her name came up a few times. Later the next year, when she landed her first part in a movie, there was an article in the Austin newspaper."

"Do you know what part she played?"

Jake nodded. "She was a hooker in an action-adventure film. I don't recall the title."

Susan remembered the movie. Angelica had been both sexy and convincingly terrified as a murder victim. The part had launched her career.

"When was the next time you heard from her?" Susan asked.

Jake's face became shadowed as the talk turned closer to the murder. "When she returned to Austin eleven days ago. She called me and asked to get together."

Now they were getting to the incriminating evidence again, Susan thought. "To renew your love affair?"

Jake sighed. "She knew I was not interested in her in that way," he said.

Susan was very aware he had sidestepped the question, not answered it directly. An important distinction. "But you went to see her anyway?" she pressed.

Jake's shoulders tensed beneath the fine wool of his suit. "As a friend."

Jake didn't look or talk as if he considered Angelica his friend, Susan thought. "Was this the first time she called you?" Susan asked, knowing there had been a good three dozen calls between them from the time Angelica had arrived in Austin until she was murdered three days later.

"It was the first time I spoke to her," Jake corrected.

"Meaning what? She called prior to that?"

"Yes."

"And you chose not to take her calls?" Susan sensed his displeasure with her question, even though his expression didn't flicker.

"I was busy."

Yeah, right, Susan thought. She made a notation on the legal pad in front of her that this subject of the calls and visits to Angelica's hotel was a "hot button" and would eventually yield some important information.

"How many times did she call before the two of you actually spoke?" Susan asked pragmatically.

"I don't recall." Again his words were bitten out.

Susan paused. She looked at Jake and their gazes clashed. For not the first time she felt the surge of electricity between them, and the barriers Jake had erected around himself.

She wondered what it would take to break down those barriers. Where was all this hurt inside him coming from . . . if not from Angelica? And was this hurt the reason for the murder?

Aware he was waiting for her to resume her questioning, Susan smiled briskly. "Well, fortunately, Mr. Lockhart, we have all sorts of records to help us jog your memory." *And so does the district attorney,* she said to herself. "In this case, phone records for the attorney general's office."

As Susan went about the formal procedure of entering Exhibit A into evidence, Jake studied his attorney.

Although her reputation as a public defender was legendary, he had never met her prior to this case. They had both gone to UT law school, but in different years. Had they met under different circumstances Jake might have enjoyed Susan; she was an attractive woman, petite, with honey blond hair and dark blue eyes.

As it was, she set his teeth on edge.

Finished putting the information into evidence, Susan folded her arms in front of her and resumed her place behind the podium.

Referring to the phone records from Jake's office, she announced, "It says here that Angelica Saint-Claire called your office ten times on November 10. Five times on the morning of November 11. And eight more times on November 12. She left a message every time, for you to call her at the Four Seasons Hotel in Austin. Is that what you remember, also?"

"It sounds right." Jake shrugged, wishing that for once Susan weren't so damn good at her job. When the world narrowed to just the two of them, as it did now, he found it hard to keep his guard up. "I wasn't counting Angelica's calls," Jake added prosaically.

Susan marched back and forth in front of the podium, her heels clicking on the polished parquet floor. "I bet you weren't," she murmured provokingly, just loud enough for Jake to hear.

She turned to face him, her gloriously tousled mane of hair moving as she did. The side-swept feathered bangs framed her piquant oval face.

Surveying her with subdued lassitude, Jake couldn't help but note how fair her skin was, or how soft her lips looked. Susan didn't wear a lot of makeup. Her cheeks had a natural color; her eyelashes were long and spiky. The ultrasuede evergreen suit was businesslike, yet soft looking to the touch. She also had great legs, Jake noted, taking in the trim skirt that stopped just above her knees. Now, if only he could communicate to her when to back off and let the circumstantial nature of his high-profile case hang itself, maybe they'd be friends one day after all.

Susan waited until Jake returned his gaze to her face before she resumed questioning. "But you were aware that Angelica was calling and that the matter she wished to speak to you about was quite urgent, were you not?"

"Everything in Angelica's life was always urgent. The word meant nothing," Jake said.

"Then why did you call her back?" Susan asked.

Because Angelica wasn't going to give up, Jake thought. "From the number of calls, I deduced it was important," Jake said.

"And was it—important?" Susan asked.

Jake shrugged. What the hell could he say to that? That he'd had the most unsettling conversation in his life with Angelica that first night in her hotel room, followed by another marathon session the next day?

"She'd had a lot of changes in her life and was having trouble dealing with her newfound fame. She knew that as attorney general I also lived in the public eye, and she sought my advice on how to handle things better."

"I see." Susan arched a brow. "She came all the way to Austin for that? Couldn't she have just called you on the phone?"

*Damn you, Susan, for pointing that out.* "She could have," Jake said tersely. "She chose not to."

Susan regarded him thoughtfully. "How would you characterize your reunion?" she asked with deceptive gentleness.

Jake braced himself for the sabotage he knew was coming. He sat back in his chair on the witness stand and regarded Susan candidly. "It was like most reunions, I guess."

Susan crossed her arms in front of her. The motion pulled her suit jacket snugly across her breasts. "Did you kiss or hug her when you met?" she asked matter-of-factly, daring him to try to evade her.

"No."

Again Susan arched a brow, implying to any juror or courtroom spectator who might be watching her face a slight disbelief in his reply. "Did Angelica express a romantic interest in you that night?"

Jake paused. This was really none of Susan's, or anyone else's, damn business. Furthermore, it had nothing whatsoever to do with Angelica's murder.

"May I remind you, Mr. Lockhart," Susan said, drawing herself up to her full five feet four inches, "that you *are* on the witness stand and under oath."

Jake glared at Susan. He did not have to be reminded that his life and integrity were on the line. "She indicated she wanted to resume our affair," he admitted reluctantly.

"And how did she indicate that to you?"

"After we talked a while, I got up to leave. She stopped me at the door and started to kiss me."

"What did you do?"

Jake met Susan Kilpatrick's probing gaze with a steadfast one of his own. "I turned my head, removed her arms and stepped back," he informed the court coldly.

"And how did she react?"

Not pleasantly, Jake remembered. "She was frustrated with my lack of interest."

"I see," Susan commented, her words weighty with implication. "Did the two of you argue about it?"

Susan's glance was so presumptuous, Jake had to struggle not to clench his hands. "We discussed it."

"And?"

"And nothing. I left."

"Mmm-hmm." Susan wasn't about to let this or any other aspect of the trial go without first digging out every nitty-gritty detail. "Please tell the court exactly what was said before you left," she instructed.

Jake sighed, his patience fading fast. He had expected Susan to be on his side, but she questioned everything, taking absolutely nothing at face value. "Angelica mentioned something about going to bed together for old times' sake. I told her that was the last thing on my mind and I left."

"Were you angry when you left her hotel room that first evening?" Susan probed.

Jake struggled not to clench his jaw as he pushed the unwelcome memories away. "I felt her pass was inappropriate, considering the circumstances," he said tightly, then realized once again that in his attempt to be totally honest in his testimony, he had said far too much.

Susan made no effort to hide her interest. "And what were the circumstances?" she asked plaintively.

Jake put aside the reasons for his hurt and anger and brought his mind back to Angelica's attempt to get him into bed. "We hadn't seen each other in a long time. We weren't in love."

Susan assessed him with a narrow glance. "And are you telling the court those are the only conditions under which you would now consider an affair?"

"These days, yes."

She smiled, made another note on the legal pad in front of her. "Meaning what? That wasn't so in the past?" she inquired silkily.

"Meaning," Jake corrected, "that in my college days, I didn't understand the consequences." Never again did he want to be ruthlessly used to fulfill someone else's agenda.

"What consequences did your relationship with Angelica Saint-Claire have?" Susan asked, for a moment looking as if she wanted to understand for herself.

And Jake, to his surprise, wanted to explain at least this small part of what had gone on with Angelica.

He wanted Susan to know there was a difference between then and now. "We entered into a sexual relationship without really getting to know each other first," he said quietly. "We ended up breaking up because of that."

For a moment, Jake saw a flash of compassion in Susan's eyes. It was soon replaced by the coolness of an attorney who doubted everything he said.

"And that was the only consequence?" she challenged matter-of-factly.

No, Jake thought grimly, but it was the only outcome he was going to tell the court, the newspapers and Susan Kilpatrick about. He'd been humiliated enough as it was.

"I'll repeat the question, Mr. Lockhart," Susan said in a strident voice. "Was the breakup the only consequence of your affair with Angelica Saint-Claire?"

Jake pondered what he could say on the stand that wouldn't hurt anyone else. Finally he offered succinctly, "My grades dropped a little while I was seeing her. I had to really work to pull them up."

"Anything else?"

Jake thought back to the overworked law student he had been at the time. Aware Susan was carefully monitoring his every movement, he shrugged and said, quite honestly, "At that time, I was primarily concerned with two things—finishing law school and passing the bar exam. My dating Angelica or breaking up with her had no impact on either of those things."

"I see." Susan smiled and looked ready to go in for the kill. "How would a love affair with Angelica affect your career aspirations in the present day?"

"I don't know." Jake felt his muscles tighten. "It's a moot point, isn't it, now that she's dead?"

With effort, Jake reined himself in. Susan was getting too close to the painful truth. Nevertheless, the sarcastic edge to his tone was not going to bode well with any jury; he couldn't allow himself to lose it like that again. As it was, Susan was regarding him thoughtfully, as though she knew she had gotten to him.

"Let's go back a bit, then, to last November, Mr. Lockhart. How would a love affair with Angelica Saint-Claire have been perceived *by your political rivals?*"

Jake knew the attack he had been expecting had just begun. "I suppose they would have been envious," he replied casually. "After all, she was a beautiful woman."

"She also had a reputation for wildness, didn't she?" Susan said bluntly. "Not exactly *wife* material for the attorney general when he's up for reelection in a few months."

"As I said," Jake repeated heavily, "it's a moot point. There was no relationship between us, so it didn't matter how it was perceived by my opponents or anyone else."

Susan regarded him with faint condescension. "Let's move on to the next time you saw Angelica. That was when?"

"The following day."

"And where did you meet?"

"Her suite at the Four Seasons."

"And what happened during that meeting?"

*We argued about what she had done to hurt me,* Jake thought. Aware Susan was still waiting for an answer, he told what he could of that night. "Angelica and I talked." Bitterly, at times. "And then I told her I'd help her find a way to maintain some privacy because of her growing fame as an actress."

"Did you discuss renewing your romance again?"

"That subject didn't come up," Jake said. He hadn't allowed it.

Now that, Susan acknowledged to herself, was hard to believe. Jake was a sexy man. "Why didn't it come up?" she asked softly, studying his face for any sign of guilt.

Jake shrugged his broad shoulders. Because Angelica knew I was still angry with her, he thought. "We had established the fact I wasn't interested in an affair when she made a pass the previous evening."

Susan let her gaze roam his handsome face. Jake was smart, personable; he was also hiding a lot. She knew he didn't want to open his relationship with Angelica to public scrutiny. Unfortunately, the only way he would ever make the jury understand what had gone on with him and Angelica was by being more forthcoming.

Jake had to know that, but he wasn't doing it voluntarily. She'd grill him some more and see what she came up with. "She didn't try again? Tell you she'd always been in love with you?"

Leave it to Susan to promptly zero in on what he least wanted to reveal under oath. "She said something about desire at the time she made her move."

Susan's face lit up. "Did she say anything about still being in love with you?"

"No."

"Were you the only man who'd ever left her?" Susan asked.

"I don't know."

Susan made a notation on the page in front of her. "How long were you with her the second evening?"

"Not that long. Maybe half an hour or so."

Susan found that strange, too. The former lovers hadn't seen each other for almost fourteen years, surely they had a lot to catch up on. "Why weren't you there long?" Susan asked, letting Jake know that she wasn't giving up. She was going to find out the truth, no matter how long she had to keep Jake on the witness stand.

"I had work to do at the office."

There was more to it than that, Susan thought. "So how did you end up at the Shady Villa Motel on the outskirts of Austin the third evening?"

"Angelica requested I meet her there."

Once again, he was leaving out huge parts of the story. "That didn't seem odd to you?" Susan said. "I mean, she had a room in a luxurious hotel. Yet she drives out to an obscure low-rent motel just outside of town. I have to ask myself why. And I imagine the jurors do, too."

"Again, she wanted some privacy."

"She couldn't get that at the Four Seasons Hotel?"

"She had been recognized by other guests. They were asking for autographs."

And Jake was a public figure, easily recognized wherever he went. Susan decided to move on. "All right," she said briskly, consulting her notes. "You got there. You parked in front of room number six, next to her car. Is this correct?"

"Yes."

"Then what?"

Jake recalled, without wanting to, the fury he'd felt that night. How badly he had wanted never to have known Angelica Saint-Claire, never mind to have slept with her.

Aware Susan was waiting, he recited the facts. "I got out of my Jeep and I walked up to the motel room. I knocked. She didn't answer. So I tried the door. It was unlocked, so I went in."

"What did you see when you entered the room, Mr. Lockhart?"

"Angelica was in bed. She appeared to be sleeping."

"Did you notice anything else?"

"Her clothes were strewn about the room, in the order she would have undressed. They were arranged in a trail that led to the bed."

Susan quirked a brow. "Was that usual?"

"No."

"Was Angelica undressed on the other occasions you saw her last November?"

"I don't recall."

Bingo. Angelica was naked at least once, Susan thought. She smiled. Jake gave her a look that wavered between contempt and exasperation. "So what happened next?" she asked.

"I said something to her. She didn't move. I couldn't tell if she was pretending to be asleep or not, so I went up to her, and I—" Jake paused, his eyes darkening in anguish, as he recalled what had happened next "—I flung the covers back."

"And what did you see?"

Images rose up, vivid, haunting. He drew a shaky breath. "There was blood pooling everywhere," Jake said hoarsely. "It hadn't soaked through the blanket to the bedspread yet, but given time, it would have."

"Where was this blood coming from?"

Jake swallowed, fighting back his emotional reaction to the horror and the all-encompassing numbness accompanying it. "A deep stab wound beneath her left breast."

"Did she appear to be in pain?"

Jake shook his head, glad about that. "She was definitely unconscious, maybe already dead. Not for very long, though."

"How do you know?"

Jake clenched his jaw and recited wearily, "Because when I touched her neck to see if she had a pulse, her body was still warm."

"And then what happened?"

*I didn't think about anything. I just reacted.* "I started for the phone. I was going to call the police, but they walked in before I could even pick up the receiver, and told me to put my hands up. The next thing I knew—" Jake shrugged helplessly "—I was being read my rights and put under arrest."

"Did they tell you who had called the police?"

"Not then. Later, at the station, I learned an anonymous tip had been phoned in a mile down the road." It had been clear to him that he had been framed, but to his increasing frustration, Jake still did not know by whom.

"Do you have any idea who might have made that call?" Susan asked.

Jake shook his head.

Susan gave him an officious smile. "Let's back up again to your arrival at the motel."

Inwardly Jake swore. How many times were they going to have to go over this before someone believed him?

"Did you argue with Angelica Saint-Claire that evening when you got to the motel?"

"No, I did not." Jake made his voice as rote as the question.

"Did she ask you to sleep with her again?"

"No."

"Did she try to seduce you?"

"No."

"Or maybe threaten to tell everyone about your past love affair?"

"No." Jake held himself rigidly in check.

"You know what I think, Mr. Lockhart?"

Susan's tone turned taunting as she approached the witness stand and leaned toward him contemptuously. She was close enough for him to smell the delicate floral scent of her perfume.

"I think you were furious with Angelica for coming back into your life. I think you asked her to meet you at that motel. You told her to get lost. She refused. And then the situation turned violent."

"That isn't the way it happened," Jake insisted, his whole body taut with all he was forced to suppress.

"There was no violence between you and Miss Saint-Claire that night?"

"No." Although, Jake thought, there might have been if he had found out that she had done anything else to him.

Susan narrowed her gaze. Once again, she had the sharp sensation that he was withholding much more than he was telling. "Then how do you explain the blood on your hands and your clothes?"

"When I realized she was bleeding, I utilized what first aid I knew—putting some direct pressure on the wound."

Again Susan consulted her notes. There was a way to get him to open up here; she just had to find it. "And you said she had already been stabbed when you arrived."

"Yes."

"By whom?"

"I don't know. There was no one else there."

*Aha,* Susan thought. "Was anyone else *supposed* to meet you there?"

"No," Jake said, but abruptly he looked uneasy again. Susan made a mental note of it. What did he *not* want her to find out about that night? Was there a love triangle going on? Something worse? Knowing she would get back to that, Susan glanced once more at her pad. "But Angelica did ask you to meet her there, did she not?"

"Yes."

Susan lifted her head. "To have sex with her?"

The grim, haunted expression was back on Jake's face. "No."

"Then why was she in bed with all her clothes off?" Susan asked.

"I don't know," he repeated irritably. Although he had a few ideas about what she might have been planning.

Susan gave Jake a look that was filled with both frustration and raging disbelief. Still he refused to be drawn in, holding himself coolly aloof.

"Where's the knife that was used to kill Angelica Saint-Claire, Mr. Lockhart?" she asked, not bothering to mask the edge of derision in her voice.

"*I don't know.*" His expression could have been carved in granite.

She arched a brow. "You never saw it?"

"No," he said softly, but with quiet fury in his eyes.

She didn't have to think to push harder for the truth. Because that was what a court of law was all about. She paced back and forth. "You never held it in your hands—maybe after the murder?" she fired back for what seemed the millionth time.

"No."

Ignoring the iron authority in Jake's denial, Susan whirled on him and tried again. "How about before the murder?"

"No."

"You're telling me that you never hid the knife after the murder?"

Jake stared at her, his jaw muscle flexing. "That's exactly what I'm saying," he said flatly.

He was nearly at the edge. One more really good push, Susan thought. She would break down his guard and find out what was really going on here.

She leaned in closer, so they were face-to-face, and went for broke. "You never took that hunting knife with the very sharp edge—that knife that no one can seem to find—and maybe thought about plunging it into Miss Saint-Claire's heart?"

"No, I did not."

"You never wanted her dead?"

"No!"

"You never wanted her out of your life, never wanted for your affair to have never happened—?"

Before she could do more than utter a soft, startled gasp, Jake was out of the witness stand. He had her by the shoulders, and was shaking her unceremoniously into his arms. He brought her roughly against him and stared down at her. The only sound in the room was their mingled breaths.

Trembling, afraid of what Jake was going to do next, Susan backed up a half step and tried to wrest herself free of his implacable hold.

Realizing what he was doing, he dropped his hands. Then he moved back abruptly, still apparently absorbing the fact he had just completely lost it.

He lifted his gaze and their eyes meshed. He saw the fear in her face, and swore in a low, guttural tone. "Damn it, Susan, don't look at me like that. You have to know I didn't kill her."

With effort, she pulled herself together. "Well, then you'd better get a handle on that temper of yours," she advised him coolly. "Because this sample of direct examination that I have just given you is nothing compared with what the district attorney is going to dish out when you take the stand during your trial."

Jake blew out an exasperated breath. "I know this was just a practice session."

Her composure regained, Susan stalked closer. She regarded him grimly. "Then also know this, Jake. You explode like that just once when the real trial starts, and it's all over. You'll go to jail for the rest of your life. And there won't be a damn thing I can do to save you."

## Chapter Two

"Look," Jake said, "obviously hiring you wasn't a very good idea."

And that, Susan thought, was almost too bitterly ironic a statement to be true. Jake Lockhart asking *her* to represent him in a criminal trial! Not that he knew the connection between them. No, he had hired her because it made good political sense to be represented by a woman.

"What are you trying to say, Jake?" she asked briskly.

"That considering the way we spar—or, more to the point, don't get along—I don't want you as my lawyer."

"What is it you don't like about me, Mr. Lockhart?" Susan questioned, cleaning up. "The fact I'm a woman or that I'm audacious enough to be good at what I do, too?"

"Your being a woman has nothing to do with the way I feel about you," he said shortly.

Susan could see that. She could also see that during the mock trial session he had noticed she was a woman. "Then it must be something else, like my relentlessness when it comes to researching a case, that's irking you so much," Susan theorized.

Jake gave her a searing once-over and didn't reply.

Finally, he sighed. His expression was filled with regret as he shoved a hand through his hair. "Look, I'm sorry for snapping just now. I've been under a lot of pressure."

"Both before and after Angelica Saint-Claire died, it would seem," Susan noted.

Jake gave her another pointed glare, angered she wasn't pulling any punches with him. She was being paid to get to the truth of the matter and craft a defense. It wasn't her fault that getting information out of him was about as easy as getting blood out of a stone.

"I know how you operate, Ms. Kilpatrick. I'm not interested in a showboat defense."

"You'd prefer not to have one at all," Susan asserted coolly, as she stuffed papers in her briefcase and snapped it shut.

"You're damn right about that."

"Well, too bad, Mr. Lockhart, because you need a lawyer and you need one badly. Contrary to the judicial system in this country, which presumes you are innocent until proven guilty, the media have all but convicted you of murder. And thanks to the sloppy investigation of the district attorney, we've got a real fight on our hands."

"You don't have to tell me that," Jake growled.

"Then why aren't you helping me?" Susan asked. *And what are you still hiding?*

Once again Jake was silent, refusing to answer.

Susan continued to study him. As much as she tried to stay objective, she couldn't help but notice what an attractive man he was.

"From everything I knew about you before I took your case, I was under the impression you had an iron-clad sense of right and wrong," she said.

"I do."

"I also know you have a reputation for not making exceptions to any rule, for anyone," she remarked casually.

"That's also right."

"You're that sure of yourself?"

"I don't think I'm God, if that's what you're implying," Jake said gruffly, tossing off his suit jacket and slinging it over the back of the sofa. "But I also know that once people step over the line, it can be awfully hard to get back on the right side of the law."

"Therefore," Susan deduced slowly as she watched him undo the first button on his starched shirt and loosen the knot of his tie, "you'd just as soon see first-time offenders tried, convicted and put away."

Jake opened his collar, exposing the tanned column of his throat. "It isn't my job as attorney general to usurp the role of district attorney and go after criminal justice."

But it had been his mission once, years ago, Susan thought bitterly, to unfairly railroad Hap Kilpatrick into jail for a crime he hadn't committed. She wondered if Jake was sorry for that now. How would he feel if he knew she was Hap Kilpatrick's daughter, and that he had started a chain of events that had destroyed Susan's family?

If she wanted vengeance, she had the perfect opportunity to take it now, simply by seeing that Jake went to jail for something he didn't do. But Susan wanted to prove to herself that she was different, that she could rise above the sins of the past and win this case.

"The attorney general is the protector of the public. People come to my office with their concerns and we work to find solutions—period. I've never once considered myself above the law, Ms. Kilpatrick," he said. "Unfortunately, because I come from a wealthy family, that's often the perception people have of me."

Susan felt for Jake in that regard. She knew what it was like to grow up in the limelight, to have had to struggle for every single honor she'd earned, yet still have people look at her with suspicion and disapproval. Because she had grown up the daughter of a convicted criminal, she needed to win this case.

Knowing Jake Lockhart didn't realize who she was gave her a feeling of power, of control. She was conflicted about that, too. As the trial progressed, there would be a lot of scrutiny of her and her background. If some industrious reporter found out about her connection, her integrity might end up being questioned.

And about that, Susan had a moment of discomfort. Should she even have taken this case? Not to mention that a bad outcome could ruin her reputation. And with Jake fighting her every step of the way, a guilty verdict seemed likely. Yet the case was too challenging to pass up. Even if it meant dealing with the man she had every reason to despise.

Samuel Lockhart, Jake's father, appeared in the doorway to the living room they had briefly turned into a "courtroom."

At sixty, Jake's father looked and dressed like the powerful rancher he was. His skin was weathered from years spent in the sun, his hair white, his tall body strong and fit. In a Western-cut suit, he had a commanding presence.

Samuel watched as Susan and Jake put aside the chair and writing table used during the questioning.

Samuel looked at Jake, then turned to Susan, his blue-gray eyes thoughtful, his manner respectful. "May I have a word with you, Miss Kilpatrick?" he asked cordially in his low, raspy voice.

"Certainly." She picked up her briefcase and followed him down the hall and to the left. He led the way into his rustically deco-

rated den. Susan noted the guns on the walls, and animal tro-
phies.

Samuel got straight to the point. "Jake giving you a hard time?"

"Nothing I can't handle," Susan said coolly, as she seated herself on the end of the leather sofa.

"What was going on in there? I thought I heard shouting."

"I like to start out a case by putting my client on the witness
stand in a mock-trial setting. Jake didn't enjoy the experience."

"Well, don't worry about him. I'll make Jake see reason,"
Samuel promised gruffly. "In the meantime, I think I know who
really killed Angelica Saint-Claire."

Susan quirked an interested eyebrow. She opened her briefcase
and took out a legal pad and pen.

"I think it was her boyfriend, back in Hollywood," Samuel
continued.

"I wasn't aware she was seeing anyone there." According to the
Los Angeles police, Angelica had maintained a separate residence
in Laurel Canyon and lived there alone.

"She and her agent, Chip Garrison, were close."

"You think he might have been jealous of Angelica's relationship with Jake?"

"Angelica had no relationship with my son. Maybe just a han-
kering that wouldn't go away," Samuel said emphatically.

If that was the case—and at this point Susan wasn't taking anything at face value alone—she wondered what kind of woman Jake
did favor. "Would you have approved if Jake had told you he was
in love with Angelica?" she asked Samuel.

"You don't have to answer that, Dad," Jake said from the
doorway. He walked in and looked at Susan. "My father isn't on
trial here. I am."

"I'm not afraid to be questioned," Samuel said.

But maybe you would be, Susan thought uncomfortably, if you
knew who I really was.

"Nevertheless," Jake explained patiently to his father, "you
need to watch what you say so you don't implicate yourself."

"I don't care who is implicated as long as you are absolved of all
the trumped-up charges," Samuel said.

Susan watched Samuel pour himself a drink as Jake prowled the
room, silently shaking his head. She took the opportunity to plunge
on. "Does this mean you think Jake is innocent?" she asked
Samuel.

Samuel ignored Jake's restless presence and didn't bat an eye. "It wouldn't matter to me if he was or wasn't," Samuel vowed. "That woman was nothing but trouble for him, from the first day they met."

Susan made a few notes. "When they were in college, you mean?"

"Yes."

"Did Angelica know you did not approve of her?"

"I made it clear to her that I saw through her, on the rare occasions Jake brought her out to the ranch. She was a chameleon, used her acting ability every chance she got."

"Did you kill Angelica, Mr. Lockhart?"

"No, but I admit there were a few times I was tempted to rid the ground of her shadow and I'll say that on the witness stand, too, if you let me."

"I'll keep that in mind."

He was angry enough at the trouble the actress had caused his only son, but not stupid.

"Anything else you want to ask me?" Samuel prodded.

"I think you've said enough for one day," Jake reprimanded gruffly.

Samuel countered, looking a little hurt, "I'm just trying to help."

"I know, Dad. I know."

But all Samuel had done, she thought, was make his son more worried. Susan said, "I think we've done enough for today." She looked at Jake. "Walk me out to my car?"

"Sure."

They were silent until they had reached Susan's dark blue Cadillac Seville. "You need to discount just about everything my father said in there," Jake declared, staying a careful distance away from her.

Susan noted he had rolled up the sleeves on his shirt to just above the elbow. His muscled forearms were suntanned and dusted with dark brown hair. She was close enough to drink in the brisk masculine scent of his after-shave. "You don't think he killed her?"

"No. Dad would never hurt another human being, even unwittingly," Jake said with quiet confidence.

"How about you?" Susan asked, noting the way his eyes turned silver in the dwindling sunlight. "Would you pin the blame on someone else just to get this all over with?"

For a second, Jake was silent, contemplating her question. Looking up into his ruggedly handsome face, Susan caught her breath. Like it or not, she was physically attracted to him.

"What do you think about your father's theory that Chip Garrison, Angelica's agent, was responsible for her murder?" Susan asked.

Jake shrugged, his broad shoulders straining against the starched white fabric of his shirt. "He put a lot of pressure on Angelica."

"What kind of pressure?"

Jake compressed his lips, the angles of his face becoming more pronounced. "She was supposed to be gearing up to do promotion for her new movie, when she came to Texas. He was unhappy that she wasn't there, getting ready for her tour."

"Why did she skip out on it?"

Jake's expression became closed. He stared out at the neatly groomed ranch. "I told you," he insisted stonily. "She had a lot of stress in her life and she needed help dealing with it. The thought of going on tour was . . . frightening for her."

Susan had the feeling Jake was telling her the truth. Even so, he was still holding back as much as he was telling. "Did Angelica have any enemies that you know of?"

Jake's thick straight brows lowered like thunderclouds over his eyes. He turned back to Susan. "Angelica could be cutthroat when it came to getting what she wanted. I'm sure there are plenty of people in the movie business who resent her."

"We're going to have to bring that out during the trial," Susan warned.

"Fine. Just keep in mind, I don't want my father used as a scapegoat."

But Jake hadn't minded when her father had been used unfairly, Susan thought bitterly.

But the past was over, Susan told herself firmly. She had a case to win. She could, however, keep an eye on Jake and make sure no other unsuspecting man was railroaded into jail for a crime he didn't commit. "I'll see you at Angelica's funeral tomorrow?"

Jake nodded grimly. "I'll be there."

"Good," Susan said, shifting her briefcase to her other hand. She hadn't been sure he'd attend. "I'll stop by here first." Susan lifted her eyes to Jake's and saw nothing but unease. "I think we should go together."

THE STRING of swear words Jake uttered as he glanced out the tinted windows of the limousine and saw the huge gathering of TV crews was enough to burn the ears off a nun. He swore again at the helicopter landing just inside the cemetery gates, as Angelica's brother, Dusty, his girlfriend and Chip Garrison all stepped out. "I should have known Angelica's agent and her no-account brother would turn what should be a somber occasion into a three-ring circus with full press coverage."

Their car halted in the center of the rural central Texas cemetery. Susan grasped Jake's arm before he could exit the car. Samuel had promised to attend the memorial service and burial, but had been ill that morning. Susan had offered to ride with Jake. Now, sitting opposite him in the back of the car, she wondered if that had been such a good idea. He was like a scorpion with its tail up, ready to lash out at anything that got in his way. Nevertheless, as his attorney, it was her job to see that he didn't make things any worse for himself than they already were. "Are you okay?"

"Why wouldn't I be?"

Jake shot Susan a contentious glance. His biceps tensed beneath her grip enough to make her drop her hand.

"I don't know." She sat back slightly and tried to keep her pulse as slow and steady as it needed to be. "Perhaps because an old friend of yours is being buried today." That would be enough to upset anyone.

"I know the services will be difficult for you emotionally," she went on.

"Counselor, you have no idea."

"But you can't afford to look angry today, Jake, no matter what your feelings for Angelica were."

"Is that a fact?"

"Yes. Furthermore," Susan continued, determined to take a pragmatic approach to the grueling event ahead of them, "it would be helpful for your case if you showed a little sadness today."

His eyes shifted to hers. She found them disconcerting in their directness, oddly mesmerizing in all they hid.

"For the cameras, you mean?" he said softly.

Something about the way he looked at her took her breath away. "Yes," Susan said, abruptly aware how dry her throat was. "It wasn't my idea to have them here. Like it or not, whatever you do today will be captured on camera, so you might as well play to them."

Jake sat back in his corner of the limo. His long muscled legs flexed beneath the fine worsted wool of his suit trousers. "Maybe I just shouldn't attend the service."

Susan shook her head, keeping her eyes locked on his face. "That's not a good idea, either."

"Why not?"

The challenge in his eyes had her pulse jumping. Susan smoothed damp palms on the clinging fabric of her black jersey dress. "Because a jury would view your absence from the funeral as unfeeling."

Pewter eyes gleaming, Jake regarded her cynically. "I see. And we want to think about appearance now, above all else, don't we?" he said sarcastically.

Susan frowned. She knew she was being blunt, but someone with Jake's political sensibilities should've understood. She drew a deep breath, then flushed as his eyes tracked the discernible rise and fall of her breasts. "Jake, you're not a child."

"Damn right I'm not," he snapped, glaring at her. "So stop treating me like one!" He pushed out of the limousine.

Susan sighed. She caught up with him just as he reached the tent. A hush went over the Hollywood celebrity-studded crowd. Jake took a seat in the middle of the outdoor sanctuary, where the memorial service was to be held. Susan slipped onto a folding chair beside him.

Blissfully, the service started moments later.

It lasted for over an hour. Angelica was eulogized by many. Her agent, Chip Garrison, called her "a legend." Film exec Toni Griffith said she was "a top talent who would be missed for years to come." Her brother, Dusty, got up and told everyone, "Angelica always promised she'd grow up to become a star and she did." But no one, Susan noted, said anything of a more personal nature. Yet, Susan thought, someone had hated Angelica enough to kill her. That person had also set Jake up for the murder. Was the real murderer here with them today?

The ceremony concluded with a prayer. Immediately afterward, the crowd began breaking up. All except for a heavyset man in the front row. Dressed in a cheap black suit, black shirt and black tie, he clutched a bunch of yellow roses in his beefy hands. His head was bent; his massive shoulders were shaking with sobs.

Susan elbowed Jake and inclined her head in the direction of the mourner with the black aviator sunglasses. "Do you know who he is?"

"An aging Elvis?" Jake said, his comment directed toward the man's black pompadour and long sideburns.

"I'm serious, Jake," Susan whispered back. "I think he needs some assistance." Determined to give it, she threaded her way through the crowd of mostly dry-eyed mourners to his side. By the time she reached him, he was hunched over the flower-draped casket that had yet to be lowered into the ground.

"Sir, are you all right?" Susan said gently. "Sir?" She touched his shoulder gently, not sure he'd heard her.

The man reacted by whirling on Susan and shoving her rudely aside. Knocked off-balance, she stumbled back into Jake. He caught her against him, back to front. "Hey—!"

Still sobbing, the mourner reverently laid the crumpled roses on the flower-draped casket, then stumbled away. Slowly Jake released Susan. Still feeling a little stunned, Susan looked at Jake. "What was that all about?" she asked.

"I don't know and I don't care," Jake muttered, still standing protectively close. "Let's get the hell out of here," he said, yanking at his tie as if it were strangling him.

Susan understood his urge to flee. But she had a job to do. "You go ahead if you want," she murmured. "I'm going to hang around for a while." There were numerous people she wanted to talk with.

"Why?" Jake asked.

He was glaring down at her, looking all the more suspicious and aggravated. Aware that a crew of television reporters was heading their way, Susan flashed a composed glance. "I want to say hello to Walter Van Cleave and his wife." Walter was a family-law attorney with a prominent Austin law firm, and an acquaintance of both Jake and herself. Then she would speak with the district attorney, Tom Peterson. And perhaps Angelica's agent, as well.

Jake narrowed his gaze. "Walter's here?"

Susan nodded and pointed discreetly to a physically fit man with closely cropped, prematurely gray hair. He was holding hands with a blond socialite. Both were in their early forties. "He and his wife, Bitsy, came in a little late, I think," Susan murmured.

"I see them now. If you don't mind, I'm not really in the mood for small talk," Jake said.

"I told you you didn't have to stay. I'll catch a ride back to town with Walter," Susan said.

Jake frowned down at her distrustfully. He looked as though he were about to argue with her, when Angelica's brother, and only surviving relative, strode up to them.

Susan knew from having read Angelica's lengthy obituary that
Dusty was a decade younger than his sister and a guitarist with a
local rock band. He had long unkempt auburn hair and was wearing black jeans, a T-shirt and an ill-fitting blazer. As he drew closer
to Jake, Susan could see the fury blazing in his green eyes. Oh, here
it comes, Susan thought, their first—and she hoped only—truly
hysterical scene of the day.

"You low-down, snake-bellied, sleazy son of a bitch. How dare
you show up here!" Dusty shouted as he charged at Jake, causing
several onlookers, including Dusty's girlfriend, drummer
"Rhythm" Malone, to scream and dart out of the way of the
coming brawl.

Jake simultaneously ducked the first punch and pushed Susan
to his left, well out of harm's way. Standing his ground grimly, Jake
put both hands up to ward off future violence and said, "I don't
want to fight you, Dusty."

"Well, isn't that just too damn bad, 'cause I'm gonna wallop the
spit out of you!" he shouted back, looking completely out of
control. He charged at Jake again.

Jake grabbed Dusty by the shoulders and pushed him back. He
landed on his backside and slid along the ground. "I said I didn't
want to fight you!" Jake warned.

Dusty glared at Jake. "Fine, have it your way," he muttered as
he started to get up. Everyone around them, including Susan,
breathed a sigh of relief. Then Dusty went for Jake's knees,
knocking him off-balance. The two crashed into the chairs, Dusty
landing on top of Jake.

Having had it with Angelica's little brother, Jake grabbed him
by the shirt. Dusty's head snapped back with the force of a blow.
Jake shoved a groaning Dusty aside and stumbled to his feet.

Blood streamed from a cut on Jake's lip. "You'll pay for this,
Lockhart!" Dusty yelled. "I swear I'll make you pay for what
you've done!"

A chill went through Susan at the threat. Fortunately, two dep-
uties who had come out to direct traffic after the services were on
their way over. One hunkered down next to Dusty and talked to
him softly. Jake held up a hand, signaling there would be no more
trouble, then moved away.

Tom Peterson, the DA, walked up, looking insufferably smug in
a custom-made, three-piece suit, his blow-dried hair cemented into
place.

He drawled, "Lucky I sent out the police today, right, Jake? We wouldn't want another murder."

Susan stepped in front of Jake. It didn't take a rocket scientist to see that Tom was enjoying Jake's and Susan's discomfiture. "There've been enough scenes for one day, don't you think?" she said pointedly.

Tom just smiled. "Oh, I don't know about that. I think things are just beginning to heat up."

Susan knew Tom would do everything in his power to stir things up. But in deference to the news cameras still headed their way, he backed off. She and Jake were promptly joined by another mourner.

"Way to go," Angelica's agent said to Jake. A fiftyish man in a double-breasted Armani suit, Chip Garrison had long blond hair, worn slicked back and caught in a ponytail at his nape, and a diamond stud in one ear. "You know this could have been a dignified occasion. Of course, if not for you, then none of us—including Angelica—would be here at all!" Chip said bitterly.

"Back off," Jake growled to Chip, pressing the back of his hand to his cut lip.

"Don't worry. I have no intention of brawling with you," Chip continued glibly.

Without warning, they were joined by Walter Van Cleave and his wife. Walter stepped between Jake and Chip. "I'll take care of this," he said. Walter looked at Susan. "You two go ahead."

"Thanks," Susan said. She grabbed Jake's arm, hoping for a quick getaway. But that, too, was not to be. The reporters surged around them. In particular, Susan noticed a man in his midthirties with short carrot-colored hair. He had a camera slung around his neck, but he wasn't taking any pictures. He also looked edgy and upset.

Susan nudged Jake. "Do you know that guy over there with the red hair?"

Jake glanced at the person she indicated and shook his head. "He looks familiar. Like I've seen him before, but I can't place him." Not waiting for a response from Susan, Jake touched her waist lightly, propelling her forward. "Come on. Let's get out of here," he said impatiently.

But before they could go, the man who had been crying uncontrollably and carrying the roses stepped in front of them, barring their way to the limousine. His lip was curled in an ugly sneer as he glared at Jake. "Sinners always pay. You will be punished for what you have done," he said, very low.

Another chill went down Susan's spine. For the second time that day, she backed up swiftly, crashing into the solid warmth that was Jake. His hand went around her waist protectively. Susan felt immeasurably safer in his arms.

"Hey, you!" the cop said to the heavyset mourner menacing them. "Do you have permission to be here?"

"Mr. Garrison invited me," the man said.

"Figures," Jake mumbled. Jerking open the door of the limo, he pushed Susan inside, then climbed in after her. "Get the hell out of here!" he instructed the driver.

The car took off with a lurch. Once they had cleared the cemetery gates and were well on their way to the ranch, Susan dared a look at Jake. His mood seemed dangerous, his emotions close to the surface. Fearful of his reaction, she decided to wait until they got back to the ranch house to question him.

As the limo rolled to a halt next to her car, Jake said dismissively, "Thanks for going today. You were, uh, you were okay."

"You're welcome." *I think.* Knowing Jake wanted nothing more at that point than to simply get rid of her, Susan got out after him. Her pulse pounding, she followed him toward the house.

He spun around toward her. "You don't have to stay."

"The cut on your lip needs some attention and so does the scrape on your cheek."

"I'll handle it."

"What about the one on the back of your neck? Are you going to handle that, too?"

Jake compressed his lips. "Suit yourself."

Striding on ahead of her, he led the way ungraciously into the sprawling ranch house, through the majestic front hall and back to the brick red-and-cream kitchen. His method was effective, Susan admitted to herself; if she hadn't needed to speak to him, she would have taken the hint and left.

Once in the state-of-the-art kitchen, he got down a first-aid kit from the top shelf of a cupboard. Susan put her purse on the table and carried a wooden bar stool from the counter to the sink while Jake shrugged out of his suit jacket. Still standing over the sink, he attempted to wash off the back of his neck first. All he succeeded in doing, Susan noted dispassionately, was working the dirt more thoroughly into the long, jagged scrape.

"Sit down, Jake." Hands on his brawny shoulders, she pushed him onto the stool. "And let me do that."

For a second, she thought he was going to argue with her. His gaze lifted to meet hers. Then he gave her a long, slow, insolent once-over. Susan tingled, as if she'd been caressed. Then he ducked his head, giving her better access to the back of his neck.

"Whatever."

Whatever, indeed, Susan thought. She was not going to let him turn this into something sexy. It was the act of a Good Samaritan. That was all. "Take off your tie and undo the first two buttons on your shirt," she ordered.

He glanced up, his pewter eyes full of question and suggestion simultaneously.

Susan put to rest the notion she had anything on her mind but nursing him back to health with one arch of her brow. "I need to fold your collar down. If I try that while you still have your tie on, you really will feel like you're choking to death."

Jake unknotted his tie and tugged it off. "Shows, huh?" he said as he undid first one button, then the next. A wealth of curly golden brown hair sprang out of the open vee between shirt and skin.

"What shows?" Susan pushed up the sleeves on her long black jersey dress, and was already efficiently folding down the collar of his shirt.

"How much I hate wearing ties," he said.

"Not good for a career politician, Jake." Susan began cleaning the back of his neck. She worked gently. Even so, he winced. Finished, she soaked a cotton ball with antiseptic and dabbed the scrape. They were close enough that she could hear the meter of his breath. Aware that Jake was strong enough to kill her with his bare hands, Susan said, "Do you want a bandage on this?"

"No," he answered curtly.

She then moved around so she was standing just to the side of his spread legs. Sliding a hand beneath his chin, she tilted his face up to hers and began to treat first the scrape on his cheekbone, then the cut on his lower lip. Jake sat stock-still while she worked, his face level with hers. Deciding it might be politic to get their minds back to his predicament, Susan reared back slightly and said, "So, what do you have against Chip?"

Jake glanced at her sharply, but did not move as she reached for the antiseptic.

"He created the circus today. He crucified me in the press. He might even be Angelica's killer. Need I say more?"

Chip had also been Angelica's lover. Was it possible Jake was jealous? Susan wondered. "Are those your only reasons for resenting Chip?"

Jake caught Susan's wrist before she could apply antiseptic to his lip. "Isn't that enough?" he shot back. Still holding her gaze, he took the cotton ball and dabbed at his lip himself.

Trying not to notice the way her skin sizzled from his touch, Susan extricated herself from his grip and handed him the tube of antibiotic cream. "What about Dusty Saint-Claire?" she asked casually.

Jake dabbed some cream on his lower lip, then handed the tube back to her. "What about him?" he asked gruffly.

Susan stepped closer and applied cream to the scrape on his cheek. Finished, she looked down into Jake's eyes and asked, "How far back does *that* animosity go?"

Jake pushed the stool back and rolled to his feet. He began to put the first-aid kit back together with much more care than was needed. "I don't know the guy," he said indifferently.

Susan capped the tube of cream and handed it to him. "Not at all?" She studied his face.

"Nope." Jake kept his expression impassive.

"He knows you," Susan persisted.

"That's his problem," Jake retorted, and gave her a testy look. He then took a step toward her and hauled her unceremoniously into his arms. They touched everywhere. Susan felt the hardness of his body pressed against hers, the strength in his arms, and lower still, the sizzling heat and pressure of his desire.

Jake gazed down at her, his eyes dark, his breathing erratic. "I wouldn't keep pushing it, if I were you," he warned silkily.

Susan couldn't help it; when pushed she just had to drive harder. "Why not?"

Jake's eyes darkened even more. His head lowered. Susan sucked in her breath and turned her head in time to avoid the touch of his lips to hers. "Don't, Jake," she ordered in a strangled voice. She couldn't get out of his arms without a struggle.

"Why not?" He tunneled his hands through her hair, his fingers luxuriating in the thick silky strands.

Susan fought and eventually silenced the moan rising in her throat. "Because I'm your lawyer," she said hoarsely, as his lips grazed her other temple, and her eyes closed.

Jake kissed her forehead, and a dizzying excitement raced through her.

"Even better—" he murmured, gently lifting her hair and pressing his lips to her ear.

"Oh, God," Susan whispered, as a hunger unlike any she had ever known raced through her. Aware she was on the verge of losing everything she had worked so hard for, she pushed at his chest again.

He lifted his head, but he did not let her go. They stared at each other. Susan's mouth felt as if it were on fire, and where her hands lay against his chest, she could feel the strong thudding of his heart.

To her consternation—or was it her satisfaction?—Jake looked taken aback by what had just transpired between them, too. But he didn't apologize. And he still didn't let her go.

Susan drew in another shaky breath, her emotions in turmoil. The back door banged shut, alerting her they were no longer alone.

She and Jake moved apart just as Samuel strode from the mudroom into the kitchen. Susan composed herself with effort and turned to look at Jake's father. Despite what Jake had told her earlier, Samuel did not appear at all sick. He did seem edgy and upset, Susan noted.

Samuel took off his Stetson and hung it on a hat rack. "How was the funeral?" he asked.

Jake shrugged and didn't answer. Figuring someone should, Susan said, "The service was okay, but afterward there were several scenes." Some of which might make the evening news.

"That bad, huh?" Samuel looked at Jake.

Jake looked back at his father. Another moment of tense silence ensued. Susan noted there were secrets they had no wish to share with her.

Finally, Jake shrugged. "You know what they say, Dad. A funeral isn't a funeral without at least one brawl."

Samuel's expression gentled. He and Jake exchanged understanding glances. "I'll be in the den if you need me," he said.

As soon as they were alone again, Susan told Jake, "We need to talk."

He shook his head. "I've had enough legal advice for one day."

Susan didn't want to leave, despite what had happened between them. Jake might be strung as tight as piano wire, but that was when people were most inclined to break down and confide in someone. "We have to start working on the case," she said urgently.

Jake regarded her cavalierly. "Tomorrow evening around five will be soon enough."

If she thought he would be catching up on sleep, Susan would not have minded the respite, but she had the feeling he was not going to be idle between now and the next time they met. "Promise me you won't do anything you'll regret."

Jake smirked. Hand on her spine, he briskly showed her to the front door.

"I'm serious." Susan dug in her heels, refusing to let him push her out the door. She had the feeling he was as much a danger to himself as he was to her, in his current emotional state. She leaned against the open portal. Her eyes lifted to his, and for a moment, she thought she could drown in the mysterious pewter depths. She wanted so badly to figure out what was going on with him. Susan stepped back, schooling herself to do her job, but to maintain her emotional distance. "Promise me you'll keep your cool," she said sternly.

Jake's lip curled sardonically. "That's a little hard to do, isn't it, when I'm set to hang for a crime I didn't commit and Angelica's murderer is still on the loose?"

"You haven't been convicted yet," Susan warned.

Jake eyed her, his emotions under lock and key once again. "I know. And I'm not going to be," he retorted grimly. "Not if I have anything to do with it."

# Chapter Three

Jake stood alone in the back of the San Marcos nightclub, watching as the drummer in Dusty's rock band, Rhythm Malone, set up onstage. He had come there to talk to Angelica's brother alone. It was imperative he find out how much Dusty knew. Jake hoped Angelica hadn't confided in her brother. If she had, he thought grimly, he would have to find some way to silence him.

Jake threaded his way through the scarred tables with the upended chairs. He stopped about ten feet away from Rhythm. "I'm looking for Dusty," he said.

"Why?" Rhythm bent to plug in an amp. "Need some more experience trying to punch his lights out?"

Jake ignored her sarcasm. "I need to talk to him. Is he around?"

Rhythm lifted the microphone to her lips and spoke into it. "Nope," she said, her low voice echoing about the empty club.

"Where is he?"

Rhythm sent Jake a bored look and switched off the microphone. "He had a meeting."

Great, Jake thought. He'd driven forty-five minutes out of Austin to make a surprise visit, only to find his intended quarry a no-show. "Where and with whom?" Jake asked impatiently.

"His sister's attorney."

"Do you know the name of that attorney?"

Rhythm shrugged. "Van something."

"Van Cleave?" Jake suggested.

"I guess." Rhythm flicked a disinterested glance over Jake. "What's it to you anyway?"

Jake decided to go for broke. Hoping to shock her into revealing something, he said, "I'm trying to figure out if Dusty had a motive to murder his sister."

Rhythm strode across the stage to retrieve her bag. Her expression was unperturbed, but her hands trembled slightly as she pulled out a pack of Virginia Slims. "Where would you get an idea like that?"

Jake leaned against one of the tables closest to the stage and watched as Rhythm quickly tapped out a cigarette. "Dusty and Angelica never did get along. He's her only living heir. She was wealthy when she died. If he profits, that gives him a motive."

Rhythm lit the cigarette and took a deep drag, avoiding Jake's eyes. "I don't see what all this has to do with me." Inhaling again, Rhythm strode back to the drums and sat down.

"Maybe Dusty had help. Maybe it was a conspiracy."

Rhythm took another deep drag on her cigarette. "You're crazy, man."

Jake watched her blow smoke rings in the air above her head. "Am I?"

Rhythm's eyes met his, accusing. "You're the one on trial for Angelica's murder," she said softly.

But to Jake's surprise, she didn't look the least bit frightened of him, even though they were in the nightclub alone. Did that mean Rhythm didn't scare easily? Jake wondered. Or simply that Rhythm knew he didn't kill Angelica, because she knew who did?

"So why are you running around asking questions?" Rhythm persisted.

"Because I didn't do it." Jake smiled tightly. "That means someone else did." *Maybe even you, Rhythm.* "The only way I'll find out is by looking into it myself."

Again, she was silent.

"If you know something about the crime or the events leading up to it, and you don't tell anyone, then that's conspiracy," Jake informed her.

Rhythm's eyes grew hard. "I've got nothing to say to you."

"Fine," Jake said smoothly. He smiled at her carelessly. "We can do it the hard way if you want."

Rhythm got up so quickly she banged into the edge of one of her drums. Panic tightened the edges of her mouth. "What are you talking about?"

Jake shrugged, switching from the role of bad cop to good cop with ease. "My attorney thinks Dusty murdered Angelica. I'm not sure I agree with Miss Kilpatrick, but she's convinced her theory has merit and as such has decided to investigate Dusty and those closest to him, starting with you of course. I thought I'd save my lawyer the time and money but if that's the way you want it—''

"Wait a minute." Rhythm walked to the very edge of the stage. "I don't want any cops breathing down my neck."

"That's right. You're still on probation from that drug charge a couple of years ago, aren't you?" Jake had called in a few markers at the police station to find that out.

"What do you want to know?"

"Did Dusty see his sister when she hit town?"

Rhythm took another deep drag. Still looking a bit panicked, she said, "He *tried.*"

Jake regarded her steadily. "Why?"

Rhythm shrugged. "The usual reason. He wanted to borrow some money from her."

"Had she given him money in the past?" Jake asked.

"Not one red cent. She was one stingy witch, according to Dusty, anyway. Me, I never met her."

Jake studied the mixture of jealousy and resentment in Rhythm's expression. Noticing she needed an ashtray, he brought her one from the bar and handed it over. "Angelica never heard her brother's band play, even once?" From what Jake had been able to glean from the club owner, the band had been together for about four years. They were popular with local crowds but had been unable to attract much attention outside the central Texas area.

Rhythm tapped her ashes into the ashtray. "Are you kidding? She didn't even want to act like she knew Dusty. If you ever notice, every time there was an article about Angelica in some newspaper or magazine, it read like she was an orphaned only child or something. She never once mentioned having a brother."

Jake sat sideways on the stage. "Dusty must've resented that."

"He probably wouldn't have minded had she used her connections out there to get us heard at a major recording studio, or loaned us the money for a demo tape."

Jake pointed to the cardboard box of independently marketed cassette tapes, which would be for sale after the concert that night for ten dollars apiece. "I notice you made one anyway."

"Yeah, but we had to pay for it ourselves," Rhythm grumbled.

"Where's the rest of the band?" Jake asked. He wanted to talk to them, too.

"They've got regular jobs, so if you want to see them you'll have to speak to them later this evening, after we're finished our gig," Rhythm said gruffly. She picked up her drumsticks and played a silent riff in the air. "Look, if that's all, I've got to get back to work here."

Jake figured he had gotten all he could out of her. Nevertheless, he still had the feeling that she knew more about Angelica's death than she was saying so far. He promised himself he would find out what she already knew, or die trying. "Tell Dusty I'll be back to talk to him," he said.

As he walked out of the club, Jake made a mental note to have Susan's private detective check out the backgrounds of all four members of Dusty's band. In the meantime, he would head on over to Walter Van Cleave's office and see what he could find out there.

DUSTY STARED at Walter incredulously. "What do you mean I'm not in my sister's will! She didn't have any other family!"

Walter regarded Dusty calmly. "The two of you were estranged for years. She made no provision for you."

That lying, conniving bitch, Dusty thought. "Then I'll contest the will," he said calmly. One way or another, he was getting his money.

Walter handed over a copy of the document. "There's no point in that, Dusty. She was broke."

Broke! What a laugh! His sister had lived like a queen, while he had scrounged every penny. Angelica had treated him like a saddle tramp in life, and now in death she was doing it again. Well, this time she wasn't going to win. He was going to take her to the cleaners if it was the last thing he ever did.

"How could Angelica have been broke?" he asked, determined to keep a level head if it killed him. "She made millions." Surely, knowing what a planner Angelica had been, she had put something away for a rainy day.

"And she spent, too." Walter sighed. He leaned forward urgently. "I want to help you, Dusty. You know that. But I've been going over the records her L.A. accountant sent. There's simply nothing left. Your sister died with considerable debts."

Walter talked on. Dusty heard none of it. All he could think about was the last time he had seen his sister. She had hated and resented him from the day he was born, making sure she got everything she needed to succeed from their mother, and he got nothing at all.

He had thought all that would stop when she died. Well, she had humiliated him for the last time, Dusty decided. Now it was time for the tables to be turned. One way or another, he was going to use Angelica to get what she had owed him.

Walter frowned at him. Belatedly, Dusty realized the attorney had stopped talking some time ago.

"Dusty... are you all right?" Walter asked.

"Why wouldn't I be?" Dusty asked.

Walter continued looking at him uneasily.

Walter was right to think he was dangerous, Dusty thought. That was a lesson his dear departed sister had never learned. Maybe if she had, she would still be alive.

Dusty stood. "Thank you," he told Walter quietly, his manner deceptively tranquil despite the fury still pouring through his veins.

"Stay in touch," Walter said.

"Oh, I'm not going anywhere," Dusty said. He leveled a bitter smile at Walter, already plotting his revenge. "Not until after the trial. And maybe not even then." Because one way or another, Jake Lockhart was going to pay for what he'd done.

"JAKE, I CAN'T tell you anything about that meeting I had with Dusty and you know it," Walter said.

"How about Angelica's will, then? Who stood to profit?"

"Also confidential."

Jake studied Walter. They had known each other for a long time, since college. Bitsy and Angelica had even belonged to the same UT sorority.

Jake knew he was putting Walter on the spot. As one of Austin's most prominent family-law attorneys, Walter had his own legal reputation to protect. "Let's talk about what you know about Dusty, then, and his relationship with the drummer in his band, Rhythm Malone. Did Angelica ever say anything to you about her brother's relationship with Rhythm?"

For a moment, Walter appeared torn between protecting the confidentiality of his deceased client and wanting to do something for Jake. Finally, he looked straight at Jake and said, "Angelica despised Rhythm. She thought Rhythm was behind Dusty's attempts to extort money from her."

"Did she use the word 'extort'?"

"I don't remember exactly. I just know that she felt Dusty took after the stepfather she hated. She wanted her half brother to make his own way, just as she had. She tried to tell him that numerous times. All Dusty could see was that Angelica wouldn't smooth the way for him to succeed, too."

"Did she confide in you about other things, as well?"

"I was her lawyer, Jake. People talk. You know that." Walter paused. "If you're asking me if I know who killed her, I don't. I'm sorry."

Jake stood. "You've been a lot of help anyway. I appreciate it." Because now Jake had his suspicions confirmed: both Rhythm and Dusty were motivated by greed.

"Jake—"

Walter's voice stopped him at the door. His private speculating on the real killer interrupted, Jake turned.

"I know what you think about Dusty," Walter said gently. "His attitude bothers me, too. But as a friend, I have to tell you. This sleuthing you're doing on your own. It can only get you into trouble."

"I can handle the legal end of it," Jake assured Walter sagely. "I know the boundaries of harassment and I'll make sure I stop just short of breaking the law and still find out what I need to know to vindicate myself."

"Yeah, but can you handle the killer?" Walter said. "What happens if you come face-to-face with the person who did Angelica in? What then?"

WALTER HAD MADE a good point, and Jake was still thinking about it when he stepped off the elevator and headed for Susan's office thirty minutes later. He wasn't a cop.

Jake located Susan's office and opened the door. Simultaneously he noted two things: her receptionist had already left for the day and she was waiting for him, arms crossed in front of her, her expression belligerent.

"What?" Jake said in response to the furious look she was still giving him. "Am I late?" He checked his watch.

"Don't play games with me!" Susan retorted hotly. "Hundred to one, you know exactly what's got me upset!"

Jake was just beginning to realize he had vastly underestimated Susan Kilpatrick. He'd known she was sharp, and therefore might be trouble, when he'd hired her. He'd also known she appealed to him in a fundamental way that was going to make it damn hard to concentrate on anything else when she was in the room. So far, he'd managed to keep the barriers up, but Jake had the feeling it wouldn't work for long.

"Suppose I don't know what has you so upset," Jake drawled, already thirsting for a repeat taste of her silky, floral-scented skin. "Then would you give me a clue?"

Susan refused to be distracted. She moved around to stand behind her desk. "I'm going to give you ten seconds to start explaining your actions today, Jake," she warned, her eyes shooting fire.

"And then what happens?" he wanted to know.

"Don't push me."

Seeing the passion in Susan's face, it was all he could do not to grin. This was the kind of diversion he had been needing all day. He pushed a chair back from her desk and sank onto it. He propped his feet on the corner of her desk and folded his hands behind his head, knowing he wanted nothing more than to push her until the sparks really flew. "What are you talking about?" he asked lazily.

"Walter called. He told me you'd been by to see him and Dusty's girlfriend, Rhythm Malone!"

Damn Walter, Jake thought.

"How did Walter know I saw Rhythm?"

"Rhythm told Dusty, who called Walter to complain. Fortunately for you, Walter talked Dusty out of notifying the DA on the promise that he would call me, instead."

"And you're supposed to do what? Whip me back into line?"

"Damn straight."

"Well, dream on, Counselor. There's no way I'm sitting around idle, not when my life is on the line."

"Do you want to have your bail revoked?"

"Do you want me to get another lawyer?"

They had reached a stalemate. She didn't like it.

Susan sighed. She picked up a file folder and threw it right back down on her desk. "Has it occurred to you, Jake, that your snooping around might put your life in danger?"

"What was Rhythm going to attack me with—one of her drumsticks?"

"Dusty might have been there—"

"I had been counting on it," Jake interrupted sarcastically.

"He might have had a knife or a gun," Susan continued. "He might even have used his bare hands. In any case, the two of you probably would've gotten into another fistfight. Jake, you don't need the trouble.''

"Gee, I thought I did.''

As Susan clamped down on her emotions, some of the bright pink color left her face. She inhaled a long, slow breath. "Do you want to get yourself arrested again?''

Jake gave Susan a bored look. "Why would that happen? I didn't break the law in going over to the club.''

"Maybe not, but you sure as hell are making yourself look bad. Damn it, Jake, you can't go around interrogating innocent people!''

Jake lowered his feet to the floor. "Who says Rhythm Malone is innocent?''

Susan sat back in her leather swivel chair. "So far, the police think she is.''

Jake remained stubbornly silent.

"I have an investigator on retainer, Ray Trevino. He's licensed and trained for this kind of work, an important consideration, since you are not.''

"Well trained or not, I'm not leaving the fate of my life up to him," Jake said. There was too much a high-caliber investigator might find out.

Susan released a slow, contemptuous breath. "Or me, either, it would seem," she said coolly.

Getting up, she moved around to lean against the front of her desk, so there were only inches between them. So that, Jake thought, he couldn't evade her.

Annoyed to find himself fighting his own attorney as well as those plotting against him, Jake rolled to his feet. Placing his hands on his waist, he towered over her. "Look, I'm the one on trial here. I'm the one who faces the end of my life if I'm convicted. Therefore, Counselor," Jake said through his teeth, "I plan on doing whatever the hell I have to do to save myself, whether you like it or not!''

She tilted back her head so she could see into his face, then she looked him up and down, her own temper simmering. "Did you have a similar attitude before Angelica's death, I wonder?''

"What's that supposed to mean?'' Jake positioned an arm on either side of her and trapped her against the desk. Smiling grimly down at her, he leaned forward. Susan moved as he moved, her motions in silent synchronization with his, until she was bent over backward, her hands braced behind her. And still, Jake noted, she wouldn't give up.

"Did you harass her? Did it get out of hand?"

No, Jake thought, it hadn't. But the situation with Susan was getting out of hand. He could smell her perfume and the minty fragrance of her breath; see the softness of her parted lips and the rapid rise and fall of her breasts. And right now he wanted a taste of that sassy mouth. Now he wanted to take her into his arms.

Aware he needed Susan, and therefore it would be foolish to alienate her further, Jake tore his gaze from her tempting mouth. He lifted his hands from the desk and backed away.

Apparently realizing a lecture on what to do would be a complete waste where Jake was concerned, Susan clenched her fingers to stop their trembling. She resumed her place behind her desk. Slipping back into a calmer mode, she gestured for him to have a seat. Slowly she released the breath she had been holding, and regarded him with a brooding look. "All right, we won't quibble any longer over what you've already done."

"Thank God," Jake said.

"Stupid as it was."

"Only in your opinion." Jake thought he'd uncovered quite a lot in a short amount of time.

Susan narrowed her eyes at him as she picked up her pen and put a legal pad squarely in front of her. "Tell me what you found out," she ordered.

Briefly Jake explained. "Can Dusty testify to any of the ugliness that went on when you and Angelica broke off your relationship years ago?"

"No," Jake said. Only he and Angelica had been privy to that....

*"You're telling me you won't go to California after we graduate?" Angelica said angrily. She sat up in bed, taking the sheet with her.*

*Jake lay flat on his back beside her, his arms folded beneath his head. He felt sated and drowsy after their evening of nonstop lovemaking, but it was clear his girlfriend was far from happy. "I can't," he explained patiently as he absently stroked her long auburn hair. "I've got to take the bar exam here, look for a job."*

*Angelica let the sheet drop to her waist. Locking her eyes with his, she rubbed her bare breast against his arm sensually. "You can do that in California."*

Jake knew that, but because of his family responsibilities it wasn't really an option. "I want to live here," he said.

Angelica swung herself lithely over top of him and sat astride him, the palms of her hands caressing his chest in a way she knew he liked. "Jake, I want a career, too," she reminded him softly.

Jake lazily cupped her breast. "So go for it," he advised gently.

Angelica undulated against him sensually. Impossibly, Jake felt himself becoming aroused once again.

"You don't care if I go to California alone?" she taunted softly, a half smile curving her lips.

Jake shrugged. He saw no reason to be a chauvinist about this. He and Angelica had been straight with each other since the beginning. Their careers came first. For now, it had to be this way. "I understand if you want a career," he said, looking into her eyes. "I want one, too."

Angelica's lower lip thrust forward in a sexy pout. "I want us to be together now."

Jake grinned. "We are." And they were both enjoying every second of it.

Angelica looked at him seriously. "I don't think you understand me, Jake," she said coldly. "This isn't an either-or proposition. If you want me, you have to come to Los Angeles."

Jake did not bend to ultimatums. Nor did he like the way she habitually tried to control him with sex. "And I told you, I can't do that," he said flatly.

Angelica regarded him dispassionately. "That's your final answer?" she asked hoarsely.

Not sure whether her dismay was real or feigned, Jake said, "Yes."

Beautiful face now set in a stubborn pout, Angelica slid off of Jake and picked up her clothes and began to dress. Tears flowed from her eyes in an unrelenting stream. "I can't believe I slept with you!" she said, playing the distressed virgin to the hilt. "I thought you were going to marry me!"

Jake admitted the idea had crossed his mind more than once. He wasn't sure he was in love with her, but he knew he desired her. "We could get married and live here," Jake said finally, thinking that might appease her.

Angelica whirled around to face him. "I can see it now. I'd be active in regional theater and be a politician-rancher's wife. No, thank you, Jake!"

*Realizing the fun-and-games part of the evening was over, Jake got up and tugged on his jeans. "Look, I've said you can leave if you want. I've offered to marry you if you stay here. What else do you want?" he asked impatiently.*

*Like a chameleon, without warning, Angelica turned soft and cuddly again. She wrapped an arm about his waist and laid her head against his bare chest. "Marry me and come with me, Jake. Live in California with me, just for a few years, until I get my career started." Holding him tightly, she pressed hot, wet kisses all up and down his neck. "I'll make it wonderful for you, I promise. We can elope tonight."*

*Jake caught her hands. He felt it only fair to tell her. "The answer is still no, Angelica."*

*Still smiling at him, eyes locked with his, she stood on tiptoe and kissed him gently on the lips. "No?" she echoed sweetly, but there was something deadly and vile in her eyes.*

*"No." Jake confirmed.*

*The next thing he knew her nails were vengefully digging into his skin. Swearing viciously, he reacted in self-defense and pushed her aside.*

*Angelica came at him again. Hands crossed in front of him, he knocked her away. She bounced against the bed, then vaulted back up. "Bastard!" she rasped with another swipe of her long nails, this time aiming at his face. "I'll make you sorry you ever double-crossed me!"*

*Jake caught her arms and forced them behind her back. "Stop it," he commanded. When she continued to struggle, he pushed her down on the bed, hands clasped behind her.*

*Gasping in fury, Angelica opened her mouth to scream. Jake knew if he didn't shut her up immediately the cops would come, so he did the only thing he could; he cut the shrill sound off with a brutal kiss—*

"You're thinking about her, aren't you?"

Susan's voice, so cool and deliberate, brought him out of his reverie. Jake looked up to see Susan standing in front of the television in the corner. He had no idea how long he had been remembering.

"It's okay, Jake," she said gently. "You have a lot to deal with at the moment. I understand that. That's why—" she popped a videotape into the machine "—I want you to take a few moments and look at these."

Jake grimaced as news photos flashed on the screen, taken outside the motel where Angelica had been found. Susan came back around to stand beside his chair. The two of them watched in silence, listening to the reports. Jake saw himself in some of the news footage. He had blood on his clothes, hands; his face was ashen. He had the dazed look of someone in shock as, hands handcuffed behind him, he was thrust into the back of a police car. He saw two men who seemed to stand out in the crowd.

"Do you remember all this?" Susan asked gently.

Jake nodded. "Unfortunately, yes. It plays over and over in my head like a bad horror movie." Just as he kept recalling the first time he'd seen Angelica again, upon her return to Austin.

He remembered walking into her hotel room, leaning against the closed door, resentment roiling inside him....

*It had been fourteen years since he had seen Angelica, and they were in the plush Four Seasons Hotel instead of the sleazy Shady Villa Motel, but his loathing of her remained unchanged. "Okay, I'm here," he announced curtly.*

*Angelica set her wineglass down with a thud. She glowered at him. "Are you going to be rude?" She advanced on him, her silk lounging pajamas flowing around her. "Because if you are, you can just get the hell out of here."*

*"Fine with me!" Jake started to go.*

*Angelica swept across the room and grabbed his arm. "Wait. Don't go. Please, Jake." She pulled him toward her urgently, her eyes wide, her expression theatrically distressed. "I need you."*

*He stared at her, wondering how he ever could have been so involved with her.*

*"You've got three minutes to tell me what this is all about," he said brusquely, "and then I'm out of here."*

*"All right." Angelica's lower lip trembled. "I'll try but it's a long story."*

*Jake's jaw set. He was not there for the long haul.*

*Tears filled her eyes, spilled down her cheeks, marring her perfectly applied makeup. "I'm in trouble, Jake," she whispered, throwing herself into his arms. Swallowing hard, she clung to him tightly and looked up at him. "Real trouble—"*

"Are you having nightmares about the murder scene?" Susan asked gently, drawing Jake back to the present once again.

He looked up at Susan. Somehow, the gentle woman was a lot more dangerous than the sassy, determined one. "Yeah," Jake admitted, feeling it would be senseless to deny it. "I am. Some-times—"

"What?"

Oh, God. He had so many regrets, nearly all of them having to do with Angelica and the furious, resentful way he had handled her. Aware Susan was waiting for an answer, he said, "I just wish it had never happened."

"Her murder?"

Any of it, Jake thought.

Susan reached over and squeezed his hand. "It'll be all right," she said softly. "I'll get you through this, I promise." She smiled, abruptly giving him a break he didn't deserve. "No matter how badly you sometimes behave."

Jake had been afraid of that. Just like Angelica, Susan was not the type of woman to give up once she had set her sights on some-thing. Right now, it was helping him. The only problem was, he didn't want her to uncover the whole truth, just bits and pieces of information that would help him craft a successful defense. His jaw clenching, he withdrew his hand from hers. "Look, if you don't mind, it's been a long day. I really ought to get home."

SUSAN SAID GOODBYE to Jake and gathered up her things, her mood dejected. Her attempt to spark his memory and get him to open up had failed miserably. It was true—she'd seen the first flash of vul-nerability in him tonight. But beyond that they hadn't accom-plished anything. He was still as intractable as hell, and she sensed that as the trial grew nearer, he would only get worse. She would just have to try again, Susan decided. Because she damn well wasn't giving up.

She turned off the lights and headed out.

She was just locking the outer door to her office, when the ele-vator slid open behind her. Jake stepped off and started walking toward her.

Unbidden, a picture of him covered with Angelica's blood flashed through her mind. She pushed the ugly picture from her mind. Nevertheless, a shiver went through her as she became aware how alone they were.

"I thought you'd left," Susan said with a casual smile. It was ridiculous for her to be afraid of Jake; he was her client. An in-nocent one.

"I decided to come back and walk you to your car," he replied enigmatically.

Once again, he seemed moody and restless.

Susan was surprised by Jake's sudden display of seemingly unwilling gallantry. A few seconds ago, he had been unable to get out of her office quickly enough. "That's not necessary." She stepped briskly into the elevator with Jake and watched the doors slide shut. "This building may be old, but it's perfectly safe." *Just as I'm fine alone here with him.*

"It's not the walk to the parking garage I'm worried about," Jake said cryptically as the elevator stopped at the lobby.

"Then what?" she asked curiously as the doors slid open.

Jake pointed toward the front door to the building. Just outside the glass-fronted lobby demonstrators and news teams surrounded the redbrick building. Seeing them, Susan muttered something wholly unladylike.

The lone night security man emerged from behind his desk. "Sorry, Miss Kilpatrick," he said. "They just got here, and so did the police. If you wait a few minutes, I think they'll all be cleared away."

Susan looked at the mob, then at Jake. She didn't want to wait, and she sensed neither did he. "We can go out the back entrance."

"No," he said flatly, his mouth taking on a grim line. "I'm not running."

Susan wasn't about to let her client indulge in any more macho posturing. "Jake—"

"I'm not running," he repeated, pushing the words through bared teeth. "I've got nothing to hide. And I'll be damned if I'll act like I do!"

That said, he pivoted sharply on his heel and headed out into the mob of demonstrators loudly chanting, "Murderer, resign!" As Susan strode out to join him TV cameras rushed to cut off the demonstrators. Microphones were shoved at Jake. Susan tried unsuccessfully to cut off his access to them.

"Mr. Lockhart! What do you say to the demand you resign?" a reporter asked.

Ignoring the quelling grip she had on his jacket sleeve, Jake stood in the middle of the crowd, looking perfectly at ease and happy to have the chance to defend himself. "I was elected attorney general to do a job. I plan to complete my term."

"What happens if you go to jail?"

"I'm not going to prison," Jake said, his expression determined.

"How do you know that, Mr. Lockhart?"

"Because I'm innocent," Jake said calmly.

Susan decided he had defended himself quite sufficiently. "Enough questions," she said. She held up a hand, cutting off the protests of reporters. "Please, we'll hold a news conference when we have something to tell you. Until then, we have work to do."

Susan and Jake started down the six steps leading from the office building to the broad city sidewalk below. As the demonstrators picked up steam, Jake laced an arm about Susan's shoulders. She did not consider herself the type of woman in need of a man's protection, but in this case she didn't mind having him there to shepherd her through the taunting crowd. The melee seemed to get worse with every passing second.

"We should have gone out the back way," Susan reiterated, her heart pounding.

"They still would have chased us down," Jake muttered back. And then all hell broke loose. In the street, there was the simultaneous sound of glass breaking, a screeching of car wheels, a horn blast. Susan whipped around in time to see a rear window on a car dissolve into flying shards of glass, while the driver and her passenger ducked and screamed in terror.

Jake swore under his breath at the violence. He put his own head down and pushed her forward. "Come on, let's get out of here!" he said.

"Watch out!" someone behind them screamed.

Fearful of what was going to happen next, Susan whirled to glance behind her. She saw a baseball-size rock cartwheeling in the air. She didn't know where it had originated, but it was coming fast and flying straight at her head.

# Chapter Four

Jake had only one thought—keep Susan safe. In a flash, he pushed her forward, covered her with his body. They hit the cement sidewalk just as the tip of the rock caught him in the back of the head.

Jake swore as people around him screamed. A cop pushed through to their side.

"Hey, Lockhart. You okay?"

Jake wasn't sure. He felt sick and dizzy as hell. But he'd be damned if he'd lie there like a whipped pup. "I think so." He stood, then helped Susan to her feet. She winced. He noted that both her hands were scraped. She looked badly shaken. He still wasn't feeling so steady himself.

The cop began shooing everyone away. "All right. Show's over, folks. Time for this demonstration to come to an end."

Jake put his arm around Susan's waist as the space cleared around them. "Sorry. I didn't mean for that to happen."

"You're the one who got hit with a rock." She frowned and gently touched his hair. "Oh, Jake."

He noticed she was looking at his collar. For the first time he became aware something warm and wet was dripping down his neck. He touched the damp area with his hand. When he drew his hand back, he saw the bright red smear of blood.

Susan put her fingertips to the edge of his jaw and turned his head slightly, so she could get a better look at the wound. "You're going to need stitches for that."

Great, Jake thought. Just what he needed on top of everything else. "Never mind about that," Jake said impatiently, as the back of his head continued to throb with the force of a giant migraine.

"I want to know who hit me." He looked at the reporters and their cameramen. "Anyone get this on tape?" Jake asked.

There was a collective mumble of dismay from the various news crews. "No." "Sorry, Jake. I'd already shut mine off." "I'm getting this now," another offered. A fourth chimed in, "Me, too."

Jake suppressed another groan as Susan fumbled in her purse and came out with a clean wad of tissues. She handed it to him and he pressed it squarely against the bleeding, aware the pain was beginning to dissipate slightly.

As the crowd dispersed reluctantly, a second cop came around the corner. He was sweating and out of breath.

Jake cut a swath through the reporters and closed the distance between them. "Did you see anything?" he asked the cop.

"No. My partner and I both had our backs to whoever it was who threw the rock. As soon as you were hit, my partner headed for y'all and I took off in the direction the rock thrower ran, but whoever it was had a head start and disappeared in one of those alleys on the other end of the parking garage."

"It was probably one of the protesters," the other cop said grimly.

"No it wasn't." A young woman with a ponytail and a UT backpack stepped forward. "The person who threw the rock was not with the protestors. At least I don't think he was."

"How do you know?" Susan asked, stepping closer to Jake.

"Because he came out of that parking garage over there, ran straight into the crowd, and threw a rock at the car, busting its window, and then another one at Mr. Lockhart and his attorney."

"Could you identify the guy who threw the rock?" Jake asked. Damn, but his head hurt, and he couldn't imagine Susan's hands or knees felt much better.

"I'm not sure. It all happened so fast. I mean, I know he was a big guy—at least six feet."

"How much did he weigh?"

"I don't know, but he was pretty heavyset."

"Anything else?" Jake asked.

"He was Caucasian and he didn't have a beard or mustache or anything."

Well, that narrowed it down, Jake thought. She could have been describing half the men in the city.

"What about his eyes?" Jake asked. "Did you get a look at his face?"

The protester shook her head. "He had on opaque black sunglasses."

Jake realized the folded face tissue in his hand was saturated.

Susan fished another thick square of tissue out of her purse. "We better get you to the hospital," she said.

Jake reluctantly decided Susan was right. He called over his shoulder. "I want to know if you find the guy that hit me."

"Will do," the cops promised.

Susan rounded the corner and strode forward to unlock the passenger side of her Seville. Jake shrugged out of his jacket, folding it beneath his head, across his shoulder, so he wouldn't get blood on the inside of her car, and slid in. "Where are we going?" he asked as she pulled away from the curb. Austin had several good hospitals.

"St. David's Emergency Room. It's closest."

Three minutes later, she pulled her Seville into the ER parking lot.

"Sit still until I open your door," Susan barked.

"Why?" Jake asked grumpily. He hated being babied.

"Because you look a little green around the gills, pal."

To Jake's chagrin, he was feeling a little woozy. The light-headedness increased when he stood. Susan slipped an arm around his waist. "Lean on me."

"If you insist," Jake muttered, his ruined suit coat still clutched in his hand. Susan's body was warm and deceptively soft pressed up against him, and she had no shortage of physical strength.

The triage nurse took one look at Jake and Susan and directed them back to a treatment room. Susan assisted Jake all the way to the stretcher. She eased him up onto it, her movements slow and steady and extremely comforting.

"You two been through a war zone, or are you just unusually clumsy?" the nurse asked.

"A little of both. Although he's the clumsy one," Susan joked.

"Fill out this form," the nurse said, handing a clipboard to Susan. She handed Jake a clean square of surgical gauze. "I'll be right back to clean up that wound and then the doctor will stitch you up."

Jake used his free hand to pull his wallet out of his back pocket. He awkwardly fished out his medical-insurance card, while Susan asked for the pertinent details of his medical history and wrote them down on the form. Finished, she put it aside. Jake noted her hands were trembling. He waved her close, and when she approached him, he took her hand in his. "Are you okay?" he asked. He wasn't used to being rescued, but now that it had happened, he was glad it was Susan who'd come to his aid.

She nodded. "Sure."

"You look a little shaken up."

"I guess I'm just now realizing what a close call that was. I mean, what if that rock had hit you in the eye or something?"

"It's all right. I'm okay."

"Hey, you're the patient," she reminded him wryly, resting her hip against the stretcher, her hand still cupped in his. "I'm supposed to be comforting you."

Jake wished her association with him had not put her in danger. Nevertheless, he admired the way she had taken the crisis in stride. Aware that he couldn't afford to let the feelings of closeness draw them together, Jake resorted to further discussion of the attack. "I'd settle for getting rid of this headache," he lamented. "And finding out who caused it."

Susan's eyes glowed with concern. "Any ideas who it might have been?" she asked casually.

Jake had a few. Unwilling to share any of his thoughts with her for fear he'd give away his dark secret, he turned from her with a shrug. "I'm a politician. I've got a lot of enemies."

Susan pulled her hand from his and studied him silently. "It might have been one of the protesters," she theorized cautiously at last.

Or someone connected with Angelica's murder, or the trouble she'd had before her death, Jake thought. Because he couldn't discuss that, he was silent.

Susan moved across the room and continued to regard Jake carefully. Instinct told him she suspected he was holding something back from her—again. But there was no helping it. There was more here at stake than just his own life. Much more.

SUSAN LEFT when the doctor came in to stitch Jake up. She washed up in the hospital bathroom. Feeling immeasurably better, she returned ten minutes later, with a small can of orange juice for each of them.

When she walked into the examining room, Jake was sitting up again. He looked anything but relaxed. Every inch of him was rigid with tension and ready to do battle. The only signs he'd been hurt were the small square bandage on the back of his head, the lingering scrape on his cheek and the healing cut on his lip. She handed him his juice.

He appeared annoyed as hell. "Thanks," he said gruffly, taking a sip.

Jake was hot tempered, arrogant and secretive, Susan thought. And he still didn't look like the cold, calculating killer the district attorney made him out to be. More like a man who'd found himself in an incredibly damning situation and was doing his best to wade through it. In the meantime, he had earned her empathy if not her trust.

Jake drained his can. He pitched it toward the wastebasket just as a shadow fell over the door. Susan frowned as Tom Peterson walked in uninvited.

"They told me I'd find you back here," Tom said, focusing in on Jake.

"How'd you know Jake was at the emergency room?" Susan asked, her expression anything but welcoming.

Tom thoughtfully stroked his black mustache. "They interrupted local programming to show the rock-hurling incident on TV. Naturally I came over to see if you were all right." Tom hooked his fingers in the pocket of his vest. "Anything I can do?"

"Yeah," Jake said. "Drop the murder charge. We both know I didn't do it."

"Tell it to a jury," Tom said. "I meant, is there anything I can do about the incident," he continued.

Jake shrugged. "Find the son of a gun who hit me."

"Unfortunately, the police at the scene don't have much to go on." Tom paused, checked his hair to see if it had moved, and smiled insipidly. "Maybe you should take this as a warning and resign as AG, Jake."

"And clear the way for you to run in the March primary?" Jake asked sarcastically. His eyes were dark and dangerous. "Don't bet on it."

"If there's anything I can do for your client in regard to this assault, let me know," Tom told Susan, both tone and expression matter-of-fact. He offered her a salute. "In the meantime, I'll see you in court, Kilpatrick."

"As usual, I'm not looking forward to it," she said sweetly.

Tom grinned and exited the room.

"He is definitely not one of my favorite people," Susan said with a beleaguered sigh.

"Mine, either," Jake admitted.

Susan watched Jake step down from the gurney. "Any particular reason why?"

Jake yanked off his tie and stuffed it in his jacket pocket. "You mean, besides the fact he's gunning for my job and had me indicted for a murder I didn't commit?"

Susan smiled. "Nice to see you haven't lost your sense of humor."

Jake folded his copy of the hospital bill and put it in his shirt pocket. "If it were up to Tom, that's all I'd have left."

Susan quickly finished her juice. "How do you know him?"

"We were rivals in law school." Jake's eyes locked with hers. "He constantly competed with me. He's still at it."

Susan hadn't expected such candor. She leaned against the wall, savoring the unexpected intimacy. "If it's any comfort, he doesn't care for me, either," she admitted.

"How come?"

She shrugged, acutely aware of Jake's nearness. "Probably because he's lost every case he's tried against me."

Jake watched her pitch her can, then returned his gaze to her face. "I noticed there's no love lost for him on your part, either," he said.

Susan readily admitted that was so, adding, "I know. I detest the way he uses the DA's office to pursue a political agenda."

Susan held out a hand. "Ready to go home?"

Jake nodded. "Since this was on the news, I'd better call my dad."

They stopped by a pay phone in the hall. Jake explained what had happened and said he was okay. As he hung up the phone he looked at her and rolled his eyes. "Dad doesn't want me to drive myself home."

"Considering what happened earlier this evening, he might be right," Susan said. "I'll drive you."

"Look, it's a long way, almost an hour out to the ranch."

"And you're my client," Susan said. When Jake still hesitated, she added, "Besides, I owe you, since that rock would have hit me if you hadn't knocked me to the ground."

"We also know if I hadn't knocked you to the pavement, you wouldn't have scraped both your knees and hands."

"Yeah, well, every cloud has its silver lining." Susan nudged him in the direction of the exit. "Let's get a move on."

"THANK GOD you're all right," Sam said when Jake entered the ranch house, Susan at his side.

Jake shook his head. "I told you so on the phone."

"Some things a father has to see for himself." Samuel looked at Susan. "I understand you drove Jake to the hospital for his stitches. Thank you."

"You're very welcome." Susan smiled at Samuel. She didn't know quite how he had done it, but he had made her feel like part of the family. She backed toward the door. "Well, I'd better get going. I have an appointment with Chip Garrison tomorrow morning."

Jake stopped her by touching her arm. He looked down at her, his gaze intense. "What time?"

"I'm supposed to meet him at his hotel at ten o'clock."

"I want to go, too." It was more a command than a request.

Susan frowned. "I don't think that would be wise, Jake. If you're there, Chip may not talk as freely."

"And maybe it won't make a difference. All I know is, my life is on the line, and I need to take an active part in this investigation," he said.

Susan understood that. "All right, you can come."

"The news is on. They're going to show Jake's impromptu remarks to the press," Samuel announced.

Susan and Jake followed Samuel into the den.

The coverage was as bad and as damaging as Susan had feared. The way the footage had been edited, Jake looked cocky one minute, grimly worried the next. The pictures of him bleeding from a rock wound were worst of all.

Because he was a lawyer himself, she was sure Jake knew why she was unhappy. But she waited until he was walking her out to address the issue.

"Just a minute, Jake." Susan paused in the front hall.

She directed him into the adjacent parlor and shut the door behind them. "Before I go, I want to talk to you about your impromptu remarks to the press tonight. You can't do that again. If a statement is to be made, we'll work on it together. Otherwise, you're to keep silent."

His eyes drifted over her. As Susan suspected, he was fully aware of the impact the negative press coverage had had on his case, but unapologetic just the same. "I had to do it. To not comment would have made me look guilty."

"You looked guilty anyway."

"At least I had my say."

Susan took a deep breath. "Look, Jake, I have come to this case late in the ball game. I didn't represent you during the inquest of Angelica's death. If I had, I never would have let you take the stand. As it is, every statement you made at the inquest and to the police at the scene can now be twisted around and taken out of context and used against you in the trial."

Jake crossed to a desk in the corner, picked up a stack of mail and threw it back down again. "Everything I've told them would have come out anyway."

"Jake, you've got to calm down and stop thinking that everyone is on your side, 'cause they're just not!"

Jake whirled around to face her and released a short contemptuous breath. "That's easy for you to say." He closed the distance between them in two long steps. "You're not the one whose reputation is being impugned every second of every day."

"If you don't start trusting me, we're never going to get anywhere." When he wouldn't look at her, she grasped his sleeve and forced him to face her. "Do you hear me, Jake? Unless you start cooperating with me, you're going to go to jail for a murder you did not commit."

He regarded her silently, a muscle working convulsively in his cheek. He braced his hands on his waist and leaned down until he was only inches from her. "Does that mean you believe I'm innocent?"

Susan tried not to think about his nearness or inhale the tantalizing woodsy scent of his after-shave. "I'm your lawyer, remember?"

"Except for during that mock-trial examination, which didn't really count, you haven't asked me if I did it," Jake said silkily, moving closer still.

Susan knew he expected her to back up, so she deliberately held her ground. "No, and I'm not going to."

"Why not?"

Aware she barely had enough room to maneuver, Susan crossed her arms in front of her. "You know the answer to that."

Jake gazed down at her, his eyes dark with an emotion she wasn't sure she wanted to identify.

"Because you couldn't defend me if I had murdered Angelica?" he asked.

"That's right." She held his gaze with effort, instructing herself sternly to react like an attorney. "I couldn't enter an innocent plea to the court if I knew that you'd killed Angelica, because legal ethics require me to tell the truth. As your attorney, I ask you what happened, and I accept that as fact.''

Jake continued to watch her in a way that made her heart pound. ''And if you find out I lied to you?''

Susan tucked her arms in close to her waist to still their trembling. ''Then I withdraw from the case. So be warned, Jake,'' she said fiercely. And knew instantly by the look on his face she had made a mistake.

Jake moved in closer, his face taut with anger. ''Maybe you're the one who made the mistake.'' He closed his hands around her upper arms. ''Maybe you picked the wrong man to represent.''

''Don't try to frighten me, Jake!'' Susan tried and failed to shake off his grip.

He backed her up until her hips touched the sofa. He looked down at her, turbulent emotion in his eyes. ''But you're frightened, aren't you?'' he taunted softly.

''I—''

''Don't lie to me, Counselor!'' he snarled.

Susan drew a ragged breath. She was shaking all over. Where they touched, she could feel him trembling, too. ''I'm not—''

''The hell you're not.'' He moved his body even closer.

And suddenly there was too much tension. Too much contact. She couldn't take her eyes off him. Couldn't help but soften in response to the need in him. With a groan of capitulation . . . or was it regret? . . . Jake lowered his head and slanted his mouth over hers. She had known from the start he was unlikely to cut anyone—especially her—any slack.

He possessed, he aroused, he brought her to dangerous new heights, all with the masterful caress of his lips over hers. Sensations swept through her, warm and wild, drawing her into a world she had always dreamed of and never known. Before Susan realized it, she was kissing him back wholeheartedly. And that was when he let her go.

Susan would've fallen had it not been for the sofa she was leaning against. Jake looked just as disoriented. And displeased. His expression brooding, shoulders taut, he swung away from her. She waited.

''If you want an apology—'' he said finally.

Susan drew herself up to her full five feet four inches. ''I think you owe me one, don't you?''

''Maybe I do.''

But he wasn't sorry he had kissed her, Susan noticed, trying hard not to feel so elated.

"You want to call it a night?" he asked huskily, a surprising tenderness in his eyes.

Disconcerted by his swift change of mood, Susan said, "Not just yet. Not until we finish talking." She was not running out of the room because of a simple kiss.

Aware her knees were still shaking, just a little, Susan sat down on the arm of the sofa. "I know this has been an extraordinarily difficult time for you, Jake. And that you're probably not your-self—"

"That's an understatement."

"But for now, let's take it one step at a time, all right?" she coached gently.

He met her eyes. "Keep going."

"For the time being, it has got to be business as usual for you and your father. I want you to keep working."

"I intend to," he said firmly.

"You also need to avoid reporters. And one more thing. Stop making passionate speeches about your innocence. Let the jury decide that for themselves."

"What if they don't decide I'm innocent?" he asked curtly.

Susan knew that if she had been in his place, she might have done exactly what Jake had done today. The need to defend one-self against slander was a powerful emotion.

Susan stood and crossed the distance between them. She touched his arm gently, reassuringly. "They will believe you. I'll see to that. I promise."

Jake relaxed slightly. Knowing she had no reason to continue touching him, Susan dropped her hand. "In the meantime, as far as the press goes, you let me handle them. I'll make sure they're given only positive information about you."

Realizing they'd dallied too long, Susan picked up her purse and moved to leave. Jake fell into step beside her. He opened the door to the hall and walked her out. Next to her car he paused. He looked incredibly handsome in the shimmering moonlight.

"What time do you want to meet tomorrow?" he asked.

"Be at my office at nine-thirty," Susan advised. "We'll go to see Chip Garrison together." She only hoped the agent had some an-swers.

"THANKS FOR AGREEING to meet with us," Susan said as the three of them sat down in a private dining room at Chip's downtown hotel.

"I figure I'd better be in on what's going on," he said. "Although I can't say I think it is particularly appropriate for me to be helping prepare the defense for the person accused of murdering my best client," he added, with a glare at Jake. "However, since Angelica's reputation still needs protecting, I agreed to come here and meet with you."

Jake met Chip's gaze equably. "I didn't kill Angelica. I am interested in finding out who did."

"We both are," Susan continued. "So anything you can tell us about her life in Los Angeles would be appreciated."

Chip took a long sip of Perrier. "What do you want to know?"

Susan pulled out a legal pad. "How did you and Angelica meet?"

"At a party about four years ago when she asked me to represent her. I had some reservations. Her career was not exactly what I would call hot, but she was beautiful and she showed promise. And she was as dedicated as they come."

"What do you mean by that?" Susan interrupted.

"Just that there wasn't anything she wouldn't do to get a role."

Amen to that, Jake thought. Although he hadn't known until just before she'd died just who she would be willing to cold-bloodedly sacrifice on the altar of her career.

"I take it you felt her perseverance was commendable," Susan said.

Chip nodded. "You gotta have it to succeed in this business." He shook his head. "That's what makes her disappearance in mid-November so stupid." His voice emotional, he said, "I mean, here she was, about to star in a big holiday theatrical release. She had publicity sessions set up for six weeks straight, and what does she do? She skips town and leaves me behind trying to make explanations."

"So I take it you fought about her leaving?" Susan said, scribbling madly.

"Hell, yes, and for good reason, it turns out. If she had just stayed and met her obligations, she never would have died."

"Did Angelica give you any reason for skipping town?" Jake asked curtly. Susan looked at him. This was obviously important. Again she wondered what Jake knew.

Chip shrugged. "Beats the hell out of me why she left."

Beside Susan, Jake began to tense.

"I thought we had something special," Chip continued. "We kept things cool for professional reasons. But in private, things were pretty hot. We'd practically been living together the past two years. But whatever was bothering her, she didn't tell me."

"Could it have had anything to do with the weird guy at her funeral, the one with the Elvis hair?" Jake asked, leaning forward in his chair.

"I don't know."

"Who was he, anyway?" Jake asked.

"I don't know!" Chip began to get defensive.

"He told the cops you invited him," Jake said.

Chip sipped his Perrier. "He lied. Obviously he was just a bereaved fan who came to pay his respects."

"But he didn't look familiar to you?" Jake persisted tensely.

Chip stared at Jake. "Not at all."

"Did you at least get his name?" Susan asked.

"It wasn't necessary," Chip said. "He left voluntarily when the cops asked him to go."

Jake sighed, his frustration evident. Susan wondered what Jake thought was so urgent about finding that strange man. If he knew something else, he hadn't shared it with her. And that ticked her off. "Back to when Angelica left California," Susan said. "Was she upset when she left?"

Chip glared at Jake. "Yeah. She seemed very high-strung. Moody."

Jake shifted uneasily in his chair.

"And that was unusual?" Susan asked, ignoring the way Jake kept glancing at his watch.

Chip stared at Jake as though Jake were to blame. "She could be difficult," he allowed, "but never . . . like that."

So something really was wrong, Susan thought. "Do you think her problems might have been stress related?" she asked, aware Jake's face was slowly losing its healthy glow.

Chip shrugged. "That's about the only thing that makes sense, isn't it? She had worked her whole life to make it to the top. Then she just leaves before she can even enjoy the fruits of her success—and for what . . . to gallivant around Texas with a former lover she hasn't seen for years? Assuming," Chip added sarcastically, with another accusing look at Jake, "that she was telling me the truth."

Jake lifted his head and glared at Chip. "We weren't in touch until a few days before she died," he said.

Chip looked at Jake, his jealousy evident.

Wondering if Chip had anything to do with Angelica's murder, Susan asked, "How did you learn of her death?"

"The paper, same as everyone else. I was in Mexico, visiting another one of my clients on a shoot, when the word came down."

Susan questioned Chip a few minutes longer. It was clear he knew or would divulge nothing else. Finally, she stood. "Thanks for staying in Austin for a few extra days to talk to us," she said graciously.

Chip nodded.

They said goodbye. The moment Susan was alone with Jake in his Jeep, she let him have it.

"All right, I want to know what you're hiding."

He gave her an innocent look and backed out of the parking space with a screech. "I don't know what you mean." He thrust the Jeep into gear.

Susan was thrown forward as he accelerated abruptly. "The hell you don't. Why did Angelica leave town?"

"I already told you. The stress." Jake jerked them to a stop at the edge of the lot.

Susan ignored the traffic whizzing by. "What else?"

"That's it."

"Why were you so interested in that weird guy at the funeral?"

"Because he might have been the killer! He certainly was acting strange."

Susan couldn't disagree with that. "Back to Angelica—"

"I've already told you everything I can."

Susan knew that cagey look. She blew out a weary breath. "I warned you once about lying to me, Jake."

"I remember." He leaned closer and gave her a Cheshire-cat grin. "I also recall what that heated argument led to," he murmured silkily, twining a strand of her golden hair around his finger. "Do you?" he whispered dangerously, letting his hand slip to the seat belt across her shoulder.

Susan flushed. Damn him for bringing up that one ill-advised kiss. She let out a slow, calming breath. Just because she had never met a more exasperating man didn't mean she couldn't handle him. "Fine, Jake. Have it your way. We won't talk about this now." It didn't mean she was going to give up.

"Where do you want to go next?" he asked.

Susan glanced at her appointment book. "Let's go over to the Four Seasons and see what we can find out from the staff there."

"What'd you think about Chip?" Jake asked as he drove.

"He seemed jealous of you."

"Enough," Jake wondered out loud, "for him to have killed Angelica in a fit of rage, then set me up to take the blame?"

"Maybe. I mean, we still don't know who called the police, just that the call was made from a pay phone down the road a mile from the motel. It could have been anyone. In the meantime, I'll have Ray Trevino check out Chip's alibi. And I'll ask him to try to identify those two men we saw on the tape yesterday, too."

Susan's beeper sounded. She turned it off and Jake headed for the nearest pay phone. She got out and when she came back, her face was grim.

"Who was it?" he asked.

"The county medical examiner's office. The toxicology reports on Angelica are in."

# Chapter Five

"Angelica had a lethal amount of glutethimide in her system when she died," Susan said, as she scanned the report that had been sent to her office.

"What's that?" Jake asked.

Susan handed him the first page of the report after she had finished reading it. "According to the coroner's report, it's a particularly strong, hence dangerous, prescription sleeping pill. She also had a .05 blood-alcohol level, which means she'd had one margarita, or the equivalent thereof. I mean, for all we know, she could have had a drink elsewhere, and the pitcher of margaritas and two glasses were just there for show, to make it appear like a seduction scene. We're going to have to check out everything, and take absolutely nothing at face value."

Jake sat down on the edge of Susan's desk. "Well, this explains a lot," he said grimly, lifting his eyes to hers.

She nodded. "Like how Angelica could have been stabbed to death without anyone else at the motel hearing a thing."

"Or there being no signs of a struggle in the room at all." Jake looked at Susan, his expression troubled. "Angelica must have been unconscious at the time she suffered her fatal wound, which means that whoever planned this went to a lot of trouble."

"The killer also cleaned up the scene before he or she exited the motel room. Probably waited until you arrived, then went down the road to make the call to the police."

Jake swore heatedly. "Well, the frame worked. I was indicted. I just wish the DA had come through with this evidence earlier, before the inquest."

Susan realized Jake had every right to be upset. "My guess is that Tom didn't want to know more. He had enough to rush this case through the grand jury, with just enough evidence to indict you. He probably knew that a bad toxicology test result could hinder his chances of making this look like an open-and-shut case. Depending on the backlog, it can take anywhere up to a month to get a written report back from the crime lab. Tom knows that. In this case, he used it to his advantage."

Jake's eyes bored into Susan's. "If Angelica was drugged first, before she was stabbed, this pretty much rules out a crime of passion, doesn't it?"

Susan nodded her agreement gravely. "The lethal amount of glutethimide in her system makes it premeditated murder, all right. A capital offense. I think you should brace yourself, Jake. The district attorney will be asking for the death sentence. And since you've already been tied publicly to the crime, at least in the minds of much of the public..."

"I can't believe this," Jake said.

Because you didn't do it? Susan wondered. Or because you just didn't think you'd get caught?

Realizing it was not her place to speculate, she pushed the troubling thought away. She had known from the outset it was going to be difficult to represent Jake. The way he held himself apart and aloof made him a dangerous risk to her, both professionally and personally.

Yet at the same time she felt Jake needed her help, maybe more than he was prepared to admit, even now. And she wanted to get to the truth of the matter. She wanted to be able to prove that he was innocent, that her own perception of him was not wrong. She felt passionately about not allowing innocent people...like her father...to be sent to jail. If Jake was innocent, it was up to her to see he was vindicated. The problem was, Susan thought uncomfortably, her gut instincts had failed her before. Having not seen the capacity for violence in her father, she was very much afraid she could be fooled again.

"You okay?" Susan asked him gently.

Jake shrugged and didn't answer, then stood and approached her desk. Once again, his expression was all business. The vulnerability he had shown her was gone. "Do you have that list of belongings the investigators found at the crime scene?"

Susan riffled through the file and handed the list over.

Jake scanned it and frowned. "There's no bottle of sleeping pills on the list."

"If we can find out where the pills came from, maybe we can pin down the murderer."

Jake's shoulders tensed. "The pills may have been hers, Susan. I saw a bottle of them on her dresser at the Four Seasons."

Susan's heartbeat picked up. If Jake had seen the pills, then he'd also had physical access to them. With effort, she pushed her suspicions aside. "Well, they weren't among the list of items from her hotel room at the Four Seasons, either."

"What do you think it means?"

That someone stole Angelica's pills from her room and used them to murder her. Susan realized uncomfortably that Jake was the only person who had mentioned knowing Angelica had been taking sleeping pills while she was in Austin.

She looked up, to see Jake watching her, his expression grim and intent. A chill went down Susan's spine. She pushed it aside. "Come on. Let's go over to the Four Seasons Hotel and see what we can find out there."

"OF COURSE I REMEMBER Angelica Saint-Claire's stay here," the maid at the hotel told Susan and Jake as they paused to talk to her in the suite she was cleaning.

"I was very upset to find out that she died," the pretty young maid said.

"So was I," Jake said quietly. He guided her to a chair and sat down adjacent to her. "That's why we're here," he continued. "We're trying to piece together what happened prior to her death."

"Did Miss Saint-Claire have any visitors while she was here?" Susan asked.

"Only one that I know of besides you—" the maid pointed at Jake "—but I don't know his name."

"Can you describe him?" he asked.

The maid nodded. "He was very tall, over six feet, I think. And older. Maybe in his sixties? He had white hair, blue eyes, leathery skin—like he'd spent a lot of time outdoors—and a deep raspy voice."

Jake immediately sent Susan a warning glance. "Don't start speculating wildly."

How could she not? she wondered, when the description matched his father.

"What was this older gentleman wearing?" Jake asked.

"A tan cowboy hat, a Western suit with pearl-snap shirt and one of those string ties."

Jake went completely still.

"Any idea what that man was doing here?" Susan said.

The maid shook her head. "All I know is that he came over late one afternoon. The second day she was staying here, I think. He was carrying a briefcase when he walked in. And he looked kind of of—"

"What?" Susan pressed.

"Angry," the maid said.

The expression in his eyes mysteriously brooding, Jake snapped impatiently, "How long did he stay?"

"About half an hour," the maid said. "I know, because I was cleaning the suite across the hall."

"Was it a quiet meeting?" Susan asked, as beside her Jake began to pace.

Again the maid shook her head. She began to appear a little frightened at the barely suppressed tension emanating from Jake. "No. I heard shouting."

"Do you know what they were fighting about?" Jake cut in abruptly, looking as though he were afraid of what was going to come out of this fact-finding mission of theirs.

The maid shook her head. "It wasn't any of my business what they were arguing about, so I kept real busy and tried not to listen. Then, about the time I was finished running the vacuum and cleaning the suite, the older gentleman left," she said respectfully.

"With the briefcase?" Jake asked swiftly.

"You know, come to think of it," she said, "he didn't have anything with him when he left. I guess he must've left his briefcase inside the suite."

"Was that the only time this gentleman visited?" Jake asked.

"I never saw him there at the hotel again."

"Did she have any other visitors?" Susan asked.

"Not that I saw. But as I said earlier, I'm only here days. I don't know anything about what goes on in the evenings. The only reason I saw you here that one night, Mr. Lockhart, is that you arrived just as I was getting off work."

"Thanks for the information," Susan told the maid.

"I know what you're thinking, Counselor, and you're wrong, damn it! It's not my father," Jake growled as soon as they were out of earshot. "The maid could be describing any number of men in this part of the country,'' he stressed as they headed back down to the lobby.

"True," Susan said. Although the description had sounded a lot like Jake's father. It would be foolish to jump to conclusions before they had gathered all the facts. "Let's have a glance at the copy of Angelica's hotel bill, see if we can find out who she called while she was here."

Jake nodded. To Susan's dismay, for the first time that day, he did not seem eager to push on.

Susan talked to the manager of the hotel—who didn't particularly want to have to deal with a subpoena. Soon they were sitting in a private conference room, with the printout of Angelica's hotel bill.

Jake scanned the list. "There are fifteen calls to my office."

"And two to the ranch." Susan looked at Jake. He looked at Susan. "We're thinking the same thing, aren't we?" she said.

"Let's hope we're wrong," Jake replied.

JAKE DROVE toward the sprawling Lockhart Ranch, Susan by his side, his thoughts in turmoil. His father couldn't have had anything to do with Angelica's murder. But even as he tried to tell himself this was so, he was recalling how much animosity there had been between the two. He'd thought she was a fortune hunter. And his father had been right, Jake acknowledged grimly, as he turned his Jeep into the long winding drive to the ranch house.

Acres of rolling green pasture, peppered with shady live oak, cedar and Arizona ash, rolled by. Behind expertly maintained dark brown fence, rust-and-white longhorn cattle grazed sedately. In another pasture, well away from the house, several brood mares roamed, their new colts by their sides.

Jake looked longingly at the palatial ranch house as it came into view. The sprawling ten-thousand-square-foot hacienda, with its arched windows and doorways, white stucco walls and red tile roof, had been his home as long as he could remember. He had hoped to raise his own family here someday. Now he wasn't sure he would ever get the chance.

So many questions needed to be answered. Why hadn't his father told him he'd been in contact with Angelica? Jake wondered. What else was his father hiding? Was this part of the reason Samuel had been too sick to attend Angelica's funeral? Damn it, why had his father lied to him?

"Are you okay?" Susan asked warily, as Jake parked the Jeep and they started up the walk.

Jake nodded, but inside he was reeling, still felt edgy and dismayed. And those feelings of gnawing unease only increased as he confronted his father with the evidence he and Susan had uncovered.

"So I talked to her and went to her hotel to see her," Samuel admitted, his manner defensive, as he met them in the front hall. "So what?"

Jake glanced at the small bottle of rifle oil and soft cotton cleaning cloth his father held in his hands. "You never said a word about seeing Angelica before she died," Jake accused.

"I didn't think it was relevant," Samuel said. Pivoting on his heel, he marched back to the den.

Jake scowled at his father and strode after him.

Susan caught up with the men at the doorway. She watched Jake's father open a cupboard next to the fireplace and pull out a canvas drop cloth. "What was your business with Angelica, Mr. Lockhart?" Susan asked.

Samuel unfolded the drop cloth with a snap. Mouth set thinly, he spread the cloth on the center of the carpet. "She called here looking for Jake. Said he wasn't returning her messages that she'd left for him at the office. She was through waiting around. Either he went to see her right away at the hotel or she was going down to the attorney general's office and make a big scene."

Jake looked even more upset by that revelation. "What did you tell her in response?" he asked his father.

Calmly Samuel walked over to the gun cabinet in the corner and brought out two rifles. "I told her if you weren't answering her messages that was the response. I suggested she take the hint and head on back to Hollywood."

Jake handed his father a low stool and went back to the cabinet to get two more rifles. "What was her reaction to that?"

"She said she meant it about making a scene." Samuel accepted the rifles Jake handed him wordlessly. "And she said it real mean, too."

Jake shoved a hand through his dark brown hair. "You should have told me she called," he said shortly.

Samuel shrugged. He checked the rifle chamber. "I figured you didn't need the hassle of dealing with her, especially when she was in such a snit."

"What happened next?" Susan asked. She didn't know if it was the sight of all the guns, or the information being discussed, but her heart was racing.

Samuel poked a thumb at his chest. "I decided to take care of things myself and I went to see her."

His face ashen, Jake towered over his father. "What was in the briefcase?" he demanded hotly. When Samuel didn't reply, Jake reiterated with a snap, "The maid at the hotel said you went in with a briefcase and came out empty-handed."

Samuel looked at Susan, then back at Jake. "I suppose you'll find out anyway," he said reluctantly. His weathered cheeks flushed. His eyes took on a guilty sheen. "I paid her off, to get lost."

Jake let out a string of swear words. He ripped off his suit jacket, then his tie, then threw them both down on the sofa, while beside him, Susan shut her eyes. Jake needed this like he needed a hole in his head, she thought.

"How much did you give her?" she asked Samuel.

"Fifty thousand dollars. I figured it was a small price to pay if I could keep her from trying to align herself with you. You know that woman's reputation, both here and in Hollywood," Samuel said, defending himself hotly. "And with you facing the primary in March and up for reelection next fall..." The look Samuel gave Jake was pleading. "I couldn't take a chance on her ruining all you had worked so hard to attain," he finished explaining.

Jake glared at his father as though he wanted to strangle him. "This money you gave Angelica, Dad?" he asked tersely. "Was it cash or check?"

"Cash."

Jake sighed, appearing slightly relieved.

Susan eyed both men. She knew Samuel loved his son, but this was nuts. "So what happened to the money you gave her?" Susan asked Samuel. "It was never found according to the police reports."

Samuel shrugged, looking completely at a loss, and as evasive as Jake. "Maybe she put it in the bank," he suggested as he routinely began to clean the rifle.

Susan shook her head, not about to let them dismiss the vital clue so easily. "The district attorney's office already subpoenaed Angelica's bank records. I reviewed the transactions made before she died. There were no large amounts of cash deposited in her accounts in the eight weeks prior to her death. But there were two other fifty-thousand-dollar cash withdrawals made, two weeks apart, in the month before her visit to Texas." And that spelled trouble.

"Maybe she had a secret account no one knew about," Jake mused, almost too nondescriptly, as he strode to the window and stared out at the winter sky. "And she was just shifting money around."

Susan made her way past Samuel and the row of rifles to Jake's side. "Maybe Angelica came back to Texas for a reason," she speculated bluntly, telling him and his father they'd better not be hiding anything from her. "Maybe she was in some kind of trouble. Was it possible she was being blackmailed, and that is why she was nervous about doing publicity? Did she come here not just to see you and cry on your shoulder, Jake, but to ask you to lend her money?"

Jake turned slowly toward her. The silence stretched out uncomfortably.

"Could it be that that was why she was so anxious to meet with you?" Susan continued. "After all, you are attorney general, besides being a former friend. It's not unreasonable to think she might ask you for help, particularly if her blackmailer came from her home state."

Jake turned away from Susan. "I don't know all that was on her mind," he said curtly, staring out the window again. "I never did."

Susan studied the rigidness of his posture. She believed Angelica had been an enigma as well as a problem to Jake. Just as she believed he still knew a lot more than he was telling her at the moment. And that would not do.

Susan glanced at Samuel, who was putting cleaning oil on the cloth in his hand. "Excuse us a minute." She grabbed Jake's sleeve and tugged him out into the hall. She released her grip.

Jake gave her a bored look. "Now what?"

"You want me to drop this part of my investigation, don't you?"

"That would be nice, yes." He pushed the words through a clenched mouth.

Susan shook her head at him. "Well, it's not gonna happen, Jake."

"Why the hell not?" He moved forward until she was inundated with the brisk masculine scent of him.

"Because you're hiding something from me and I don't like it."

He shook his head at her. His eyes mocked her. "Your imagination is working overtime, Counselor."

"I don't think so." Susan's lips curved into a taunting smile. "I think you suspect your father had something to do with Angelica's death."

Hand to her shoulder, he pushed her away, then strode past her. "Like hell I do!"

Susan raced after him. "Then who are you protecting?"

Swearing his frustration, he spun around again. "No one!" He was seething.

Susan just looked at him. Hands knotted into fists at her sides, she paraded past him and marched back into the den. Jake was fast on her heels and so close she could feel the warmth of his breath on her neck. Susan eyed Samuel. "Can you account for your whereabouts at the time of Angelica's death?"

Samuel shot Jake an unamused glance and said, "I was home alone, watching television that night."

Susan swore silently to herself. "Was there anyone here who can attest to that?"

"Nope. My housekeeper had gone hours before. The bunkhouse and barns are on the other side of the property."

Jake sent Susan a sharp warning look. He had known when he hired her that she might uncover more than he wanted. Having it actually happen added a nightmarish quality to a life that had already spun out of control. He had to rein her in. "Don't use my father as a scapegoat," he said sharply.

Color flushed Susan's cheeks. "You're an attorney, Jake. You know the laws about evidence." She turned to Samuel and explained, "The DA is bound by law to share whatever evidence he has with the accused and his attorney—it's known as the discovery process. So far, there's been nothing about Samuel. But I think you both should brace yourself. If we can find out about Samuel's visit to the Four Seasons, then so can the district attorney."

"Then we'll cross that bridge when we come to it," Jake decided autocratically.

Again silence fell between them.

Susan wished she knew what was going on. Then she brought herself up short. She did not allow herself to get emotionally involved with her clients so that her ability to remain objective was hampered. She couldn't let that happen here, either.

"I've got to meet with my private investigator, Ray Trevino. I want to fill him in on everything we've found out so far. As well as ask him to check out Chip Garrison's story about being in Mexico at the time of Angelica's death." And then there was the prescription sleeping pills, Susan thought. Ray could look into finding out who Angelica's physician had been.

She gathered up her things. "Do you want to sit in on this meeting with me?" she asked Jake.

He shook his head. "I've got to do a few things here, before I head on back to town. But I'll talk to you first thing tomorrow morning."

Susan nodded.

Jake might think he was fooling her with this casual act of his, but she knew the truth. He was very upset with his father. If Samuel hadn't been involved in Angelica's death, as Jake asserted, what exactly had he done to alienate his son? And what was Jake still hiding?

"YOU KNOW, don't you?" Jake said in a choked, angry voice as soon as Susan had left. He wondered if the news had been as much a shock for his father as it had been for him.

Samuel nodded, his expression compassionate. He clamped a reassuring hand on Jake's shoulder. "I know what Angelica did to you, how she betrayed you."

"But you didn't tell me."

Samuel rammed the cleaning rod down the barrel of the rifle and worked it around. "What purpose would that have served?"

Jake had no answer for that. He had kept his father in the dark for the same reason, because he was trying to protect him. "Is that why you paid her off? Or did she ask you for money?"

Samuel handed the rifle to Jake. He went to the bar and poured two shot glasses of whiskey. They clinked glasses, then Samuel downed his drink. Finished, he wiped his mouth with the back of his hand. "She asked me for half of what I gave her. Prettied it up with a lot of flowery words and the term 'borrow' but the end result was the same," Samuel admitted gruffly.

"So in other words, she was blackmailing you," Jake said. The hatred he felt for Angelica grew by leaps and bounds. He hadn't suspected her of extorting money from his father.

Samuel put down his empty glass. Restless, he walked over to the gun cabinet in the corner. "I gave her the money on one condition—that she never bother you with what I found out."

"Is that what you were arguing about in the hotel?"

Samuel shrugged and paced over to the flagstone hearth. He knelt slowly and stoked up the fire. "She blamed me for the breakup between the two of you years ago."

Jake sighed. It hadn't been that way at all. But Angelica had never believed that.

"She hated me for thinking that she still wasn't good enough for you, even after her Hollywood success," Samuel continued. "And when I found out what she had done to you back then, well, I admit I hated her just as much as she despised me." Tears glistened in Samuel's eyes. He clenched the fireplace poker. "She took what was ours, and she had no right to do that, Jake."

Jake swallowed around the knot of emotion in his throat. He wasn't prepared for the feelings he was having. The growing sense of loss he felt. The helplessness to do anything about it. He downed the rest of his whiskey and brought himself rigidly back under control. "Much as I'd like to, we can't change what happened, Dad. And we can't let anyone else find out," he warned. "Not even Susan."

Samuel was silent. "What do you think Susan would do if she knew?"

"As tenacious as she is? She'd probably use it in my defense, and Dad, I can't let that happen. There's a lot at stake here. Promise me, you'll tell no one what you've learned," he said passionately. "Even if they put you under oath."

Samuel looked conflicted. But he also understood Jake's need for secrecy. He knew who he was trying to protect. "I promise," Samuel said, just as the phone rang.

Jake reached over to get it. "Hello," he answered gruffly.

"Jake? It's Dusty Saint-Claire."

OTIS KINGSLEY removed his aviator sunglasses and smoothed back his jet-black pompadour before he knelt and opened the briefcase he had brought from Vegas. Inside was a stack of black construction paper and a carton of push pins.

Removing a fresh pair of surgical gloves from the box in the pocket, he inched them on. Then, ever so carefully, he began lifting the pages from the case, spreading them out in precise order on the bed.

Each piece held a single photo of Angelica.

Otis paused as he came to the picture of Angelica taken during her first appearance in Vegas. Lovingly he lifted it and gently kissed

Angelica on the mouth, then set it reverently back down on the bed.

"My beautiful angel," he murmured.

He would never see her again.

And it was all Jake Lockhart's fault.

But that, too, would be taken care of, Otis thought, as rising, he lifted the last piece of construction paper from the case. On it was the photo of Jake taken during the last campaign. He was smiling.

But he wouldn't be happy for long, Otis told himself complacently, as he pinned the picture of Jake on his motel room wall. Like Angelica, Jake was doomed to a short life. Like Angelica, Otis thought as he drew a sharp-bladed hunting knife from his case, Jake was going to have to pay for his mistakes. . . .

# Chapter Six

Jake walked into the deserted nightclub. Dusty was sitting on a stool, playing riffs on his electric guitar. They appeared to be alone, but Jake was taking no chances. He had a revolver tucked into the back of his pants and a knife strapped to his leg.

"What do you want?" Jake asked. First he'd been jerked around by Angelica and now her brother.

"That's no way to talk to someone you owe," Dusty chided.

He had done a remarkable job of shelving his grief, Jake thought contemptuously. But then, like his sister, Dusty always had a selfish agenda of his own. "How do you figure that?" Jake demanded gruffly.

"'Cause I think I know why you killed my sister."

"Impossible," Jake said. Angelica had hated Dusty and never would have confided in him.

Dusty just smiled smugly and didn't disagree. "I also know you never got over her, that you had been carrying a torch for her for years."

"That's a lie!"

"I bet the district attorney would believe me."

Probably so, Jake thought grimly. "What do you want?" he snapped.

"A reason to keep my mouth shut."

How about this? Jake wanted to say as he pulled out his gun. But aware this could be a setup, he kept silent and left his gun where it was. "My band and I have been wanting to make a video to go with our demo tape for some time. Maybe you know some financial backers who might be interested in helping us out?" Dusty suggested slyly.

Jake stared at him. To pay or not to—that was the question....

SUSAN WAITED as long as she could for Jake in the downtown hotel lobby. When it was time for her appointment, she went on up to speak to Dr. Torres alone.

"I thought Mr. Lockhart was coming with you," he said, as he showed her into his hotel suite.

"So did I," Susan said. "But he must have been unavoidably delayed. Either that or we got our wires crossed, so I'll fill him in later."

"Of course. Now, how can I be of help to you?" Dr. Torres asked graciously.

"Thanks for agreeing to speak with me about your patient Angelica Saint-Claire." A family practitioner in his early fifties, he looked like a nice man and seemed, Susan thought, both genuinely concerned and eager to help. Susan got out her notepad and pen. "You understand that legally, all this information is going to be made public in the trial anyway."

Dr. Torres shifted uneasily in his seat. "Yes, the DA's office has already served me with a subpoena to testify for the prosecution." He frowned, admitting with a sad shake of his head, "Her death was such a shock to us all."

Susan noted he seemed nervous, now that they were talking about the murder. "Had you known her for long?"

He nodded, his affection for Angelica quickly becoming evident. "She was my patient for the past ten years."

"So you know her fairly well?" Susan stated.

Dr. Torres's round face broke into a smile of fond remembrance. "Yes, I think so."

Susan made a note that there was some closeness there. "And you had time to look at the toxicology reports that I faxed to you this morning?" she continued.

Again he nodded. Abruptly his expression turned grim. "She came to see me the first week of November. She said she had been under a lot of pressure and was having trouble sleeping. She looked fatigued, so I prescribed the glutethimide for her."

"Did she know not to take the medication with alcohol?"

"Oh, yes. I was very clear on that when I gave her the prescription, and I also had a warning written on the bottle."

"Supposing someone mixed glutethimide with a margarita anyway—three or four tablets' worth—what would happen?"

"That person would become dizzy and disoriented and pass out, probably within fifteen minutes."

"They wouldn't get sick first?"

"No. The medication is very strong. Even taken with water in that dosage, a person would pass out rather quickly."

"Once the person had passed out, would it be possible to rouse them?" Susan asked.

"No."

"So they could be shot or stabbed and never know it?"

"That's correct."

"Does the DA's office know all this?"

"They only asked me if I prescribed the medication, and that's all they want me to testify to under oath."

That was Tom Peterson, Susan thought, picking out the information that would help his case, ignoring the rest. At any rate, the overdose explained a lot about why no one else had heard anything that night. "Back to the last time you saw Angelica," Susan said. "Did she tell you what kind of anxiety she had been having?" Susan asked.

Opposite her, Dr. Torres tensed.

"No."

"Had Angelica ever had problems with anxiety before?"

Dr. Torres nodded, his expression guarded. He was beginning to look nervous again.

"From time to time in the past, she had trouble sleeping, usually at the start of a new movie, and that's when I prescribed something for her."

"Glutethimide again?"

"No. Trialozolam, which is milder."

"Why didn't you give her trialozolam again?"

"Because it wasn't working anymore. So I gave her something a little stronger."

"How much glutethimide did you give her?"

"Fourteen pills, or two weeks' worth."

"How was she directed to take the medication?"

"One pill at bedtime."

"How many pills would constitute a lethal dose?"

"Two grams, or four tablets."

"Were you concerned about giving her two weeks' worth of medication then?" Susan asked. After all, that would be enough to kill three and a half people.

"Normally I would only prescribe three to seven days' worth, but because I knew Angelica and she was going to be out of town for a couple weeks, I gave her more."

"Was there a refill?"

"No." Dr. Torres flushed guiltily. "I told her she would have to see me again if her problems persisted. I cared a great deal about her, you see. I didn't want her suffering unnecessarily."

Susan studied Dr. Torres. His concern for Angelica seemed unusually personal. "Did she appear suicidal?"

"No. Definitely not." He paused and glanced at his watch. "If that's all—"

He looked abruptly anxious to end the interview. He also looked as if he had let slip more than he'd intended. "Yes, it is. Thank you, Doctor," she said.

As Susan left his room and headed back to the lobby, she couldn't help but wonder about Dr. Torres. He'd been almost too helpful, Susan thought. It could be guilt causing such a reaction. After all, he had prescribed the medication that had knocked Angelica out.

There was nothing odd about a physician caring for his patient. But to come halfway across the country to attend said patient's funeral... Susan couldn't shake the sense that the good doctor harbored some unrequited feelings for the dead actress. Maybe those feelings had been paternal in nature, Susan mused as she stepped out of the elevator and into the dimly lit hotel parking lodge. But why had Dr. Torres felt it necessary to emphasize how much he had cared for Angelica? Why had he acted so nervous and guilty?

Deciding she should have Ray do a background check on Dr. Torres, too, Susan pulled her car keys from her handbag. She was just closing the clasp, when she rounded the section that she'd parked in. At the far end of the aisle, she could see the front end of a dark green Jeep. Thinking it might be Jake, having found her car, she started for it, waving her arm in greeting.

Without warning, the Jeep shifted from park to drive. Bright lights on, it rounded the corner with a roar and headed for her. Her heart pounding and a scream of pure terror rising in her throat, Susan barely had time to ditch her briefcase and leap out of the way.

The Jeep sped past, screeched to a halt and began to back up swiftly.

Crouching to car level, Susan ran the length of the aisle, her body bent over crablike. The Jeep halted just as she reached the end of the row. A shot whizzed past her head, landing in the concrete wall just above her.

Susan screamed for help and in a panic rounded the corner and dashed up onto the next level. Another shot whizzed past her just as she turned the corner. On the other side of the divider, the Jeep started up again. Susan kept screaming, even as the vehicle lurched to a halt. On the other side of the divider, she heard a car door open and close. Footsteps. Her heart racing, every survival instinct on high, Susan continued to run, and was still going as she heard the Jeep back up again, coming toward her.

No longer screaming, Susan hit the cement floor facedown and slid under a pickup truck just as the Jeep careened around the corner. It stopped two cars away, idled menacingly. Knowing she was dead if she was seen, she stayed where she was, lying in a pool of grimy motor oil, barely daring to breathe.

Above her, on the next floor up, Susan heard footsteps and the sound of another car starting up. Realizing this might be her only chance to get out of there alive, she let out another bloodcurdling scream for help. A car horn honked in return, and there were promises of aid. The Jeep took off with a screech of wheels, heading for the garage exit the next level up.

Susan turned her head as it roared past, and caught a glimpse of the license plate—LKH ART2—and a shadow of a Stetson on the head of the tall driver....

Susan lay there a second longer, trying to get her bearings, absorb what had just happened to her and figure out what to do next. Had that been Jake who'd just shot at her and tried to run her down? Was this why he hadn't shown up to meet Dr. Torres with her?

Hysterical sobs bubbled up in her throat. This was ridiculous. Clients didn't try to kill her.

But someone just had.

Every inch of her feeling like jelly, Susan pressed her hands flat against the concrete. Footsteps sounded and she saw a pair of cowboy boots dash past. Friend or foe? she thought, and froze.

"Nothing down here!" one excited male voice said.

More footsteps, then someone springing past her.

"Nothing over there, either. Let's try the next level, then. The way she was screaming and carrying on, she couldn't have gotten far!"

Again the footsteps took off, faded.

Susan waited until she was sure the two men who were looking for her were gone. Belatedly, she realized the voices were not those of either Samuel or Jake. They could be her volunteer rescuers from the next floor up, but right now she couldn't risk trusting anyone. Her goal was simply getting out of there alive.

Trembling, she grabbed her purse and scooted stealthily across the concrete floor until she cleared the pickup, then struggled to her feet and stood on legs that barely seemed to work. She began to run toward the garage elevators. Just as she reached them, the door slid open. Jake Lockhart strode out and stopped short when he saw Susan. He took one look at her disheveled state. "Susan, what's going on here?"

"Stay away from me!" Fear poured through Susan. She backed up and panicked, then began to run.

Jake sprinted after her. He caught her before she could go six steps. His arms tightened around her like an iron band, cutting off her air. In a panic, she opened her mouth to scream again. Jake saw her intent and swore.

Clamping a hand over her mouth, he jerked her into the elevator, pushed the Door Close button and trapped her against the back rail, well away from the control buttons.

Slowly, deliberately, his eyes locked with hers. He dropped his hand from her mouth, letting it rest on her shoulders, instead.

Aware he could cut off her windpipe with one hand, Susan calmed down. At least for the moment. Her only recourse was to use every bit of persuasive speaking ability and talk her way out of this. "Jake, you are in enough trouble," she said softly. "You do not want to add kidnap and assault charges to the ones you are already facing. So—" her eyes still locked on his, Susan tried to sidle past him "—let me go."

Jake moved with her, his expression determined. He grasped her arm and held her close. "Not until you tell me what happened to you just now."

Susan took a deep breath. Fury washed away her fear. She was not going to play these games. "Stop it, Jake." Angry tears filling her eyes, she shoved him away from her. "I saw your Jeep!"

Jake dogged her steps to the other corner of the elevator. "What are you talking about?" He stared at her in confusion.

The tears she'd been withholding spilled down her cheeks. "You know!" Susan accused.

"The hell I do! I've been looking all over the hotel for you. Dr. Torres wasn't in his room."

Susan wondered where Jake had been. He'd had plenty of opportunities to set up an attack on her. She slipped her trembling hands in the pockets of her blazer. "You were late," she reminded him suspiciously.

"Yeah, well, I'm sorry about that," he said irritably, his expression fierce. "It couldn't be helped."

Susan stared at Jake, weighing her options, wanting so badly to believe him. "Damn it, Jake, I want out of here." *And if he really is innocent,* she thought, *he'll let me go.*

He shook his head and braced his arms on either side of her. He leaned in close. "Not until you talk to me." His glance slid over her critically. "How'd you get oil all over your suit?"

*As if you don't know.* Susan swept a shaking hand through her hair. "Someone tried to kill me. That person was driving your Jeep."

His expression went from angry to concerned in a second. "Kill you how?" he interrupted.

"By trying to run me down and then shooting at me."

"Where did this happen?" he demanded.

Susan heard the shock and disbelief in his voice and fell stonily silent.

He grabbed her shoulders and shook her. "Damn it, Susan, answer me!"

"On the next level down."

"I parked my car two levels down!"

"Before or after you chased me in it?"

Jake glared at her, looking as though he didn't know whether to kiss her or shake some sense into her. Susan drew a quick breath, stepped back, until she was flush against the wall without an inch to maneuver.

Eyes darkening, Jake began to move in.

"Don't—" Susan said, resting a hand on his chest.

"Don't what?" Jake whispered.

Beneath her fingers, she felt the strong steady beat of his heart. As he lifted her face to his, she felt the urgency in his touch, the gentleness. Were these the hands of a killer? Susan wondered, even as his head lowered and, of her own volition, her lips began to part....

Without warning, the elevator doors slid open. Jake and Susan broke apart. To her relief, two policemen stood on the other side.

"Everything okay in here?" they asked. "Miss, you all right?"

Susan nodded, though at this point she wasn't really sure. And then, as smooth as silk, Jake turned to the officers and began to explain.

SUSAN STOOD numbly by while Jake related everything that had happened. Her emotions were in turmoil. Looking at him now, listening to him converse with the police officers, it was hard to believe him capable of any violence, she thought. But she had seen the icy resolve in his eyes just now, felt the raw strength in his grip. He could have strangled her with his bare hands if he'd had a mind to.

So did that mean she was a fool to suspect Jake of the attack? Or a fool not to?

The only thing Susan knew for certain was that she was still Jake's attorney, and as such, had a responsibility to her client. If he wasn't guilty of trying to run her down . . . then they needed to find out who had done it, and why.

Still feeling a little dazed by all that had happened, Susan moved with the group to the level where her car was parked. The officers found the two bullets, lodged in the concrete wall. Remembering she had been carrying her briefcase full of notes when she'd left Dr. Torres's hotel room, she looked around, then swore her frustration. "My briefcase is gone," she said.

"Anything important in it?" the officer asked.

"Notes on a murder trial I'm investigating," Susan replied tightly.

"Any idea who would have wanted these?"

Jake, maybe? Again she felt a bubble of hysterical laughter welling up in her throat. "Just the murderer," she murmured, feeling abruptly on the verge of losing it.

The frown lines between Jake's eyes deepened at the jokelike delivery of her answer and the way her hands were still trembling slightly. The cops exchanged a worried look.

"Are you sure you're all right, Miss Kilpatrick? Maybe we'd better send you to the hospital, just to be sure."

Susan shook her head. She clamped down on her emotions. "I'm fine," she insisted, just as another cop came up to join them. She couldn't afford to fall apart the way her father had, at the first sign of trouble. She had to get hold of herself, discover the truth and continue to do her job.

"Mr. Lockhart, we found your car. It was about a half block from here, in another garage. The door lock had been jimmied, the ignition wires pulled."

Jake did not appear surprised by that revelation, Susan noted.

A shiver went down her spine. Noticing, Jake shrugged out of his suit jacket and slipped it around her shoulders. She was immediately inundated in his warmth and scent and, to her chagrin, still couldn't stop shivering. She couldn't afford to lean on Jake, yet part of her wanted to, especially now that she knew at least some of his story stood up to police scrutiny.

"Did you find a gun?" Jake asked the cops.

"No sign of one," the third cop said.

Jake nodded. He put his hands on his waist, looking anything but relaxed, and continued to glance around, scanning the area for anything they might have missed. Meanwhile, other cops were searching for the missing gun.

"You know this might have been gang related," the first cop suggested. "We're starting to have some of those problems in the area."

Except no one in a gang wore a cowboy hat, Susan thought. And again she thought of the only person she knew who still wore one—Jake's father Samuel Lockhart. Could he be in on this, too? Or was she really reaching here?


"YOU DON'T KNOW whether to believe me or not, do you?" Jake said, after his truck had been checked for fingerprints by the police and then towed away for repair.

Feeling considerably calmer, Susan walked toward her car. As a test of her courage, and his innocence or guilt, she had agreed to give Jake a ride back to her office building.

She slipped behind the wheel of her car, already feeling a little achy. "I'm not your judge and jury, Jake, just your attorney," she said wearily.

He slid in beside her. Their eyes met. For an instant, Susan thought he was going to argue with her, but he let the moment pass.

Silence strung out between them.

Abruptly aware she still had his jacket wrapped around her, Susan started to shrug out of it. Jake held up a palm to stop her. "You can keep it on."

Being wrapped in his coat was like being caressed in Jake's arms. And that was a luxury she couldn't afford. "No, thanks. I'm fine now." She handed it over.

"Tell me what you found out in your meeting with Dr. Torres," Jake said.

Glad to have something to talk about, Susan started driving the half-dozen blocks to her office building. Briefly she filled Jake in on the facts as they walked up to her office. "Did Angelica ever seem suicidal to you?'' she asked as she parked. "I mean, is it possible that she wanted you to find her after the fact, as some sort of punishment?"

Jake shook his head. As they headed inside, he said, "Absolutely not. She was a real survivor. She'd never go down without one hell of a fight."

"So whoever murdered her probably knew that," Susan commented once they were inside. She brought out two soft drinks for them.

Susan frowned. She got up to pace her office restlessly. "If Angelica took sleeping pills at the beginning of every movie, I'm sure Chip Garrison knew it. He was obviously very jealous that Angelica had returned to Texas to see you," Susan added, watching Jake's face carefully. "But was he jealous enough to kill her, then set you up for her murder?"

Jake shrugged. "He might have been jealous enough, but she was just starting to make him a lot of money. I mean, why would he kill her, when he'd put all that time into building her career?"

"You've got a point there," Susan said slowly.

"And let's not forget that I saw a prescription bottle out on the dresser the first night I went to see her," Jake said. "And it was there the next night, too."

"Did it look full?" Susan asked.

"Yes."

"You're sure it was the glutethimide?"

"Yes, I remember reading the label and seeing the warning not to mix the medication with alcohol."

"So anyone who saw her there would have known?"

"Even the maid, probably," Jake said. "But that doesn't mean that they would have known exactly what the lethal dose of glutethimide was, or what the reaction would be if it was mixed with alcohol."

"Well, this certainly doesn't help us narrow anything down," Susan said. She ran her hands through her hair.

Without warning, Susan heard her outer office door open. "Excuse me." She got up to see what was going on.

A freckle-faced man with red hair stood in the portal. Susan recognized him from Angelica's funeral. In fact, she couldn't be sure, but thought he might even be wearing the same clothes. He even had a camera slung around his neck.

"Ms. Kilpatrick?" he said. "I'm Vince Boyer. And I have a proposition for you. For a price, I'll launch a smear campaign against Angelica in the tabloids so it'll look like she deserved to be murdered.''

Jake came out to join Susan. She could tell Jake had the same thought—this guy was trouble.

Susan gave Vince a tight-lipped smile. "I don't operate that way, Mr. Boyer. I deal in the truth.''

"That's all a smear campaign would be—the ugly truth about her, in print," Vince said.

Susan saw the resentment glittering in Vince Boyer's eyes. She sat back and pretended to consider his offer. "You talk as if your crusade against Angelica is personal," Susan remarked.

"It is. Like Jake here, I'm one of Angelica's castoffs," Vince remarked. "I know what a selfish witch she could be. Hell, I'll even testify to that at the trial if you want.''

"Were you with her the night she was murdered?" Susan asked.

Abruptly Vince's face glowed a bright angry red. "Hey, you're not going to pin this on me!" he said. "I was just trying to do you a favor. And this is the reward I get!''

"Thanks, but those are the kinds of favors I can do without," Jake said. "In fact, I'd prefer not to see pictures of Angelica in the tabloids at all," he continued.

"No way, man. No can do," Vince said passionately. "After all, this is a high-profile case. Murder in Texas. A famous actress and a high-ranking politician . . . makes for lots of sales, you know?''

Jake looked at Susan as if he'd had just about enough. She knew how he felt.

"Thank you for stopping by, Mr. Boyer, but we'll pass," Susan said. She started to show Vince the door, but he refused to leave without first making another pitch.

"How about this, then?" he said. "I'll pay you for tips on how the defense strategy is going.''

"No, thanks," Susan said.

Jake walked around Vince and opened the door to the outer office. "Got any more suspects on the line?" Vince asked.

Susan did, but Vince Boyer was the last person she would ever have confided in. He was now near the top of the list of people she intended to investigate.

"Everything we have to say will be said in court," Susan declared firmly. "I'm afraid you'll just have to wait. Now, if you don't mind—''

"Something's going to be printed anyway, even if it's only speculation," Vince warned.

"I'd think twice if I were you before you libel my family or anyone close to me," Jake said grimly. "And that goes for Angelica, too."

Vince glared at Jake again. "You threatening to sue me?" he asked.

"If the shoe fits," Jake said mildly, with an affability that didn't begin to reach his eyes.

Vince paused. A pulse throbbed mightily in his neck. "Why do you care what happened to that broad?" he asked.

Why, indeed? Susan wondered, and once more puzzled over what Jake was hiding, why he was so protective of a woman he was now accused of murdering.

"She made your life hell, both before and after her death," Vince continued smugly.

Jake leaned toward Vince. Before Susan could do anything to stop it, Jake had both edges of Vince's jean jacket clasped in his fists. He jerked Vince threateningly close. "How do you know that?" Jake thundered.

Beads of perspiration broke out on Vince's forehead as he struggled unsuccessfully to break free of the grip. "Because I followed her here to Texas," he said. "And I saw how you looked after your first meeting with her at the Four Seasons Hotel. Hell, I even got photos of you storming back down to the lobby afterward. I tried to get photos of you in her suite, but she had the drapes closed."

Jake looked as though he were going to throw Vince against the wall at any second. Susan touched Jake's arm. Unprepared for the violence, she felt her heart pounding.

"Jake, please!" Susan said.

For a moment, Susan didn't think Jake was going to heed her. But after another moment's thought, he took a deep breath and reluctantly let Vince go. Susan was trembling as Vince stumbled against the portal. "Think you're tough, don't you?" Vince taunted. "Well, maybe you'll change your tune when you see those photos. Front page, too."

Susan swore. Just what they needed. "Out!" She pointed to the door.

His expression impassive, Jake took Vince's arm and escorted him out. Breathing a sigh of relief that Jake had resisted the violence simmering in him, Susan picked up the phone and dialed security. "Please see Mr. Boyer out. I don't want him in this building again. Period."

While Jake looked on, Susan called Ray Trevino. "Find out everything you can on Vince Boyer."

"Think we got another suspect here?" Jake asked after Susan had hung up.

"Don't you? He certainly seems very self-serving and capable of being involved in something criminal."

"But Vince Boyer doesn't seem like someone Angelica would let into her motel room voluntarily."

"Unless he had something on her."

Again Jake looked uncomfortable, as if he knew exactly what Angelica was hiding.

"Do you think Vince Boyer could have been blackmailing Angelica about something?"

"I don't know," Jake said shortly. He got up and headed for the door, his expression remote, his shoulders tense. "Look, if that's all you wanted to talk to me about, I need to get out to the ranch to see my dad," he said. "I promised him I'd stop by and update him on the defense."

Susan knew why he was in such a hurry to get out of there. She was beginning to read him better all the time—and that drove him crazy. Unfortunately, the more she knew about Jake, the more confused she became.

She put her thoughts aside and said, "Jake, there is one more thing."

He waited, every inch of him impatient.

"Vince did have one idea that was worth discussing. What are your feelings about launching a Darrow defense, which would so inflame the jury that they'd want to hang the deceased. I know the DA's strategy will be to prove that Angelica was an angel."

"I don't want you to destroy Angelica to save me." Jake's decision was firm.

Susan paused. "Why not? I thought you hated her."

Jake gave Susan a contemptuous once-over. "She's dead, Susan."

Susan held his glance defiantly. "And you're going to go to jail for her murder unless we can show the jury others wanted Angelica dead, too."

Jake moved away from the door. "Any information we dig up on her could backfire."

"So?" Susan shot back, irked he was stonewalling again. She moved toward Jake imploringly. "Let's dig up everything we can on her anyway and use what we think we can get away with. We don't have to prove someone else murdered her, Jake, only reasonable doubt."

Jake gritted his teeth. "I know that."

"And you're still reluctant. Why?"

He whirled away from her and retrieved his soda can. His back to her, he took a long thirsty drink. "Back off."

Susan's heartbeat accelerated at the edge in his voice. She folded her arms in front of her. "I'm not getting paid to do that."

Jake crumpled the can with one squeeze of his fist. He swung around to face her. "Well, now you are."

She ignored her cue to surrender. "Uh-uh, Jake." She shook her head at him. "I do my job or not at all."

He closed the distance between them. "You just have to keep pushing, don't you?"

"And you just have to keep throwing up roadblocks. Why?"

"Maybe I don't like defaming a dead person."

"And maybe," Susan said softly, "there's dirt on you, too. Information that links you both and might ruin your political career."

Jake was silent, a muscle working convulsively in his cheek.

"I'm right, aren't I?" Susan said.

"Are you finished playing these silly little games?" he asked.

Susan caught the dark glint in his eyes and decided to heed it—for the moment, anyway. "What if it looks like a Clarence Darrow defense is the only way we can save you?" she asked quietly.

"Then I'd tell you to find another way."

Their eyes clashed, held.

Finally, Jake sighed, abruptly becoming more reasonable. "The case against me is based on circumstantial evidence. That's all the DA has and is going to get—period. I know I didn't kill her. When I take the stand the jury will know that, too."

Susan shrugged. "You've got all the aces in this situation, Jake. If you choose to hold back information from me there may not be a heck of a lot I can do for you. But I have to warn you, if you take that same attitude into court, you're asking for nothing but trouble."

VINCE BOYER SWORE as he climbed into the Dumpster behind Susan's office building shortly after midnight. He'd thought slandering people for a living was bad, but sorting through garbage was the absolute pits. Not that he didn't enjoy his job, he mused, as he pulled out the long-bladed knife and sliced open a bag. Hell, he loved watching people squirm.

Seeing Angelica get what she deserved had been an unspeakable pleasure. Just as paying back Jake and his fancy lawyer was going to be a hoot, too. The only question was, Vince thought, as he studied the moonlight glinting off his silver knife blade, how was he going to do it?

# Chapter Seven

"Miss Kilpatrick! What's your response to the DA's statement that if Jake Lockhart really had the best interests of the people of Texas at heart, he would resign?" a reporter shouted.

Susan paused on the steps to her office building. Her new briefcase in hand, she smiled for the cameras. "Jake Lockhart has done a wonderful job as attorney general and will continue to do so. As for the trial, I have been actively gathering the facts surrounding the case. Once this case comes to trial, then Jake Lockhart will be vindicated."

The reporter stepped forward. "What can you tell us about the evidence that will be revealed, Miss Kilpatrick?"

Susan knew the key to winning any case was making sure the jury had an open mind. Therefore, she had to do all she could to discredit Tom Peterson's allegations that this was an open-and-shut case. "All I can say is that this trial is going to hold some real surprises," she answered coyly.

"Will that vindicate Jake Lockhart?" the reporter asked.

"Let's just say I am absolutely certain justice will prevail in this case." Susan smiled confidently, wishing she really felt that way. "Thank you. That's all I have for you at this time." She turned and went into her office building.

Jake was waiting for her upstairs. She knew he was still irritated with the way she had pushed him to confide in her the evening before. "I saw you got accosted by the mob," he said casually.

"Don't worry about it. Being dogged by reporters and cameras comes with the territory," Susan reassured him as she snapped open her briefcase.

"I suppose you heard Tom Peterson's latest assertions," Jake said.

Susan nodded grimly. "He's dreaming if he thinks you're going to resign. Or that I would ever allow him to railroad anyone out of a political office just so that he could run for it."

Jake's expression was both worried and remote. "You think everyone sees through Tom Peterson as clearly as you and I do?" he asked.

Susan nodded. "I do." She took a closer look. "You seem tired," she said.

Jake shrugged. "I just haven't had a lot of sleep."

Susan's gut feeling said it was more than that, but she sensed Jake was not ready to tell her anything else. She would have to wait until he trusted her more. But one thing was certain: she couldn't go into trial knowing half the story of what had gone on between Jake and Angelica.

"You said you had some interviews set up that you wanted me to sit in on this morning?" Jake asked.

Susan nodded. "The first is with the head of Worldwide Pictures, Toni Griffith. You may remember her from the funeral. She's in town to meet with the Texas Film Commission. She's agreed to talk to us this morning, if we go over to her hotel."

"YOU DIDN'T TELL ME she was going to be getting a massage while we spoke with her," Jake whispered as he and Susan entered Toni Griffith's suite a couple of hours later.

"That's 'cause I didn't know."

Tanned, thin, beautiful, Toni was a powerful person in her own right, and not the least bit uncomfortable, it seemed, conducting a meeting practically in the nude. The three of them said hello and Susan got right down to business.

"What can you tell us about Vince Boyer?"

Toni sighed as her masseur worked his nimble magic on her shoulders. "Angelica met Vince in an acting class soon after she arrived in Hollywood. He was already acting in bad horror movies, and he helped her get some bit parts."

Jake had moved so that he was looking out the window, rather than at Toni. "How long were they together?"

Toni rested her cheek on her hand. "They lived together on and off for about nine or ten years."

"Were they happy during that time?"

Toni sighed and shifted. The sheet dropped a little lower on her hips. "I don't think happiness came into it. They were both trying to survive in a tough town. It isn't easy to break into this business. They had that in common, and that was about it."

"What happened to break them up?"

"Angelica met Chip Garrison at a party up in Malibu. The next thing I heard, she had moved in with him and he had agreed to represent her. That surprised me. Angelica was still a nobody at that time, and Chip had major stars in his lineup of clients. It was unlike him to take on a complete unknown at that point in his career. But it turned out to be a wise decision. He has since made a lot of money off her."

"How did Vince Boyer take all of this?" Jake asked. He turned from his vantage point at the window to face Toni.

Toni sent Jake a frankly flirtatious look that had Susan's blood boiling.

"It was no secret in Hollywood that Vince was very ticked off with Angelica for walking out on him," Toni said. "However, it was also clear that he probably could have been mollified if Angelica had helped him get better roles."

"Why didn't she help him?" Susan asked, recalling how bitter and angry Vince had seemed as he'd offered to destroy Angelica in the tabloids.

"A couple of reasons, I think," Toni said. "One, she just wanted to forget she had been forced to live with someone who wasn't a mover and a shaker in this town, just to make ends meet. Two, Vince just never was a very talented actor.

"When Angelica refused to help Vince out," Toni continued, "he turned to dogging her and selling stories and photographs of her to the tabloids."

"How did she feel about that?" Susan asked.

"Her past relationship with Vince was a constant source of embarrassment to her. We did what we could for her in that regard, by barring him from our studio lots and all Worldwide Pictures sets."

"Did he adhere to that?"

"Vince?" Toni laughed and dismissed her masseur with a wave of her hand. Gathering the sheet around her middle, she rolled over and sat up. "Of course not. He was always trying to disguise himself and sneak his way in. Finally, last summer, we had him arrested for trespassing."

"And?" Jake prodded, watching Toni Griffith closely as she swept a hand through her mop of short black hair.

"The security guards at the scene said Vince vowed revenge."

"Was he able to get near Angelica again?" Susan asked.

"Not on our sets. Probably not at Chip Garrison's, either. He's got electric gates, an alarm system. And Angelica had a security system in her place in Laurel Canyon, too. But Vince might have run into her in public. If that did happen, though, I didn't hear about it."

"So, in other words, Vince kept dogging her every move, even after he was arrested by the movie studio," Jake ascertained thoughtfully.

"Right," Toni Griffith said. She tilted a bottle of Evian water against her lips and drank deeply. "He just couldn't do it on our movie sets."

"How did you feel about her shirking her promotion duties on the last movie she did?" Susan asked.

Toni Griffith frowned. Her beautiful face became pinched. "We were very unhappy, as you might well imagine," Toni said tightly, taking a sip of mineral water.

"Did you send anyone to Texas to talk to her?"

"We would've, had we known where she was. But we didn't, so no." Toni glanced at her watch. "I'm sorry. That's all the time I can give you."

"Just one more quick question," Susan said. "Was Angelica being hounded by any deranged fans?"

"No. Had she been, we would have known about it, and so would the Los Angeles police. Now I really have to go," Toni said.

They thanked her and left the suite. Susan wasn't sure if Toni had been coming on to Jake or not. She was certain, however, that Jake had not responded to Toni in the least.

"What do you think?" Susan asked Jake, as they stopped for coffee. In his usual starched white shirt and tie, he looked very handsome. She knew she shouldn't be noticing how he looked and she shouldn't care whether another woman came on to him or not. He was a client . . . not a date.

"It looks like Vince Boyer had motive to kill Angelica," Jake said with a frown. "He was a spurned lover, he blamed her for not helping him with his career and he vowed revenge for his arrest last summer. That all adds up."

"To a motive for murder?" Susan said, as she and Jake both reached for the cream and sugar simultaneously. Their hands touched briefly in the process.

Jake shrugged as he watched Susan stir cream into her coffee. "Love is a powerful emotion."

Yes, thought Susan, it was. "He also had opportunity," she said, since by his own admission, Vince followed Angelica to Texas and was here, dogging her steps when she died.

"But why would he wait so long to kill her?" Susan mused. "They'd been apart for years."

"Who knows?" Jake shrugged, looking remote again. "Maybe Angelica did something else to Vince recently?"

"Do you think Vince could've been blackmailing Angelica?" Susan asked.

"I don't know." Looking irritable again, Jake quaffed his coffee in a rush. He tossed five dollars on the table and stood. "What's next?"

"Meeting back at my office with a clerk from the health club at the Four Seasons," Susan explained. "I figured that since Angelica was an actress and needed to stay in shape, she might have used the hotel's facilities while she was in town. I had Ray Trevino check it out for me. He found a clerk, Luke Porter, who has agreed to come in and speak with us."

SUSAN'S FIRST impression upon meeting Luke Porter was that he was very young. He couldn't have been more than twenty or so. Her second was that he was very nervous. He was still in his hotel uniform, and he was sweating profusely.

Susan introduced herself, then Jake. They all shook hands and Luke took a seat. "I understand you had occasion to assist Angelica Saint-Claire at the health club," Susan said as she poured Luke a cup of coffee.

Luke Porter nodded. "Miss Saint-Claire worked out every day. And one day she even signed out a bicycle to ride around the lake."

"My investigator said you noticed something unusual that day," Susan said. "Could you tell us about it?"

"Well, Miss Saint-Claire took the bike out around nine that morning. I remember, because it was the same day that she later got murdered. She took off alone, and she looked pretty happy, considering it was early in the morning and everything. Anyway, she came back about ten-thirty and she was all hot and sweaty and upset looking, you know. I went to help her with the bike and she snapped at me to hurry up. Then this guy came up to her. She didn't seem to want to talk to him at all.''

''Who was it—do you know?''

Luke paused. ''I heard her call him 'Chip'. He didn't have a Texas accent, so I just figured he was one of her friends from Hollywood.''

Susan pulled a black-and-white photo of Chip Garrison out of a manila file folder. She slid it across her desk to Luke. ''Is this the guy?''

''It sure is,'' he said, his face lighting up. ''Who is he, anyway?''

''Chip Garrison, Angelica's agent,'' Susan said.

''Oh.''

''What happened next?'' Jake prodded.

''Well, that guy said she needed 'to come back and do the publicity, like she had promised.' She said she couldn't do it because she wasn't up to it, and he should just leave her alone.''

Susan and Jake exchanged a look. Chip had not mentioned following Angelica to Austin when they questioned him. Susan was sure the oversight was no accident. ''How did Chip react to that?'' Susan asked.

''He got real angry. He grabbed her arm and kind of pulled her outside. They walked down this path a little ways, and he pushed her up against this tree. They were arguing real bad. Then he took her in his arms and—'' Luke hesitated ''—I'm not sure I should tell this next part.''

''It's okay, Luke,'' Susan said gently. ''Just tell us everything, then Jake and I'll sort it all out and decide if it means anything or not.''

Luke took a deep breath. ''Then this Chip guy started to kiss her and she started struggling.''

''Was she screaming?'' Jake interjected quickly.

''No.'' Luke frowned. ''But she didn't look like she was enjoying it much, either.''

''What did you do?'' Susan asked.

Luke looked embarrassed. ''I didn't know what to do.''

''So you did nothing,'' Jake said.

Luke nodded in relief. ''Then this other dude comes up.''

''Who?'' Jake asked, leaning forward suddenly in his chair.

''I don't know.'' Luke shrugged. ''He was real tall, and he had white hair, wore Western clothes and a Stetson.''

Susan took another picture out of her desk. She showed it to Jake. "That's him all right." He pointed to a photograph of Samuel Lockhart.

Jake sucked in a shocked breath. His slate gray eyes igniting with temper, he sat all the way back in his chair.

"Anyway," Luke said, resuming his story, "this man wants to know if I'd seen Miss Saint-Claire, 'cause he had an appointment to talk to her. And I said yeah, and he asked me where she was, and I point down the path behind the hotel. He took one look at what was going on, raced down there and grabbed hold of the guy with the ponytail—"

"Chip Garrison," Susan said, aware that Jake was now avoiding her eyes altogether.

"Right, and he pulls him off Miss Saint-Claire, real rough like, and tells him the lady wants him to take a hike. You woulda thought Miss Saint-Claire would be all grateful like—?"

"But she wasn't?" Susan interrupted.

"No. She said she called the shots in her life, not him. And the rancher guy told her that as long as she was in Texas, he was calling the shots. Then she got this scared look on her face and got real quiet."

Susan glanced at Jake out of the corner of her eye. He got up and paced around the office restlessly. "Then what happened after that?" she asked.

"Miss Saint-Claire told both men to get lost and she went on up to her room."

"Did either of them try to follow her?"

"Yeah, both did, and she turned around and threatened to call hotel security. I was afraid there was going to be trouble by that time, so I escorted her to her room."

"And then what happened."

Luke Porter blushed. He ducked his head a little as he admitted, "She said I was sweet to come to her rescue like that and she kissed me on the cheek and went inside her room and shut the door. I hung around for a few minutes, just to make sure there was no more trouble. Then I went back downstairs. Both the rancher and Chip were nowhere around. And that was all."

"Did you see Miss Saint-Claire again?"

Luke Porter shook his head. "I got off at noon. I'm a student over at UT, so I only work at the hotel part-time. Miss Saint-Claire was killed later that same night, so when I got to work the next morning . . . her death was on the front page of the papers. I went to the district attorney's office, and told them what I knew."

Susan hadn't heard any of this. She wondered what else Tom Peterson was keeping from them.

"Thank you. You've been a lot of help." Susan showed Luke out.

When she came back in, she shut the door. "I take it you didn't know that your father was with Angelica the morning she died?"

Jake shook his head no. "Just because my father was there again, doesn't make him Angelica's murderer," Jake said.

Susan refilled their coffee cups. "I know this is difficult for you."

Jake promptly quaffed half a cup. "And then some," he admitted grimly.

"But unless you start confiding in me, crafting a defense for you is going to be like threading a needle in the dark. Without your full cooperation, we haven't got a prayer," Susan finished.

Jake whirled on her so fast she bumped up against her desk, trying to avoid coming into physical contact with him. "You think I don't know that?" he returned gruffly.

Susan's heart pounded at Jake's nearness, but she kept her demeanor calm. "Knowing it and being able to let your guard down are two different things." Susan sighed. "Let's start with your father's relationship with Angelica. Obviously there was no love lost between them."

"Right."

"Why? Was he instrumental in breaking the two of you up?" Susan asked.

Jake shook his head. "Angelica did that herself."

"How heartbroken were you?" Susan asked, aware she was asking for herself now.

"I felt used. Angelica had really put one over on me, with her sweet and loving ways. Until the night I told her I wasn't going to Hollywood—and she exploded."

"So you weren't in love with her back then?" Susan asked.

"Truth of the matter is that at that stage of my life, I didn't know the difference between my hormones and love."

"Do you now?" Susan asked.

"Yes," Jake said flatly, draining the rest of his coffee in a single gulp. "I do." He looked at Susan steadily. "Making love is a commitment for me these days...not a way to ease a physical ache. And I'll say that on the witness stand."

Susan's breath caught in her chest. She hadn't expected such candor from Jake, especially not in such an intimate area of his life. More important, she had the strong feeling that he hadn't told her because she was his attorney, but because he simply wanted her to know how he now felt about that area of his life.

Jake sighed. He jerked loose the knot of his tie, swore in obvious frustration. "Spoken out loud, that sounds like a line, doesn't it?"

"Maybe from someone else," Susan allowed with a smile. "Not from you."

Had Jake told this to Angelica, too? she wondered. Had they quarreled about it? "Had Angelica grown up in this respect, as well?" Susan asked.

Jake frowned. Some of the bitterness was back in his face. "For Angelica, I think making love was a means to an end. Period," he said tersely.

"Did that bother you?"

"It bothered me that I hadn't seen her clearly before, for who and what she was." Jake blew out a weary breath and raked both hands through his hair. "Understand that I never meant to take advantage of Angelica. At the time, I didn't think I was. But now in retrospect I know I should have passed on the opportunity to sleep with her. If I had—" the brooding light was back in his eyes "—it would have been better for all of us."

"We all make mistakes, Jake," she said quietly. "Especially when we're that age. But you can't keep letting your regret about what happened then affect what happens now."

He turned to her. "It's not that easy, Susan."

"I know," she said gently. "But you've got to try, Jake."

"Why?" He regarded her impatiently.

"Because, damn it, Jake, if you don't find a way to come to terms with it, people are going to assume the conflict you're feeling has to do with Angelica's death, not making love to her when you had no intention of marrying her."

"I know what you're saying."

"But you're making no promise you'll comply, right?" Susan asked, wishing she could find a way to shake some sense into him.

"I can't, Susan," Jake said roughly.

Again she studied him. She thought how odd it was to know so much about some aspects of his life and so little about the rest of it. And she realized something else. The two of them had become a team.

She wasn't as unhappy about that growing closeness as she knew she should be.

Her secretary buzzed her. "Ray Trevino, line one."

Susan reached for the phone. She was glad Ray was checking in while Jake was still there with her. "Hello. What have you got for us on Chip Garrison's whereabouts the day Angelica died?" she asked.

She listened, then thanked him and hung up. She turned to Jake, who was anxiously waiting for the latest word. "Ray talked to everyone on the movie set. Chip was not in Mexico visiting another client, as he claimed."

Jake, like Susan, was not at all surprised by that revelation.

"So that makes two corroborations," Susan continued, writing down the information. "The first being Luke Porter and now the movie set. Plus Chip was seen arguing with, and trying to force his attentions on, Angelica earlier in the day."

"That makes two spurned lovers on the list of suspects," Jake said thoughtfully. "Chip Garrison and Vince Boyer."

"And both had motive and opportunity." Susan smiled. Jake's defense was looking up, but they weren't out of the woods yet. "Can you meet me here this evening, say about seven-thirty? I want to go out to the Shady Villa Motel."

"Why?" Jake felt wary and alarmed.

"I want to go over everything that happened from the moment you arrived at the motel to meet Angelica. I think being there will assist in your recall of even the tiniest details," she explained.

"All right," Jake agreed reluctantly after a moment. But he wasn't happy about it. "I'll pick you up at seventy-thirty," he said, "and we can both go in my car."

"The building is locked up every evening at six. After that, only people with keys can get in. So I'll meet you out front," Susan said.

Jake paused in the doorway. "You're sure you want to do this?"

Susan gazed at him. "Aren't you?"

"Mr. Lockhart didn't look too happy about going to the crime scene this evening," Susan's secretary, Maizie, said as she prepared to leave for the day.

Susan looked up from the questions she was compiling. "I know, but it's a necessary evil. See you tomorrow, Maizie."

Maizie nodded. "Be careful leaving this building. It gets spooky when everyone goes home for the day."

"I'm always careful," Susan said with a smile. She went back to her questions. At seven-fifteen, she slipped on her coat, grabbed her things and headed out of her office. Everyone else on her floor seemed to have gone home and it was eerily quiet as Susan locked up the outer door, then made her way to the elevators.

She pushed the down button and waited. And waited. She pushed it again. Still nothing. Susan walked across the hall to the other set of elevators. She pushed those buttons, too. Again nothing.

Swearing, she glanced at her watch. Seven-twenty. Jake would be there shortly. She was anxious to get out to the Shady Villa Motel and see what he could recall. Not looking forward to descending seven flights of stairs in her heels, she nevertheless started for the emergency exit at the end of the hall. As she neared the stairwell, she noticed the stairs were dark. Susan paused, a chill running up her spine. That was strange. Although the elevators frequently were on the blink, the stairwell lights were never out. She didn't like this at all.

Getting out her keys, she turned briskly on her heel and headed back in the direction of her office. Without warning, the door to the stairwell opened behind her. Susan whirled just as a fire fighter stepped out. To her surprise, he was dressed in full gear: heavy heat-proof yellow-and-black jacket, pants, boots, gloves, helmet and face mask.

Susan frowned, her heart rate picking up. She tried not to panic. There was now a fire fighter in the building wearing a mask and she didn't smell smoke. There were no alarms sounding in the building. Oh, God, Susan thought.

The fire fighter motioned Susan toward him with one big gloved hand, then pointed behind him toward the stairs. In an emergency situation, Susan wouldn't have hesitated to follow instructions. But this was no emergency; this was some sort of trap.

Her heart pounding, regretting the fact she was in heels, not sneakers, Susan kicked off her shoes and broke into a run. Heavy footsteps pounded behind her, gained on her, closing in with terrifying speed. *Oh, God, she wasn't going to be able to outrun him.*

Susan waited until the footsteps were almost upon her, then she turned and swung hard with her briefcase, aiming right for her follower's middle. As it connected, her masked attacker grunted in pain. Taking advantage of his momentary incapacitation, Susan dashed for the safety of her office door. Her attacker lumbered wordlessly after her, surprisingly agile for all the heavy cumbersome gear.

Knowing she would never be able to get her key in the door and the office door unlocked before he was on her again, she put all her energy into saving herself by sprinting toward the other stairwell. Again, he was almost upon her. Susan screamed and lunged, whacking him with her purse, forcing him to back off. She hit him once, and then— Oh, God. Too late, she saw the glint of a hunting knife in his gloved hand. There was a sickening rip as it thrust forward and lacerated the leather of her purse.

Sobbing hysterically, she broke away from him and ran on. He was struggling with the purse, and the knife, trying to pull the blade free of the leather exterior just as she reached the fire alarm. Susan felt for it along the wall, located it blindly and yanked on it as hard as she could. The deafening peal of the alarm sounded throughout the building. Her attacker made one last lunge with the knife, slashing her across the body from shoulder to chest, ripping through the wool of her coat, then turned and ran, the knife still glinting silver in his gloved hand as he headed back toward the emergency stairwell.

# Chapter Eight

"You sure you're all right, Ms. Kilpatrick?" the policeman asked gently as Susan stood in front of the office building, between the officer and a fire fighter. Inside the building, a search was being conducted for her attacker. Outside, the whole block was cordoned off. Fire trucks were parked in front of the building.

Susan nodded, and pressed her folded arms closer to her middle. "I'm just a little shaken up is all." Now that it was over, she couldn't seem to stop shaking.

She noticed that the policeman writing the report glanced at the jagged tear in the front of her coat. Had she not had her coat on she would have been badly hurt from just that one vicious swipe. Had she not been able to reach the fire alarm, she might be dead. But she couldn't think like that, she told herself firmly. She had to remember as much as possible and help catch the person who had attacked her.

"Do you feel up to going over what happened one more time?" the officer inquired.

"Sure." Susan wanted her attacker caught. Briefly she explained the frightening episode.

When she had finished, the police officer asked, "Are you sure the fire gear was authentic and not a costume? Halloween wasn't too long ago, and it wouldn't be the first time costumes have been used as disguises in robberies."

"It seemed real—heavy and cumbersome, like it was impeding his ability to move quickly and agilely."

"Sounds like real gear, all right," the fire fighter said.

The policeman looked at the fire fighter. "Any idea how this could have happened?"

"We had some fire gear stolen over the weekend during an open house. So I suppose whoever took it could have done this." He turned to Susan. "You didn't get a good look at your attacker?"

Susan shook her head. "He had that mask over his face and a fire hat on his head."

The policeman made a couple of notes. "What about height and weight? Were you able to estimate either of those?"

Again Susan shook her head. "I know he was a lot bigger than I am, broader of shoulder. But the clothes were so bulky he could have been skinny, for all I know." She sighed. "I'm not being very much help, am I?"

"You're doing fine. You said something about meeting someone here earlier."

Susan nodded and tried her best to short-circuit another shudder. "One of my clients," she said through teeth that chattered. "Jake Lockhart."

The policeman narrowed his glance. "Where is he?"

"I don't know." Susan looked at her watch and saw it was seven-fifty. "I haven't seen him." And it wasn't like Jake to be late. Usually he was early.

Suspicion formed in her mind. Deliberately she pushed it away. "Did anyone else know you were going to be here at this time tonight?" the policeman continued.

"Just Jake," Susan said. "But my coming out of the building at this time of night is not unusual. I often work late. Anyone who knows me, knows that."

"Uh-huh." The murmured word carried a wealth of innuendo. "How well do you know Mr. Lockhart?" the policeman asked.

Susan stiffened. She knew what he was getting at and she didn't like it. "Jake Lockhart didn't do this," she said.

"He has been accused of murder," the policeman responded matter-of-factly.

Susan didn't like what he was suggesting. Shivers started up and down her spine once again. Her knees were trembling. "He's innocent of that crime," she said.

The policeman and fire fighter exchanged skeptical looks. "Just the same," the fire fighter said, "perhaps you shouldn't be alone with him."

That was ridiculous, Susan thought as she pushed her fingers through her hair. Jake wouldn't hurt her. Or would he? Her intuition about what a person was or was not capable of had failed her before. She had believed in her father and he had killed a man in the heat of passionate anger.

"Do you have any enemies?" the fire chief asked, dragging Susan out of her troubled reverie.

She gestured lamely. "I'm a criminal lawyer. Not everyone is happy with the job I do." *Including Jake sometimes, when I press too hard, too fast.*

"That's right," the policeman mused as Susan turned her face into the winter wind. "There was a group of protesters here a few days ago, wasn't there? A rock-throwing incident?"

Susan nodded. That rock had been aimed at her, too. Only Jake's quick thinking had saved her from being the one who had needed stitches.

"What about your family? Any enemies there?" the policeman continued.

"My family's gone," Susan said numbly. Though inwardly she was thinking about Jake and how he'd put her father in jail. *What would he think if he knew she had lied to him from the first, if only by omission?*

To her left, there was a commotion, some cops yelling at someone to stop. Susan turned to see Jake pushing his way through the crowd.

"Damn it, let me through!" he said. His face was flushed, his expression grim. "Susan!" He stopped just short of her, searching her face. "What happened? Are you all right?"

She nodded. The policeman and fire fighter regarded Jake distrustfully. They noted, as did she, the perspiration streaming down his neck, onto his collar, the rumpled state of his suit and shirt and the fact that he wasn't wearing an overcoat.

"There was an attack on Ms. Kilpatrick tonight as she left her office," the police officer said. He peered at Jake. "You wouldn't happen to know anything about that, would you?"

Jake scowled. "Of course not. I just got here."

"But you're late," the fire fighter commented, eyes narrowing. "And you look a little worse for wear."

"Because I had to park three blocks away and fight my way through the crowd back there and your line of officers," Jake said hotly.

For a moment, Susan thought he was going to lose his temper. Fortunately, just then, some policemen and fire fighters came back out of the building.

"We couldn't find anyone," one reported. He looked at Susan. "We did find out why the elevators weren't working, though. Someone had shut off the power to them downstairs—about seven-fifteen near as we can figure. Then he must have headed on up those back stairs, and that's when you ran into him."

"Did anyone else see him?" Susan asked.

The fire fighter shook his head. "There was an accountant working late on the other side of the building, but he had no idea anything was going on until the fire alarm sounded."

"What about the security guard downstairs?" Susan hadn't had a chance to talk to him herself yet.

"He was by the front desk. Says no one at all came in or out of the building since it closed down at six o'clock. As you know, the cleaning crew doesn't arrive until ten. So...your description of the attacker is all we have to go on."

Silence fell. "They're fingerprinting down by the switch boxes in the basement, but because you said your attacker was wearing gloves, they don't expect to find anything."

Susan nodded. She had expected that, too.

"We're going to have to ask you for your coat and your purse, though," the policeman said. He pointed out the deep slash marks in each. "Material evidence, you know, in case this ever does come to trial."

Susan emptied the contents of her purse into her briefcase and shrugged out of her coat. "If that's all, officers, I think I'd like to go now," she said.

"Sure thing. We'll call you tomorrow if we need anything else from you. And—" one of the officers cast a censuring look at Jake before he turned back to Susan "—be careful now, Ms. Kilpatrick."

Susan swallowed. She blinked back tears of fatigue. "I will." She walked off, Jake at her side.

"Let me drive you home," he said kindly.

Susan took a long, deep breath. "I'm fine, Jake." She had handled worse things in her life.

Jake shrugged out of his suit jacket and put it around her shoulders. It was warm with his body heat, and scented with the brisk, masculine scent of his cologne. Just having it wrapped around her somehow made her feel safer. "You look like hell," he remarked protectively, his eyes narrowed in concern.

"Thanks," Susan said dryly, and moved a little away from him.

Jake moved closer and placed a comforting arm about her shoulders. "After what happened tonight, you should go home and soak in a hot bath and have a glass of wine and forget about all this."

The way Angelica had soaked in a tub and then had a drug-laced margarita? Susan wondered. She pushed the thought away. She had to stop this. She was letting her anxiety get the best of her, and she never did that.

"I'm sorry. I had no right to tell you what to do." He took her briefcase so she could hold the suit jacket closed. "I'm just trying to help."

"I know that." Susan stalked across the street. Despite her doubts and fears, with Jake close at her side she began to feel a little bit better, a little safer.

They moved down the block, walking briskly into the winter wind. "Would you prefer I took you somewhere else? A friend's house?"

Susan recalled how much Jake had not wanted to return to the crime scene earlier. The attack on her was not going to circumvent the task, however. He needed to get this over with, and she needed to lose herself in her work. "We still have work to do tonight, remember?" she prodded. "Plus I've already made the arrangements. We have a policeman out there, waiting on us. I called from the front desk after the attack, to let him know we'd be a little late."

He regarded her incredulously as they moved into the parking garage and headed toward his vehicle. "You still want to go, after everything that's happened tonight?"

"Look, Jake, the trial isn't going to wait just because I got assaulted tonight." Susan stopped just short of his Jeep. "So yes, let's go."

JAKE PARKED in front of the Shady Villa Motel. At Susan's request, he waited while she walked in to talk to the motel manager and the young uniformed cop.

So much had started here, so much had ended, Jake thought, as he stared at room number six. It seemed the place wouldn't let go of him, nor would the memories. And then, he thought with a troubled sigh, there was the future.

Without warning, Susan was stepping out of the manager's office, the cop at her side. Together they walked toward room number six, which was still under seal.

An adhesive notice was affixed to the door, stating that the room was a crime scene and that entry was forbidden.

"I'm going to have to frisk both of you before you go in," the officer said with an apologetic smile at Susan.

"No problem," she replied.

Next their IDs were checked and the court order allowing them access to the scene perused. Finally they were let into the room.

"Don't touch anything," the cop said.

The officer stood across the room, in the doorway, arms folded across his chest. Jake looked around reluctantly. The room was just as it had been when he'd walked in that night. Angelica's clothing was strewn about. The pitcher of margaritas had been emptied and so had the glasses, but they were still there, next to the vase of dead flowers.

Susan motioned Jake close. "You okay?" she whispered in his ear.

He looked at the tape outline of Angelica's body on the bed, the dried traces of her blood on the white hotel sheets. "Okay" seemed a relative term. "Let's get this over with," he said, feeling none of the grim curiosity she did. He just wanted to get the hell out of there, put this all behind him.

Looking as if she had completely recovered from the attack on her earlier, Susan nodded. She activated the tape recorder in her hand and began to question him, in the same whispery tone.

"When you arrived that night, was the light on?" Susan asked.

"Yes."

"Any sound coming out from the room? TV? Radio?"

Jake closed his eyes briefly. "No."

"What did you see when you walked in?" Susan asked.

Jake tried to shut the picture out of his mind, but he couldn't. Rubbing at his forehead, he turned toward the chalk outline. "Angelica was lying in the center of the bed. The covers were pulled up above her breasts and tucked beneath her arms. It didn't look like she was wearing anything at all."

Susan's glance gentled, as if she knew how hard this was for him. "Do you recall what you were thinking and feeling?"

Jake nodded, the bitterness coming back over him in waves, warring with the need to keep the most secret things about that night from Susan, while still telling her what she wanted, needed, to know to defend him. Jake drew a bracing breath and wished he had some of the whiskey his dad kept in his den at the ranch. "I wondered what kind of game she was playing with me now."

"Game?" Susan asked.

Jake brought himself up short. He was revealing too much again. "She was an actress. She liked drama in every aspect of her life, including her lovemaking," Jake said truthfully, avoiding Susan's eyes.

Aware that the cop in the doorway was straining to hear every word they said, Susan stepped even closer. Her shoulder brushed Jake's arm. "Did you expect her to be in bed when you arrived?"

"No. It was early yet, only about ten p.m."

"So what'd you think when you saw her?"

Jake shrugged, a surge of uneasiness rising in his gut. "That she wasn't really asleep, just pretending to be, to get me over to the bed."

"Did you say anything?"

"Something like 'Okay, Angelica, I'm here.'"

"What happened next? Did she make any sounds or movements?"

"No. She was perfectly still, which is what led me to go over to the bed. I admit I was irritated as I reached her side because I still thought at that point that she was trying to play games with me. So I said, 'Enough of this, Angelica!' And I ripped back the covers, trying to get her to react, and that was when I saw . . . the blood," Jake said hoarsely.

Without warning, he flashed back to the scene, then pushed the ugly memory away.

"Tell me everything you see, Jake," Susan urged quietly.

He clenched his jaw. This was even harder than he'd expected. The anxiety was coming at him again, full force. "It was like a nightmare," he said in a choked voice, "only it was real." He shook his head, as the tight web of fear inside him grew and grew. Swallowing hard, he forced himself to concentrate on the murder scene. "For a second, I just stood there, staring, unable to believe this was really happening."

"And then?" Susan probed.

Jake shrugged, his world taking on a dreamlike state again. "And then I located the wound and put pressure on it to see if I could stem the bleeding. With my other hand, I felt for a pulse in her neck. There didn't seem to be one, so I forced her mouth open and blew some air into her lungs. She didn't appear to respond. But she was still warm." Jake released a shaky sigh, remembering the utter panic he had felt. "I started for the phone, and that's when the police burst in the door and told me to freeze."

"Why was the motel room set for a seduction? Had you given her a reason to think the two of you could reconcile?"

"No," Jake said vehemently. Angelica had known, at that point, how much he hated her. And it had infuriated and frustrated her....

*"Jake, please!" Angelica hugged him around the middle, dragging him down even as he made his way toward the door. "You've got to try and understand!"*

*Jake pried her arms from his middle and pushed her away from him. He stared down into her flushed face and fever-bright eyes. "I understand all right," he told her with deadly calm, aware it was taking all his self-control not to strangle her here and now. "I understand you were a selfish, lying, manipulative little con artist even then!"*

*"You're responsible for what happened!" Angelica cried.*

*Jake had expected the anger at seeing her again, but he hadn't expected the smoldering fury, the feeling of being just on this side of control, the feeling that he might snap at any minute. He closed the distance between them slowly. Keeping his hands to himself with effort, he glared down at her. "And how the hell do you figure that?"*

*Angelica blinked back huge crocodile tears. "If you had just done what I wanted—"*

*"What you wanted," Jake repeated, a muscle working in his jaw as he towered over her. He picked her up by the waist and pressed her back against the wall. "That was always it, wasn't it, Angelica? You never cared about anyone but yourself and you still don't." He tightened his grip on her until she gasped. "Well, you can rot in hell for all I care!"*

*Her sobbing gasps for breath ringing in his ears, the heavy scent of her perfume choking him, Jake dropped his hold and spun away from her. He had to get out of there, he thought. Had to...before something else happened.*

*But already she was regaining her cool. Sauntering implacably after him. Working hard to get in the last word.*

*"Before you walk out that door, Jake, be warned," she said silkily. "You let me hang on this one by myself and I swear I'll ruin you," she threatened destructively.*

*Jake turned very slowly. Her threat had just pushed him over the line.*

*He strode back to Angelica, closing the distance between them in an instant. Grabbing her by the arms, he pulled her up off the floor and held her there, so her feet dangled helplessly beneath her. "Don't you ever threaten me again!"*

"Are you sure?' Susan asked, pressing the point, her voice dragging Jake back into the present. "Maybe she took your willingness to see her at all as a sign you wanted to rekindle things, too."

"No. She knew how I felt," Jake muttered shortly, "especially after—"

"Especially after what?" Susan asked, when he didn't go on. She searched his eyes, her determination evident. "Did the two of you fight when she returned to Texas, Jake? Relive the breakup? What happened? You said she came to you for help, but just now you looked angry."

Susan was seeing too much. As an elected public servant, Jake had prided himself on his ability to keep his feelings in check, but when he was with Susan he had this constant urge to let his guard down.

She continued to press. "Could Angelica have been hoping for reconciliation?"

Jake turned away. "I had given her no hope of that," he said after a moment.

"But she would have liked to get you back into bed," Susan ventured, closing the distance between them.

Mindful of the cop still lingering in the doorway, he said, "Angelica manipulated men with sex. That's how she always got what she wanted." Except for that last time, Jake thought.

"And she wanted to manipulate you?"

Jake swore silently. The more he explained to Susan the worse it sounded, yet he had to tell her some of what had gone on, or risk her digging around on her own. He walked into the tiny bathroom, looked around. Angelica's expensive toiletries were still there, a silent testament to the care she had always lavished on herself.

"Why did she want to meet you here, when she had already rented a luxuriously appointed suite at the Four Seasons?" Susan continued, stepping into the bathroom, too.

Jake grimaced. He didn't see what any of that had to do with Angelica's murder. Yet it was something that could be found out by someone as tenacious as Susan.

"Did this place have some special significance to the two of you?" she persisted.

Again Jake hesitated. He had to be careful here. There was too much at stake.

"Fine." Susan threw up her hands in exasperation. "Don't tell me then. I'll find out some other way."

Reluctantly Jake clamped a hand on her shoulder and pulled her back before she could exit the bathroom. His frustration evident, he said in a low voice, "This motel is the place where Angelica and I first made love, same room. Satisfied?"

"Actually—" Susan gave him a humorless smile "—I've just started to get everything I want to know out of you." Susan paused, studied his face. They both looked at the policeman. Reassured that he couldn't hear, they remained in the bathroom doorway, in plain view and went on quietly.

"So, how did she talk you into coming here?" Susan whispered.

"She didn't, exactly, because we never talked about it." Susan sent him a confused look, and he was forced to continue. "She sent me flowers at the office. In them was a card with this address and room number and the time I was supposed to get here. Ten p.m. She said the door would be open."

"Who else saw that card?"

Jake shrugged. He had thought about that himself many a time. "No one. I pocketed it as soon as I got it."

"Did you try to decline the invitation?"

"No."

"Why not, if you weren't interested?"

"Because like I said, when she arrived here, she appeared to be having some difficulty coping with the stresses...in her life. I didn't know what she might do." I didn't know who she might hurt.

"Did you think she was suicidal?" Susan asked.

"No." Jake shook his head. "Absolutely not."

"So the overdose of glutethimide and margarita—"

"Had to have been done to her by someone else," Jake said firmly, "without her knowledge."

Susan frowned. "So why stab her if death could be caused with the pills alone and it could be made to look like a suicide?"

"Because someone wanted me to be framed!" Jake told her with a shrug.

Arms folded in front of her, Susan leaned back against the jamb, her look and manner increasingly speculative. "Someone who knew you would be arriving at ten that night."

"Right." Jake leaned against the opposite jamb.

"Is it possible Angelica told someone she was meeting you here that night?" Susan looked up into his face.

Jake paused. He had no answer to that. "Maybe. I don't know."

"We know two of her former lovers, Vince Boyer and Chip Garrison, followed her to Texas. Both were giving her grief."

"What's your point?" Jake asked curiously. It was clear that in this one instance she was miles ahead of him.

"You said Angelica used sex to manipulate men and get what she wanted. . . ."

Yes, she had done that, Jake thought, remembering. . . .

*Angelica let him into her hotel suite, wearing nothing but a pale pink silk robe, open at the waist, and a semitransparent white teddy. Her auburn hair was arranged in a mass of silky curls; her classically beautiful face would have been flawless in any light. Glass of champagne in hand, Angelica moved about the room in a drift of heavy perfume.*

*"I hope you've calmed down now, Jake."*

*Reining in his anger, Jake roamed her suite restlessly. "If you're asking me if I hate you for what you did, the answer is yes."*

*"Then that makes us even, because I hated you once, too, Jake. More than you'll ever know. You were the only man I ever met who I couldn't—" She floundered, searching for a phrase.*

*"Manipulate?" Jake offered.*

*Angelica set her glass down and paused in front of the mirror. "I was going to say, get to love me back."*

*Jake watched her impassively. "I wouldn't call what we shared love."*

*Angelica spared him an accusing look. "You thought it was at the time."*

*Jake shrugged. Roaming again, he noticed a prescription bottle next to her purse. "I was a kid. I didn't know the difference between sex and love."*

*"And now you do?" Angelica taunted softly, slipping into the adjoining bedroom.*

*"Yes. Thank God." Jake turned. Through the open doorway, he saw Angelica slip off her robe, as she'd meant him to. The teddy came next. Naked, she walked to the closet, pored over the selection of silk dresses, finally bringing out a short black sheath.*

*"Back to our situation,"* Angelica said, as she unzipped the dress and took it off the hanger. *"I need money."*

Jake continued watching her. *"I told you. I'm not giving you any."*

Angelica stepped into the clinging low-cut dress. Her eyes locked on his, she drew it ever so slowly up her body. Jake wondered what she expected him to do—act like a randy kid or lose it all and beat her senseless. He had to admit the odds were on the latter.

*"I was hoping you'd changed your mind,"* she said.

Smiling seductively, completely oblivious of the danger she was in, she sashayed toward him. Turning around in front of him, she pointed to the back of her dress. The zipper was a long one and ended at the small of her back.

Her hand cupping his, she placed it between the silk of her dress and the heat of her skin.

*"Would you do the honors?"* she said....

"Jake, stay with me here!" Susan said irritably. "Was it possible that Angelica was using her past relationship with you to get what she wanted out of Chip? Could it be she set this up and told someone else about it in advance, in the hopes that this other person would arrive and find her in bed with you? I mean, is it possible that she might have been using you to make someone else jealous?"

Jake sighed. If he knew for sure who had been there with Angelica that night, then he would have had to put aside his agendas, his need to protect and take care of his own. But he didn't know, and until he did, he wouldn't go around accusing anyone of murder.

"You can look around more if you want, but I've got to get out of here," Jake said. He turned and headed out the room.

"Jake, wait." Susan rushed after him.

"You done in here?" the policeman asked.

"Yes!" Jake said.

"I'm not sure," Susan said. She smiled at the policeman. "Give us a moment alone. Please?"

"I'm going to have to frisk you first. You get frisked going in and coming out. Those are the rules," he said.

"Fine."

Satisfied they had taken nothing with them, the policeman went back inside the motel room. Jake moved toward the Jeep, Susan at his heels.

"Come on," she said pleadingly. "Just stay a while longer and answer a few more questions. Please—"

Without warning, Jake felt a singing sound whiz by his face, and another past Susan's head. Simultaneously the crackling echo of two rifle shots reverberated in the air. "Get down!" he shouted.

Arm around her neck, Jake knocked her to the ground and fell on top of her. Three more shots, whistling close. Then the sounds of shouting, and someone a few rooms down yelling that the police had been called. Jake stayed where he was, head down, heart pounding. It was happening again, he thought. His life was turning into an endless nightmare. But he was damned if he was going to be a sitting duck this time. Another shot whizzed by his ear.

"The hell with this," Jake said, scrambling to his feet. He dived across the front seat of the Jeep and yanked open the glove compartment. He removed a small black handgun. It was already loaded and ready to go.

Glass shattered the rear window, eliciting another scream from Susan. Extra ammunition in hand, Jake dived back out. Grabbing Susan, he kept her low and pushed her back into the motel room. The policeman helped Susan to safety, then came barreling out, his own gun drawn. Still kneeling, Jake motioned toward the woods. "The shots are coming from over there," he said.

Taking cover behind the front end of the Jeep beside Jake, the police deputy began returning fire. So did Jake.

Just as abruptly as they had started, the gunshots in the woods stopped. Jake swore again as he quickly reloaded his gun. "Ten to one, they're going to make a run for it now," he said grimly. He turned to the deputy, his decision made. "Cover me. I'm going over to the woods to see what I can find."

Whatever argument the deputy may have voiced was lost in another barrage of gunfire from the woods. Jake dashed down the row of cars parked in front of the motel, keeping low, while the deputy returned fire.

In the distance, a siren wailed.

Again the gunfire stopped. Jake moved across the road into the woods. His heart was pounding, his gun drawn. It was so damn dark he couldn't see much of anything.

Carefully, quietly, he began to move from tree to tree in the direction the shots had come. Nothing. The wail of sirens grew nearer. An eerie wind blew through the trees. And that was when Jake saw it, a shadow, all in black, backing stealthily toward him.

"HOLD IT right there," Jake said grimly.

The bulky figure with the pompadour froze. "Hands above your head. Now!" Jake ordered in a guttural voice. "Do it or I swear I'll blow your head off!"

"All right, all right, don't shoot!" the man said in a panicked tone. He raised his beefy hands slowly.

A chill went through Jake as he noticed that his opponent's hands were clad in surgical gloves. Was this the man who had killed Angelica? At the thought, Jake's stomach lurched, even as his anger built.

"Lockhart, you all right in there?" the deputy called from the roadway.

"Fine! I've got the culprit, too!" Jake said. Though where the man's gun was, he didn't know.

"Hey, I didn't shoot anyone!" the heavyset man whined.

"Tell it to the deputy," Jake growled. "Now, start moving . . . slowly . . . toward the roadway."

The deputy met them at the edge of the woods, a broad-beamed flashlight in one hand, his gun in the other. Two patrol cars pulled up almost simultaneously. More officers piled out, guns drawn. Within seconds, the heavyset man was surrounded and spread-eagled against the side of the car. "Well, what do you know?" the deputy said, pulling out a long-bladed hunting knife from a sheath strapped to the guy's leg. "Look what I found!"

Susan joined the group. Jake noted she looked shaken, disheveled and angry. She pointed at the suspect. "This man was at Angelica Saint-Claire's funeral. He also matches the description of the man who threw a rock at Jake and me, and cost Jake a couple of stitches."

"Hey, I had nothing to do with that," the guy said.

A deputy was already pulling out his wallet. "Driver's license says his name is Otis Kingsley. Address is Las Vegas, Nevada. What are you doing here, Otis? Why were you shooting at these people? And where's the gun you used?"

Otis's meaty jaw clenched. He stared across the top of the squad car with lethal calm. "I'm the President of the Angelica Saint-Claire Fan Club, and I'm in town to mourn her death. That is why I was at her funeral. And that is absolutely all I am saying until I get an attorney!"

ONCE AGAIN, the motel parking lot was filled with police vehicles. Jake and Susan stood outside, patiently explaining to the police what had happened and why they had been there in the first place.

As soon as they were done, Susan moved off to the side, taking Jake with her. An in-depth search was going on across the road. Spotlights were trained on the woods. So far, no weapon had been found. And, Jake thought, no search of the other motel rooms had yet been made. He looked at Susan, caught the speculative gleam in her eyes. "Are you thinking the same thing I am?" he asked.

"That Otis Kingsley is awfully strange and quite preoccupied with Angelica?" Susan said.

"And Angelica died here," Jake added.

Susan's glance met Jake's. "Which would make the Shady Villa a very important place to Otis, wouldn't it?" she mused.

"And if Otis was telling the truth, about just going over to check out the gunshots, then he had to have been in the vicinity when the gunfire started," Jake continued.

Susan nodded her agreement. "And since we didn't see Otis hanging around outside, or in the motel office when we arrived, that means he might have been inside one of the motel rooms when we did arrive," Susan said.

"The question is, which motel room," Jake said.

Determined to find out, they walked briskly toward the Shady Villa office. The manager, a seedy looking fellow in his late twenties with acne-scarred skin and stringy brown hair, was seated behind the desk, looking understandably unhappy about all the police milling around the place. "Is Otis Kingsley a guest here?" Jake asked.

The manager frowned and shot a nervous glance toward the door. "I can't give out information like that. That's confidential."

Jake had the feeling it wouldn't take long to discover this guy's price. He opened his billfold and ignoring Susan's barely audible sigh of dismay, withdrew a hundred dollar bill. He folded the bill discreetly into his hand and rested his hand on the counter. The sign above the desk said rooms rented for twenty dollars a night, or five dollars an hour.

"Suppose I asked to rent a room for the next hour," Jake said. He dropped the hundred on the other side of the counter. "One occupied by a Mr. Otis Kingsley. If all Miss Kilpatrick and I did was look inside, there'd be no harm done now, would there?" Jake asked persuasively.

The manager stared greedily at the hundred-dollar bill. "I don't want any more trouble. I already had enough."

"I don't want trouble, either," Jake said. "I just want the truth. So what do you say, Mr—"

"You can call me 'Bubba.'"

"Bubba? Do Miss Kilpatrick and I have the room we want? Or don't we?"

BUBBA ACCEPTED the money, then handed over the key to room number two. "If anyone asks me how you got in, I know nothing about it," he said, then went back to watching TV on the wall-mounted set.

Susan and Jake headed for room two.

"You know, if Otis's story is true . . . the room he rented should be unlocked, shouldn't it?" Susan asked.

Jake shrugged. "I don't know. You'd think he wouldn't have been concerned about locking the door behind him if he was chasing down a potential murderer with a gun. . . ."

As it turned out, the room was locked. Jake didn't know quite what to make of that, and from the expression on Susan's face, neither did she. He unlocked the door and swung it open.

At first glance, Jake noted the room seemed empty. But something about it—he couldn't say exactly what—gave him the creeps. He walked in and Susan followed. Taking a tissue from the box, he gingerly opened the closet doors. Nothing. The bathroom appeared untouched. As did the bed. Only the glasses beside the sink looked disturbed. One was filled with water, the other with stale cola. A single empty can was in the wastebasket.

"There's nothing here," Susan said, disappointed. "Nothing incriminating, anyway."

Jake paced back and forth. "I don't know what was going on here, but it's time to talk to Bubba again."

Susan and Jake returned to the motel office. "How long was Otis Kingsley staying here?" Jake asked.

Bubba grinned as if he knew something, but said nothing.

Getting the drift, Jake handed over another hundred. And then a third.

Bubba finally said, "Otis Kingsley checked in the night after Miss Saint-Claire died."

"Did you see him around here before that?" Jake asked.

Bubba shook his head. His gaze was candid. "Nope. And Otis is the kind of guy you don't easily forget, you know?"

Susan and Jake knew. With that bouffant Elvis hairdo, Otis was hard to miss.

"Has he been sleeping here?" Susan asked.

"No. At least, the maids haven't had to make up his bed or nothing. He just comes and goes a couple of times a day."

Susan and Jake exchanged a look. Jake could tell she was just as baffled by what they had discovered as he was. "How long is he paid up for?" Jake asked.

"So far, he's been renting the room a week at a time," Bubba said. He gazed past them, at the police coming out of the woods. "Looks like they're about to give up out there," he said.

Susan and Jake slipped back outside, just as another car pulled up. District Attorney Tom Peterson got out. He sauntered over to Susan and Jake. "Can't stay out of trouble, either of you?"

"Fancy meeting you here, Tom," Susan said sarcastically. "Just happen to be in the neighborhood?"

Jake knew what she was implying—that it was odd Tom just happened to be in the vicinity of the Shady Villa at the time an attempt had been made on their lives.

"I doubt there's anyone in Austin who doesn't know what happened here tonight," Tom continued. "It's all over the news. The motel owner phoned it in to one of the television stations. I expect camera crews here momentarily."

"Great," Jake said.

Tom smiled. "I thought you'd think so. Resigning your post sounds better all the time, doesn't it, Jake? Although if I were you two, I'd be ashamed of myself."

"What are you talking about?" Susan asked, inching closer to Jake.

"Come on, Counselors. Drumming up sympathy for the defendant is an old ploy in courtroom tactics. Although I would say you two have reached a new low here by pretending Jake is in danger."

"Those bullet holes in the wall behind us are real," Susan said tightly.

"And so are the tracks in the mud in the wooded area across the street," Jake added.

"Oh, I know someone shot at you," the DA said smugly. "I also know you have money, Lockhart. For all I know, you hired it done. Or maybe your attorney here did."

"If anyone is acting unprofessionally, Tom, it is you," Susan said.

Jake touched Susan's shoulder. He nodded at a television news truck pulling into the lot. "We should get out of here."

"You do that," Tom said, as they started for Jake's Jeep. "Before it gets any hotter."

"SORRY ABOUT THAT," Jake said, as soon as they were headed away from the motel.

"Why? It's not your fault we were shot at," Susan said. And then thought, to her chagrin, is it?

"No, it's not." Jake's mouth thinned unhappily. "But it's my fault you're in the middle of this."

Susan couldn't disagree with that. Nor could she discount the fact that both times Jake had known where to find her.

"When did you begin carrying a gun, Jake?"

He slanted her a sidelong glance.

"Since the incident in the hotel when you were shot at and almost run down."

Without warning, Jake turned the Jeep into a long gravel lane. It lurched to a halt. He put it in Park and cut the lights, but left the motor running. "You okay?"

"Yes." Susan turned toward him slightly. Her pulse hammered in her throat. Her palms were damp. "Why do you ask?"

"I don't know." Jake slid a hand beneath her chin. He guided her face up to his. He skimmed his thumb lightly across her lips. "You look scared all of a sudden," he said softly.

Susan swallowed and tried hard not to notice how handsome he appeared in the shadowy light of the dash. "That's because I am a little," she confided on a shaky breath. "I'm not used to having my life in danger." But since Jake had entered her life, her whole world seemed to be turning upside down, to the point that she was no longer sure who or what to trust.

He took her hand in his and slid his palm warmly over the back of hers, eliciting tingles everywhere he touched. He wrapped his arms around her, smoothed his hands in her hair.

"Why don't you come back to the ranch with me, at least for the night. No reporters will be able to get to you." He moved back slightly and his gaze deepened. "You'll be safe there," he promised, bending to plant a light, teasing kiss on her lips.

But she wouldn't be safe from him. Her conscience shuddered with the knowledge that she didn't want to stop him from kissing her. She wanted him more and more. But that couldn't happen, she told herself sternly.

Susan withdrew from his embrace. "I just want to go back into town, pick up my car and head home."

"You're sure?" Jake asked.

Susan nodded, not daring to look at him for fear she would throw caution to the wind and end up in his arms again. "Please, Jake, just take me back to my car."

He regarded her another long moment, then put the Jeep in gear. Once they were on their way, Susan drew another shaky breath and said, "Do you mind if I use your car phone to call Ray?"

"Go ahead, I'd like to know what, if anything, he's turned up, too," Jake said.

Susan put Ray on the speaker. "What have you got for us?" she asked.

"Angelica's brother played a gig the night she died, but neither Dusty nor Rhythm was there. They had other musicians filling in for them."

"Any idea where they were?" Susan asked.

"Nope."

"Any idea where they are tonight?" Jake asked.

"Yeah, that club in San Marcos. They're supposed to be working till midnight."

THE BAND was still playing when they arrived. Dusty looked strung out, as though he hadn't been eating or sleeping much, and his voice was hoarse, cracking on many of the vocals. Rhythm put in a lackadaisical performance. She didn't seem happy to see them in the club.

Jake and Susan both ordered sodas. Jake pulled his chair over next to Susan, slipped his arm around her shoulders and stretched his long legs out in front of him. He leaned over to whisper in her ear, "Wanna play Good Cop Bad Cop?"

Susan acted completely unaffected. "Let me guess. I get to be the good cop. Right?"

"Depends on who we can goad into talking first," Jake said.

The band ended. The last few patrons filtered out. Dusty and Rhythm exchanged apprehensive glances. Susan and Jake stood and sauntered over to the bandstand.

"Got some more questions for you," Susan said.

Dusty glared at her. "Go to hell."

"Fine." Jake shrugged and turned to Susan disinterestedly. "We'll let the district attorney ask them what they were both doing the night Angelica was killed."

Dusty was off the stage in two steps. He grabbed Jake by the shirtfront. "You implying I had something to do with my sister's death?"

Rhythm pulled Dusty off Jake. "We had a gig that night."

"Your band had a gig," Susan said quietly. "The two of you had subs."

Dusty was silent. Rhythm's cheeks were flushed bright red.

"We already know what you were up to that night," Jake said, looking completely confident, when Susan knew damn well it was a bluff. "So if you want to explain, this is your chance." His expression hardened menacingly. "Your only chance."

"Hey, it wasn't my idea to follow her over there!" Rhythm said.

"Shut up!" Dusty whirled on his girlfriend.

"I'm not taking the rap for something we didn't do!" Rhythm retorted testily.

"Then why did you go to the motel?" Susan asked.

"Because Dusty figured that if we started following his sister around, sooner or later we'd get some dirt on her and be able to get some money in exchange for our silence. So we trailed her to the motel around seven that evening."

"And?" Jake said.

"And nothing. Dusty figured, judging from the stuff she carried into the motel room, that she was probably gonna meet someone there and be around for a while. So we went to get something to eat. When we got back around eight-thirty, nothing seemed to be happening, so—"

"Shut up, Rhythm," Dusty said. "Just keep quiet right now."

"If you don't tell me now, I'll put you under subpoena and you'll have to tell us then," Susan warned.

Rhythm shot an uneasy look at Jake. "So we went up to the window and looked through the curtains, and that's when we heard her laughing real meanlike and telling him—" Rhythm pointed to Jake "—that he was a fool and always had been, and she'd used him from the first, but that it was all over. She was through sleeping with men to get what she wanted. And she was through sleeping with him!"

"I DID NOT HAVE a discussion with Angelica that night," Jake said tightly as soon as they reached his Jeep. He paused, his key in the lock. "She was already dead when I got to the Shady Villa."

"Did I say you did?" Susan asked.

"No, but you're thinking it," he snapped back.

Susan knew he was right. Deliberately she pushed her uneasiness away. "Look, Rhythm admitted they never saw the face of the man who was with Angelica, only a shadowy outline of him through the curtain. And his voice would have been muffled. What's important is that it's now clear someone was with her that night before she was killed. Someone male." Someone hopefully not Jake. Susan frowned. "If only they hadn't been chased off by the man a couple of doors down, they might have seen a whole lot more."

"Maybe that's part of why Dusty is so angry," Jake said. "Maybe he cared about Angelica after all. Maybe he feels guilty."

"Maybe," Susan said slowly. She tilted her head back to look at Jake. Moonlight gilded his masculine features and lent a romantic aura to the emotion-filled night. "The question is, Jake, if it wasn't you with her that night, then who?"

Jake shook his head. "The list of her lovers is long. It could have been almost anyone. Chip Garrison, Vince Boyer, even our illustrious district attorney, Tom Peterson."

"You know, Tom does seem awfully involved in this case," Susan said slowly.

"His cutthroat tactics could be just political payback for both of us," Jake said. His expression turned brooding. "Then again, maybe we should make it our business to try to find out if Tom had any contact with Angelica prior to her death."

Susan nodded. "Especially the night she died."

# Chapter Nine

"I tried to get you at your house last night, to confirm where we were going to meet," Walter Van Cleave said over lunch the next day. "But you weren't home."

After meeting with Ray Trevino and asking him to check out both the slashing and the shooting incidents that evening, Susan had packed a bag and spent the night in the Marriott. "I wasn't expecting any calls."

She had wanted time to sort things out. And although she was no closer to understanding her growing feelings for Jake, she had managed to compile a list of questions for Walter, who had handled Angelica's personal affairs as her attorney. "The DA and I have looked at Angelica's phone records for the months prior to her death," Susan continued genially. "I noticed you had called her several times, and she had also called you back."

Walter nodded. He was as perfectly attired as he had been the day of Angelica's funeral. "That's right."

"How did the two of you get acquainted?"

Walter adjusted a gold cuff link. "We met at a UT Prelaw Society party when Angelica was still dating Jake. My wife Bitsy and I both met her then."

"Was Angelica's breakup with Jake an amiable one?" Susan asked.

"Well, Jake seemed to take it in stride. I'm not sure she did."

Susan toyed with the silverware beside her plate. "Are you saying she was in love with him?"

"I don't know about that," Walter said carefully, trying his best to be honest and still not impugn Jake. "But I know she was counting on him to go west with her. The fact that he was more concerned with his own educational and career goals than her desire to make it as an actress hurt."

"Did she date anyone else at the time?"

Walter shifted impatiently in his chair. "Not that I know of."

"How is it that you kept in touch with her after she moved west?" Susan asked.

Walter gave a self-deprecating smile. "I'd like to say it was because I was a crackerjack lawyer, but I think the reality is that I was probably the only attorney she knew who was softhearted enough to give her free legal advice, at a time when she simply could not afford to pay for it. At any rate, whenever she had a legal problem or question, she called me. When she was first getting started, she'd send me her contracts to look over. When she signed on with Chip Garrison, she moved into the big time, and after that, he reviewed her contracts. But I still handled her personal legal work, such as her will. And I've done some things for her brother Dusty, too."

Susan leaned back to let the waiter put her chef salad in front of her. "Did she ever come back to Texas to visit?"

"No." Walter picked up his fork and speared a piece of shrimp. "Not until the week that she died. But I did see her a few times the past year, when I was in Los Angeles on business for another client."

"When you saw her then, did she seem like the same old Angelica?"

"Yes and no. The Angelica in college was very sexy, but it was in a youthfully exuberant way. Her years in Hollywood changed all that."

"What do you mean?" Susan asked.

Walter shrugged. "Her legendary lack of... Sometimes when you see some of those *Playboy* centerfolds on TV talk shows, you say... wait a minute, that plain Jane was the sexy Playmate in the magazine? With Angelica, what you saw was the real thing. She turned a lot of guys on just by walking into a room."

"Did she ever talk to you about Jake?" Susan asked.

Walter hesitated.

"I need to know," she insisted.

Walter struggled with his answer. "The truth is, I think she still carried a torch for him."

"Even though she was living with Chip Garrison at the time of her death?"

Walter said, "Maybe it was the fact that Jake was the only guy I ever knew of who dropped her. There was lingering anger on her part, and also some . . . I don't know, I guess . . . desire. When she talked about him, it was as if she still wanted to make him pay for dumping her. If the rumors are true that the two were arguing in the days before her death, that's probably why, because Angelica had yet to extract her revenge on Jake.''

Susan's heart began to race. This was not what Jake had told her, but it could very well be part of what he kept leaving out. ''Is that why you think she came back to Texas?'' she asked Walter. ''Because she wanted to get revenge on him?''

''I don't know what she had on her mind,'' Walter said frankly. ''I wish I did.''

''How was she the last time you did see her?''

''That was when she was in California. And she was under stress.''

This did fit with what Jake had said. ''Why?'' Susan asked.

''She hated the fact that people who had helped her on the way up were now coming back into her life, demanding their due. I told her quite candidly that was only to be expected, but she couldn't accept it. She felt she was at a new plateau in her life, and she wanted nothing to do with anyone or anything that had happened to her on the way up.''

Susan finished her salad and pushed it aside. ''You disapproved of this attitude?''

''I think it's an attitude that invites problems,'' Walter admitted with a troubled sigh. ''Celebrities don't need enemies. If Angelica had felt differently, she wouldn't have had Vince Boyer shadowing her. I mean, what would it have cost her to pull some strings and get him a part in one of her movies? She refused to do it and he started selling everything he knew about her to the tabloids.''

''You knew about that, too?''

Walter nodded. ''I'm one of many who advised her to have him barred from the studio lot. Frankly, I wouldn't be surprised if Vince had something to do with her death.'' Walter frowned and looked where Susan was gazing. ''I didn't know Jake had planned to join us today,'' he said.

Until this moment, she hadn't known, either.

His expression matter-of-fact, Jake headed toward Susan and Walter. He greeted them genially. ''Mind if I join you?'' He pulled out a chair. ''Sorry to interrupt, but your secretary told me I'd find you here,'' he said to Susan.

She had the feeling that Jake wasn't sorry at all . . . that he was worried about what Walter might say.

Walter looked at Jake meaningfully. "You should know my first priority is maintaining any sort of privacy Angelica had left at the time of her death. My second is helping with your defense, in whatever way I can."

Jake nodded, his gratitude to Walter apparent, even to her. Susan had the uneasy feeling that now Jake and Walter shared a secret, too.

Walter glanced at his watch. "I apologize for cutting our meal short, Susan, but I'd better get going. I'm due in court." Walter turned to Jake. "If there's anything I can do to help, you just let me know," he said.

"Thanks, Walter, I appreciate that," Jake said absently.

He was still gazing at Susan in a way that made her heart race.

Walter left. The waiter came to the table. "I'd like some more coffee, please," Susan said. "Jake?"

He nodded.

"What did you need to talk to me about?" she asked.

Jake shrugged, his feelings well hidden. "I wanted to see if you were all right. You didn't look well when I left you at your car last night, and just for the record, I didn't like doing that. I would have much preferred you come back to the ranch with me."

Susan knew he wanted her under his control. And that would never happen.

Yet she remained hopelessly drawn to him. He made her aware how alone she had been most of her adult life. He made her want what she had never had—a happy family life. She wanted to go home at the end of the day and know there was someone there who genuinely cared for her. She was beginning to think that Jake might actually be the man for her. And that, Susan knew, was dangerous.

"Not only would you be safer at the ranch," he continued, "but it'd be a lot easier for the two of us to get together to craft my defense. I wouldn't have to keep chasing you down and vice versa."

Susan recalled how wonderful and right it had felt to be drawn against him when he protected her. She couldn't let those feelings grow. Not while she was still representing him. "I don't think it's advisable for us to spend that much time together, Jake."

His eyes were steady. "Why not?"

"I don't want to lose my objectivity."

"I don't want that, either." He nudged her knee with his under the table. "Nevertheless," he continued, "I was still worried about you last night."

Susan had worried, too. So she did what she always did when she was afraid of something—put it out of her mind. She traced her coffee cup with the tips of her fingers. "I've been on my own for a long time, Jake."

"How long?" he asked.

Susan tensed. She didn't want him to know about her potential conflict of interest in taking his case. "My father died when I was in junior high. He had a heart attack."

"And your mother?"

"She passed away soon after I opened my law practice."

"But she was proud of you."

Susan nodded. Graduating law school was one of the few things she had ever done that had ever pleased her mother. "Yes."

Jake's expression turned wistful. "I wish my mom had been around to see me grow up."

"What happened?"

"She had a stroke when I was eight. I have some memories of her, but mostly it's just me and my dad that I remember."

"What was Samuel like when you were growing up?"

"A hard taskmaster. Everything had to be perfect. He didn't tolerate any excuses."

And neither had Jake when he was twenty and running the Lockhart Ranch.

"It must've been hard trying to measure up," Susan said, making an effort to understand.

"Yes. It was. But his pushing me to always be my best and do what had to be done, no matter how difficult that was, had its advantages, too. I learned how to be tough and withstand adversity. That lesson has stood me well as attorney general." He paused. "What was it like for you losing your dad?"

"Tough." Especially since the end of his life had been so fraught with an unfairness that had led to violence.

"Was it hard adjusting to not having him around?" Jake asked.

Susan reined in her feelings, adopting a poker face. "My mother and he had divorced a few years prior to that, and I wasn't able to see him much after that."

Jake's eyes lit up compassionately. "Why not?" he asked softly.

Because he was in prison, and you, Jake, are every bit as responsible for his ending up there as he was. "I lived in Kerrville. He was over in Huntsville."

"Oh. I'm sorry."

*So was I,* Susan thought wearily. *More than you'll ever know.*

"The reason I showed up here is that I'd like to hear questions about my case. I thought I'd made that clear," Jake said firmly. So she'd been right—he had meant to interrupt her and Walter.

"That's not always advisable," Susan said with an inner calm she couldn't begin to feel. "People close to Angelica may not speak as freely with you around."

"I don't care." Jake's jaw took on a stubborn tilt. "I want to be around to witness what is being said."

Susan thought about Walter's version of Jake and Angelica's relationship. Had Jake been there, she doubted Walter would have spoken half as candidly. "Why? Are you afraid I will find out something you don't want me to know?"

Jake was silent. The flip comeback she'd half expected did not materialize. It seemed she had caught him off guard.

"I would just prefer you concentrate on my case, instead of Angelica's life," he said quietly.

The waiter returned. He refilled the coffee cups, laid the check on the table and disappeared.

As soon as he was gone, Susan continued in a low voice, "Someone close to Angelica killed her, Jake. No one broke into that motel room. She let the killer in. She had drinks with the killer. She might have even gotten in bed with him."

Jake's patience with her point of view faded abruptly. "This isn't Perry Mason. We can't prove my innocence in court simply by pointing the finger at someone else."

"But we can discover enough about the real killer that the district attorney will drop the case before it ever comes to court."

Jake frowned. And once again, Susan had that feeling he was holding back. She leaned across the table urgently. "What aren't you telling me, Jake? Damn it, I want you to come clean with me."

His eyes filled with sadness and regret. "I've told you all I can," he said.

"You mean all you will," Susan corrected.

Jake didn't deny it. He put cream in his coffee, set the pitcher back down, picked up his spoon and stirred, all without saying a word.

Jake Lockhart was without a doubt the most maddening client she had ever had, she thought. Which made her personal interest in him all the more dangerous.

"Just don't meet with any other material witnesses without my knowing about it," Jake warned, lifting his coffee cup to his lips.

"I cannot and will not represent you with one hand tied behind my back."

SUSAN WALKED into the district attorney's office. Tom Peterson was waiting for her. "I heard you released Otis Kingsley on his own recognizance," Susan said furiously.

Tom inclined his head dismissively. "We had no reason to hold him."

"I see." Susan set her briefcase down on a chair and crossed her arms in front of her. "Shooting at Jake and me last night wasn't reason enough?" she asked tenaciously.

"We had no evidence of that," Tom said with a disinterested shrug. "No smoking gun, as it were. Besides, as it turns out, Otis had rented a room at the Shady Villa Motel. So his story that he heard someone shooting and went over to the woods to check it out holds up."

Like hell it did, Susan thought, narrowing her eyes at Tom. There was something creepy about Otis, and Tom knew it. "How long has he been staying at the motel?" she asked.

"A while." Tom let his glance drift over her. "Why?"

Susan kept her eyes leveled on Tom's. "Don't you find that odd?"

"He's a fan. Angelica died there. Makes perfect sense to me."

Susan wondered if Tom knew that Otis had no luggage at the motel. "Did you check out his room at the motel?"

Tom unwrapped a piece of spearmint gum and stuck it in his mouth. "Are you Otis Kingsley's attorney? 'Cause unless you are...there's no reason in hell that information should be given to you."

"I represent Jake. Jake could sue Otis in civil court."

Tom gave a noncommittal smile and continued to chew his gum. "You'd have to have grounds first. Right now you've got no grounds. You can't sue someone for being in the wrong place at the wrong time, Counselor."

Susan suppressed a sigh and tried again. "If Otis was innocent, why was he wearing surgical gloves when Jake found him?" Susan asked.

"He says he's eccentric." Tom propped his feet on the edge of his desk. Crumpling the gum wrapper, he tossed it into the wastebasket beside his desk. "That's certainly confirmed by the way Otis looks and dresses."

Susan fumed. "What about the rock-throwing incident in front of my office building? Otis Kingsley matches the description given there, too."

Tom smiled at her brightly. "Well, that's a problem. We seem to have misplaced the name and address of the eyewitness, but we're looking for the info. In the meantime, we asked Otis where he was that night and guess what . . . he was eating dinner at the Chili's restaurant on Burnet, and he had the credit card slip to prove it."

"May I see it?"

Tom opened a file on his desk and slid a photocopy of the alibi over to her. Susan examined the paper. "This just has the date. There's no time. He could have eaten there at noon, for all you know."

"Ah, but the staff there remember Otis. They recall he came in during the dinner hour and sat at the bar in the center of the restaurant, nursing a root-beer float, for at least an hour before he asked for a table and ordered dinner. He was wearing a white rhinestone-studded leather jumpsuit at the time. So there's no mistaking he was there."

"So maybe he went there after he threw the rock at Jake and me."

Holding her stare, Tom said, "The person who threw the rock was dressed all in black. That much I recall."

"So maybe Otis changed clothes before he went to Chili's," Susan suggested grimly.

Tom smiled flippantly. "Prove it."

Susan could see she was going to get nowhere with Tom. He didn't want to arrest anyone and he didn't want to let Jake off the hook for Angelica's murder. Therefore, she would have to absolve Jake of all charges herself. Impatience coloring her low tone, she said, "I understand you have some additional evidence in Jake Lockhart's case." Under state statutes, he was required to make them available to Jake and his defense team prior to trial.

Tom smiled smugly. "As they say in this case, the evidence just keeps a coming."

Susan looked at the cardboard box stacked on the meeting table. It contained documents, police reports and witness statements. Considering what was at stake in this trial, it didn't seem like much. Yet she knew that if she didn't do her job properly, the small amount of evidence in the box might just be enough to send Jake to jail.

"So how's it going, Susan?" Tom kicked back in his chair and propped his dress boots up on the corner edge of his desk. He had a well-thumbed copy of *Vanity Fair* on his lap; Angelica was on the cover. "Ready to try to plea-bargain yet? Not that I'd be amenable to reducing a sentence or passing on the opportunity to try this case, you understand."

Susan understood all right. Tom Peterson wanted Jake out of the way so he'd have a clear shot at attorney general.

"But I'd still like to see you try," Tom finished smugly.

Susan thumbed through the contents of the box. "Don't hold your breath," she said absently.

"You know, Susan, I'd heard you were losing sight of your professional responsibilities in this case and were getting involved with your client, but I never would've believed it if I hadn't seen the two of you together last night. He was hovering over you like a paid bodyguard."

"What are you getting at?"

Tom smiled with the barest hint of amusement. "You're falling for Jake Lockhart."

Susan knew it was true. But not about to let Tom know that, she said out loud, "You're making a mistake if you think this trial will have anything but an absolutely just and fair outcome."

"This may be one case against me that you won't win."

"If so, it'd be the first, wouldn't it?" Susan said, jabbing right back.

Tom frowned at her as she struggled to contain a sigh. It wasn't like her to sling mud, no matter how down and dirty her opponents. "I don't suppose you have separated out what documents are new and which ones I've already seen?" she said.

"Sorry." Tom shrugged without genuine apology. "There hasn't been time."

Right, Susan thought. "What copier can I use?" she asked curtly.

Tom hooked a finger over his shoulder. "The one in the conference room next door. A bailiff will stay with you while you work."

Susan spent the next hour copying the "proof" against Jake, then she took the pages back to her office. She immediately telephoned her investigator. "Ray, I need you to do two more things for me. One, find out where Otis Kingsley is really staying. He's got to have all his luggage stored somewhere in town. Two, locate the eyewitness to the rock-throwing incident for me. I want to see if she'll ID Kingsley as the culprit. And find out where Tom Peterson was the night Angelica was murdered."

"I'll get on it right away," Ray promised.

Satisfied, Susan spent the rest of the afternoon reviewing the evidence. As she studied the phone records from Angelica's Laurel Canyon home, she noticed an interesting pattern that brought forth all sorts of implications.

Susan buzzed her secretary. "Get Jake Lockhart on the phone for me."

Minutes later, Maizie buzzed her back. "I talked to his office. They said he just left for the ranch."

Susan grabbed her briefcase and the stack of evidence. "Tell him I'm on my way, and not to leave there until after I've talked to him."

"So WHAT WAS that important you had to see me right away?" Jake asked as he used long, smooth strokes to brush down the horse he had just ridden.

"There's a pattern to these phone calls, Jake. Angelica received and or returned half a dozen calls from Walter Van Cleave in the last few weeks before her death. Immediately after every call from Walter, is a call to you."

Jake tensed. He dropped the brush and backed his horse up into the stall, shut the door and came back to stand in the aisle, his feet braced apart.

"So?"

It was the first time Susan had seen him in anything but a suit. In jeans and a chambray shirt, he looked even more ruggedly appealing. She refused to let that throw her. She moved closer, her high heels rapping on the cement floor of the barn. "Is it possible that Walter was threatening Angelica in some way?"

"More like trying to help her. After all, he was her lawyer."

"Help her with what?"

"How the hell would I know?"

"Then why would she call you immediately afterward?"

"Maybe Walter wasn't telling her what she wanted to hear."

"Which was what exactly?"

Jake picked up his bucket of grooming equipment. "That the price of fame was worth whatever difficulties she was having," he said shortly.

"It's got to be more than that," Susan said stubbornly, pulling out her cellular phone.

Jake caught her hand before she could dial Walter's office. "Leave it alone, Susan," he said gruffly.

They studied each other, silently doing battle. "I can't do that," she said softly. "Not when I remember what you and Walter both told me about how Angelica was bothered by the pressures of being in the public spotlight. Not when Walter told me that she was upset because people from her past were suddenly coming forward again, making demands on her. Was Walter one of those people, Jake? Or did he know who was bothering Angelica and why?"

Jake shrugged. He turned and headed for the tack room, saddle over one brawny shoulder. "How would I know?"

Susan watched him put his saddle on the shelf, the bucket of grooming gear on the floor beneath that. She folded her arms in front of her, wishing she had on jeans, too. "Because I think you do."

"Based on what, Counselor?"

"Based on the fact that you and Angelica hadn't talked in years, and yet she calls you up out of the blue because she has problems dealing with the pressures of public life. Hollywood is full of people who share those same problems, Jake."

"So?"

"So, there must have been some other reason that she came to you after all that time. And there must be something behind that veiled promise Walter made to you at lunch today—something about his simultaneously protecting her and helping you, wasn't it?"

Jake's shoulders tensed. A muscle worked in his jaw. He looked as though he wanted to punch something. "Stop badgering me," he ordered, and lunged for the door.

Susan moved sideways to block the exit. "I will when you start telling me the whole story."

Jake braced his hands on his hips and scowled over at her from beneath the brim of his hat. "I've told you everything I can."

Susan lifted her brow. "Can or will?" Knowing she was treading on dangerous ground, she stepped a little closer, anyway. "Was Walter one of those people from Angelica's past who'd come out of the woodwork? Did he know something about her past that she didn't want made public?"

Jake's face changed, going from anger to worry in an instant. "What would make you think that?"

Susan shrugged. "Something in his face when he was talking about her. After looking at these phone records, I had the feeling there was more between them than what he'd said during our lunch. Also, he seemed to know a lot about how she manipulated men in a sexual sense."

"So?"

"So I got to wondering this afternoon. Maybe there was a little unrequited love there. And taking it one step further, maybe Walter was bothered by Angelica's lack of romantic interest in him."

Susan could tell from the look on Jake's face that he had thought about that, too. But he wouldn't admit it, perhaps because the two men had known each other for years. "Was Walter ever interested in Angelica when she lived in Texas? Were the two of you ever in any kind of rivalry over her?"

Jake scowled. "Walter was married to Bitsy at the time he met Angelica, Susan. And I have never been interested in being a rival with anyone over anything."

Susan stepped nearer. She could feel the tension thrumming in Jake. "Married men have been known to have affairs."

"Bitsy never would've stood for that."

"They're a happy couple, then?"

Jake shrugged. "Who can tell these days, but they certainly seem devoted to each other and their three kids. If you want the names of thwarted suitors, add Tom Peterson to the list. He knew Angelica then, too, and I know he had a thing for her, even though they never dated."

"Tom had a well-thumbed copy of *Vanity Fair* on his desk when I was over there. Angelica was the cover girl."

Jake paused. Not surprised, exactly, but wary again. And worried. "Tom Peterson's trying to railroad me into a conviction." Jake's mouth flattened into a thin line. "Who better than the district attorney to set up a crime-of-passion scene and then hang me with it?"

"There's someone else who could have profited from your misery here. Vince Boyer. You've seen how eager he is for a story. Is it possible he set you up?"

"I DON'T LIKE THIS, Jake," Susan said as they pulled up in front of the motel where Vince Boyer was staying. "It's too dangerous. If we get caught, we could both get disbarred."

"Then let me go in alone, as I wanted."

"No."

"Why not?"

*Because I care about you,* Susan thought, shocking herself. Deciding this was a question best not answered, she turned away from Jake. "Look, you have fifteen minutes from the time I walk Vince down to the bar for a drink. I'll make sure his hotel room door is left unlocked. Get in and get out, and for heaven's sake, don't get caught."

Susan got out beneath the portico. Jake drove off to park her car in the lot. She walked into the hotel. Vince Boyer was not in his room, waiting for her to arrive, as she had requested. Instead he was in the hotel lobby, camera slung around his neck, hands stuffed into the pockets of his cheap jean jacket.

Susan swore silently, but put a bright smile on her face. His eyes were bloodshot, as if he had been drinking and were hung over.

"Hi, Vince, I'm glad you could see me this late."

His expression was both sulky and suspicious. "I was surprised you called."

Out of her peripheral vision, Susan saw Jake approaching the lobby from the side exit, next to the parking lot. Linking arms with Vince, she led him toward the bar. She hoped Jake would see her, figure out what had happened and improvise. Otherwise, this was probably all going to be for naught.

JAKE SAW Susan lead Vince into the hotel bar, where a jazz combo was playing energetically. He ducked into the stairwell and took the steps to the second floor.

As suspected, the door to Vince's room was locked. Seeing that it opened only with an electronic card, he realized that breaking in was impossible.

Thinking quickly, Jake headed for the maid's closet. He stepped in and grabbed an ice bucket, and went down to the machine at the other end of the hall. He filled the bucket, then went off in search of a maid. He found one at the other end of the L-shaped corridor.

He offered her a sheepish smile and held the ice bucket up for her to see. "Miss? I seem to have locked myself out of my room. Would you mind . . . ?"

Seconds later, he was in Vince Boyer's room, aware a good five minutes had passed.

Jake had been hoping the place would be a wreck: it was incredibly tidy. The suitcase was empty, save for a well-marked map of Austin and another of Central Texas. Vince had a travel-size shaving kit. Socks, underwear and T-shirts and an extra pair of jeans were folded neatly in a bureau drawer.

Jake frowned. He was about ready to give up, when he noticed one back pocket of the jeans was stiffer than the other. He reached in and pulled out a small savings passbook. Angelica's name was typed on the front. Bingo, Jake thought.

He pocketed the passbook and folded the jeans back into the bureau. He dumped the ice in the sink, ran hot water over it until it melted. Empty bucket in hand, he headed for the door—and came to a swift, soundless halt as he heard voices in the hallway. It was Susan's and Vince's. Jake swore beneath his breath and stepped into the only available hiding place—the mirrored closet. Now what?

"VINCE, I REALLY don't feel comfortable talking in your room," Susan said loudly, as he swung open the door. Where the heck was Jake? Had he been in and out already, or was he still there hiding somewhere? she wondered, beginning to panic.

Vince grinned at her stupidly, confirming her suspicions that he couldn't begin to handle two shots of tequila back to back, particularly when it looked as though he hadn't slept for days.

"You think I'm going to put the moves on you?" Vince sneered.

He leaned close, smelling of liquor, and Susan felt her initial impression of him—that he was inept and harmless—fade. He had a cruel streak. Maybe he hadn't been doing as much acting in all those horror movies as he'd wanted everyone to believe. Maybe he had wielded the knife that had killed Angelica. Susan fought a shiver and caught a glimpse of herself in the closet mirror. She looked pale.

Vince snickered. "Well, relax, you're not my type." Hot breath fanning her face, he pointed drunkenly to the reflection of her breasts. "You're not busty enough. Angelica was my type."

Susan smiled tightly. Trying to keep some sense of humor about what she was putting herself through for Jake's sake, she deadpanned, "Thanks, Vince, I appreciate that." Breezing past him, she moved the curtain back and glanced out the window, down at the parking lot. No sign of Jake. Damn.

"Besides, the band downstairs was way too loud," Vince continued. He flopped down on the bed and folded his hands behind him. "Ya wanna make a deal? Let's deal."

Susan went into a paroxysm of coughing. She thumped her chest dramatically and struggled for breath, then said hoarsely, "I really need a soft drink first." She edged toward the door. "I'll go get it."

"No. You stay here." Vince's look was grim. "I'll go get it."

"Sure?" Susan asked brightly, digging in her purse and bringing up a handful of quarters. "I could—"

"Stay here," Vince said. He glared at Susan, fast moving to the brawling stage of drunkenness, and took the change from her palm. "I'll be right back."

He staggered out the door. No sooner was he gone than Jake slid the closet door open. Susan stared at him stonily. "I thought I smelled your after-shave," she hissed. "Good thing Vince was too drunk to smell it."

"Let's go." Jake waited for the coast to be clear, then pushed her out the door and into the elevator. He headed for the stairs.

THEY MET in the hotel parking lot, got into the car and took off quickly. Susan half expected Vince to come running out after them, but he didn't. "He's going to be ticked off," she predicted, laying her head on the back of the seat.

"More so than you know," Jake said. He was starting to let his guard down with Susan. He wondered what it would be like if he wasn't hamstrung by what Angelica had done and he could confide in her.

He pulled into a crowded Sonic Drive-In and parked next to a speaker in the rear. "Look what I found among Vince's possessions." He pulled out the bank book.

He and Susan perused it. "These entries date back almost fourteen years," she said.

"Yep, and notice the amounts of the deposits. Ten thousand here, another two here. Thirty-three thousand here."

Susan pulled her billfold out of her purse and opened the checkbook side. She began punching numbers into the calculator. "Jake, there's nearly three hundred thousand dollars total here in deposits," Susan gasped. Quickly Jake read off the withdrawals while she calculated. "And two hundred ninety-seven thousand in withdrawals."

"Which leaves her with the three thousand in her account at the time of her death," Jake said.

"Where was she getting this kind of money? Especially early on in her career!"

"I don't know," Jake said grimly, waving away the car hop approaching them and starting up the car again. "But there's one person who might know. Let's pay a visit to Walter Van Cleave."

EVEN THOUGH IT WAS barely ten o'clock, they got Walter out of bed. Clad in pajamas and a robe, he looked a little less rested than usual. But then, Susan thought, Angelica's death had been hard on all of them.

"Sorry to drop by so late," Jake said.

"No problem." Walter waved off the apology. "I assume it must be important."

"Very." Jake handed over the bank passbook with Angelica's name on it. "Do you know anything about this?"

Walter frowned. "Where did you get this?"

"We can't say," Susan said. "And really you'd be better off not knowing."

"You did Angelica's taxes, didn't you?" Jake said.

"Only for the first five years or so that she was in Los Angeles. Once she started making money from the movies, she hired an accountant."

"Did you know about this account?"

"No." Walter's mouth thinned into an uncompromising line. "I didn't," he said unhappily.

Jake swore.

"She didn't report this as income, did she?" Susan guessed.

Walter shook his head. "Not a dime of it...and from the amounts...well, as you can imagine, she would've had to pay a lot of taxes on the money."

"Is it possible she could have had this account and the IRS not know about it?" Jake asked.

"Years ago, yes. Now, with everything being computerized and this account being registered in her social-security number, it's possible the IRS would've discovered her on the oversight."

"So...someone could have known about her dodging taxes and called her on it?" Susan theorized.

"I suppose," Walter said.

"But as a motive for murder?" Jake said. "I just don't quite buy it." Jake reached for the passbook and took it out of Walter's hand. "There had to be something more here if the passbook was the reason for the blackmail," he said. "Something that had been going on for years."

"Something that didn't involve you," Susan speculated, looking at Jake.

"Apparently."

"Walter?" Bitsy appeared at the head of the stairs. Seeing they had company, she came down. Unlike Walter, she was not dressed for bed, but was wearing a black cocktail dress. "What are you doing here?" she demanded of Jake and Susan in a slurred voice. "It's about Angelica Saint-Claire again, isn't it? Damn you, Walter. I told you I was sick of hearing about that woman!" she raged.

Walter leapt up, his slippers squeaking slightly on the parquet floor. "Bitsy, honey—" he soothed.

"We're not at the funeral now and we're not in public, and I will not pretend I liked that woman or cared one whit about her," Bitsy continued ranting as she weaved unsteadily into the room. "Any more than she cared about us!" she raged, slipping into a wing chair.

"Did you know her well, then?" Jake asked Bitsy.

Walter glared at Jake. He moved behind Bitsy and put his hands on her shoulders in an effort to calm her down.

"How could I?" Bitsy shrugged insouciantly. "The witch never accepted our invitation."

"What invitation?" Susan asked, aware she was being unforgivably nosy, but unable to help it.

This time Walter answered, though he still looked annoyed. "Bitsy wanted to have Angelica over to the house for a party when she arrived in Austin," Walter explained. "She thought it would be fun for our friends to meet her."

"But the witch refused to come—she told us she was too busy. Walter said he understood and that I should let it go."

Bitsy extricated herself from Walter's grip and staggered to her feet. "But why should I forgive such a slap in the face? All our friends knew she was in town! They knew Walter and I had been acquainted with her for years. They expected to meet her! I was so humiliated."

"Bitsy, please!" Walter said. "Think about what you are saying here!"

Bitsy collapsed in the chair. Her face was ashen. "I'm sorry. I—I'm overtired."

"We all are," Susan said quickly. She exchanged a concerned look with Jake. "Maybe it's time we were going," Susan said, getting to her feet. It was obvious Walter had his hands full.

"Please excuse Bitsy's behavior," Walter said, as he walked them to the door. "She hasn't been herself. I think having someone we knew murdered...well." Walter looked at Jake. "You know what I'm saying, I guess."

Jake nodded. "Thanks for the information."

Walter shook his head. "Let me know if there's anything else I can do. I want the murderer caught as much as you do."

"So what do you think?" Susan asked, as she and Jake headed back to the car.

"Bitsy didn't seem drunk exactly."

"Just stoned . . . as if she'd taken too much antidepressant medication or something," Susan said.

They sighed in unison. "Do you think—?" Jake began, as Susan finished his thought.

"Possibly—but a social slight as motive to kill?"

Maybe Bitsy had drugged Angelica in a fit of rage. Then someone else had come along, found her unconscious and stabbed her and framed Jake.

Susan made a mental note to check out Bitsy's whereabouts the night of the murder.


"YOUR HUNCH WAS right," Ray told Susan later the same evening over the speakerphone. "Tom Peterson did have contact with Angelica in recent months. According to one of the secretaries at the studio where she made her films, Tom wrote a letter to Angelica, asking her to consider campaigning for him in the future, since she was a native of Austin, Texas, and they had known each other during their college days. He felt they had many of the same concerns, and that she could be a real asset to his campaign."

"Wait a minute," Susan said. "This letter was dated last summer? Tom isn't set to run as district attorney again for another two years." She looked at Jake.

"Right."

"Did he say specifically when he wanted Angelica to campaign for him?" Jake asked Ray.

"No," Ray said. "He didn't. It was a very general letter, with no specific time frame mentioned. I can tell you, however, what Angelica's written response to his request was. She said she didn't get involved in politics—period. She thanked him for his interest, wished him well, and that was it."

"So in other words, she brushed him off," Jake said.

"Right," Ray said. "I don't have copies of the letters at the moment. The secretary was going to see if she could get them for me, without us having to subpoena them. I should have an answer in a day or two."

"Was there any other contact between Tom and Angelica?" Jake asked.

"Not that I've been able to discover so far," Ray said. "All I found are the letters. So that one exchange may have been the extent of it. I'm still checking."

"Where was Tom the night Angelica died?"

"Still working on that. He had no official duties scheduled. But I did locate the eyewitness to the rock-throwing incident. She's a waitress on Sixth Street. You want me to see her, or would you rather do it yourself?" Ray asked.

"We'll go," Susan said.

"Good work, Ray," she said. They hung up.

On the drive to the restaurant, she asked Jake, "What do you want to do about Tom Peterson? We could ask the judge for a subpoena, suggest conflict of interest on Tom's part and request that he withdraw himself from the case."

"I don't really see that would do any good," Jake said. "Tom would just appoint an assistant district attorney to prosecute the case, and direct the machinations from a distance."

"I suppose you're right," Susan said slowly. "It's gone so far now they have to prosecute, even if they fail to win, to avoid looking like total fools. And for all we know, Tom could have sent out letters to many celebrities from Texas. You'd think, though, that he would realize that sooner or later his relationship with Angelica would've come out."

"Since he wasn't close to either Angelica or me, he probably didn't think it would matter much. We'll just have to keep plugging away," Jake said. "And hope that the truth wins out in the end. Either way—" Jake looked at Susan directly, letting her know how much he was counting on her "—I want this over with as soon as possible." He took her hand and squeezed it tightly, then let out a ragged sigh. "I want to be able to go on with my life."

"YEAH, I remember you," the young, ponytailed waitress at the Old Pecan Street Café said. "How's your head?" she asked Jake with a warm smile.

"Okay. What we wanted to ask you about was the guy who threw the rock," Jake said.

Susan withdrew from her briefcase a copy of the mug shots of Otis Kingsley taken at the police station. "Do you think this was the guy?" she asked.

The waitress shook her head. "Nope, it's not him."

"You're sure?" Jake asked urgently, leaning forward. "I mean, think of him with sunglasses on."

"It wasn't him," the waitress reiterated firmly. "For one thing, his face wasn't that fat. And for another, the guy that threw the rock didn't have any sideburns at all, and certainly not the kind like this—" the waitress pointed to the mug shot "—that come partially down to his jaw. In fact," she said slowly, "come to think of it, he could've been wearing a wig, 'cause it was kind of fake looking."

"Great," Jake muttered, "now we've got an Otis impersonator on our hands, too."

It seemed that way, Susan thought dispiritedly, as she took another sip of her coffee. "Is there anything else you can remember?" she asked the waitress.

The girl shrugged as she glanced at her watch. "Just that the black leather biker jacket the guy was wearing looked and smelled brand-spanking new. Listen, I've really got to get back to work."

"Thanks for the time," Susan said with a smile.

"You've been a big help," Jake added appreciatively.

Jake paid for their coffees. He and Susan walked out of the restaurant, their steps meshing perfectly, in the way of people emotionally and intellectually in sync. "Are you thinking the same thing I am?" Jake asked Susan.

She gazed up at him, her heart racing. She rested against the side of the building and wished desperately she could throw caution to the wind and make love with Jake. "That someone framed you, and now someone is trying to frame Otis, as well."

Jake nodded. He braced his hand on the wall beside her and leaned in close, the warmth of his breath stirring her hair and feeling like a lover's caress.

"The question is why?" Jake asked softly, perplexed. "Assuming for a second that Otis is innocent, what has he done to anyone . . . to deserve being framed?" Jake's mouth thinned. "And what do he and I have in common?"

## Chapter Ten

Samuel Lockhart met Susan at the door of the ranch house early the following evening. "Did you see this?" He thrust a copy of a supermarket tabloid at her.

Susan saw Jake's picture, right next to Angelica's. The headline screamed, "High-ranking Texas Politician Kills Movie Star In Love Nest."

"It's not as damaging as it could be," Susan said with a sigh.

"You haven't seen the *National Tattler*," Samuel said. "Take a look at this. Then we'll talk about damage."

Susan gazed at the front cover. On it were color photos taken at the motel the night of Angelica's death. In the first, Jake was being led from the motel room. He looked shell-shocked. The next photo was that of a black body bag being put into the coroner's wagon.

Susan bit back an oath. In tiny print next to the photos was the name Vince Boyer. He had taken these photos only minutes after Angelica's body had been discovered by Jake. What was Vince doing there? Susan wondered. It was something she vowed to find out when he was on the witness stand.

"I don't know how my son is going to get a fair trial when garbage like this is printed every day," Samuel growled.

Susan set down her files. "Where's Jake?" She had been under the impression, when Samuel had called, that this work session tonight would include all three of them.

Samuel helped Susan take her trench coat off. "He called and said he would be late."

"Is he still at the office?" Susan started for the phone.

"No." Samuel hung up her coat, which was dusted with a light winter rain. His back to her, Samuel said, "He's not there."

Susan studied the new bit of color coming into the older man's leathery cheeks. "How do you know?"

"Because—" Samuel floundered briefly "—he left there a while ago, right after he called."

Susan waited. "And?" she asked, when no other explanation was forthcoming.

"And he had some errands to do," Samuel said. He led the way to the dining room briskly.

Susan picked up her briefcase and fell into step behind him. "Jake's not doing any more sleuthing on his own, is he?" Susan had warned him about that.

"You mean regarding the murder charge against him?" Samuel asked, as he examined a stack of pencils, checking the ends to see if they were sharpened.

"What else could he be investigating?" Susan wondered out loud.

Samuel shrugged. "He is attorney general. They get all sorts of complaints—"

"And Jake has a staff of attorneys in his office, several of whom are assigned to criminal enforcement. He does not have to play cop. Furthermore, his job is to decide which cases to pursue."

Respect glowed in Samuel's eyes. "Sounds like you know a lot about it."

"It's my job to know a lot about my clients," Susan said. "Even when they are avoiding full disclosure."

"Like I said," Samuel drawled, ignoring her not-so-subtle hint to tell what his son was doing, "Jake'll be home in a little bit."

"I would think he'd be more eager to hear what new information the DA had added to the discovery process," Susan said.

"I'm sure he'll get here as soon as he can," Samuel repeated. "Like I said, he wants to read through the information, too. In the meantime, I'm here, and I'm ready to roll up my sleeves and get to work."

Susan couldn't dispute the fact that she needed the help of everyone involved if she was going to break through this case. They were going to trial now in a matter of days, and although she had discovered Angelica Saint-Claire had garnered many more enemies than friends, she still had no clear idea of who had killed her.

Susan looked at Jake's father. To her irritation, she felt that like his son, Samuel was not telling her everything he knew.

Susan set her briefcase on the table and sat down reluctantly.

"Do these files of yours include all the notes you've made about the case?" Samuel asked.

She shook her head. "No, I have some I consider private."

"At your office, you mean?"

"You're annoyed that you can't see them?"

"I'm just not sure it's fair." Samuel paused, then asked her bluntly, "You do believe in my son's innocence, don't you?"

"What I believe doesn't matter," Susan said crisply. "I'm not on the jury."

"You're dodging the question," Samuel chided.

"On purpose," Susan agreed, "because it does us no good to speculate. What I want to do here is look for the truth. It's not easy, when information is being held from me."

"If you're talking about Jake, maybe he's telling you enough to solve this case," Samuel said meaningfully. "Just because he doesn't want to clutter your mind with unnecessary facts doesn't mean he's lying to you."

Susan put her elbow on the table and rested her chin on her hand. "You don't believe in sins of omission?"

"I believe in my son," Samuel said quietly. "The question is, do you?"

The back door slammed. "I'll see if that's Jake or one of the men," Samuel said, getting up.

Susan continued working at the table. Five minutes passed. Susan wondered what was keeping Samuel. Had there been word about Jake?

She got up from the table and walked quietly across the carpeted floor. Down the hall, past an entertainment room and Samuel's den. She heard men's voices as she neared the kitchen.

"I thought we'd both decided it would be best if you stayed as far away as possible from him."

Samuel was speaking in a low hushed voice Susan had to really strain to make out.

Leery of interrupting something private, but not wanting to be excluded if the talk had anything to do with the case, Susan paused. And then heard Jake's voice, hot and defensive.

"I had to see for myself, Dad."

"You should have waited, damn it," Samuel shot back in an irked voice.

"I couldn't," Jake said, defiant again.

There was a moment's silence, then Susan heard Samuel's raspy voice asking Jake tremulously, "Then everything's okay?"

Jake's sigh was audible, even from where Susan was standing. "From what I saw tonight, yes. I'll check into it further as soon as my trial is over, but so far, so good."

Check into what? Susan wondered.

"You know I never liked her, but this must be terrible for you," Samuel replied gently.

"The worst thing is I don't know what to do long-term," Jake confessed.

"You do know what to do," Samuel stated softly. "We talked about this."

So there was some sort of conspiracy between father and son, Susan confirmed. Her hunch was right. The two men were protecting each other!

"I know what my first inclination was," Jake argued.

"And it was right," Samuel replied stubbornly.

"Now that I've seen...it's a lot more real to me, and a lot more difficult to deal with," Jake said hoarsely.

Seen what? Susan wondered.

"But you will deal with it, son, and I'll help you," Samuel whispered.

"How? You know how I've always felt about cover-ups of any kind, Dad," Jake said tersely. He glared at his father. Even from the side view, Susan could see his expression was anguished. "What if my decision now comes back to haunt me?"

"You'll deal with that then," Samuel snapped back impatiently.

Jake scowled as he drove his fingers through his hair. "It isn't going to be easy acting like nothing has happened, because it has. For one thing, who's going to believe that I didn't know?"

"I realize it's going to be hard for you, son, but you have to consider everything here, not just what you want," Samuel said grimly. "Coming on the heels of this murder charge...well, you're in a heap of trouble."

Jake nodded grimly. Still facing his dad, he braced both his hands on his waist. "I know. Any disclosure that was in any way related to me wouldn't exactly be welcome news, would it?" Jake asked.

"I wouldn't think so, no," Samuel said.

Jake shook his head in silent remonstration, then turned his glance away from his father. Unfortunately, it was also in Susan's direction.

Susan wanted to duck out of sight, but she had already been spotted. Damn!

"Susan?" Jake's tone had a sharp edge. "How long have you been standing there?" he demanded.

"Just a second."

Samuel appeared just as disgruntled to find her eavesdropping. He started in her direction. Jake caught his father's arm, halting his progress. "Dad." Jake eyed Samuel meaningfully. "I'll handle this. It'll be all right, I promise."

Meaning what? Susan wondered. That Jake planned to manipulate her again with smooth talk and lies? He was in something nefarious, and he was in it up to his neck!

"You go back and start reading through the files," Jake continued. Samuel finally nodded at his son, gave Susan a long, subduing look and exited the room.

Jake also looked at Susan. Judging by the frown on his face, he did not like what he saw in her eyes. Wordlessly he grabbed her wrist and tugged her into the kitchen. The next thing she knew her back was to the counter and he was in front of her. He planted a hand on the countertop on either side of her. "Okay, how much did you overhear?" he demanded, as if it weren't all that big a deal.

Susan leaned back slightly and tried not to think how strong and warm his thighs felt pressing against hers, as she folded her arms defiantly in front of her.

"How much did you hear?" Jake repeated impatiently, leaning in even closer.

Susan straightened to her full five feet four inches. She mocked him with a glance. "Enough to know you were doing more than casual errands tonight. Enough—" she flattened a hand on his chest and shoved him back as far as she could "—to know you're withholding something very important from me."

Ignoring the hand she still had flattened over his chest, Jake hooked a hand beneath her chin. He tilted her face up to his, held it there. "What else did you hear?" he demanded in a low, silky voice that made her pulse race.

"Whoa, there. I think you have this backward. Isn't there something you want to tell me?" Susan was bartering, hoping he would inadvertently reveal more than she already knew.

Jake searched her eyes. Apparently satisfied that she didn't hear everything, he backed away from her as abruptly as he had taken her into his arms, and said mildly, "How about giving me a hand rustling up something to eat." Turning his back to her, he rolled up his sleeves. "I haven't had dinner yet. And I'll never make it through a prolonged work session unless I give my body some fuel."

Susan stared at him. Then realized in frustration, she wasn't getting any further information out of him, not now, and maybe not ever. And that meant only one thing. She would have to work with what she had, and hope that one day soon he would trust her with the rest of the story, whatever it was.

By midnight, Susan had gone over every bit of evidence with Samuel and Jake. Together, they had rehashed the inconsistencies and weaknesses in each area of the prosecution's case.

"Dad, you look exhausted. Why don't you go on to bed?" Jake said finally.

Samuel regarded his son. "You sure?"

Jake nodded. "We'll be all right." Again the words seemed heavy with hidden meaning to Susan.

While Susan was still debating silently whether to ask Jake again about the conversation she'd overheard, Samuel said good-night. Finally they were alone. An awkward silence fell. They eyed each other over the table. Jake's expression was so deliberately impassive it was impossible to tell what he was thinking, but the faint smudges beneath his eyes told her how long it had been since he had slept.

"If we're going to keep going, I need another pot of coffee," Jake said gruffly. He pushed away from the table.

"Maybe we should call it a night, too," Susan suggested. Her thoughts were definitely starting to stray into forbidden territory. She picked up the tray. "You seem—"

"What?" Jake asked when she didn't go on.

Aware of his eyes upon her, Susan shrugged. "Distracted. As though you've had something on your mind all night." Something he sensed might upset her, too, if she knew about it.

"I guess I have been distracted," Jake admitted quietly as he picked up the tray and carried it to the kitchen. "Everything just seems so unreal to me, especially tonight. I can't believe it's all really happening."

Susan nodded, wishing she could take Jake in her arms and hold him close. "Most people in trouble feel that way."

"Are you speaking from experience now?" he asked.

Susan thought about the way her own life had been turned upside down when her father had been arrested. For so long she had blamed Jake and his father—wrongly, she was beginning to suspect. It bothered her she hadn't told Jake the truth from the outset.

Susan busied herself rinsing the dishes and loading them in the dishwasher. "I had a tough time when I was a teenager. When my family split up, it seemed as though my whole world came apart. I imagine that must be how you feel now," she said softly.

Jake cleaned the coffeepot and wiped down the counters. "How old were you when your family split up?"

"Thirteen."

Abruptly Jake looked troubled, for reasons, Susan thought, that had nothing to do with her. He switched off the overhead kitchen light, so that the only one that remained on was the dim light over the stove. "You remember it all clearly, I suppose?"

Susan nodded. "It was traumatizing. For a while, it seemed as if everyone I had ever believed in had let me down, and that everything I had believed about the fairness of life in general was a lie." She shook her head, the remembered misery almost overwhelming. "There were so many days when I just wanted to die."

"It's a hard age, anyway," Jake said with a sigh.

"Yeah, it is," Susan agreed, thinking how strange it was to be standing there with Jake, in the near dark, chatting, when just hours before they had been going head to head about all the secrets he was still keeping from her.

"You're in the middle of puberty and all that girl-boy stuff," he said.

Susan nodded. "Not to mention the difficulty of trying to figure out who you are and what you want to do with your life." *When everyone in town knows you have a convicted murderer for a father.*

Jake lounged against the counter, looking in no hurry to end the evening. Susan knew how he felt. The kitchen was cozy, and their conversation becoming as intimate as their glances. "What was your life like when you were growing up?"

Susan looked into his dark gray eyes. She was standing so close she could feel the warmth of his body. "My dad was a rodeo cowboy. Despite his fierce love for the sport, he never earned enough prize money to live on. To make ends meet, or maybe just get away from my mother, who could be pretty miserable to live with, he worked as a hired hand on a lot of ranches, usually for short periods of time. My mother got tired of moving from place to place. So she returned to Kerrville, where she had grown up, and she got a job as a waitress. Unfortunately she hated her job, and our home life became even worse.''

"She had no right to make you all so miserable," he said gently, taking her into his arms.

His understanding attitude made it easier to go on. Susan smiled ruefully and laid her head on Jake's shoulder. "In retrospect, I don't think she really meant to make us feel as bad as she did. It's just that everything in her life revolved around the commitments she'd made and she felt trapped and helpless. She felt it was her duty to stand by my father, even though they made each other miserable."

"You said they later divorced."

Susan moved back slightly. "Yes. When I was thirteen."

"And that's when your dad moved to Huntsville?"

Susan nodded. Absently she smoothed her hand across the starched fabric of his shirtfront. "Even then, she kept up the martyr act, insisting I visit my father." Realizing what she was doing, Susan dropped her hand.

Jake put her palm back on his chest and held it there. "You didn't want to?"

Susan drank in the solid feel of him beneath her hand and went back to absently stroking his chest. "My dad had really let us down. I couldn't forgive him at first. And then he had a heart attack, so I had no chance to try to work things out."

"Would you have?"

Susan sighed her ambivalence. "Now I'd like to think so. But . . . realistically there was a lot of hurt. So I don't know. But it made me stronger in the end, so something good did come of all that turmoil in my life."

The question was, would something good come of her association with Jake? Susan wondered. Or would she at some point rue the day she had ever met him?

As if sensing her doubts, Jake reached out and tugged her into his arms. He held her against him. "I know what you're worrying about. But I haven't lied to you about what happened that night, Susan," he said in a low, silken voice. "I had nothing to do with Angelica's death."

She knew that deep in her heart. But what she didn't know was what he was still so very afraid she would learn. She had been hoping her confession might spur one of his own. Instead, all it did was seem to make him want to ask more questions about her past.

She looked up at Jake. The mention of the murder had brought the brooding expression back into his eyes. Once again, he seemed a million miles away. "Are you okay?" she asked.

"Sure. I'm fine." Pushing whatever troublesome thoughts he'd been thinking aside, Jake held her away from him and gazed down at her fondly. He laced an affectionate arm around her shoulders. "Come on, I'll walk you to your car. You're right. It is time we called it a night."

"Were you able to contact Jake and tell him that the ranch is being searched again tonight?" Susan asked his father the next afternoon as she strode past the line of police cars parked in front of the Lockhart ranch house.

"Yes. I got the message to him the same time I called you," Samuel said. "He should be here any minute, too. At least, I hope so."

"Is Tom Peterson here?"

"Yes. He's upstairs in Jake's bedroom. It's the second room on the left."

Susan found Tom directing a drawer-by-drawer search of Jake's room. Outside, policemen with dogs and metal detectors combed the ranch.

Susan leaned against the jamb. "Is this really necessary?" Particularly, she thought, when they had already done it prior to this, before she was representing Jake.

Tom shrugged. "Material evidence is still missing. It's my job to see that it's all located before the trial."

"See it or plant it?" Susan asked.

Tom grinned victoriously. "I have a feeling you're going to be a sore loser when this trial is over."

Susan straightened, moving away from the jamb. "I'm not going to lose."

"Make anything of this?" One of the cops handed Tom a white program.

Tom glanced at it. "Nah." He tossed it down on the dresser. "Keep looking. And do a thorough check of the medicine cabinet in there, too."

Footsteps sounded in the hall. Susan turned to see Jake striding purposefully toward her. He looked harried, tense.

But perhaps that wasn't unusual, Susan thought. Having strange people combing through one's home would be enough to unnerve anyone. It didn't necessarily mean Jake was worried they might find something incriminating.

"I'll take over here," Jake announced to Susan, after trading accusing glares with Tom Peterson.

Jake looked at Susan, his eyes dark and hooded. He told her in a brusque, steely tone, "Maybe you could go help my dad oversee things downstairs."

Susan knew when she wasn't wanted. His pushing her away stung, maybe because it was so unexpected, and it brought up echoes of the past.

She had promised herself she would never live that way again, never have to feel as though she were in the way. And yet here she was, doing exactly that. Like the worst kind of fool, she kept hoping for a closeness and honesty between her and Jake.

Susan caught Tom Peterson's look, knew he was watching her and Jake with a jaundiced eye.

Susan forced a cooperative smile at Jake. "No problem," she said cheerfully. Heart aching, she turned her back on Jake and Tom and left.

JAKE FOUND Susan in his father's den several hours later. She was on the floor, kneeling in front of a bookcase, replacing numerous books that had been taken out of their place during the search. Still feeling like a heel for sending her out of the room as though she meant nothing to him, he knelt beside her. "Here let me help you with that," he offered.

"It's okay, really, damn it, Jake, I can manage!" Susan's tone was tense.

He put his hands on her shoulders, turned her to him despite her resistance. "I hurt your feelings earlier, didn't I?" he said softly. *Because I was in a panic, worrying what the police might've already found.*

Susan shrugged. "It was nothing."

"I made you feel unwelcome here." Despite the way he had been forced to shut her out, he didn't know what he would've done without Susan in his life the past few weeks. She might have been a thorn in his side regarding her demands he tell her everything, but she had also been his rock.

"Look, don't worry about it. I've been unwelcome before. I've lived through it," she said matter-of-factly.

Jake paused, no longer caring about the search that was still ongoing at that very minute. "What do you mean you've been unwelcome before?" He gripped her hands, refusing to allow her to put back the book she held until she answered his question.

Susan gazed down at the book caught between them. She muttered something he couldn't quite catch, then said, "My mother never wanted me around. There, now you know. Satisfied?"

"What do you mean she didn't want you around?" Jake asked, appalled.

Susan sat back on her heels. She had kicked off her shoes. Damn him for making her want what she had never had, a happy family life. Her slim straight skirt was hiked up over her knees. She shook her head at him as she tugged her skirt down. "I don't know why I started this," she said in exasperation. "It has nothing to do with the trial, or you and me."

"The hell it doesn't," he said. "Everything about you concerns me. Don't you know that by now?"

She was beginning to, Susan thought, as Jake's father walked in. And the knowledge wasn't nearly as troubling as it perhaps should have been....

"Tom Peterson and the police are finally leaving!" Samuel announced.

"Thank God," Jake said with undisguised relief, forgetting all about their conversation. He looked at Susan. "I'll be right back."

SUSAN WAITED ten minutes for Jake to return. When he didn't, she glanced at her watch. She had to get back to the office. She hadn't planned to be out at the ranch today, but then, she hadn't known the search was going to happen, either.

She went upstairs to track down Jake and tell him she was leaving. He was in his bedroom. It, too, had been completely dismantled.

The logical thing, of course, would've been to put everything back. Instead, Jake was on his knees, going through the pockets of the suit jacket he had been wearing the last time she had seen him.

Susan stood in the doorway and watched him search the coat pocket, find it empty and sigh. "Missing something?" she said.

Jake looked up. "I had a paper in here," he said calmly.

Susan nodded, recalling the DA had already found and discarded it. "I know." She walked to the bureau and searched it out. "Is this what you're looking for, a program from a junior high school band concert, dated the night you were supposed to be going over the discovery files with your dad and me? Is that where you were, Jake? Why couldn't you have just told me you were at a band concert? Though I must say I think it's a little odd for you to be out relaxing when your life is on the line and there's still work to be done."

Jake took the program from her hands. He folded it and put it in his shirt pocket.

He was sorry she had followed him up here and she knew it, but then, what was different about that? She was understanding him better all the time.

He was becoming much more intimately involved with her than he had a right to be, under the circumstances. He never should have touched her, taken her in his arms or kissed her . . . not even to get her off the track. But he hadn't been able to help himself. And that couldn't be explained, either. Since Angelica, he hadn't allowed anyone to get too close to him.

"Leave it alone, Susan," Jake said gruffly. He didn't want to hurt her and he didn't want to explain.

"The way I'm supposed to leave everything else alone?" she asked sweetly, her frustration with him mounting.

"Yes!"

"I can't do that."

"Well, you have no choice."

Susan raised a silky brow. "It seems to me that I could quit, ask the judge for a continuance while you find yourself a new lawyer," she said smoothly.

Jake stiffened at the implied threat in her low tone. "That isn't necessary," he said, the flush of exasperation coloring his face.

"Says you." Susan angled a thumb at her chest for emphasis. "I, however, see it differently."

"Susan, wait—" Jake took two long steps to her side.

She whirled on him.

Until he'd met her, he hadn't found anyone as fiercely honest as he was, as willing to cut through the bull to get to the heart of the matter. It was just a damn shame, Jake lamented passionately to himself, that he'd met her at a time when he'd had so much to hide. . . . "What's it going to take to make you stay?"

Susan glared at him. "I want you to open up to me, to tell me everything you can about the night Angelica was killed, as well as all the events surrounding it, *because you want to tell me*."

Jake pulled himself together and away from her. "I have told you everything there is to tell," he said, his eyes hardening.

"No, Jake." Susan stepped around so he had to look at her. "What you have done, to date, is dole out information only as you absolutely have to. Well, guess what? I don't take cases where a client doesn't trust me with his or her life, because I don't think it makes for a very good defense." Susan threw up both her hands in aggravation. "And I don't have to put up with this."

He scowled. Suddenly she had his undivided attention. "You're asking too much."

His bluntly spoken words stopped her cold. She took a deep breath and tried one last time to reach him. "Look, Jake, I understand where you're coming from. I really do. I don't trust people easily, either. But I can't work this way any longer. I can't go on not knowing what you're up to half the time."

"How about one-third of the time, then?" he teased.

She didn't respond.

He let out a defeated breath. "Okay, what do you want me to do?"

Susan kept her eyes on his. "For starters, tell me why you were at that junior high band concert the other night."

He shrugged. His eyes lit on everything in the room but her face. "I heard Hill Country Middle School had a great band program."

Susan shook her head. *Not good enough, Jake, not nearly.* "I'm outta here."

"All right." He beat her to the door and barred her exit. "I'll tell you why I was there. I'll fill in all the missing details. But first—" Jake looked at her solemnly "—I want a promise from you."

## Chapter Eleven

"What kind of promise?" Susan asked suspiciously.

He reached around behind him and shut the door to his bedroom. "That what I tell you will be part of the attorney-client privilege and cannot, under any circumstances, be brought into my trial."

"How can I promise you that when I don't even know what the information is?"

"Because it is the only way I'll give the details to you."

Susan stepped over the piles of clothes left out by the search. Sensing this was going to be a long conversation, she perched on Jake's bed. "I'll consider the information privileged. And I promise I won't use it unless you give me your permission."

"I'm telling you right now that I won't give permission," Jake stipulated firmly as he crossed the room and sat down opposite her.

"Then I reserve the right to convince you otherwise if it is the only way justice will be done."

Jake studied Susan's upturned face. He had never wanted to trust any woman as much as he wanted to trust her. "Let's go downstairs, to my father's den. I've got some papers I want to show you."

Susan sat on the sofa while Jake stoked up the fire and poured them each a glass of wine. "You were right when you thought Angelica had a specific reason for coming back to Texas to see me. The first night we met she told me she was being blackmailed. Someone, and I never was able to learn who, had found out that she'd had a baby boy before she'd left Texas. She said . . . the baby was mine, and that she'd had him in secret and given him up for adoption."

Susan regarded Jake soberly. She'd never expected this. So this was who he had been protecting, she thought.

Jake went to the safe behind the Remington painting. He opened it, then removed the shelves and the false bottom. Realizing there was at least one hiding place on the ranch that the DA didn't know about, Susan watched as he pulled out two papers and handed them both to her, before continuing with his story.

"I didn't believe her at first. I couldn't imagine her shouldering a burden like that alone. But she showed me that birth certificate and told me the name of the adoptive parents our son, Jaime, had been placed with."

Her mind and heart reeling, Susan scanned the documents carefully. "It says here Angelica had the baby in Fort Worth and she listed the father as unknown."

Jake nodded. "The baby's birth date is eight months after we broke up and consistent with the time we were dating."

"So you believe you're the father," Susan said slowly, not sure how she felt about that.

"Yeah, I do."

"Why didn't she tell you she was pregnant?"

"She said she wanted to punish me. Robbing me of my child was the best way she knew to do that."

"You must have been very upset with her for not telling you she was pregnant," Susan said, guessing.

Jake nodded, his expression grim as he recalled. "I was furious with her self-centered, selfish behavior, her lies and betrayal. That's why we argued that first night. I knew I had to leave the hotel room or I would end up exploding. So I left and took the documents with me. The next morning I checked out the birth certificate. It was valid. And there was a couple by that name living in Westlake Hills, just as she'd said, who had a thirteen-year-old son, Jaime."

"Then how did you feel?"

Briefly Jake's anguish showed on his face. "So betrayed that my first inclination was to walk away from her and never look back, but there was a child involved. Our child. And I knew I had to protect our son at any cost."

"So you went back to the hotel to see her a second time," Susan said.

"Right. It turned out the blackmailer had already extracted two payments from her, of fifty thousand each. Now he was demanding a third."

Jake stood and began to pace the den restively. "I told Angelica that the only way to end this was to go to the police, and I would go with her. She said she couldn't. I told her people gave babies up for adoption every day. She might not have been proud of the fact she'd had a child out of wedlock, but her fans would understand.

"She said I was the one who didn't understand. And besides, it wasn't that simple. I asked her what she meant, and then she dropped her next bombshell. She looked at me and said she had...*sold* our child for twenty-five thousand dollars and used the money to start her career."

"She knew that it was against the law to accept anything other than living expenses and medical care during her pregnancy from the prospective parents?" Susan commented carefully.

"Oh, yeah, that was obvious. And that was why she was so scared. She was afraid that if she went to the police the news about the blackmail and the baby would leak out. Then the public would turn on her, and her career would be over."

"She must have been pretty sure you'd help her, to reveal all this to you," Susan said slowly.

"Even though I hadn't known about Jaime, at the time he was born, she figured it was now my problem, too."

"Who handled the adoption for her?"

Jake frowned. "A former law partner at Walter Van Cleave's firm, who is now deceased. He handled the work privately, after he retired."

No wonder Jake shared a secret with Van Cleave, Susan thought. "Did Walter or this other attorney know the child was yours?" Susan asked.

"According to Angelica, she never told anyone who Jaime's father was, but it's not out of the question that Walter guessed I was the father. Particularly since he knew we were dating during the time Angelica became pregnant. But Walter swears to me he had no idea the adoption was illegal. In fact, he didn't know that it had been until Angelica called and told him so in the weeks before the other attorney's death. Hence all the phone calls from Walter to Angelica to me."

"Is it possible someone close to this other attorney could be the blackmailer?"

"No, Walter and I both checked into it."

"How did they manage to sell the baby and not get caught?"

"Apparently, the adoptive parents never knew there was anything amiss. And there's no reason they should have suspected anything. Van Cleave's firm has a squeaky-clean reputation. The adoptive parents thought they had a legal, though very expensive, adoption. They had been told that the birth mother was going to have a difficult pregnancy. Part of the deal was paying her private college tuition while she was pregnant. Of course all that was false, and the records of Angelica's expenditures—especially her medical expenses—were padded to the point that she came out with twenty-five thousand over and above the actual costs during her pregnancy."

"Didn't Angelica have any pangs of conscience about that?" Susan asked, aghast.

"Not really. She knew Jaime was going to have a good home, and she would have enough money to make a fresh start elsewhere and stake her acting career. I was free of her, which was what I had wanted. She thought she had done what was best for all of us." Jake knelt to stoke up the fire again.

"Did she tell you who the blackmailer was?"

"No. She refused to tell me anything more until I agreed no police. I saw no end to the blackmail unless we did involve the police, and I wouldn't agree. Again we argued."

"And this was the second night you saw her, over at the Four Seasons."

"Right. Anyway, since all she wanted to do was keep on paying her blackmailer, and I couldn't convince her to do otherwise, I felt I had no choice but to walk away from the situation, and her."

"So you left the hotel again?"

Jake nodded. "The following day, I got a bouquet of flowers with a note telling me to meet her at our old rendezvous, at ten that night. I was ticked off at her, and I didn't want to go, but under the circumstances, I also felt I had to. So I showed up at the motel, and found her dead when I got there."

Jake came back and sat beside her on the sofa. Without thinking about it, Susan twined her fingers with his. "What do you think was going on there that night?"

"From the looks of things and the place she chose for us to meet, I can only assume that she hoped to seduce me into doing things her way, but it wouldn't have worked in any case. Unfortunately, now I don't know who the blackmailer is."

"Have you had any threats?"

"Dusty Saint-Claire tried to extort money out of me a day or so after the funeral, but it was to keep him from talking bad about me to the press. I refused to pay and threatened to go to the district attorney if he tried again, so he backed off. I feel sure that if he'd known about the baby, he would've used it," Jake said.

"Then again, maybe he's just biding his time, waiting for you to get closer to trial before he tries again. We know he and Rhythm wanted money from Angelica and she refused to pay. We've placed them at the motel around the time of her death."

Jake tightened his hand on hers. He turned toward her slightly, his expression questioning. "It may also be that the blackmailer, whoever he or she is, doesn't know I'm the father. Only that she had a baby."

"Who do you think the blackmailer could be?"

Jake shrugged. "I've done nothing but speculate about that since this whole mess started. Chip Garrison was furious with Angelica for refusing to promote her new movie. He had created her and she had turned on him."

"We know from the kid at the health club that they'd argued," Susan added, taking a sip of her wine.

"And he lied about being in Mexico," Jake added. "Which gives him motive and opportunity."

"Then there's Vince Boyer," Susan continued. "He had been shadowing her. We know Vince vowed revenge."

Jake nodded. "He could have dug into her past and uncovered the baby. Known how she would feel about it, and blackmailed her."

"Afraid of the law, he could have killed her after she turned to you for help," Susan said. "And we also know he was here in Austin at the time of the murder. So that gives him motive and opportunity, also."

"And then there's Walter Van Cleave," Jake said.

"Her actions put his professional reputation at risk, since he was the one who had referred her to this other lawyer."

"Of course, in exposing Angelica for wrongdoing, Walter would have then been exposing himself to possible criminal action and a lot of bad publicity," Susan said thoughtfully. "I mean, no lawyer wants to get mixed up in anything like that."

"Maybe he never figured it would get that far," Jake stated bluntly. "Maybe he just wanted to shake her up and get her to go to bed with him. It didn't look to me like he had a very happy marriage," he said.

"And we know Bitsy was jealous and resentful of Angelica. So she had motive, too," Susan said.

"Then there's our pal Tom Peterson," Jake said. "He couldn't have been very happy with Angelica's refusal to help promote his political agenda. He wrote to her last summer. The blackmail started in October. As DA, Tom had the resources to dig into Angelica's past. . . ."

"Plus, I think it's odd that Tom hasn't mentioned the fact that Angelica may have been the victim of extortion and blackmail, in any of his leaks to the press," Susan said.

"Which means that either he has done a very sloppy job in prosecuting my case or he has chosen to overlook the blackmail patterns you easily uncovered," Jake said.

"As DA, he has plenty of access to police files."

Jake nodded grimly. "We can't forget that he wants my job and has shown in the past how ruthless he can be."

Susan's cellular phone rang. She picked it up, listened intently and sighed loudly at what she heard. Jake was watching her as she put the phone down.

"More bad news?" he asked as he took the papers and put them carefully back in the false bottom of the safe. He replaced the shelves, shut the door and covered the safe with the Remington painting.

"It was the police. My home has just been broken into."

"If you wait while I grab my coat and go upstairs to tell my father where I'm going, I'll drive you."

Normally Susan would have insisted on driving herself, but as time was at a premium and she still had much she wanted to talk to Jake about, she acquiesced.

To her frustration, he kept her waiting nearly five minutes. When he came back downstairs, he had on a casual sweater and a winter jacket with lots of zip pockets. Susan realized it was the first time she had seen him in anything but a shirt and tie or ranch gear. "Everything okay?" she asked.

Jake nodded. "My father was upset when I told him your place had been broken into. He wants you to come back here and stay the night."

"I don't think that's necessary, Jake," Susan said.

"We'll talk about it later," he said, as they headed out the door.

Once en route back to Austin, Susan picked up where they'd left off. "Jake?"

"Hmm?"

"I'm sorry about Jaime, the fact that you never knew you had a son." She understood better than most how deep the hurt was when a person close to you betrayed you unexpectedly.

"Thanks. That means a lot to me."

"Were you able to find out anything else about the adoptive family?"

"I have a friend who's a retired police detective. He nosed around and discovered that the parents are architects. They love Jaime with all their hearts. He's an honor student, plays the trumpet, has a real talent for soccer and a way with the girls."

Susan smiled. "That must be a relief to you," she said softly.

"Yeah. It is."

"Is that why you went to the band concert the other night?"

Jake nodded, his expression grim in the dim light of the dash. "I had to see for myself he was okay."

"And is he?"

"Great! He's a beautiful kid. Looks happy, too. That's why I can't let this get out. If it did—if he found out his birth mother was Angelica and she sold him to stake her acting career—it would devastate him."

"So how do we stop it?" Susan asked, frowning, too.

"For one thing, we keep it out of the trial."

Susan paused. "Have you thought any more about going to the police?"

"I did, before I was indicted. The problem is Tom Peterson. Since he has access to the police department, I'm afraid he'll find out about Jaime. And because Angelica and I didn't go to the police before she died—and most of the proof she was being blackmailed was her word—it might look as if I'm just making all this up to find a nefarious scapegoat to pin her murder on."

Susan knew Jake was right. Tom Peterson would accuse him of just that. "What about the FBI? They could guarantee you confidentiality."

"But would they believe me? I still have very little proof, and right now, no one is being blackmailed."

Susan sighed. "I see your point. We are between a rock and a hard place."

Jake steered the car onto the shoulder without warning and put it in Park. He left the motor running. "So I have your word you won't tell anyone about Jaime or the blackmailer?" he asked.

Susan knew how hard it was for him to reveal his private thoughts and feelings to anyone. They had come a very long way in a very short time. So far, in fact, she was having trouble taking it all in.

"You have my word," she said softly. Then had to add honestly, "For now." She was making no promises about later.

TWO PATROL CARS were still parked in front of Susan's condo when they drove up. "The guy that broke in says you may not want to press charges," one of the cops said, coming up to Susan.

She followed the officer over to the patrol car. Vince Boyer was seated in the back, his hands cuffed behind him.

"Can you give us a moment alone?" Vince Boyer asked.

The officer looked at Susan. "Up to you, Ms. Kilpatrick."

Susan looked at Jake. She knew instantly that he was wondering if Vince had some information to trade for his release. "We'll hear him out," she said.

"Okay, start talking," Jake said, as soon as the cop was out of earshot.

"I'm not negotiating with you, only with her," Vince said. "How's about we cut a deal?" he said bluntly.

"What kind of a deal?" Susan asked, folding her hands in front of her.

"You don't press charges against me for breaking one of your bedroom windows, and I won't print any more information about you or your client in the *National Tattler*."

Susan smirked. "Not much of a deal, Vince. Particularly from someone who is still a suspect in Angelica's murder, as far as I'm concerned. What were you doing here tonight?"

"Nothing in particular." Vince shrugged. "I was just looking for something to sell to the *Tattler*."

Susan quirked a brow. "And you feel that gives you license to break into my home?"

"You want me to pay for the window?" he said innocently.

"How did you know I wouldn't be home?" Susan asked.

"I saw you drive out to the ranch this afternoon. I spotted all the squad cars and figured they were doing another search, so I knew now would be a good time to get in here and see what you'd cooked up for the defense. I just didn't think your neighbors would be peering over the privacy fence around your backyard and catch me climbing in the window."

"Is today the first time you've followed me?" Susan asked.

Vince's ears glowed a self-conscious red. "What do you mean?" he asked.

"I mean, I was shot at the other night outside the motel where Angelica was killed. Someone hit Jake with a rock that was aimed at me and I was attacked in my office building."

"Hey, I didn't have anything to do with any of that," Vince said, incensed.

Just looking at his face, Susan would have believed his declaration of innocence, but she had learned the hard way not to trust her gut instincts when it came to predicting what criminals might do.

She turned on her heel, stepped over to the officer and told him she did indeed want to press charges. After the squad car left, Susan and Jake walked into her condo. It had not just been broken into, it had been trashed. Every paper and file had been scattered, as if to the wind. Drawers were upended. Silky lingerie mixed with the contents of her jewelry box.

Susan felt violated just seeing the mess. "You okay?" Jake said. "You look a little pale."

"I guess I'm just tired." She groped behind her until she reached the edge of her bed, and sat down. "Vince Boyer is such a low-life creep. I have an image in my mind of him slashing people to death in those bad horror movies he made, then I think of him in here, touching my things." Susan shuddered again.

"Not exactly the usual drawbacks of being a defense attorney, is it?" Jake sympathized with a sigh, wanting to take her into his arms and hold her close.

Susan wanted that, too. But aware of the nature of their relationship, she kept her distance and contented herself with the emotional intimacy of confiding in him. "It's funny," she admitted slowly. "I've defended all sorts of people. But until I took your case, I was never personally attacked."

Jake frowned. "Look, if you want to withdraw from the case—"

Susan shook her head. "I promised to defend you as long as you told me the truth. You more than did that when you told me about the baby. Now I'm going to keep my commitment to you. Besides—" Susan flashed a weary smile "—I'm stubborn. I don't want anyone to get the idea they can push me off a case, even if they do sorely try my patience." She cast another glance at the mess around her.

"Look, there's no reason for you to have to clean this up alone," Jake said, pitching his coat aside. "Show me where things go and I'll clean up in here while you do your personal papers in the living room."

Susan hesitated. "You don't mind?"

"I think I owe you." Jake smiled.

It took a good half an hour for Susan to restore order to her living room. Finished, she went to see if Jake was done. He was kneeling beside her bed, peeking beneath it.

Catching her glance, he stood and faced her, empty-handed. "Looking for someone?" she said dryly.

"For some*thing*," Jake corrected. He pointed to the open jewelry box. "I wanted to make sure that I had picked up all the jewelry. The way Vince tossed it open, jewelry could have landed anywhere."

Susan hadn't thought about that. "True."

"But I think I got it all."

The phone rang. Susan walked over to get it. For the second time that night, she listened grimly while Jake watched her. "You're kidding. Yeah. Small comfort. Thanks for letting me know."

"What happened?"

"That was the arresting officer. He said Vince Boyer just made bail. He's out on the street again." Susan glanced down at her hands. They were trembling.

"The cops warned Vince they'd be keeping an eye on him."

Jake was silent, his face mirroring his concern. "Vince would have to be pretty stupid to come back here tonight," he said.

"I know."

His eyes glowed with a compassionate light and he looked as though he wanted very much to take her in his arms and hold her close. Susan had the feeling that if she hadn't been his attorney, he would have done just that.

"You still seem a little shaken up," he observed.

"I'll be all right," she told him defiantly.

"Yeah, you will," Jake said in a tone of voice that said he would see to it that she was. He strode past her and headed for her kitchen. "Where do you keep your brandy?"

Susan followed him into the kitchen, a rueful smile curving her lips. "I don't have any brandy," she confessed.

"How about wine or whiskey, then?"

Susan shrugged. "Don't have any of that, either."

He crooked a brow. "Beer?"

She pointed to the refrigerator. "Bottom shelf." He pulled out a can and popped the top. He took a long draft, then handed it to her.

Susan studied the can. "You're being ridiculous."

"Humor me anyway." She took a small sip and admitted the icy golden brew did make her feel better.

Jake continued to study her. "You're not used to being taken care of, are you?" he asked gently.

Susan shrugged. He was getting close to her again. She wasn't used to being put on the defensive. She liked to be the one asking the questions. "I think I indicated to you earlier that my family life was not like yours. And besides, there's never been any need for someone to take care of me, when I could do it just as well myself."

"I'll buy that as far as your parents go." Jake leaned against the counter. "What about the rest of the people in your life?"

"I have a secretary," Susan said.

"That's not what I mean."

Susan took another drink. She was no longer upset about the break-in. Her unease now came from a different source. "I have a lot of friends, most of whom are lawyers," Susan answered diffidently, not meeting his eyes.

"That's not what I meant, either," Jake said.

She knew. She had just been hoping he wouldn't push it. Obviously, that wasn't the case.

Susan tipped her head up. "You're asking me if I'm involved with someone?"

Jake grinned. "Looks like it, doesn't it?"

Their eyes held. She knew by answering that she was allowing him into another area of her life. "No, I am not involved with anyone," Susan said slowly. Then she grinned, trying to take some of the intimate edge off the question. "Not that this is anything we should be discussing," she noted sagely, taking another sip.

"It seems to me we've discussed a lot of things we shouldn't have tonight."

Jake pried the can from her fingers, set it aside and took her in his arms. He lowered his head with breathtaking slowness.

"Maybe it's time we did something we're not supposed to do, too."

His kiss was everything she had wanted it to be, all that she had hoped for, and more. Susan wreathed her arms about his neck and leaned against him, reveling in his tenderness, his warmth. The pleasure was so intense, so sizzling hot, it frightened her. And yet beneath the fear were urges she had never dreamed of. His chest was warm and solid against her breasts, his arms strong and protective as they wrapped around her. And everywhere they touched . . . and places they didn't . . . she tingled and burned with the ache, the need, for more.

As if he knew what was already in her heart and her soul, Jake pressed closer, molding his thighs to hers, until she made a soft, involuntary sound in the back of her throat. She was trembling all over. Her body was a wildfire of desire, and still she couldn't get enough of him, or of the feel of his mouth over hers.

Finally he leaned back. His breath uneven, he looked down at her.

Aware how close she was to giving in to him and the desire flowing through her, Susan pushed him away. She pressed her lips together to keep them from trembling and took a ragged breath. "Jake, we can't do this. We can't get involved. Not now."

Disappointment glittered in his eyes. He touched her face gently with the back of his hand. "We're already involved, Susan," he said softly. "But you're right." He frowned as reality came crashing back. He wound his fingers through her hair. "This part of our relationship is going to have to wait until I'm free to give you the kind of love and attention you deserve. As much as I wish it were otherwise," he said, the yearning catch in his voice belying the pragmatic glint of his eyes, "preparations for my trial can't wait."

Susan's heart was still pounding. All she wanted to do was go back into his arms, but she knew she couldn't allow herself to be distracted that way, not when Jake's future was hanging in the balance. She drew a stabilizing breath and brought her glance back to his face. "Speaking of the trial, it's really late." Susan took note of the time on her wristwatch.

But was it too late to work? She didn't want Jake to leave. . . .

He didn't seem to want to go, either. Jake drew her close again and wrapped his arms around her. "With that broken window, and Vince Boyer on the loose again, I don't think you should stay here tonight," he said softly, stroking his hands through her hair. "Why don't you come back to the ranch with me? We only have one more day to trial. We could work tomorrow, go over the questions, the order of witnesses."

He was right. Their trial-preparation time was running out. They still had much to do to ready him. "I'll go, but only on one condition."

Jake smiled as if he had won something mysteriously pleasing. "And that is?"

Susan stepped away from him and put a safe distance between them. "That you understand the parameters of our relationship, at least for now," she said gently. "No more kisses. No more hovering over me like a male with territorial rights. Not until after the trial," she added firmly.

"And then?"

"Then—" Susan drew a deep breath "—we'll see."

Jake grinned triumphantly. "Okay, Counselor. No more hovering over you," he promised softly, "at least for the time being."

Susan nodded, her pulse beating quickly. When Jake looked at her like that, as though he wanted very much to make wild, passionate love with her, the urge to head right back into his arms was almost overpowering.

Susan moved away from Jake as the phone rang. She picked it up and listened intently a moment, then said, "We'll be right there."

"What is it?" Jake asked.

Susan grabbed her keys. "Ray found the hotel where Otis Kingsley's really been staying."

RAY MET THEM in the parking lot of a cheap motel in South Austin. Jake and Susan joined him in the back of his surveillance van. "He's staying in room 212," Ray said, passing out takeout containers of hot coffee.

"Have you talked to him?" Susan asked.

Ray shook his head. "I knocked on the door, but there was no answer."

"Did you speak to the motel staff?" Jake asked.

"Apparently Kingsley hasn't been seen by the maid for five days, but his bill is paid up through the rest of the month, so they've left his room alone."

"Has anyone been in there since he was last seen?" Susan asked.

"Just the maid, and only once to clean. She checks on it daily and then leaves," Ray said.

"Have you seen the room?" Jake asked, his expression anxious.

Ray shook his head. "I haven't been able to get permission to enter it."

Susan looked at Jake. She knew his curiosity was as potent as her own. "You're thinking what I'm thinking, aren't you?"

He nodded. She sighed. "I can't believe I'm doing this." And yet for Jake's safety, for her own, she had to find out what Otis Kingsley was up to.

Minutes later, the three of them slipped into the room, thanks to Ray's lock-picking skills and equipment. They shut the door quietly behind them.

At first glance, everything appeared in order. The bed was made. An array of Elvis clothing was hanging neatly in the closet. Toiletries were lined up carefully on the bathroom sink. The bureau drawers were empty, save for a briefcase. It, too, was locked. While Jake and Ray went to work on that, Susan studied the contents of the closet again. "There's no new leather biker jacket in here, Jake," she said. "No wigs." Susan turned back to Jake and Ray just as the briefcase lid swung open.

The first thing Susan noticed inside the case, as she walked over to join them, was the box of push pins. The second was the box of disposable surgical gloves, still half-full. Beneath that was a stack of black construction paper with cutout photos of Angelica pasted on each one. Susan wasn't sure why, but the pictures gave her the creeps.

Jake got to the bottom of the stack. "Is that all that's in there?" Susan asked, feeling almost limp with relief that they'd discovered nothing more psychopathic.

"Just one more, here in the pocket," Jake said, pulling it out for them all to see.

"Oh, God," Susan said, feeling as though she were going to get sick at any minute. Her hands trembling, she took it from him. "It's a photo of you, Jake. And there's a bloodred X marked through your face."

## Chapter Twelve

"I think Tom Peterson is going to inject this trial with as much sex and violence as he can when he gives his opening statement."

Jake sighed as he drove toward the ranch, Susan in the passenger seat beside him. "I agree. As far as our illustrious DA is concerned, the more publicity the better," Jake said.

"Right." Susan bit into the softness of her lower lip, thinking. "And since our motion to bar television coverage of the trial was denied, we're going to have a national audience watching every titillating second."

"Why do I have the feeling you're leading up to something?" Jake asked, as he turned into the drive.

"Because I am." Susan held her pen poised over the legal pad on her lap. She slipped off her seat belt and turned to face him. "I need to know who you were dating before your arrest."

Jake parked in front of the ranch house and cut the engine. He studied her face and tried to decide if her questions were business or personal. And that in turn made him reluctant to divulge what she wanted to know. He would have much preferred to forget there had ever been any woman in his life but Susan. He rested a hand along the back of the seat, just inches from the soft spill of her honey blond hair. "Why do you ask?" he asked warily.

"Because we need to back up your assertion that you weren't chasing Angelica at the time she returned to Texas. And since you don't want your son mentioned—"

"I forbid my son to be brought up," Jake stated bluntly.

Susan paused. "Is there anyone who might testify to being involved with you?"

Jake pushed wearily from the car. He circled around to the back and got Susan's overnight bag out. "This isn't going to help."

Looking as if she would prefer to be the judge of that, Susan merely quirked a brow and followed him into the ranch house.

Jake gestured toward the stairs and wordlessly led the way to the guest bedroom at the far end of the upstairs hall. As he passed his bedroom, he saw it was still in a state of disarray.

Sighing, Jake carried Susan's bag into the guest room. Because it was sparsely furnished, there had been much less damage done during the search. Still, the bed needed to be remade, the towels put back in the linen closet.

Jake stepped into the bathroom. By the time he had put everything in its original place, Susan had made the bed.

Satisfied everything was okay, and that Susan was indeed set for the night, Jake started to leave. She blocked his path and shut the door.

She stepped in front of him, her chin tilted up defiantly. "We didn't finish our conversation, Jake."

He had been afraid she just wouldn't let it go.

"Why won't it help to have any woman you've dated lately testify on your behalf?"

"Because any woman I've dated lately is likely to say I was emotionally distant," he replied testily.

"And were you?"

Jake was beginning to feel he was on the witness stand again, but he forced himself to give the conversation another try. "Yes."

Looking more intrigued than ever, Susan sat on the edge of the bed. "And why was that?" she asked softly.

Her voice invited all kinds of late-night confidences, Jake knew. He turned his glance away from the sexiness of her crossed legs and sat on the other end of the bed. "Because that's just the kind of guy I am," he said.

Susan opened the briefcase she'd dropped onto the bed. "And why is that?" she asked with lawyerlike efficiency, taking out her yellow legal pad again. When he didn't answer right away, she regarded him steadily, waiting.

"I'm distant because I'm cautious," Jake said finally, wondering if he could ever find the words to explain just how foolish and gullible he'd felt when he'd finally seen Angelica for the self-serving woman she was.

Susan began to write. She was doing a fine job pretending her interest was purely professional, Jake thought, even though he knew damn well it wasn't.

"In what respect?" she asked, her quiet voice filled with purpose.

Jake hesitated, then decided, what the hell, he might as well confess; she would probably discover the truth one way or another. "I don't trust my judgment when it comes to women," he said bluntly, gazing into her eyes.

To his surprise, Susan seemed to understand his lack of confidence in that area all too well. But the look of compassion in her blue eyes faded almost as soon as it appeared. She tapped her pencil against her chin and twisted her delicious mouth into a contemplative pout as she began to talk defense strategy.

"You know, I'd bet my bottom dollar the DA is going to try to build a case of unrequited love here. So we need to find some way to demonstrate to the jury that you *did* get over Angelica, that you were able to be serious about someone again."

Jake looked at the fiercely analytical gleam in Susan's eyes and figured they were going to be together for a while. Not sure he could be locked in there for much longer and not be tempted to make love with her, he got up and began to pace the room restlessly. "I see where you're going with this, Susan, but I don't have anything I can offer up for testimony in the trial." He paused in front of the window, shifting his stance.

"So in other words, your relationship with Angelica was your only serious one?" Susan desperately hoped that was not the case.

"It's not that I didn't try to find someone I could fall in love with and marry," Jake said slowly as he picked up the desk chair, turned it around backward and sat down. He folded his arms over the back of the chair and continued to regard Susan seriously. "But my experience with Angelica taught me I could be fooled by a woman. A career in politics and having wealth are sometimes more important than the man involved." The corners of his mouth turned up ruefully. A cynical glint appeared in his eyes. "Even now, I find I'm always looking for people's hidden agendas when it comes to me. Sadly—" Jake shrugged "—I often find them."

"But you have dated?" Susan persisted.

He nodded, knowing that she could, and probably would, check out anything he said. Like him, she didn't trust easily.

"Well—" Susan sighed "—that'll help defuse the unrequited-love theory, at least a little bit." She scribbled a few more notes, then glanced up with studied indifference. "How would you characterize your relationships with these women?"

"Superficial. Emotionally unfulfilling."

"And were you looking to get married when you were dating any of the aforementioned women?"

Jake shrugged. Knowing Susan would probe until she got every inch of truth out of him, he answered carefully. "At first, I was still on the rebound from Angelica. When I was just getting started in politics, I didn't have the time to really get to know anyone seriously. Later, when I was finally ready to settle down, I couldn't find my Ms. Right."

"And your Ms. Right is?" Susan asked, leaning forward slightly.

"A woman I could love and be comfortable with. Someone who won't play games with me, who will accept the demands being married to me would make on her and who shares my beliefs, my passion for law and fair play for everyone. Yet has a fulfilling life of her own, too." It was a tall order. Jake knew it. So did Susan. But unlike some of the other women, she didn't seem bowled over by it.

"And how have the candidates you've entertained so far measured up?" Susan asked.

"Not well, so I've stayed single, but not so much by choice these days as by circumstance."

Susan nodded thoughtfully. She laid her legal pad aside and put down her pen. "I think a jury will identify with that, if it becomes necessary for us to open that Pandora's box."

"You seem to understand," Jake said softly.

Susan got up to pace the room restlessly. "Oh, I do understand. Most of the men I've dated resent the long hours I put in. I have always been very unwilling to change that aspect of my life."

"And now?" Jake asked, aware his heart was pounding for no reason at all.

Susan shrugged. She turned to face him. "Now I'm beginning to see that maybe it is time I took on an assistant counsel to help shoulder the load. Maybe it's time I had a personal life."

"Have you dated much?"

"Yes." She grinned ruefully, crossing her arms in front of her. "But not very satisfactorily. I've been told I push too hard, too fast."

Jake grinned, knowing it was true. "And why is that?" he teased.

Susan kept her eyes locked with his. "Probably because I won't allow anything, no matter how slight, to go ignored or undiscussed."

"And yet you keep pushing too hard," Jake noted, sensing her cautiousness went deeper than that. Something had happened that had made her afraid to open up, to give her heart.

"I can't help it. It's *just the way I am*, to quote another source." Susan mocked him with a teasing smile, then continued, a tad more seriously, as she began to roam the room restlessly once again. "If there's even the possibility of my getting involved with someone, then I have to know absolutely everything about him, before I ever start to give my heart. Unfortunately, most men don't appreciate my thoroughness." Her lips curved as she leaned against the bureau and regarded Jake wryly. "Going on a date with me has been compared to going on a job interview."

Jake could believe that. He stood and roamed closer. "You want children?"

"Yes, very much."

"And what are the criteria for a husband?" Jake asked.

"Hey." Susan pointed to her chest. "I'm asking the questions here."

"And I've answered plenty," Jake replied, enjoying the detour into flirtatiousness. "Your turn, Counselor. Fess up. What criteria do you have for a husband?"

She smiled slightly. "At the risk of sounding like a broken record, mine are much like yours. I want to marry a man who is as passionately interested in the law as I am, someone who understands the need for fair play in our judicial system and the part I play in that."

"Ah. Someone who won't resent it when you stay up late preparing for a trial," Jake guessed.

"Right." Her smiled broadened, meshed with his.

It seemed they had a lot more in common than he'd first thought, Jake mused. It was just too bad the trial had to get in the way. If not for that, he would have pursued her with everything he had. Susan Kilpatrick was one woman he didn't want to see get away.

"Well, I think we've exhausted my supply of mental energy for today," she said.

She slipped past him and walked purposefully to the door. She paused with her hand on the knob. Jake followed reluctantly. He knew she was kicking him out. It was nearly two-thirty in the morning. He shouldn't have stayed as long as he had.

She lifted her eyes to his. "First thing tomorrow, we get back at it?" she asked.

Jake nodded. Like it or not, the trial was looming closer. Starting the day after tomorrow, his life would be on the line, and his defense would be in Susan's hands.

SUSAN AWOKE to the sound of gunshots. In a blind panic, she bolted upright, for a second forgetting where she was and why. Then she recalled. She was in a guest room at the Lockhart Ranch.

The gunshots sounded again, rippling through the quiet morning air, making her jump. Heart pounding, Susan untangled herself from the covers, went to the window and peered out from behind the blinds. It was only eight o'clock in the morning, but Jake and his dad were already up and dressed and out in the backyard. Rifles pressed against their shoulders, they were shooting at a row of tin cans along the fence that separated the house grounds from the rest of the working ranch.

She breathed a sigh of relief, glad it was only target practice. She got dressed hurriedly in a pair of jeans and a sweater. Grabbing a jacket, she went out to join them.

By the time she reached the Lockhart men, they were reloading their rifles.

"Did we wake you?" Jake asked casually.

Susan crossed her arms in front of her. She wasn't happy with his choice of pastimes. With the trial beginning tomorrow, there were many more beneficial things he could be doing. "What do you think?"

Samuel offered Susan his rifle, choosing, she thought, to sidestep her aggravation.

"Want to shoot a few rounds?" he asked her.

Susan shook her head wordlessly. She hated guns, and with good reason; one had caused a great deal of misery in her life. "No."

Samuel shrugged. "Suit yourself." He braced the rifle against his shoulder.

Jake looked at the row of tin cans he'd set up. "Third can on your left," he said, baiting his dad, as if it were a matter of life and death.

"How many inches from the top?" Samuel challenged.

Jake peered at the can. "Two."

Samuel aimed and fired, the rifle shot reverberating in the sti[ll] morning air. The third can from the left toppled off the top of th[e] fence. Grinning, Jake went to get it. He brought it back. It ha[d] been shot two inches from the top.

"Your turn," Samuel said to his son. "How about the one o[n] the far left, bottom inch of it. And don't hit the damn fence."

Jake gave his dad a droll look. "Yeah, right." He braced the gu[n] against his shoulder, peered through the sight and pulled the trig-ger. The can on the far left fell to the ground. Jake retrieved it. Sur[e] enough, there was a hit in the bottom inch of it.

"Pure luck," Samuel teased.

"You only wish," Jake said.

The match continued. Neither missed a single shot. Watching Susan shook her head. Although being able to shoot a rifle was [a] skill a rancher was supposed to have, it was rare to be such a per-fect shot. "Do you two ever miss?" she asked.

Jake shook his head. "Nope."

"If you haven't got a shot lined up, don't take it, I always say,"' Samuel said.

"And as a consequence he could shoot the feather off some-one's cap without a qualm," Jake said.

With a flash of uneasiness, Susan recalled how she and Jake ha[d] been shot at, and missed, outside that hotel. Jake had not bee[n] nearly as shaken up as she had after the incident. Was it possibl[e] that Samuel had fired off those shots? Maybe the whole episod[e] had been set up by the two Lockhart men to shed immediate sus-picion on someone else besides Jake, as the DA had suggested a[t] the scene. No, she was just being paranoid. Samuel would neve[r] take such a chance with his son, Susan reassured herself firmly.

Jake turned to look at Susan. He immediately noted the way th[e] color had drained from her face. "You okay?" he asked.

How did she answer that? And how could she fault him for be-ing duplicitous—about anything—when she had yet to level wit[h] him about who she really was?

Samuel glanced at Jake, then Susan, then back at his son again[.] "I'll let you two get on with whatever it is you need to talk about."' Samuel turned and, rifle in hand, headed for the house. Jak[e] picked up the ammunition box.

Susan waited. "Are you ready to get down to work?"

He shook his head grimly, not about to capitulate. "If I do an[y] more preparation for this trial, I'm going to go nuts."

"Jake, we—"

He held up both hands, palms out. "Look, you do whatever you need to do, whatever you have to do." He reloaded his rifle, put the safety on, pocketed the rest of the ammunition and strode toward the stable. "As for me, this may be the last day of absolute freedom I have in a very long while, so I plan to enjoy it."

Susan followed him, because she had no choice. "Where are you going?"

"Out riding."

She didn't think he should be alone, not when he was like this. She caught up with him stubbornly. "Then I'm going with you," she said.

Jake's mouth set. "You won't be able to keep up."

"Watch me."

"Suit yourself."

They saddled up, and he took the lead. They rode hard, flying over the rolling hills and endless pastures of the Lockhart Ranch. Finally Jake dismounted and let his horse drink from the stream that cut jaggedly through the property. Susan followed suit. Still not looking at her, he advised, "If you head straight south, you'll make it to the house."

"I don't want to go back."

Jake swallowed, still holding himself aloof. "You said you had a lot to do today," he reminded her.

"And you clearly want to be alone," she noted softly.

He inclined his head slightly to the left and let out an exasperated sigh. "You're catching on."

"The problem is—" Susan tethered her horse to a tree, and, arms folded in front of her, moved nearer to Jake "—I don't think you should be alone."

He leaned against the tree. The ranch spread out far and wide around them. "Spare me the legal baby-sitting."

"Running away won't stop the trial, Jake," she said softly, keeping a careful distance. He didn't need to be crowded right now. He needed to be helped.

He glanced over at her, pain reflected in his eyes. "How do you know I want to run?" he asked in a soft, contemptuous tone of voice.

Susan quirked a brow. "Don't you?"

Silence fell between them. Susan wished she could take him in her arms. But he didn't need her to be his lover right now; he needed her to be his lawyer. So she reined in her desire and waited for him to reach out to her emotionally once again.

Finally he blew out a weary breath. "What if Tom Peterson's railroad job is successful?" Jake asked, his voice raw with anguish. He turned to her abruptly. "What if I'm convicted of Angelica's murder?"

She didn't want him having any doubts when he entered that courtroom. "It's not going to happen," she aid firmly, though inwardly she was a little less sure.

"You know as well as I do that once the trial starts anything can happen," Jake growled, shoving both hands through his hair. "If it was just me, it wouldn't matter if I went to jail. But there's my father . . . and my son. My son," Jake repeated thickly.

It was the first time he had allowed himself to show any emotion when the subject of the child he'd lost had come up. Susan wanted so much to comfort him, to find some way to help him. "It's killing you not to be able to acknowledge Jaime, isn't it?" she asked softly.

"There's a part of me that is so full of joy," Jake said in a husky voice, the strain he'd been through the past few weeks finally showing. He shook his head. "I keep thinking, over and over, I have a son." Tears glistening in his eyes, he reached down and picked up a rock. He tossed it into the stream. "And then in the next instant I realize I can never claim him, at least not at this point in his life. All I can do is view him from afar and try to make sure he is safe."

Susan watched Jake skip another rock across the water, then another. "Maybe when he's older," she said softly.

For a moment, he looked as if that were so much less than what he wanted. Then he pulled himself together. Mouth set firmly, he pivoted to face her. The sorrow was still in his eyes, along with the grim acceptance that the situation was what it was and couldn't be changed. "Maybe when Jaime's older, he'll want to search out his biological parents. If that happens—" Jake paused a moment, his expression bleak and hopeful all at once, his voice choked "—I'll be there for him."

Susan knew he would be.

He drew a shaky breath. "But in the meantime, all I can do is wait and hope that nothing of this scandal touches him."

Susan worried about what would happen if the media got hold of this news. "Do you think there's any possibility his parents have been blackmailed?" she asked gently.

"No. I think they would have gone to the police, or at the very least be showing signs of tremendous strain. But that's not the case, thank God," he admitted softly, then drew a weary breath. "If we can keep Jaime out of the courtroom, then that's all I care about."

His goal was noble. Susan just didn't know if it was workable. She closed the distance between them. "Unfortunately, we still don't know who the blackmailer is," she said. "And as long as he or she is out there, then the threat to you and Jaime exists, Jake." She paused, her heart racing as she looked up into his face. "We'll never have peace of mind until the real killer and blackmailer are caught," she added.

Jake frowned. "It bothers me that I haven't been blackmailed," he said. His eyes arrowed into hers. "It's as though there's someone out there lying in wait."

"Is that why you and your dad had rifle practice this morning?" Susan asked. Is that why he had brought the gun with him on this ride?

Jake shrugged and turned away again. "I'd rather be at that end of a gun or knife than the other."

"If only we could go to the DA," Susan lamented.

Jake held up a cautioning hand. There was no compromise in his expression. "We can't trust Tom Peterson with sensitive information on Jaime."

Susan gazed at him, her heart pounding. Like Jake, she couldn't seem to shake the feeling that there was disaster lurking just around the corner. "Do you think Tom Peterson knows about Jaime?"

Jake frowned again and looked even more worried. "We'll find out tomorrow, when the trial starts."

# Chapter Thirteen

The Austin courtroom was packed as Tom Peterson faced the jury. "The evidence will show that Jack Lockhart and Angelica Saint-Claire were lovers when they were in college. Their relationship ended badly when Angelica rejected Jake's proposal of marriage in lieu of a career of her own. Years later, she returned to Austin. Again she and Jake became lovers. Again he asked her to stay and be his wife. When she refused, he felt humiliated and murdered her in coldblood. Jake Lockhart is a dedicated public servant, but that does not excuse his actions. A life has been taken. Hold him accountable for what he has done."

The jury glared at Jake accusingly as Tom sat down.

Ignoring the ire the DA had just conjured up with his opening statement, Susan stood and faced the jury as if they were old friends. "Having a killer on the loose makes us all nervous," she began empathetically. "The district attorney worked to get this case wrapped up . . . and quickly."

Susan regarded the jury somberly. "Angelica's death was a tragedy. And she will be missed. But an even greater mistake would be convicting Jake Lockhart for a murder he *did not* commit. The evidence will show that when Mr. Lockhart arrived at the motel that evening for his scheduled meeting with Angelica Saint-Claire, she was already dead, by someone else's cruel hand. The evidence will show Jake Lockhart was framed."

She sat down, aware that she'd caught the jurors' attention and had raised some doubt in their minds. Satisfied they were off to a good start, Susan smiled. It was time to begin.

Tom Peterson put Vince Boyer on the stand. He entered the photos Vince had taken since arriving in Texas into evidence. "Can you describe for the jury where and when this first picture was taken?" Tom asked, pointing to a photograph of an angry-looking Jake.

Vince sat tall in the stand, happy to be the center of attention in such a well-publicized trial. "It was taken outside the Four Seasons Hotel, two days before Angelica died."

"And who is the man in the picture?"

"The attorney general of Texas, Jake Lockhart."

"And when and where was this next photo taken?" Tom asked.

"It's at the Shady Villa Motel, and it was taken right after Angelica Saint-Claire's body was discovered," Vince explained.

"What was going on at the time?"

"The defendant, Jake Lockhart, was being led out of the motel room by the police."

"This man here?" Tom pointed to Jake in the photo.

"Yes." Vince nodded. "The one with his hands cuffed and the blood on his shirt."

The sight of the bright red blood on Jake's shirt hit the jury hard. Score one for the prosecutor, Susan thought.

"No more questions, Your Honor." Satisfied, Tom sat down.

Susan stood. She folded her arms in front of her. "Why were you in Texas, Mr. Boyer?"

"I was taking photographs of Angelica Saint-Claire."

"For the *National Tattler?*"

"Yes."

"At Miss Saint-Claire's request?"

"No." Vince shifted uncomfortably on the witness stand. "She didn't ask me to be here."

"In fact, she asked you not to follow her around, taking pictures, isn't that correct, Mr. Boyer?"

Vince scowled at Jake. "Not in Texas she didn't."

"But in Hollywood that request was made, was it not?" Susan persisted.

Vince was silent. He glowered at Susan.

"Answer the question, Mr. Boyer," the judge directed.

"She asked me not to photograph her," Vince grumbled.

Susan smiled. "She did more than that, didn't she? You made such a nuisance of yourself that she had you thrown off the set and barred from the studio lot where she worked."

Vince folded his arms in front of him. "Yeah, so what if she did?" he replied belligerently.

Susan looked down at her notes. "How did you meet Miss Saint-Claire, Mr. Boyer?"

"We were actors in the same movie."

"What was your relationship then?"

"We were lovers."

"In fact, you lived together?"

"Yes. For nine, nearly ten, years."

"What happened?"

"She decided I was cramping her style and left."

"And it was then that you started taking photographs of her for the *National Tattler*. Correct?"

"Correct."

"Was your relationship with Miss Saint-Claire a friendly one in recent years?"

"No," Vince admitted uncomfortably. "It wasn't."

"Back to the night of her murder. How did you know to show up at the Shady Villa Motel?"

Vince looked around at the courtroom walls, as if the answer might be printed there somewhere. "I heard it on the police radio."

"You weren't following her that night?"

Vince shook his head. "No."

"But you have followed her in the past?"

"Yes."

"Without her knowing it?" Susan asked coolly.

Vince glared at Susan. "Yes."

Susan regarded Vince contemptuously, letting the jury know what she thought of him. "The pictures of her death scene made you a lot of money, didn't they, Mr. Boyer?"

The jury glared at Vince.

"I don't know about a lot," Vince said, squirming in the witness chair.

Susan smiled tolerantly. "I can subpoena the exact dollar figure from the *National Tattler*, Mr. Boyer, but it would be so much easier if you would just tell us the information." *Unless,* she added silently, *you have something to hide.*

"Approximately one hundred thousand dollars."

"Thank you." Susan went back to the table and sat down. "No more questions, Your Honor."

The jury continued to look at Vince suspiciously.

"Hey!" Vince stood up and pointed a finger at Susan. "I know what you're trying to do, but you can't blame me for her death!"

"Mr. Boyer, you may step down!" the judge said sternly.

Vince stared at Susan, contained himself with visible effort and stormed out of the courtroom.

"Nice job with the cross-examination" Jake wrote on the legal pad. Susan nodded ever so slightly.

"The prosecution would like to call Chip Garrison," Tom Peterson said, looking determined to make up for the ground they had lost with Vince. Chip assumed the stand. "Mr. Garrison, would you please tell the court what your relationship with Miss Saint-Claire was?"

"I was her agent."

"Did Miss Saint-Claire confide in you?"

"Yes, we were very close."

Chip looked suitably distraught. What an actor, Susan thought, recalling how he had displayed no such grief when she and Jake had interviewed him at his hotel.

"Do you know why she returned to Texas?" Tom asked.

Chip pointed an accusing finger at Jake. "It had something to do with the defendant, Jake Lockhart."

Tom smiled slyly. "Did she tell you what her business with Mr. Lockhart was?"

"No, just that she was afraid of him," Chip said.

There was an audible gasp from the jury box. "Objection, hearsay," Susan said matter-of-factly. "The witness cannot testify to how Miss Saint-Claire might or might not have felt about the defendant."

"Sustained," the judge agreed. "The comment will be stricken from the record. The jury is instructed to disregard it."

Looking at the faces of the jury, however, Susan feared damage had already been done.

Undaunted, Tom Peterson tried again. "Mr. Garrison, were you aware of any friendship between Miss Saint-Claire and Jake Lockhart?"

"No," Chip Garrison said. "Her *friends* were all in Hollywood."

"Thank you. No more questions." Tom sat down.

Susan stood. "How would you describe your relationship with Miss Saint-Claire, Mr. Garrison?"

"It was a close, loving relationship."

"You were, in fact, very responsible for her success."

"I molded her career."

"How is that done?" Susan smiled at Chip encouragingly, knowing that Svengalis liked to talk about their creations. "Can you describe the process?"

Chip eyed the jury. "I helped her change her looks. Got her started with the best acting coach on the West Coast. Had her take elocution lessons to lose her Texas twang so she could play a broader range of parts."

"And in the time you were her agent, her career soared. Correct?"

"You could say that," Chip announced smugly. "Under my tutelage, Angelica went from playing the victim in bad horror movies to being one of the top-ten movie actresses in the country."

"Her new movie was slated to be a success, then?" Susan asked naively.

"It already is. It's breaking records at the box office as we speak," Chip said proudly.

"And the publicity from her murder has spurred an extraordinary amount of interest in her last film, hasn't it?" Susan asked, determined to show that Chip had profited from Angelica's death just as he had from her life.

"Objection." Tom Peterson was on his feet. "There's no way that statement can be proven."

"I withdraw the question." Susan turned back to Chip. "Were you happy with Miss Saint-Claire's decision not to promote her new movie before she left for Texas?"

Chip studied Susan, his expression much less genial now. "No," he said so quietly the jury had to strain to hear him. "I wasn't."

"Did you argue about her decision before she left?"

Chip hesitated, just a fraction too long. "Yes, we did. But in the end I understood that she thought it was important, and so I deferred to that decision," Chip said.

Susan nodded, as if she were absorbing that. The jury leaned forward in interest. "Did she spend a lot of money maintaining her new looks?" Susan asked.

"As they say, beauty doesn't come cheap," Chip answered, and the jury chuckled. The judge frowned. "Yes, she did," Chip added hastily.

Susan looked at her notes. "Approximately how much?"

Chip shrugged. "About three thousand a month, on just routine visits to the Beverly Hills hair salon where she had her hair done, and all that."

"Did she go to health spas?"

"Yeah. Usually for a week or so once every few months."

"And how much does a week's stay cost at the places she frequented?"

Again Chip shrugged. "About three thousand per week, not including airfare."

"What about clothes?"

"Oh, she spent a lot on clothes."

"An estimate?"

Chip had to think about that one. "Twenty, thirty thousand dollars minimum."

"A year?" Susan asked innocently.

"A month. Her clothes were all designer originals now," Chip said.

Susan could see the expression of the jurors—they were astounded. "No further questions at this time, Your Honor," Susan said. "But I reserve the right to recall this witness at a later time."

Chip looked at Susan, as if wondering what she was leading up to.

Susan sat down at the table. Jake wrote on the legal pad: "I don't know where you're going with that witness, Counselor, but you've got the jury thinking maybe this isn't such an open-and-shut case after all. Congratulations."

Susan smiled. She jotted a note on her own pad: "Just keep thinking the words *reasonable doubt.*"

Next Walter Van Cleave took the stand. Swiftly the DA covered how Walter and Angelica had met at a Prelaw Society meeting in college, and had remained friends ever since. "Were you in touch with her when she arrived in Austin?"

"I read in the paper that she was in town. I remember being surprised that she hadn't let me know she was here, and I telephoned her at the Four Seasons and asked her if she wanted to get together, as was usually the case when we were in the same city."

"And what did she tell you?"

"The one night my wife and I were free to go to dinner with her she said she couldn't." Walter frowned and looked distressed.

"He's acting" Jake wrote on the legal pad.

"Why not?" a sympathetic Tom asked Walter Van Cleave.

"I don't know. Angelica wouldn't tell me. But I sensed she was in some kind of trouble," Walter said frankly, accompanying his words with a troubled expression.

The jury glared at Jake. Satisfied he'd cast some more guilt Jake's way, Tom sat down. "Thank you, that's all," he said.

Susan gazed at the jury and knew they had the same doubts about Jake's innocence that she'd had when she'd first taken the case. It was up to her to dispel them. Suppressing a sigh of exasperation, she stood.

"Mr. Van Cleave, I have here the deposition you gave police about your relationship with Miss Saint-Claire. In it, you state that you routinely provided legal advice for her during the past fourteen years. Is this correct?"

"Yes."

"Did you charge Miss Saint-Claire for your services?"

"No, I did not. I did it as a favor to a friend."

"Were you ever intimate with her?"

The "Court TV" camera went in for a close-up. No doubt thinking of his wife, Walter froze and for a second looked like a deer caught in the headlights. "No," he said finally.

"I mean intimate in a physical sense," Susan specified, aware once again she had the jury's full interest.

"Objection," Tom cut in. "Counsel is badgering the witness. Mr. Van Cleave has already answered that question."

Susan shrugged. "There are many different types of intimacy, Your Honor. I am just trying to clarify Mr. Van Cleave's relationship with Miss Saint-Claire for the jury."

"Witness may answer the question," the judge instructed.

"No, we were not physically involved," Walter said curtly. He began to turn a pale shade of pink.

Susan didn't wonder about that; his wife and children were probably at home watching the trial on TV. And if they weren't now, they would be later. She pressed on. "Emotionally intimate, then?"

"Um—no," Walter said. His shoulders visibly relaxed.

"So you weren't physically and emotionally intimate with Miss Saint-Claire... Correct?"

"Correct," Walter replied.

"Then it's not surprising that Angelica might not have had time to meet with you and your wife upon her return to Texas, is it?"

Walter looked at Susan warily. He sensed that she was setting a mine trap. "I guess not," Walter said slowly.

"And because you weren't physically and emotionally intimate with Miss Saint-Claire, then you wouldn't necessarily know, for instance, if she was upset about not being able to promote her brand-new movie or running out of her favorite bubble bath or even having a bad-hair day," Susan said as the jury began to chuckle.

Tom glared at Susan, but said nothing.

"Right?" Susan persisted.

"That's correct," Walter said, guessing he'd just been made a fool of on "Court TV," in front of millions of viewers.

"Thank you. No more questions," Susan said.

"How do you think it's going?" Jake asked over a catered lunch in the anteroom.

"Okay, so far," she told him and his dad. She reached over and touched Samuel's hand. "But I'm going to need to cross-examine you on the stand, after the prosecutor is finished with the direct examination. Are you up to it?"

Samuel nodded. "Anything to save my son," he said.

The first witness after lunch was not on Susan's list. She protested immediately and asked to approach the bench. "Your Honor, we've had no prior warning about this witness," she complained.

"That's because she just came forward yesterday," Tom Peterson told the judge. "Her testimony is vital to my case."

"I'll allow it this once," the judge said. "Proceed."

The witness, Mary Lou Breyers, took the stand.

She was a well-coiffed woman in her midthirties. While she was being sworn in, Susan scribbled "Who is she?" on the legal pad in front of her. Jake responded with a written "I don't know."

Tom Peterson looked smug. Susan wanted to choke him. Her only comfort was the knowledge she had a few of her own tricks up her sleeve.

"Can you tell the jury how and when you became acquainted with Miss Saint-Claire and Mr. Lockhart?" Tom Peterson asked.

Mary Lou Breyers faced the camera. If not for the disapproving look from the judge, Susan was sure Mary Lou would have touched her hair, just to make sure every glistening strawberry blond strand was in place. "Angelica was in my sorority at the University of Texas. I met Jake when she was dating him."

"Still can't recall her" Jake scribbled on the pad in front of him.

Susan wasn't surprised. Televising trials brought out all sorts of publicity hounds wanting their fifteen minutes of fame. She wrote back "Stay cool. Maybe the connection will come to you."

"Were you friends with Angelica at the time Jake and Angelica were dating?" Tom continued.

"Oh, yes. She used to talk about him all the time. At first, she thought he was absolutely top drawer. But then she got to know him."

"Objection, hearsay," Susan interjected in a bored tone. She let the jury know that she thought the witness was wasting all their time.

"Objection sustained. The witness will testify only to things she actually saw or heard, not anything merely told to her."

Tom tried again. "Did you witness the breakup of Jake and Angelica?"

"Yes."

"When and where did this occur?"

"Jake brought her back to the sorority house around midnight. I was upstairs studying, and I had the window open to enjoy the spring air."

Or in other words, Susan thought, you were eavesdropping.

"I remember seeing Jake park his brand-new pickup truck in front of the sorority house. Before he had even come to a complete stop, Angelica opened the door and vaulted out!"

To Susan's dismay, every eyebrow in the jury raised, as if the jury members were wondering what had occurred to cause that.

"What happened then?" Tom asked almost gleefully.

"Jake jumped out after her and circled around to her side. He tried to grab her arm, but she shook him off."

"Your Honor, I fail to see where this is relevant to the current trial," Susan said.

"The prosecution is trying to establish what the relationship between the murder victim and the defendant was at the time she left Texas," Tom Peterson said.

"Objection, prosecution's language is prejudicial to my client," Susan said.

"Ms. Kilpatrick, please give the court time to rule on one objection before you voice another," the judge said.

The jury chuckled. Susan grinned, too; she had successfully broken the tension and suspense the DA was building. "The defense apologizes, Your Honor," Susan demurred politely.

"Thank you." The judge pushed his glasses farther up his nose. "The first objection is overruled, so the questioning may continue. The second is sustained. Watch your language, Mr. Peterson."

"Yes, Your Honor." Tom cast a sidelong glare at Susan, then seemed to struggle to pick up where he had left off.

"Ms. Saint-Claire and Mr. Lockhart were standing in front of the sorority house..." the judge prompted, somewhat impatiently.

"Yes. You stated the defendant had hold of Miss Saint-Claire's arm," Tom said to Mary Lou.

"Right."

"Was it a gentle hold?" Tom asked.

"Objection," Susan said. "There's no way that could be accurately judged from a distance."

The judge frowned. "Sustained. Please try to get to the point, Mr. Peterson."

Tom frowned. "What could you hear being said while Mr. Lockhart held Ms. Saint-Claire's arm?"

Mary Lou frowned. "He said, and I quote, 'You fooled me, too.'"

"Go on."

"Then she said, and I quote, 'I never want to see you again, Jake Lockhart!' And she stormed inside the sorority house, went straight upstairs to her room, threw herself on her bed and started crying like there was no tomorrow," Mary Lou finished reciting in a breathlessly excited voice.

Jake wrote, "That sounds like vintage Angelica...always dramatic."

Tom's expression grew sympathetic as the "Court TV" camera focused on Mary Lou once again. "Did you ask Angelica what had happened?" he queried in the same breathlessly excited manner.

"Why, certainly I did. I marched into her room and said, 'Angelica, what happened, honey?' She looked up, and her face was all red and streaky with tears, and she said that he wasn't the person she thought he was and she was so very sorry she had ever dated him, because he had really let her down."

Which was, Susan thought triumphantly, exactly what Jake had told her. Tom didn't know it, but he had just confirmed a big part of Jake's story.

"Anything else?" Tom asked Mary Lou.

She shook her head dramatically. "No, she just started crying again like her heart was gonna break."

The jury looked sympathetic. Susan passed the chance to object. Better to get this over with as soon as possible, she thought.

"Did you ever discuss the incident that night with the defendant, Jake Lockhart?"

Mary Lou leaned forward. "As a matter of fact, I did. I saw him in the student union, buying stamps, and I asked him straight out. I said, 'Jake, how are you feeling about the breakup with Angelica?' And he said to me, 'How should I feel, when she's going around campus telling everyone the reason the two of us broke up is that I just didn't measure up?'"

Susan swore. That sounded like a motive for sexual revenge of some sort. Score another for the prosecution, she thought.

Jake scrawled, "Angelica did say that, and it ticked me off, but I can't recall *ever* having a conversation with Mary Lou, and she gets on my nerves so bad already I feel sure I would recall it if I had."

"No further questions, Your Honor." The damage he'd intended done, Tom sat down.

Susan stood. She smiled at Mary Lou. "Am I correct in my understanding that you and Angelica were very good friends while you were at UT?"

"Yes, you are." Mary Lou flashed a smile for the TV camera.

The general rule of thumb for a trial attorney was to never ask a question you didn't already know the answer to. But in this case Susan went with her gut instinct. She smiled warmly at Mary Lou in an attempt to put her at ease. "How did the two of you meet?"

"In drama class."

Susan raised her brow, as if suitably impressed. "So, you're an actress, too?" she said.

"Oh, yes, I appear regularly in community theater," Mary Lou stated proudly.

"Have you ever acted outside the state?"

Mary Lou's cheeks grew pink, confirming Susan's suspicions that she was out for the fifteen minutes of fame she thought due her. "I went to Hollywood for one summer, and New York another," she volunteered.

"Did you find work?"

For a millisecond, Mary Lou looked stricken. "Oh, yes."

"Perhaps I should be more specific," Susan continued. "Did you find work as an actress?"

"No. I did not."

Susan gave the jury time to wonder if maybe there wasn't a little envy going on here as she studied her legal pad. When she was sure the jury had doubts again, she looked up and asked Mary Lou,

"Did Angelica keep in touch with you after she moved to Hollywood?"

"No."

"Had you seen or talked to her since she'd left Texas years ago?" Susan pressed.

"No."

"Have you seen or talked to Jake Lockhart since your days at UT?" Susan asked.

"No."

"Not even once?"

Mary Lou squirmed on the witness stand. "No."

"Did you send him a Christmas card?"

"No."

Susan knew she was reaching again, but she felt there was something here. Something Mary Lou would rather she not know. Susan smiled. "Did you work on his political campaign?"

"No."

"Have you worked on any political campaigns?"

Again those cheeks of hers turned pink. "Yes," Mary Lou allowed reluctantly.

"Whose campaign?"

"Objection, irrelevant," Tom Peterson said, beginning to look a little panicked.

The judge noticed, too. "Objection overruled. Witness may answer."

Mary Lou announced proudly, "I worked on Franklin Holt's campaign during the past three elections."

Susan frowned. "He's not of the same political party as Mr. Lockhart, is he?" she asked.

"No, he isn't," Mary Lou admitted.

Susan allowed the shock, the personal questions about Mary Lou's integrity, to flash across her face. Noting Tom was about to voice another objection, she held up a palm to stop him and addressed the court. "Thank you. No further questions."

"You may step down," the judge told Mary Lou.

"Just because I didn't vote for Jake Lockhart doesn't mean I'm not telling the truth," she muttered, but loud enough for everyone to hear.

"The jury will disregard that remark," the judge said. "The witness is finished."

Mary Lou skulked out of the courtroom.

"Prosecution calls Samuel Lockhart."

Jake stared straight ahead as Samuel took the stand. Susan could tell he was nervous about having his father up there. So was she. She would have preferred to call and introduce the witness herself, and hence control the jury's first impression of Jake's father, but Tom had beat her to the punch.

"Jake Lockhart is your only son, is that correct?" Tom asked.

"Yes."

"And you love him very much."

Samuel settled back in the witness chair, every inch the Texas rancher in his Western suit. "Yes, I do."

"You've also led a very active part in his campaigns, have you not?"

Samuel put his custom boots flat on the floor. "I have."

Tom regarded Samuel patiently, like a barracuda going in for the kill. "Do you take pride in your son's accomplishments?"

"Yes, I do."

"Is your son facing a crowded field in the next election?"

"That depends on what you mean by 'crowded,'" Samuel replied. "Fix or six have expressed an interest in running against him in the primary."

"What would be the effect of any *personal* scandal on Jake's reelection?"

To Susan's relief, Samuel held his own as he answered.

"That's hard to say. It would depend on the scandal."

"How about a *sex scandal?*" Tom asked.

"Objection!" Susan glared at Tom. "The prosecution is using innuendo instead of building a case!"

Tom held up his hand before the judge could rule. "I withdraw the question, Your Honor."

Next, Tom brought out the phone records from Angelica's hotel room and entered them into evidence. "Angelica called both the ranch and the attorney general's office, asking to speak to Jake, numerous times upon her arrival in Austin?"

Susan sent Samuel a look that said, Keep your cool! "Yes," Samuel said, "she did."

"You spoke to her?" Tom lifted his brows incriminatingly.

"Yes."

"Would you tell the court what was said?"

Samuel turned to the jury. "She wanted to speak to Jake. I told her he wasn't at the ranch. He was at the office."

"Is that all that was said?" Tom pressed.

Samuel looked at Tom proudly, as if he had nothing to hide. "She said she was staying at the Four Seasons and wanted to talk to him. When Jake remained unavailable and she still wanted to meet, I went over to the hotel to see her myself."

"Was it a pleasant meeting?"

Samuel grinned for the benefit of the jury and stroked his jaw wryly. "We never did get along."

There was a chuckle in the courtroom. The judge admonished the jury with a look.

"Then why did you go?" Tom continued.

Samuel shrugged. "My mama raised me to be polite. At the time it seemed like the thing to do."

"And now?" Tom persisted.

"I wish she had never come back to Texas, of course," Samuel admitted.

Susan—and many of the jurors, it seemed—considered such honesty quite heroic under the circumstances. Watching him, it was easy to see where Jake got his guts, Susan thought.

"Why do you wish Angelica had never come back to Texas?" Tom asked, narrowing his eyes at Samuel, as if there were something sinister behind the feeling.

"I don't know. My son's on trial for her murder," he said sarcastically. "You figure it out."

The jury erupted into laughter. Tom Peterson looked humiliated.

"Settle down, everyone," the judge said.

But Susan could feel the jury was on Samuel's side.

Next, Tom entered several magazines and half a dozen tabloids into evidence. All featured unflattering articles about Angelica. "Were you aware of these publications?" he asked.

"I don't read the supermarket tabloids, if that's what you're asking," Samuel replied calmly, looking at Tom.

"But you were aware that Angelica had a reputation for living with men, posing half clothed for magazines and appearing in movies with R ratings, were you not?" Tom asked pointedly.

The courtroom hushed as everyone waited for Samuel to answer.

"I knew she was in the movies. I don't know if the other is true," Samuel allowed slowly. He regarded Tom cautiously.

"You don't read *Playboy?*" Tom raised a brow.

"No, I don't," Samuel said. He looked straight at the district attorney. "Do you?"

Again the jury chuckled and again Tom flushed.

Sensing things were about to get out of control, the judge said, "The witness will answer the question and refrain from making additional irrelevant comments."

Tom studied the notes in front of him. When the courtroom had quieted once more, he looked up. "Did you want your son to become involved with Angelica again?" he asked.

Samuel shrugged. "Jake is thirty-seven years old. He decides who he sees or doesn't see. Frankly, it's none of my business."

There was another sympathetic murmur through the jury box.

Tom tried again. "I assume you have helped out on your son's campaigns, though."

"Yes, I have," Samuel admitted. "Many times."

"Do you offer advice on his political career?"

"Yes, I do."

"Unsolicited advice?"

"Sometimes."

Tom smiled at Samuel, knowing, as did Susan, that he probably had him now. "Mr. Lockhart, did you ever caution your son, Jake, about the potential damage to his political career if he did indeed become involved with Angelica Saint-Claire again?" Tom asked.

"Yes, I did," Samuel said, without delay.

"And what was your son's response?" Tom asked.

Susan felt herself grow tenser by the second.

Samuel shrugged. "He didn't want to discuss it."

"Did you tell Jake that it would be best for his political career if he did stay away from her?"

Samuel thought back. "I believe that was my advice, yes."

"But he didn't do that, did he?" Tom said.

"Obviously not," Samuel concurred dryly.

The DA looked down at his notes. "Let's move on," he said brusquely. "Was it in your nature to interfere in your son's romantic life?"

Samuel folded his arms in front of him. "Absolutely not."

"But you did go to the Four Seasons Hotel to see Angelica Saint-Claire, did you not?"

"Yes, I did," Samuel said.

Tom referred to his notes with a casual studiedness that had alarm bells sounding in Susan's head.

"Did you also go to the Shady Villa Motel, perhaps the night Angelica was killed?"

"I don't know what you're talking about," Samuel said hotly. He shot a confused look at the judge, then the courtroom in general. "I was never there!"

"I remind the witness of the penalties for perjury in this state," Tom Peterson said.

"Objection, badgering the witness," Susan said.

"Jury disregard that last remark," the judge said. "Counselors, approach the bench." The judge waited until Susan and Tom stood before him. He pointed his finger at Tom. "That last remark was totally without foundation. There's been no evidence this witness was ever at the Shady Villa Motel, and unless you have something to show me right this instant . . ."

"No, Your Honor." Tom ducked his head in mute apology.

"Do that again and I'll cite you for contempt of court," the judge warned.

"Yes, Your Honor," Tom said.

But Susan knew the dirty deed had already been done. He had successfully planted a seed in the jury's mind that Samuel might be somehow involved in Angelica's murder. It would be up to her to set them straight.

## Chapter Fourteen

"Tom Peterson is just full of dirty tricks, isn't he?" Samuel muttered in the anteroom.

"He has a reputation for it, Dad," Jake said. He touched his father's shoulder. "Don't let it get you down."

"I'll undo any damage when I put you back on the stand for my cross-examination," Susan promised.

"But some of this looks and sounds so bad," Samuel complained.

Susan knew what he meant. Some of it was very incriminating. "We'll defuse every bit of evidence we think the DA is going to introduce by mentioning it first whenever possible and second when we have to do it that way. Okay? By putting our own spin on all the evidence, we can take the wind out of Tom Peterson's sails."

"She's right, Dad. She's doing a very good job."

Jake met Susan's glance. She felt a moment's closeness to him, one that would intensify once the trial was over.

With effort, Susan dropped her gaze. She had a job to do.

Samuel turned back to Susan. "How do you think we're doing so far?"

"We're doing fine," she reassured him.

"Did you find out where Tom Peterson was the night Angelica was killed?" Jake asked.

Susan nodded. Ray had given her a report that morning. "He was at a barbecue for the Optimists Club. There were tons of witnesses who saw him there, politicking all evening." Which meant he couldn't have murdered Angelica.

"What about Bitsy Van Cleave?"

"She and Walter had tickets to the Austin Symphony. Walter was late arriving—he was busy bailing a teenage client out of jail—but both were there and at a party afterward. They have witnesses, including the court records and the teenage defendant's family, who couldn't stop telling Ray how wonderful Walter was."

Jake seemed disappointed. "I was hoping—"

"I know," Susan said. She had wanted to find the murderer, too. She knew Jake and his dad were both depending on her. Not about to let them down, she wasted no time getting right to the heart of matters when she put Samuel back on the witness stand.

"Mr. Lockhart, you try to help your son Jake out in any way that you can, don't you?"

"Yes, ma'am, I do," he said respectfully.

"When Miss Saint-Claire telephoned the ranch, did she express an urgent need to see your son?"

"Yes, she did."

"Was she in any sort of trouble?" Susan asked.

"I had the feeling she might be," Samuel admitted frankly. "That's why I went to the hotel to see her."

Susan nodded. "What did Miss Saint-Claire say when she saw you at her hotel?"

Samuel sighed. "She asked me where Jake was. I told her still working. She said she wanted to see him and not me."

"Was she speaking in a normal tone of voice?"

"No. She was shouting."

"Describe her appearance."

"She had dark circles under her eyes. Her hand shook as she lit a cigarette."

"What happened next?"

"The phone rang in her suite. She asked me to get it and find out who it was."

"And did you?"

"Yes. The person on the other end said he was from the Hollywood movie studio where she worked. I covered the mouthpiece and told her. She frowned and grabbed the phone from my hand and started talking."

"Did you overhear anything of what was being said?" Susan asked.

"Only her voice, not what was being said on the other end of the line."

"Just tell us what you heard," Susan said. Out of the corner of her eye, she could see the jury was sitting on the edge of their seats.

"She said she was going to get back to Hollywood as soon as she could, and she knew damn well what the promotion schedule looked like."

"And then what happened?"

"She hung up the phone and told me to tell Jake that she wanted to see him. Then she told me she had a headache and wasn't feeling well."

"Did you see her take any medication while you were there with her?"

"No, but there was a bottle of prescription pills on her dresser, sitting out plain as day."

"Did you happen to notice what kind they were?"

"No. It wasn't my business to read the label."

The jury nodded sympathetically. Although Samuel was careful to speak respectfully of the late actress, her rude behavior made her sound like a witch on wheels. The kind of woman any loving parent would want to keep away from their son.

"Then what happened?" Susan asked.

"I left."

Susan looked down at her notes, acutely aware of all she had promised Jake she would not introduce at the trial.

Unfortunately there were some things she had to cover, lest they come up in later testimony. With the case being televised, there was no telling who would call up the DA's office and volunteer to testify.

"Was there any other time you met with Miss Saint-Claire while she was in Austin?" Susan asked.

"Yes. I went back to see her the next day, just to check up on her. The clerk at the front desk told me she had checked out a bicycle and that I should look for her on the paths behind the hotel, along the lake."

"Did you?"

Samuel nodded. "Yes. And that's when I saw her with Mr. Garrison. He had her backed up against the tree, and he was kissing her. She was flailing her arms trying to get away, so I went up and grabbed the back of his shirt and pulled him off her."

"Objection." Tom Peterson was on his feet. "This information is not relevant to this case."

Susan thought the question was very important, and so did the jury, judging from the intensely interested looks on their faces. "Your Honor, the defense is trying to establish a chronology of events leading up to Miss Saint-Claire's death. Not just those that unfairly incriminate my client,'' Susan said dryly.

The judge said to Tom Peterson, ''Your objection is overruled. This line of questioning may continue.''

''What was Miss Saint-Claire's reaction when you cut short Mr. Garrison's amorous advances?'' Susan asked.

Samuel blew out a weary breath, completely exasperated. ''She told me to mind my own business.''

''Then what happened?''

Samuel shrugged. ''I figured if she didn't mind being treated so roughly it wasn't my business to mind, either, and I left.''

''Did you ever see her again?''

''No.''

''That's all. Witness is excused.''

''Does the prosecution wish to redirect?''

''No, Your Honor.''

Tom Peterson spent most of the rest of the day introducing police photos and reports on the crime scene. Finally the medical examiner was called to the stand, to go over the autopsy and toxicology reports.

''In your opinion, what was the cause of Angelica Saint-Claire's death?'' Tom asked, after all the information had been formally entered into evidence.

''She died of two things. A stab wound to her heart and an overdose of glutethimide—a prescription sleeping tablet.''

''Could she have died simply from the overdose?'' Tom asked.

''Yes.''

''What about the single wound to the heart?''

''That was also a mortal wound.''

''Were there signs of a struggle? Bruises?''

''None.''

''Have you had a chance to compare Ms. Saint-Claire's blood with that found on Jake Lockhart's clothing?''

''Yes. DNA reports confirm it was Miss Saint-Claire's blood on his clothing.''

Tom gave Susan a satisfied smile and sat down. She stood.

''Is the amount and location of the blood on Jake Lockhart's clothing consistent with that of a person who had tried to stem the bleeding with direct pressure of his bare hand?''

''Yes.''

''Thank you. I have no more questions at this time.''

"Ms. KILPATRICK! How do you think the case is going so far?" the "Court TV" reporter asked, thrusting a microphone in Susan's face the moment she stepped outside the courthouse.

What could she say? That Tom Peterson had taken politicizing a case to new heights with his shoddy investigation of Angelica's death? "It went pretty much as I expected," she replied confidently.

"Do you feel ready to start presenting the defense case tomorrow?" another reporter asked.

"Yes. I do. In fact, I'm anxious to get started," Susan said with a smile.

"Jake, anything to say?" a reporter asked.

"I think Ms. Kilpatrick is doing an excellent job. I look forward to getting this over so I can go back to work," Jake answered.

"Samuel? Anything to say?" someone shouted.

"My son is innocent." Samuel looked straight into the cameras as flashbulbs went off. "This entire trial is a travesty. A waste of taxpayer's time and money."

Susan held up her hands. "We'll have more to say when the trial is over, I promise. Now, if you'll excuse us, it's been a very long day." The three of them moved through the crowd of reporters, to a full-size van emblazoned with the words Lockhart Ranch. Ray Trevino had agreed to make himself available to drive them back and forth each day. Samuel climbed in the front. Jake and Susan headed for the captain-style chairs in the middle of the van.

Ray drove off, making his way carefully through the crush of television-station trucks. "What a day," Susan said, as she looked out the tinted windows. In addition to the reporters, there was a small group of protestors with signs, still demanding Jake's immediate resignation as attorney general.

"I thought it went very well," Jake said.

Susan nodded. She looked back at Jake, marveling at how close they had become in so short a time. "We put a dent in it," she said, "but we still have a lot to do to prepare for tomorrow."

Jake nodded. Again she was aware how much he was depending on her and how he had come to trust her. She hoped she did not betray that new feeling. More than ever, she was aware she held his life in her hands.

"DEFENSE CALLS Dr. Enrique Torres."

"How long have you been Angelica's physician?"

"Since she first moved to Los Angeles fourteen years ago."

"Did she ever come to you for sleeping problems?"

"Yes. At the start of a new movie, she often had trouble for the first week or so. When that happened, I prescribed trialozolam, a mild sleeping tablet."

"Did you recently prescribe medication for her?"

"Yes."

"Trialozolam again?"

"No. When she came in, she told me it was not working and she asked me for something stronger."

"And did you prescribe something stronger?"

"Yes. I gave her two weeks, or fourteen pills, of glutethimide, a very strong medication."

Susan could see the jury was thoroughly caught up in Dr. Torres's testimony. "Did you caution Miss Saint-Claire about the potential dangers of such a strong medication?"

"Yes, I did."

"Had she ever mixed alcohol and sleeping tablets to your knowledge?"

"No, she had not."

"Were you worried she might this time?"

Dr. Torres shook his head. "Absolutely not."

"Thank you. That's all." Susan sat down.

Tom Peterson stood. "Did Miss Saint-Claire tell you why she couldn't sleep?"

"She said she had personal problems, and that she was returning to Texas to take care of them."

Tom sent Jake a long accusing look, then turned back to Dr. Torres. "Thank you. That's all for now."

Susan frowned. That had not gone as well as she'd hoped, but they were just getting started. "Permission to redirect, Your Honor?"

"Go ahead."

"Dr. Torres, when Angelica came into your office, did she mention how long she had been having sleeping problems this time?"

"Yes. Well over a month."

"A month before she came to Texas," Susan repeated slowly.

"Yes."

"So it's feasible whatever problems she was having started in California, not Texas?"

"I suppose—"

"Objection." Tom Peterson was on his feet. "Hearsay."

"I withdraw the question, Your Honor," Susan said with a smile. Her point made, she dismissed the witness and Dr. Enrique Torres stepped down.

"Defense calls Detective Martin O'Reilly, from the Travis County sheriff's office."

"You were in charge of the investigation at the Shady Villa Motel, were you not?" Susan began, after he had been sworn in.

"Yes, ma'am, I was."

"The medical examiner has told us that Angelica suffered a stab wound to the chest and an overdose of glutethimide. Dr. Torres stated he prescribed glutethimide for Ms. Saint-Claire. Was a prescription bottle found at the murder scene?"

"No."

"A knife or sharp-bladed instrument of any kind?"

"No."

"Was the motel room searched?"

"Yes, as well as the general area around the hotel."

"What about Jake Lockhart? Was he searched at the scene?"

"Yes. Neither item was found on him."

"What about Mr. Lockhart's vehicle, the ranch house where he lives with his father. Were those searched?"

"Quite thoroughly. The vehicle that evening and the ranch the next day. And then we went back again, a few days ago, with a full crew."

"And still didn't find anything?"

"Right."

Susan worried over this. "Was it possible the items were simply overlooked?"

"No, ma'am. If they'd have been there, we'd have found them."

Susan let that sink in a moment. She put up several pictures on display. "Let's go back to the crime-scene photos for a moment. To the left of the bed here, in the motel room, is a combination dresser, television stand, vanity table and chair." Susan used her pointer to identify the two small silver cases, hairbrush and comb laid out on the table. "Can you tell the jury what was in these cases?" Susan asked the detective.

"It was makeup. The rectangular case contained blush and a flat-handled blusher brush. The tube contained a lipstick."

"Were there fingerprints on these two cases?"

"No."

"None?"

"None."

Susan frowned. "Would a person leave fingerprints on the makeup case if he or she picked it up and used it?"

"Oh, yes."

"No doubt about it?" Susan questioned.

"No doubt about it," the detective confirmed.

"Would it be possible to pick the cases up without leaving any fingerprints on them?"

"Not unless you were wearing gloves."

"Objection, irrelevant," Tom Peterson said.

"Your Honor, it's the defense's position that every item at the crime scene is extremely relevant, as it may yield a clue as to what did or did not happen that night."

The judge nodded his agreement. "Overruled. Counsel may continue."

Susan put down her pointer, folded her arms in front of her and walked away from the photos. "Let's go back to the night Miss Saint-Claire was murdered. You were not just in charge of this investigation, Detective O'Reilly, you were the first person on the scene, were you not?"

"Yes."

"The first person to enter the motel room?"

"Yes."

"Tell us what you saw when you walked in."

"Jake Lockhart was standing next to the body of Miss Saint-Claire. He had blood on his hands and his clothes and he was reaching for the phone."

"He had not yet dialed."

"No."

"And you are absolutely certain you saw this?"

"Yes. Absolutely."

"Is it possible he heard you coming and then grabbed for the phone?"

"No. My partner and I approached the room with extreme caution and stealth. There's no way he could have heard us."

"Thank you," Susan said. "No further questions at this time."

Tom Peterson got up. He smiled smugly at the jury. "What were Jake Lockhart's first words to you when you entered the room?"

"He said we had to get help."

"For Miss Saint-Claire?"

"Yes."

"Is it possible he was just pretending to be helpful?" Tom asked slyly.

"Objection, Your Honor. Counsel is asking the witness to characterize defendant's thoughts and feelings, and he has no way of knowing either."

"Sustained," the judge said. "Move to strike."

Too late, Susan thought, the damage was already done.

THEY TOOK a brief recess. As soon as they returned, Susan called the next witness. "Please state your name and occupation for the court."

"Rob Kinzler. I tend bar at the Lone Star Saloon, which is about half a mile down the road from the Shady Villa Motel."

"Were you working the night Angelica Saint-Claire was killed?"

"Yes, ma'am." He nodded. "I answered the phone when she called the bar."

"What time was this?"

"About seven-thirty. She wanted a pitcher of eight margaritas and a bucket of ice delivered to the Shady Villa right away, along with a couple of glasses. She said there'd be a great tip if I got there within the half hour." Rob grinned proudly, recounting, "I got there within twenty minutes. She tipped me twenty bucks, too."

Susan smiled at Rob. "Not bad for just one delivery."

"No, ma'am."

"What was Miss Saint-Claire doing when you arrived?"

Rob looked at the jury. "She was running a bubble bath. I remember 'cause I saw the bubbles just foaming up over the rim of the tub."

"Was she dressed?"

"She had her shoes off, but she was wearing a short black suede skirt and a red silk blouse, black panty hose."

"Do you remember anything else?"

"Yeah. The whole room smelled like perfume, and she had flowers on the dresser."

"Was she frowning?"

"No. She was smiling. Humming to herself, kind of dancing around."

"Thank you."

Peterson waived his right to cross-examine. Susan went on to her next exhibit. "Your Honor, I'd like permission to show this videotape, *Makeup by Angelica,* to the jury."

Tom Peterson emitted a long-suffering sigh. "Your Honor, this is irrelevant."

"I plan to demonstrate relevancy," Susan said.

"The court will indulge you, but it had better be worth the court's time," the judge warned.

"Thank you, Your Honor."

For the next fifteen minutes, they watched Angelica put blusher on her cheeks and lipstick on her lips. It was a long, tedious process, but the results were perfect.

Next, Susan showed still photos of Angelica to the jury. Again her makeup was perfectly applied. Finally Susan called a set makeup artist from Angelica's last movie.

"Oh, yeah, she always insisted on doing her own makeup, always," the makeup artist said. "She was never satisfied with the way anyone else did it. The same with the lighting. She always wanted to check it herself. She was a real perfectionist, obsessed with the way she looked."

Susan turned once more to the crime-scene photos. She tacked close-ups of Angelica's face on the bulletin board. Her eyes were closed. Her hair was spread around her face like a soft halo.

"Tell me what you see when you look at these photos," Susan said.

The makeup artist smirked. "Well, it's clear that a rank amateur made her up."

Susan noticed the jury was frowning. "Why do you say that?"

"See how inexpertly the blush has been put on here...how it has been applied from cheekbone clear down to the jaw?"

"In your expert opinion, could Angelica have applied her blush herself in these pictures?"

"Absolutely not."

"Thank you."

Tom Peterson stood. "What if Miss Saint-Claire were upset—say, her hand was shaking? Would her makeup be flawed then?"

"I suppose, but—"

"Thank you. That's all. No further questions." Tom sat down.

"We'll break for lunch," the judge said.

"THE TESTIMONY about the makeup didn't turn out as well as we'd hoped," Jake said glumly, as he and Susan retired to the anteroom for a meal.

"We made our points," she said. "Besides, it's when we close that things will really jell for the jurors. They're already evidencing quite a bit of doubt. I should be able to bring it all together when we offer our closing arguments later today."

Jake nodded.

Susan yearned to offer some physical comfort, but she knew she couldn't. She had to keep a professional distance through the rest of the trial. She looked at him. "Are you ready to take the stand?"

Jake nodded.

The courtroom filled with a hushed, expectant silence as Jake was sworn in.

"How and when did you meet Angelica?" Susan began.

"We met at a football game at the University of Texas. We started dating right away."

"Were you in love with her?"

Jake looked at Susan; his demeanor was relaxed. "I thought I was at the time. Now that I'm older, I think it was more like infatuation."

"Why did the two of you break off your relationship?"

"She wanted me to move to California so that we could be together and get married while she started her career. I wanted to stay in Texas and practice law. Neither of us was willing to compromise. When we realized that, we ended our relationship. It was a mutual decision."

"Did you see her after that?"

Jake shook his head. "Not for almost fifteen years."

"Were you in touch with her?"

"No."

"Why didn't you return her phone calls initially?"

Jake sighed. "Our relationship was over. I didn't want to restart it."

"But when she came back to Austin and checked into the Four Seasons Hotel, you did go and see her. Why?"

"I thought she needed a friend."

Susan nodded. "And were you able to be a friend to her?" she asked Jake gently.

"No, not really."

"Why not?"

"Because—" Jake chose his words carefully as he looked at the jury "—whatever compatibility we had once shared was gone. We viewed the world differently. My whole life revolved around my commitment to public service and making Texas a better place to live. She lived from movie to movie. Years ago, we had little in common except that we were both students at UT. When she came back to Texas, we didn't even have that anymore."

"So her reappearance in your life, and your eventual reunion, made you feel how?"

"Let down, I guess."

Susan gave the jury a moment to assimilate that. "Was there a resurgence of romance between the two of you?" Susan asked sympathetically.

"No."

Susan regarded Jake curiously. "Then why did you meet her at the Shady Villa Motel?"

Jake lifted his hands, palm out. "She sent me a bouquet of flowers and a note asking me to meet her there that evening."

"But by that time, you knew that you did not want to restart your romance with her, correct?"

"Correct."

Susan knew she had to ask the hard questions, before the DA did. "So why go?" Susan persisted, and was relieved to see Jake stay cool and collected despite the testy edge in her voice.

Jake frowned. He took another deep breath. "I wanted to make it clear to her that the relationship was over."

Susan looked him up and down. She hoped with all her heart that the jury believed him as fervently as she did. "And did you get that chance?" she asked.

"No," Jake said.

Susan took him through the discovery of the body, detail by excruciating detail. "Did you murder Angelica Saint-Claire?" Susan asked.

"No," Jake said firmly, his voice ringing in the silence of the courtroom, "I did not."

Tom Peterson stood. "Mr. Lockhart, your career means everything to you, doesn't it?"

Jake stiffened. "I enjoy my work. I consider the pursuit of justice an important one to the people of this great state."

"Ah, spoken like a true politician," Tom replied condescendingly.

Susan's right hand clenched inside the circle of her left. *Takes one to know one, Peterson,* she thought.

"An association with Angelica Saint-Claire would have hurt your chances for reelection, would it not?"

"I don't think so," Jake said quietly. He met Tom's gaze equably. "I think the people of Texas would understand if I or any other politician were in love with an actress. I don't think the majority of voters would mix up the fantasy of a movie role with the reality of life."

The jury smiled, looking as if they were very much in Jake's court. Clearly, Susan thought, suppressing a smile, this cross-examination wasn't going the way Tom wanted.

Tom scratched the back of his neck and studied his legal pad. "You've been asked about the nature of your relationship with Miss Saint-Claire. Reminding you of the penalty of perjury in this state, I'll ask you again if you restarted your love affair with her when she returned to Texas."

"No, I did not. And if I'm not mistaken, the autopsy reports support my statement. There was no evidence that Miss Saint-Claire made love prior to her death, or in the immediate time period prior to that."

Tom frowned. He seemed at a loss. Everything he threw at Jake, Jake threw back. Nevertheless, the assault on Jake's word continued for another two hours. Tom made no headway. Finally, there was nothing left to do except offer up closing arguments.

Tom began his with zeal. "Politicians are not above the law. Angelica Saint-Claire was murdered in coldblood. She was drugged, disrobed, laid out and then stabbed in the heart.

"The defense is right. We have no murder weapon, no empty pill bottle. But we do have the equivalent of the smoking gun. We have Jake Lockhart standing over the body, blood on his hands and clothes.

"Angelica Saint-Claire is dead. Sadly, we cannot bring her back. But justice can still be done. I ask you, the jury, to render a verdict of guilty and send a message to all those who feel they are above the law. Let the criminals know that no matter how prominent they are, or how wealthy, that if they commit the crime, they will indeed do the time."

It was all Susan could do not to shake her head as Tom Peterson sat down. His summation had sounded like a campaign speech. Judging from the look on the judge's face, he had noticed, too.

She stood and faced the jury. She smiled at them and spoke in a warm, folksy tone. "You would never know it from what you've seen here in the past few days, but a courtroom is not a place to begin a political campaign or railroad one's political rival out of office. We are not here to find a scapegoat or send a message. We are here to seek the truth about what happened the night Angelica Saint-Claire died.

"The district attorney wants you to believe that Jake Lockhart killed her. He believes this, even though he has established no motive, found no murder weapon and has no eyewitness to the crime. What he does have is a lot of circumstantial evidence. But circumstantial evidence alone is not nearly enough to prove, *beyond a reasonable doubt or even an unreasonable doubt,* that a crime has been committed." Susan gave the jury a moment to assimilate that, then she continued.

"Let us take a moment and review the facts of this case as they have been entered into evidence. Jake Lockhart walked into the Shady Villa Motel and found an old college friend unconscious and the victim of a stab wound to the chest. He was shocked and horrified, but he did what we hope any one of us would have done in his place. He immediately utilized what first aid he knew. He put direct pressure on the stab wound and looked for a pulse. In the process, he got blood on his hands and on his clothing. When he was unable to find a pulse, he reached for a phone so that he could dial 911.

"And it was at that moment, as he was reaching out for help, without any thought to himself or the possible political or personal consequences, that the police walked in and he was arrested, his life made into a nonstop hell of innuendo and speculation.

"To convict Jake Lockhart of a murder he did not commit is not justice, ladies and gentlemen of the jury. And we are here to find justice, to seek the truth. We are not here to railroad an innocent man into prison for the rest of his life."

"HOW MUCH LONGER before they render a verdict?" Samuel asked.

"I don't know," Susan said. She looked at Jake; she could feel him distancing himself from her and his father. "It could be hours or it could be days."

Samuel blew out a weary breath. "Well, I'm going down to get a soda from the machine," Samuel said.

"You doing okay?" Susan asked Jake, after his father had left.

He shrugged, as if the waiting were nothing. "It's only been two days," Jake said.

"Two days that seem like a lifetime," Susan said gently.

Jake turned to look at her. His slate gray eyes warmed. She could feel him reaching out to her.

"You do understand," he said.

"It's my job to understand," Susan said. Just the way it seemed, with every moment they spent together, it was her job to care for him as a woman loved her man. Susan was stunned to realize this was so.

Jake gazed at her. He released a shaky breath and shoved a hand through his hair. "I don't think I could have gotten through this without you," he said raggedly, his anguish about the outcome clearly building.

Acting purely on instinct, Susan stepped closer. As their glances meshed, she saw more than gratitude in his eyes. She saw desire and a yearning for closeness that mirrored her own. Aware of where they were, that they could be walked in on at any moment, Susan struggled to keep a professional perspective on the situation. She touched his arm reassuringly. "Pretty soon this will all be behind you," she predicted calmly, her voice intentionally even and relaxed.

Jake covered her hand with his own. He looked deep into her eyes. He was about to speak, when the door burst open. Samuel rushed in, followed by a bailiff.

"The verdict's in."

# Chapter Fifteen

"All rise."

Susan stood beside Jake as the judge came into the courtroom and resumed his seat on the bench. Her heart was pounding. Every doubt she'd had about this case surfaced.

"Have you reached a verdict?" the judge asked.

The jury foreman stood. "We have, Your Honor."

A bailiff carried a copy of the verdict to the judge. He read it, his expression impassive, then instructed, "Read the verdict for the court."

"The jury finds the defendant, Jake Lockhart, not guilty."

Voices rose behind them, some exultant, some outraged. Tom Peterson glared at Susan from the prosecutor's table.

"Mr. Lockhart, you are free to leave," the judge said.

Susan turned to him. He reached over and hugged her tight, then he leaned across the rail that separated the spectator section from the defense table, and he hugged his father. Susan had tears in her eyes. She ducked her head and picked up her briefcase. "I promised to talk to the reporters out front."

Jake caught her arm before she could exit the courtroom. "I'll go with you."

"If you don't mind, son, I think I'll skip the press conference and go on back to the ranch," Samuel said.

"I'll meet you there later. I want to take Susan to dinner."

"You go right ahead." Samuel leaned over and hugged her, too. "There isn't a finer lawyer in all of Texas," he told her warmly.

The reporters were waiting outside. Susan stepped up to the microphones. The "Court TV" reporter asked, "How do you feel about the victory, Susan?"

She smiled at the circle of press around her. "Good."

"What do you have to say about the district attorney's office?"

"Angelica Saint-Claire made a lot of enemies on her path to success. None of those enemies was investigated by the DA's office. From the very beginning, they ignored the obvious frame job against Jake. And as both a private citizen and defense attorney, that upsets me. As for the accusation against Jake, I've never seen a sloppier, weaker case. I think the speed with which the jury was able to acquit my client verifies that."

"Are you saying the charge against your client was politically motivated?" the reporter asked.

Susan smiled circumspectly. "I think we should let the voters decide that when it comes time to elect a district attorney next November." In fact, she hoped that Tom Peterson was booted out of office, as he deserved to be.

"Jake, do you feel justice was done?"

"No," he said grimly, "I don't." A hush went through the crowd as they waited expectantly. Jake continued, "Angelica's murderer is still out there. Justice won't be done until he or she is found and brought to trial."

"Do you think that can be done now, after everything that's happened?" the reporter asked.

"I don't know. I'd like to see someone try," Jake said.

"But without the murder weapon or the pill bottle . . . wouldn't the DA be left with another no-win case?" the reporter asked.

"It's my hope that someone out there saw or heard something. Someone who maybe hasn't come forward yet, or who tried to and was rebuffed."

Susan saw Chip Garrison lingering on the courthouse steps. He was standing apart from Vince Boyer. Both were in earshot of all that was being said. Both were glaring at Susan and Jake.

"You sound like a man with a mission," the reporter remarked to Jake, as Tom Peterson and the rest of his staff walked out to join the fray.

"I guess I am."

"It was risky, what you said back there," Susan noted as she got in her car and slid behind the wheel.

"Yeah, I know."

She looked at Jake as they both buckled their seat belts. "You could be stirring up a brand-new controversy."

He settled comfortably in the passenger seat. "It needed to be done. Her killer is still out there. Furthermore, for all we know, the two of us could still be in danger, Susan."

A shiver of fear rushed through her as she recalled the earlier attacks on her life, ones that had mysteriously ceased during the course of the trial.

Jake frowned as Susan drove out of the parking lot. "Just because I haven't been blackmailed yet, doesn't mean I won't be, and the same goes for my son."

"Thank goodness there have been no indications that Jaime's family is being blackmailed so far."

"I don't like having a threat hanging over my head."

"There's no guarantee that the DA's office could discover who the murderer is any more than we could. We had four suspects, and despite all the checking we did, we were still unable to narrow it down."

Jake's jaw set firmly. "Someone out there has to know or suspect something." Abruptly he relaxed. "But I don't want to think about that now. Tonight I just want to celebrate my acquittal. Tomorrow will be soon enough to look for Angelica's murderer again."

Tonight. What was Jake expecting?

"About dinner..." Susan began, not sure she trusted herself to be alone with him in the mood she was in.

He grinned and lifted a lock of her golden hair from her shoulder. He twirled it around his finger as he teased, "Backing out on me?"

Susan drew an equalizing breath, realizing that with the end of the trial had come the end of the physical and emotional barriers she had put up. "I just meant you don't have to do this," she said awkwardly, as they stopped at a traffic light.

"I know, but I want to."

Jake had corrected her softly, in a way that had turned her insides to mush. "Because you feel grateful?" Susan asked quietly, her eyes connecting with his.

"No. Because I feel this."

Hand on her shoulder, Jake leaned over and touched his lips to hers. The kiss sent desire sizzling through her veins. His hands sifted sensually through her hair, but a harbinger of things to come. Susan sat back in her seat. "Oh, my," she said.

Jake grinned as horns honked behind them. Realizing the light had changed while they were kissing, Susan drove on self-consciously. "Where do you want to go?"

She steadied her throbbing pulse with effort. "How about someplace quiet and casual?" she said.

Jake smiled over at her. "Name it."

"THIS WASN'T exactly what I had in mind," he said.

"But I didn't hear your protesting," Susan said as she un-locked the door to her condominium. She held the door and Jake carried in brown bags filled with foil-wrapped trays of spicy Tex-Mex enchiladas. Crisp green salad, tortilla chips and salsa and a six-pack of cold Mexican beer rounded out the meal.

"Hell, no. I love Tex-Mex," Jake said, setting the papers on the counter.

"That makes two of us," Susan said, turning toward him. Jake grinned, and it hit her; he was free, and so was she. There was nothing to keep them apart any longer.

The next thing she knew his strong arms were closing around her. His mouth was on hers, and all the pent-up emotions they'd felt over the past weeks came pouring out in a sizzling embrace. She returned the kiss eagerly. This was exactly what she wanted. To be loved by Jake. To be swept away by his need for her, to forget all the ugly accusations.

His mouth was hot, determined, giving, and Susan gloried in the blunt eroticism as he touched his tongue to hers, then swept her mouth in a slow, exquisitely voluptuous exploration. "Oh, Jake," she whispered, twining her arms around his neck.

Clamping a strong arm about her waist, he dragged her even closer, until her breasts were pressed against the hardness of his chest. She could feel his desire for her, the hard thudding of his heart and the underlying tenderness and passion in his touch, and another flood of pleasure rushed through her. "I've wanted you for so long," she whispered as his hands slid beneath her jacket and stroked up and down her back.

"I wanted you, too," Jake murmured against her hair.

"But we couldn't," she said on a broken sigh, as his hands moved around her rib cage and up, to warmly cup her breasts through the silk of her bra.

"Not as long as the trial was going on," he agreed, caressing her intimately, "but now all that is over. I'm a free man, and there's absolutely nothing standing in the way of our being together."

*Except my past and my father,* Susan thought. But already Jake was sweeping her up into his arms, carrying her down the hall and into her bedroom. Sliding his hand beneath her chin, he tilted her head up and lowered his mouth to hers. They kissed until all thoughts of resistance fled, until they were so in sync they might have been one. And it was only then that he began undressing her.

Her suit jacket and skirt fell to the floor as he continued raining hot passionate kisses over her temple, down her cheek, throat, shoulders. She was drowning in the warm fragrant scent of him, in the pleasure and tenderness he so easily evoked. She clung to him, wanting this closeness, wanting the honest pleasure in a way she had never wanted it before. Always before, she had been afraid to need. Scared to open herself up to hurt. But no more, she thought as he slowly finished undressing her and lowered her to the bed.

She watched as he shed his clothes, a thrill going through her as she took in the masculine beauty of him. And then he was reclining beside her, reaching for her again, making her feel deliciously warm and sexy and wanted. She leaned over to kiss him and found herself spun on her back, his weight on top of her, his hands in her hair, his mouth on hers. She slid her palms over his shoulders, feeling the strength in them beneath the smooth warm skin. He felt so good, all of him, against all of her. This felt so right. Susan knew only that she never wanted to let him go, she never wanted this to end.

And for a very long while, it didn't. For a long time there was only passion she had never even dreamed existed.

Afterward, lying wrapped in each other's arms, Jake stroked his hands through her hair. "I feel I should apologize for rushing you into bed, and yet it feels like it's been years in coming," he murmured against her skin.

"I know what you mean," Susan said, tracing loving, lacy patterns on his chest with her fingertip. "This wasn't how I expected to be spending tonight, either," she teased.

Jake grinned down at her. "But you hoped?"

"Yes," she said softly, secure enough to be totally honest with him. "Somewhere deep inside of me, I hoped."

"In case I didn't tell you, having you come into my life is the best thing that's ever happened to me," Jake murmured hoarsely, "trial or no trial."

*I love you, too, Jake,* Susan thought. Aware it was a little soon for them to be saying all that, though, she touched his face.

"I've never felt closer to anyone than I do to you right now," he said.

Susan only wished there were no secrets between them, but she knew that wasn't quite true. *I've got to tell him about my father,* she thought, as she struggled with her guilt and her lingering inability to trust her own judgment about the people closest to her. *In fact, I should probably tell him now, tonight.* But, wanting to savor their closeness, she smiled at Jake. "You must be hungry," she said, slipping into a robe.

"I'm starved," Jake admitted as he got up and put on his pants.

Together they headed out to the kitchen. Susan turned on the oven. Jake tossed the salad and set the table. While he checked out her selection of CDs, she went back to the bedroom to hunt for her bedroom slippers. She spotted one near the beside table. Figuring the other must have slipped beneath the bed, she got down on the floor, picked up the dust ruffle and looked beneath. Her heart stopped at what she saw. Next to her slipper was a long-bladed hunting knife, crusted with what appeared to be dried blood. Susan froze, her heart pounding, all her thoughts in disarray. It was like the nightmare of her past, coming back to haunt her.

Footsteps sounded behind her. Jake paused in the bedroom doorway. "What are you doing down there?" he asked with a frown.

Pulse pounding, Susan withdrew her slipper, left the knife and replaced the dust ruffle. Feeling the blood rushing to her face, she held up the slipper for Jake to see. "I just needed this," she said with forced casualness. *There's no need to panic. Jake doesn't know I discovered anything.* "It, uh, got kicked under the dust ruffle."

"Oh." He seemed both wary and relieved. Still watching her intently, he said just as casually, "I opened a couple of beers for us and put some music on. Are you coming back out soon?"

Susan forced her hands to stop shaking. "Yeah, in a minute. I think I just want to put some jeans and a sweater on." She needed time to think. To absorb what she had just found.

"Okay."

Jake's glance dropped to her throat, lingered for a second on the pulse that was pounding out of control. His eyes returned to hers. They were a dark, unreadable gray.

"I'll wait out there for you," he said slowly.

Susan nodded. As soon as he was gone, she grabbed her clothes and slipped into the bathroom. A glance in the mirror confirmed her worst fears. Her face was chalky white, her eyes wide with suppressed terror. Her hands were trembling so she could barely get dressed. Just because there was a knife under her bed did not mean Jake had put it there, she argued sternly. But even as she fervently denied his guilt, she was remembering his anger, the attack in the hallway outside her office... when her coat and her shoulder bag had been slashed to ribbons with a big brutal-looking knife.

He had shown up long minutes later, sweating and out of breath. He had tried to dissuade her from going to the crime scene at the Shady Villa Motel, but she had insisted anyway. As she'd left the room, she had been shot at.

Jake and his father were both expert riflemen, able to hit within a half inch of their target at fifty feet.

Yes, Jake had confided in her—but only when she'd been close to discovering the truth and he'd needed her to keep silent.

But now the trial was over. He had been acquitted. No one knew about the baby, except Susan and his father.

Was it possible, she wondered shakily, that she had misjudged Jake? How had the knife gotten there?

Without warning, her mind flashed back to the night her condominium had been broken into. She remembered how Jake had offered to help her clean up. She recalled his kneeling next to her bed, ostensibly looking for something, but coming up empty-handed when she walked in. She recalled the many searches of his home, vehicle and the murder site by the sheriff's department.

Could he have hidden the weapon the night of the murder, before he called police, then moved it to her apartment, figuring that no one would ever think to search her place? Had the gunshots that night as they'd left the motel been a cover? Had he instructed her to stay down and gone over into the woods or back into the motel room to retrieve the weapon from some secret place, while Susan and the police deputy had been distracted by the arrival of Tom Peterson and even more police?

Susan froze as the next thought hit. Had he wanted to come back to her place tonight to retrieve the knife?

"Susan?" Jake rapped on the door. "You okay in there?"

"Yes." She turned the water on and reached for the cabinet above the sink. "I'm just washing my face and cleaning up a little. I'll be right out."

"You sure you're okay?" he persisted. "You're not sick or anything."

Susan splashed cold water on her face with one hand, and reached for the jar of Noxema skin cream with the other. She lifted it off the shelf, then caught sight of another bottle . . . a prescription bottle on the top shelf, stuck behind some aspirin, and felt her fingers go nerveless. The navy blue plastic jar bounced as it hit the counter, then rolled off and landed on the bath rug with a muted thud.

"Susan?" Jake said.

She moved the aspirin bottle aside and stared straight ahead, her eyes glued to the brown prescription bottle that had "Angelica Saint-Claire. Take one tablet every night before bed" printed on the white label.

The other piece of evidence was hidden in her medicine cabinet! Susan began to shake. Had she just made love with a murderer?

"Susan!" Jake said again, his voice low and fierce. *"Are you all right?"*

She knew she had to answer. "I'm fine," she said in a loud clear voice. She grabbed a tissue from the decorative holder and wrapped it around the missing evidence. Being careful not to touch it, she fitted the bottle in the pocket of her jeans and tugged her sweatshirt down to cover the bulge. Carefully she replaced the aspirin bottle.

"I just think I saw a baby chameleon," Susan lied. She opened the door, faced Jake and delivered the first of what she knew were going to be many bold-faced lies. "It startled me so much I dropped the Noxema."

"Where was it?" Jake asked, regarding her suspiciously.

"Right along the underside of the medicine cabinet. You know how they change color," Susan chattered on nervously. "Going from gray to beige to green to brown . . . depending on their environment . . . well, it was a silvery color, just like the mirror, only it moved, and well, it startled me."

Jake bent to pick up her Noxema. He looked beneath the commode, around the tub, his expression both suspicious and perplexed. "Where did it go?"

"I don't know," Susan said. She shivered uncontrollably.

Jake moved past her and opened the medicine cabinet. His eyes tracked the empty place on the shelf behind the aspirin, where the pill bottle had been. Susan watched with dismay as his frown deepened. Oh, God, he knew the pill bottle had been there and now it was missing. She backed out of the bathroom. She had to find a way to get that knife.

Inspired, she let out a little scream. Jake whirled around, his expression startled. Susan pointed down the hall. She didn't have to pretend to be excited and upset. "Oh, God, the lizard went that way, Jake!" she cried. "He's about this long." She spread her fingers four inches apart, then, unable to suppress a shudder, she hugged her arms close to her chest.

Jake gave her another weird look. "Is this a common problem?" he asked casually, as he ever so gently shut the medicine-cabinet door, picked up a water glass and glanced down the hall.

"It only happens about once every year or so. I think they slip in from the patio." Susan grabbed her shoes and sat down to put them on. He mustn't suspect a thing. "What are you doing with that glass?"

"I have to have something to put the lizard in when I catch him." His tall frame braced for action, Jake headed off toward the hall. "Don't worry," he said over his shoulder. "If there's a lizard in here, even a baby one, I'll find him."

As soon as he'd turned the corner, Susan grabbed a dry wash-cloth and towel from the bathroom rack. Perspiration dripped down her forehead as she got down on her hands and knees and grabbed the knife with the cloth. Carefully she pulled it from beneath the bed and stuck it inside a thick towel so it wasn't visible. Then she stood and screamed again, as if she had just stumbled across another lizard.

Jake came running. He appeared not to even notice the red flush in her face as she pointed to the master bedroom closet. "There's a whole nest of baby lizards in there. There must be, because I just saw three more." Susan added another short scream for effect.

"Calm down," Jake said impatiently. "Lizards don't bite."

Towel clutched firmly in her arms, Susan let Jake slip past. "I know, but I hate them just the same," she said, as she danced around nervously behind him.

Jake switched on the overhead light. He cast her a brief, exasperated look over his shoulder. "If it makes you feel any better, they're probably just as scared," he reassured her wryly, as he searched high and low for the lizards.

"I'll go out to the garage and get the broom!" she volunteered. She yelled over her shoulder, already breaking into a run, "Don't let any of them get away!"

She grabbed her keys off the counter and slipped into the garage. Seconds later, she had started the car, backed out of the garage and was headed for the police station.

## Chapter Sixteen

Susan sat in front of the police station, the towel-wrapped murder weapon in her lap, the pills in her pocket. Safety was mere feet away. All she had to do was get out of her car and walk in. Then it would be out of her hands. She would have upheld the law.

Jake wasn't going to go to jail for Angelica's murder, no matter what. He had been acquitted. The law did not permit him to be tried twice for the same crime.

She, on the other hand, could still be arrested for obstructing justice. She might still be in danger. So what was stopping her from getting out of her car and going into the station house? The fact that she was in love with him? Or the fact that despite everything, she still believed in his innocence?

JAKE DRESSED SLOWLY, not sure what had gone wrong, knowing only that he'd severely misjudged a woman again. He shoved his hands through his hair. He didn't know where she had run off to, but considering the crazy way she was behaving, maybe it was just as well. He was pretty sure there'd been no lizards in her condo. The only chameleon there was Susan....

He was getting ready to leave her condo, when she walked back in the door. She looked paler than ever. She was carrying a folded bath towel in her hands. He stared at her. After she'd left, he'd called himself every name in the book for allowing this to happen tonight, when they were both particularly vulnerable. Now that she was back, he felt even more ridiculously naive.

Swallowing hard, she walked over to the table, put the towel down. She took a deep breath. "I'm glad you're still here," she said in a voice that shook almost as badly as her hands.

Jake regarded her silently. He could see she was very upset.

Her gaze was unwavering as she faced him and said, "I have something to show you." Wordlessly she unwrapped the towel, then the washcloth.

Jake didn't want to stay and watch whatever the hell it was she was doing, but curiosity made him look. And once he had, he couldn't help but stare down at a blood-encrusted hunting knife with a two-inch blade. Was this the murder weapon that had killed Angelica? he wondered. He swore softly, then lifted his gaze to her face.

Still pale, but her expression determined, Susan reached into her pocket. With a hand that shook, she drew out what looked like a wad of tissue. Carefully she unwrapped it and exposed the pill bottle with Angelica's name on it.

Susan had the rest of the evidence!

"Where did you get these?" Jake asked, stunned.

She took a long deep breath. Putting a hand on the table to steady herself, she related, "The knife was under my bed. The pills were in my medicine cabinet, behind a bottle of aspirin."

Suddenly everything made sense to Jake. Understanding flowed through him. "That's why you ran. Why you were acting so crazy."

Susan nodded. She looked at him persuasively. "I panicked. When I thought about it, I realized you had been framed once. Why not again? It's obvious someone wants you out of the way, and now—maybe me, too."

"Correct again, Susan," a low male voice said.

Susan and Jake whirled as a heavyset man with black poufy Elvis hair and opaque aviator sunglasses slipped inside the condo. He was wearing surgical gloves and had a black revolver with a silencer pointed at them. But it wasn't Otis Kingsley, Susan noted as she stared at the intruder.

"Hands above your head, both of you," he ordered.

Recognizing his madness, Susan and Jake complied.

"Now, down on your knees, Lockhart!" he demanded. He pulled back the hammer and pointed the gun at Susan. Looking both distracted and frantic, he shouted, "Do it or I'll shoot her first!"

Jake wasn't worried about himself as much as he was concerned about Susan. Figuring it would buy him time to figure out some way to disarm their accoster before he could get off even one shot, Jake got down on his knees next to Susan, his hands clasped behind his head.

The person impersonating Otis pointed to the bottle of pills. "Open it and shake the tablets out on the table. Do it!" he instructed nervously, still waving the gun, as if he couldn't decide who to point it at. "Now!"

Afraid he would shoot Jake if she didn't do as ordered, Susan slowly worked off the lid. She shook the pills out on the table. She swore silently to herself as she counted seven tablets, and knew there was enough for two lethal doses. "You can't mean to kill us both," she said softly.

He shrugged and took a step nearer. "It didn't have to be this way, Susan. All you had to do was turn that evidence in to the police."

"You saw me drive to the station?" A shudder went through her.

The intruder's mouth curled with satisfaction. "I followed you there," he admitted smugly.

Fury erupted inside Susan as she thought about how naively she had walked into the impostor's trap. If she had listened to her heart about Jake, she never would have been duped. "What if I hadn't looked under the bed?" she asked with a coolness she was far from feeling.

He backed up slightly. Gun still pointed their way, he reached behind him and turned the dead bolt. "Wouldn't have mattered. Your toothbrush was in the medicine cabinet, on the shelf below the pills."

"And if I still hadn't seen?" Susan asked, keeping up the rapid flow of questions. The more he bragged, the longer she and Jake would have to devise escape plans. She knew from the fact he'd hardly spoken that Jake was planning something.

"Then I would have called you from a pay phone and tipped you off," he said, strolling back.

"Just the way you tipped off the police from a pay phone the night Angelica was murdered," Susan said.

He smiled. "Some things you don't want to leave to chance. And it worked, too. Until you came onto the case."

"But why plant the evidence here now?" Susan asked, slowly dropping her hands to shoulder height. If she could just grab the knife... which was on the table....

"You left me no choice. With your convincing closing arguments and speech on the courthouse steps after the verdict, you had the press and the police looking for Angelica's murderer again. So I had to do something to shift suspicion back to Jake, and maybe you, too."

"Because if you didn't get them thinking Jake killed Angelica again, you were afraid they would discover you were the one who killed her?" Susan said grimly.

"I always knew you were smart." The murderer waved the gun at them again, looking as if he were in the grip of a dangerous anxiety. "Put your hands behind your head, Susan. Clasp them tightly."

Doing her best to hide her tenseness, she complied, inching a little closer to Jake as she did so. "The question is why?"

The man with the gun smiled, his fury and madness evident as he spoke in that strange hoarse voice. "The lying bitch deserved to die."

Another chill darted down Susan's back. She wished she could see Jake's eyes so she could know what he was planning, but she didn't dare stop looking at the madman, who seemed to be slipping over some invisible precipice.

"Let me guess," Jake said sarcastically, beginning to have an idea who was hiding beneath the disguise. "Angelica did a number on you, too." He faced their accoster, wishing the man weren't beyond reason. But if it was who he thought it was, the guy had to be absolutely insane. And yet, clever enough to have concocted an alibi for himself that appeared to have held up.

"Yeah, she did a number on me, just the way she did with you," the killer concurred. His face was flushed and he was breathing heavily. "Angelica used to laugh about it, you know, when we were in the sack. She'd tell me how easy it was with noble men like you, or self-serving men like Vince and Chip, to give them what they wanted, just by doing a little acting. In your case, it was a loving angel and potential wife. In Vince's case, it was a fellow actor struggling to carve out a career in a heartless town. With Chip, it was the Pygmalion thing. He molded her into a star, and in return she made him millions."

"So where did you fit into all of this?" Susan asked.

"And when did your relationship with her turn intimate?" Jake added.

The man smiled proudly. "Angelica came on to me from the very first," he boasted, switching on an eerily sentimental grin. "She knew from the first moment we saw each other that I found life here in Austin boring as hell. I knew she wanted to build another kind of life for herself as much as I did." He waved his gun dramatically and he moved a little closer to the table and the knife. Sweat broke out on his brow and dripped down his forehead.

"Unfortunately, I had few options then financially, too, as I was already married at the time."

"My God!" Susan gasped, suddenly putting it all together. She stared at the murderer in shock. "Walter?"

He whipped off his sunglasses. "That's right," Walter said softly. He patted his padded belly. "Pretty good disguise, wouldn't you say?"

And then some, Susan thought, as she considered going for the knife first, then decided it was too risky. Jake was still in the line of fire, and on his knees. Walter might panic. She would just have to try to stall, talk him down, convince him to give himself up. "Why didn't you just get a divorce if you were in love with Angelica?" she asked gently, feeling suddenly detached now that she knew who the killer was.

"Because I needed a job and the entrée into society my wife's family provided." Walter picked up the knife with his left hand. "I also thought that by marrying the boss's daughter I would be a senior partner in no time."

"Instead you've remained an associate, while others have been promoted ahead of you," Jake said.

"Right. I don't know what I would have done without Angelica." Walter sighed. "She was the one bright spot in a very dull world."

"You said you slept with her," Susan noted.

"When did that start?" Jake asked gruffly, watching with Susan as Walter slid the knife in his belt.

"After she moved to California. Why? Are you jealous?" Walter taunted. Jake didn't reply and he continued smugly, "Well, you should have been. She came to me a couple of weeks after you two broke up. She was pregnant and she needed money to pay for an abortion. But I convinced her I had a better plan. I knew a couple who wanted a healthy newborn baby desperately. I knew they would be willing to pay big bucks. All she had to do was let them put her up in a posh apartment in Dallas, while she waited to deliver the baby, collect the money and then head on out to L.A. I would take care of everything else, and I did. We got fifty thousand bucks for the kid, over and above the actual costs, and we split the profits down the middle."

Jake looked sick. "I ought to rip your throat out for that," he said.

"Unfortunately, you won't have the chance," Walter taunted snidely.

"I still don't understand why you killed her," Susan said. She was determined to keep him talking as long as she could.

"Because of the way she turned on me. We were supposed to have a life together once she made it big. When that happened, I was going to divorce Bitsy and move out to California with her. She was going to set me up in private practice out there, just the way I helped her all those years when she was trying to make it."

"How did you help her, Walter?" Susan asked.

"I let her borrow money from me and I gave her free legal advice on her contracts. Whenever she needed me, I went out there. And whatever she needed when I got there, I saw that she had. I bought her clothes for her biggest auditions. I paid for her visits to the posh spas. I even bought her a car at one point."

"Did Vince and Chip know about you?"

"No. It was our delicious little secret. Every time we were together it was like a honeymoon. And it stayed that way, until she hit it big."

Susan felt sick just thinking about what he had done. Unbidden, the crime-scene photos flashed in her mind. "And then what happened?"

"She didn't need me anymore, so she turned her back on me. Told me not to call her, not to try to see her. It was over. Just like that." Tears glistened in his eyes.

"So what did you do?" Jake asked.

Walter's voice turned petulant. "I suggested she pay back all the money she owed me, right then. She laughed. I brought up her child. She turned pale. And paid. Not once, but twice."

"You must've felt some satisfaction about that," Susan murmured.

Walter shook his head, obviously distressed. "I tried to hurt her the way she had me, but she was tough. So I demanded a third payment. That's when she came to Texas. And saw you and told you she was being blackmailed."

"Only I refused to pay until she revealed to me who was blackmailing her," Jake said, surreptitiously nudging Susan slightly to the left, toward the table, with his elbow.

*He wants me out of the line of fire,* Susan thought. *He's getting ready to make his move.*

"Instead," Jake continued, recounting his story grimly, "Angelica quarreled with me for two days. Finally, I walked out on her. Hours later, she sent a note over to my office that was delivered in a bouquet of flowers, asking me to meet her at the motel later that night." Jake nudged Susan again, and she moved until her hip rested against the edge of the table.

"And in the meantime, she called and asked me to meet you both at the motel," Walter said. Still waving the gun, he took another step closer. "I had a feeling what was coming, and it wasn't good. So, knowing how Angelica liked to set the stage whenever she prepared for any emotional or domestic drama, I arrived a good hour before you."

Walter's eyes grew dreamy. "She was just getting out of the bath when I arrived. The whole place smelled like perfume. A pitcher of margaritas was on the bed stand. She opened the door wearing just a towel. Bubbles were still clinging to her skin. She wasn't happy to see me, but she didn't let it rattle her, either. She let me in, and told me after I shut the door that you would be there at any minute. Well, I knew that wasn't true," Walter said smugly. "She didn't have her face on yet, and Angelica never did anything without first spending at least an hour applying her makeup and fixing her hair.

"I could tell that she was planning to seduce you—and that ticked me off even more. But mindful of the stakes, I played it cool while she sat down in front of the mirror and began to carefully apply her makeup.

"I told her it wasn't too late, that we could still go back to the way things had been. She said no. She was through sleeping with men to get where she wanted and what she wanted. She was on top now. She would sleep with whomever she chose, and right then, she said, she chose Jake.

"I told her she was making a mistake," Walter said matter-of-factly, madness gleaming in his eyes.

"She turned around and she looked at me, and said I was the one who was making the mistake. That soon Jake would know I was the one who had been blackmailing her. And she said that you had no qualms about blowing the whistle on me if I made it necessary. On the other hand, if I cooperated and kept silent about the child being sold for profit, then the two of you would keep quiet, too. It was my choice. But either way, no more money was going to change hands. And absolutely no damage was going to be done to *her* career.

"I knew she meant it, and that she would do whatever she could to prevent the news about her selling her own child from coming out. But Jake here—he was another matter." Walter's composure was slipping, like a mask coming loose. "He had a reputation for integrity and honesty. He might do what he could to protect his son for a while, but then his conscience would start getting to him. He would start wondering if my operation was still going on, and it was, and he would think about his responsibility as attorney general for the state of Texas. He would shut me down, even if it meant bringing immeasurable grief to himself. So I had no choice. I had to get rid of both Jake and Angelica," Walter said, as if his plan made perfect sense.

"And that's when you decided to kill Angelica," Susan said, as her stomach did a slow, sickening lurch.

Walter nodded.

"After all, the bitch in all her cunning had provided me with the perfect setting. And I knew that with their history Jake would make the perfect scapegoat. Figuring it was going to come to that inevitably anyway, I had brought a hunting knife with me—it was in a sheath strapped to my waist."

*Just like now,* Susan thought, as her knees began to tremble.

Susan was within reach of the flower vase on the table, far enough away from Walter that he couldn't hit them both without turning and taking aim twice. But was it enough time for them to survive? "And Angelica didn't suspect how furious you were?" she asked.

"Of course not. After all, she had manipulated me for the past fifteen years. She had no reason to think she couldn't do it again, especially since I pretended to be thoroughly intimidated by the thought of having to deal with Jake. I told her that maybe I had been wrong and there was some way the three of us could make a deal. I let her see my hands shake and I told her I needed a drink. She laughed at me and told me to help myself. Then she went back to applying her makeup with those slow, careful strokes. When her back was turned, I lifted the sleeping pills from her purse."

Susan had seen Angelica apply makeup in the video. She did indeed give the process her full artistic attention. It would have been easy enough for Walter to put his plan into action without her even noticing.

Walter smiled as he reminisced, the depth of his madness becoming more evident with every second that passed. "While I poured a margarita for myself, I poured one for her, and I slipped three glutethimide tablets in it when she wasn't looking. She was so sure of herself—of her power over men—it never occurred to her that I had drugged her with her own medication. By the time she figured out something was wrong, she was too woozy to do anything about it. She passed out about five minutes later, before she could even get to the phone.

"Then it was easy enough," Walter continued with a depth of emotional satisfaction Susan found chilling. "I carried her to the bed, put her in the middle and positioned her body to make it look as though she were waiting for a lover. I finished applying her makeup. Brushed her hair so it swirled out around her. Then I stabbed her in the heart once, withdrew the knife, wiped most, but not all, the blood off and put it back beneath my clothes. Quickly I wiped my fingerprints off of everything I had touched, grabbed the pill bottle and the motel room towel and slipped from the room.

"I got in my car, drove a mile down the road. As soon as I saw Jake drive by I called the police from the pay phone, reported the murder and drove on back to town to change clothes and join Bitsy at the symphony concert."

He grabbed an open bottle of Mexican beer and shoved it at her.

"Pick up three of those pills and put them in your mouth, Susan," Walter ordered. "Now!" he said when she hesitated. "Do it or I'll shoot lover boy here."

Susan knew he was just crazy enough to do it. Pretending cooperation, she picked up three of the white glutethimide tablets. Tears glistened in her eyes.

"You can wash them down with beer. It'll work faster that way," Walter said.

Aware he was watching her, that he was losing patience and the gun was trained on Jake, she put the tablets in her mouth one by one.

"Susan, don't—" Jake said, his voice cracking with the depth of his fear for her.

"You shut up," Walter snapped viciously. He glared at Jake. "You're next."

She lifted the bottle of beer and took a long, slow drink.

"See how easy that was?" Walter said silkily, as Susan wiped her mouth with the back of her hand. "You're going to die an easy, painless death."

Susan tried to stay calm and prayed the pills would dissolve in the beer before Walter figured out she hadn't swallowed them.

"You're next." Walter looked at Jake.

"Before I die, I want to know everything else that happened since that night," he said. "Did you throw the rock that almost hit Susan?" he demanded.

Walter glanced at Susan. "I knew you were the one person who could get Jake off, Susan...."

Feigning dizziness Susan put a hand flat on the table, that much closer to the only weapon she had, the flower vase. "What about the shots that were fired at Jake and me the night we visited the Shady Villa Motel?" she asked.

Walter smugly fixed his gaze on her. "I did that, too. Again, to try to get you to resign from the case."

"When did you plant the knife and the pill bottle in my house?" Susan asked, able to see Jake inching in the opposite direction, toward the wall to his left. She figured he was going to make his move any second now, and when he did, she was going to, also.

"While you were waiting for the jury to come in with a verdict. I had watched the proceedings live on 'Court TV.' I heard your summation. I had a feeling they were going to acquit and start looking for the real murderer. So I headed straight for your home, Susan." Walter chuckled to himself. "I jimmied open a kitchen window, next to the breakfast nook, slipped in when no one was looking and planted the evidence."

"Why didn't you plant it on me earlier, before my case came to trial?" Jake asked, even as Walter picked up the four remaining glutethimide tablets and pushed them at Jake. "With evidence like that against me, the DA might have had a whole different case."

"I wanted to, but the police were keeping such a close watch on you that I was afraid I might be seen planting it. I didn't think I was going to need it, anyway. I was sure they were going to convict. But I underestimated both of you." Walter regarded them sourly. "I won't do it again. Now, get over there and swallow the pills, Lockhart. Do it, or I'll shoot your girlfriend and she *will* die a slow, painful death."

Jake started ever so slowly to get to his feet. The next thing Susan knew Jake was stretched out and diving toward Walter's knees. She grabbed the vase of flowers. Then several things happened all at once. Walter swore and, knocked completely off-balance, went flying headfirst over Jake, the gun folded inward, toward his chest. He did an awkward racing dive into the wall, one he could have recovered from, just as Susan smashed the vase down on his skull; Walter crashed to the floor and the gun went off with a muffled, deadly ping.

When the smoke had cleared, Susan and Jake were standing, only Walter lay inert. Blood streamed from a cut on his head and a bullet wound near his heart. Working quickly but efficiently, Jake removed the gun from Walter's hand, emptied it of bullets. A cautious eye still on him, Jake grabbed for Susan.

She knew the root of his concern and answered it immediately. "I didn't swallow the pills. I spit them back in the bottle, along with the beer."

"Thank God," Jake said, holding her tight.

"THAT'S QUITE A STORY," Samuel said hours later, when Jake and Susan told him what had happened. "I'm relieved you're both all right. And I'm glad you were able to convince the police that the information about Jaime should not be released to the press, even though his parents will have to be notified the adoption was illegal."

"With Walter dead by his own gun, there was no need," Jake replied. "Besides, I think when they look into it, they'll find plenty of confirmation of his affair with Angelica and his other shady dealings."

"And I think they also understand that Jaime needs to be protected," Susan said. "From everything we know, his parents never realized they'd done anything wrong. They thought they were paying only what was legally permissible under the law. It was Walter and Angelica who falsified the records of the adoption expenses, for private gain."

"Well, it's good to know my grandson will be protected, even if I can't acknowledge him as such just yet," he said. "As for the rest of your story—" Samuel, who was in his pajamas and robe, took a good look at Susan as the first light of dawn lit the morning sky "—I think you only left out one little thing," he continued slyly.

"What?" Susan grinned at the teasing note in Jake's father's voice.

He pointed from Jake to Susan. "What's going on between the two of you? Am I wrong, or are there some sparks here?"

Susan blushed.

"Okay, Dad, enough," Jake declared.

"I was right, wasn't I?" Samuel asked.

"I'm going to show Susan to a room upstairs," Jake said.

"Make yourself at home," Samuel said, patting Susan's shoulder fondly.

"I will," she promised.

It was funny, Susan thought, the Lockhart Ranch was the last place she had ever expected to feel like home. And yet, here with

Jake and his dad, she felt as if she had found a sense of family again.

"You okay?" Jake carried her overnight bag into the room she had occupied once before.

Susan nodded. She had so much she wanted to talk to him about she hardly knew where to start. "I didn't get a chance to say it earlier, but I shouldn't have run out on you. I should have trusted you."

"I told you I understood," he said gently.

But would he understand what she had yet to confess? Susan wondered.

"There's something I have to tell you," she said, swallowing hard. "Something I should have told you a long time ago."

# Chapter Seventeen

Jake waited for Susan to go on, feeling wary and unreceptive. He thought his nightmare had ended with his acquittal. The look on Susan's face told him it was only starting again.

"You remember the night we talked about what it felt like to have your life turned upside down by a charge of criminal wrong-doing?" Susan asked cautiously, her face ashen.

Jake frowned. "Are you trying to tell me you've also been arrested?"

She gave a small sigh. "No, but my father was."

Jake's eyes darkened compassionately. So that's all it was. She thought he wouldn't love her if she had something unsavory in her family's past. His body softening with relief, he reached for her. "What happened?" he asked gently, drawing her close, feeling her softness melt against him.

Susan made him sit on the bed beside her. "You recall I told you that my dad rodeoed for a living and worked at ranches in between?" Jake nodded. "The trouble started when he hired on as a hand at a new ranch. Late one night, one of his bosses rousted him out of bed and told him to move the prize bull to another ranch for a few weeks. It wasn't his job to ask questions. The next day, the bull was reported stolen to the police. The same person who'd told him to move the animal pointed the finger at him as the thief and denied giving him any orders."

This story was starting to sound hauntingly familiar. He stared at her, waiting for her to go on.

Her cheeks flushed, Susan did. "My father denied it. He even tried explaining to the ranchers who employed him that he'd only been following orders, but because he hadn't worked at that ranch for very long and had a pretty bad work record, it was widely accepted that he had done it, and he was put in jail anyway. By the time the real thieves were found, my father had spent nearly three months in jail.'' Susan's eyes filled with helpless anger and shame.

She moved away from the bed, shaking her head in silent remorse. ''If my father had just left it at that . . . But he didn't,'' she related sadly, twisting her hands in front of her.

Wordlessly Jake watched her pace back and forth, her arms pressed tightly to her waist.

''Like the hotheaded cowboy that he was, the first thing he did when he got out was track down his boss who had set him up. The two of them ended up having a fistfight.'' Susan came to an abrupt halt and looked at Jake, her eyes filled with abject misery. ''When the other man went for his rifle in the back of his pickup, my father went for his.'' She swallowed, her face flooding with barely contained shame once again. ''He killed him and was convicted for manslaughter.''

Jake pieced together everything Susan had already told him; her story was identical to an incident that had happened on his family's ranch. ''And then your father got sent to prison in Huntsville, where he later died in jail?'' Jake said, his voice intense.

Susan nodded, her need to vindicate herself clear. ''Of a heart attack.''

It was too much of a coincidence to think they were talking about two different situations. Jake stared at her, his heart racing. ''Hap Kilpatrick was your father?'' he asked hoarsely, stunned.

Susan nodded, her expression even more taut.

Unable to sit still a second longer, Jake pushed away from the bed. He paced restlessly, then turned and faced Susan incredulously. ''You know I'm the one who had Hap arrested. I was running the ranch that summer.''

Susan nodded, looking even paler. ''I know.''

''And yet you took my case anyway?'' Jake said, his gaze narrowing. He couldn't believe she had kept this from him. She had lied to him so well.

Susan shrugged and pushed her hands through her hair. ''When you left a message at my office that first time, I thought you had to know who I was. But it didn't make sense that you'd want to hire me as your attorney. So I contented myself with savoring the irony of the situation—you coming to me for help.''

''And as an added bonus, you were able to make a complete fool out of me in the process,'' Jake said sarcastically. ''Not only was I stupid enough to get myself railroaded into a murder charge, but I picked the last person on earth who should possibly represent me, too."

Susan's jaw took on the stubborn tilt he knew so well. The moments drew out between them and the embattled silence continued.

"It wasn't like that, Jake," she insisted finally.

"Then why did you take my case, when you had an obvious conflict of interest here? Revenge? Were you trying to see me put unfairly in the slammer, too? Kind of an eye-for-an-eye thing?"

The denial Jake was expecting never came.

Susan shrugged. "I wish I could tell you in all honesty that the thought never crossed my mind. But it did, in the very beginning," she admitted honestly.

"I see," he said grimly.

"No, you don't." She lifted her hands and looked at him, imploring him to understand. "I couldn't do it, Jake."

"Right," Jake agreed. He was so angry and hurt he couldn't think straight. "Because you couldn't bear the thought of losing a case to Tom Peterson."

She sent him an aggrieved look. "That isn't why I worked to save you," she said flatly.

"No? You forget," Jake said sarcastically, "I know how much your career means to you, Susan. You've shown me more than once that your work is everything to you."

"And it still is," she insisted bluntly. "But as for this being some sort of payback, Jake, revenge isn't in me, and even if it were, I could never have let an innocent man go to jail. It goes against everything I stand for."

"Too bad full disclosure isn't among your treasure trove of talents." Jake braced his hands on his waist and loomed over her. "You realize I could file a complaint with the state bar association over this?"

"Yes. But that isn't what you want, Jake," Susan said firmly.

She thought she knew him, just as he had thought he knew her. Jake turned away from her. "Congratulations, Susan," he said bitterly, hardly able to believe he'd been so thoroughly hoodwinked by a woman. Again. "You're even better than Angelica was," he remarked bitterly.

He thought he saw the first hint of tears glimmering in her eyes. Her voice trembled as it rose.

"Jake, please. Calm down. Give us a chance to work this out. Don't do anything now that you'll regret."

"I have plenty of regrets, lady, the first of which is becoming emotionally involved with you. And to think I actually took you into my bed tonight!" he said roughly, pivoting away from her. He stalked to the window, watched as the rising sun threw a misty pink light across the sky. "I must have a real thing for vipers!"

Susan crossed to his side. She gave him a sharp look that made his heart race.

"You don't mean that," she said stonily.

"Don't I?" Jake regarded her. He had never felt more pained in his life. They faced each other.

"You don't want to hurt me," Susan continued.

Jake shook his head at her. Now she was the one being the fool. "What did you think? That you would just confess everything to me now and I would say okay? That I wouldn't care that you lied about your motives here."

Susan crossed her arms in front of her. "I didn't have to tell you this now," she remarked stubbornly.

"But you would've had to eventually? Because when I asked you to marry me—it all would have come out."

"I've already said that I regret not telling you before," Susan said stiffly, as the tears she had been withholding began to flow.

"Oh, I just bet you do," Jake said.

"You can't leave, not like this," she said emotionally. She would've done anything to spare him this pain, after all he'd been through.

"Can't I?" Jake retorted, very quietly.

Susan could tell he'd stopped listening to her, but she had to try to get through to him anyway. "This isn't what you want. You're not a man who is incapable of forgiveness. I know you, Jake." Susan moved to block his path to the door. "You have a very big heart. We just need to talk this through, not bottle it all up inside," she continued. But already, she could feel the barriers between them going up once more.

Jake refused to meet her gaze. "Wrong again, babe," he said defiantly. He put his hands on her shoulders and moved her aside. "Revenge is in me. I'm just beginning to discover how deep the feeling goes. I was played for a fool by Angelica. Then by Walter." He drew a deep, steadying breath. "Never again."

"IT'S BEEN two weeks now. You're still grumpy as a bear full of buckshot," Samuel told Jake over breakfast.

"Dad. Don't start," Jake said. "I'm not in the mood to hear any of your Texas homilies."

"Too bad, 'cause you need a Sermon on the Mount to shake some sense into you."

Jake glared at his father over the sports page.

"When are you going to get it through that thick skull of yours that you are in love with Susan Kilpatrick?"

"I told you, Dad. She lied to me."

"Yeah, yeah. She didn't tell you about Hap Kilpatrick being her daddy. Well, so what? She probably knew if you knew that you'da fired her on the spot."

"With due cause," Jake commented calmly.

"More likely with no cause. You'da run from her so fast you woulda run smack dab into your past. Which seems to be the case here anyway."

Jake put down his newspaper. "What's that supposed to mean?"

"It means, son, that you had bad luck with Angelica Saint-Claire, just like every other man who ever crossed her path. Susan Kilpatrick, on the other hand, is a lot like you." Samuel lifted his craggy brow for emphasis. "Maybe more than you want to admit."

"I beg to differ with you there, Dad."

Samuel shrugged. "Beg to differ all you like, son. It doesn't change the facts. Susan has dedicated her life to seeing that innocent people do not go to jail. You have dedicated your life to seeing that justice in this state is served. All that do-gooding must give you and Susan something in common.

"Then," Samuel continued affably as he speared a piece of bacon with his fork, "there's the fact that she saved you from going to jail."

"Is this going to be a long Sermon on the Mount?" Jake asked sarcastically, getting up from the table. "'Cause if it is, I need another cup of coffee."

Samuel speared another piece of bacon imperturbably. "You're going to be sorry if you let her go," he warned.

"I have no choice," Jake said tersely.

"You have a choice. Did you think things between your mama and me were always perfect? No, sir, they sure weren't."

This was something Jake had never heard before. He turned to face his father. "I never heard her lie to you."

"No. You didn't," Samuel agreed.

"In fact—" Jake narrowed his gaze "—I can't recall ever seeing you fight."

"That's because we never did it in front of you. We had our squabbles in private. But we had them, Jake. Sometimes your mama was so mad at me she would've like to wring my damn fool neck, and I had times when I was eating fire and spitting smoke, too. But there always came a time when we snuffed out the lamp and closed the range. It's time for you to do the same, Jake."

Jake hated it when his dad reverted to using so many Texasisms. But that was the only way Samuel could back his way into a discussion of emotions. He sighed. "What are you telling me?"

Samuel stood and looked at Jake sternly. "It's time for you to go see that young woman, hat in hand," he said in a tone that was strictly man to man. "Beg her forgiveness. Get down on bended knee. Do whatever you have to, but don't—under any circumstances—let her get away."

SUSAN FINISHED writing the rough draft of her brief and turned off the computer. Her secretary stood in the portal. "You need to go home, Susan."

What was at home? Susan thought. Endless space. Lonely hours. A mindful of memories of Jake and a heart that ached? "I think I'll stay on shortly."

"Well, I've got to get home to my family. Say...do you want to come home and have dinner with us?"

Spending time with someone else's loving family at this point would only remind her of all she might have had with Jake. Susan swallowed around the knot of pain gathering in her throat. "How about a rain check?"

The outer door opened, closed. "I'll see who it is," Maizie said.

Susan heard a murmur of voices. Her secretary returned and popped her head in the door.

"Got time for one more client?"

*Why not?* Susan thought. Maybe it would take her mind off Jake. "Sure." She moved behind her desk. "Send 'em in."

"Okay, then I'm heading on home."

Susan heard another murmur of voices. The outer door opened and shut once again. A long shadow fell over the door. Jake walked in. He had shadows beneath his eyes, which meant that, like her, he wasn't sleeping. The familiar scent of after-shave clinging to his skin sent her already-overloaded senses into high gear.

Telling herself that this was probably just some formality on his part—after two weeks of utter silence it couldn't be anything else—Susan steeled herself against any more hurt. "I thought your case was over," she said quietly.

"You know what they say." Jake gave her a level look filled with hidden meaning. "It ain't over till it's over."

"Don't tell me Tom Peterson's still on the warpath?"

"No. Everything's cool on the legal and political scene. I'm here about something much more important. I'm here about us."

"What about us?" Susan asked hesitantly.

Jake came in and sat on the edge of her desk. "I said a lot of mean things the night you told me you were Hap's daughter."

As Susan recalled that awful night, her hopes for a reconciliation with Jake fell a little. "I remember every single one of them," she said stiffly.

"I guess I didn't mince my words, did I?" Jake asked ruefully.

"No, you didn't." Susan sighed and got up to roam her office restlessly. She tucked her hands in the pockets of her blazer. "But in all fairness, you had every reason to be ticked off at me. I should have leveled with you."

Jake hesitated. He searched her face. "Why didn't you tell me?" he asked softly.

For the first time since he'd entered her office, he looked as if he really wanted to understand her.

Susan shrugged, as her face filled with emotion. "There's a stigma of growing up the child of a convicted criminal. People always look at you a little funny, as though they're wondering if you're a bad seed, too. I struggled against that prejudice from the time I was thirteen, when my dad was first arrested. And my mother didn't help matters, because she constantly lamented the fact to anyone who would listen that she had married the most worthless, reckless jailbird on earth. By the time I went to college and law school, I just wanted to put it behind me. So I did. I haven't talked about it for years."

"But you still think about it," Jake said.

Susan nodded seriously. "Every time I defend a client. That's why I became a defense lawyer. I don't want to see what happened to my father—the guilty-until-proven-innocent routine—happen to anyone else. Ever."

"If it'll make you feel better, your father's arrest and the gun-fight that followed later had a profound effect on my life, too." He shook his head, his regret obvious. "I never should have taken the crew boss's word that your father had acted alone and on his own initiative. I should have done my own thorough investigation, but I didn't, and that has haunted me to this day."

Susan accepted his apology, because she knew it was genuine. She nodded brusquely. "I'm glad you came by," she said politely, feeling as though she were going to burst into tears if she didn't get rid of him. She circled back toward her desk. "But if that's all, I have to get back to work."

It was killing her to be this close to him and not be able to touch him. One look at his face told her he was feeling the same pain.

"It's not all," Jake said huskily, cutting her off at the pass. He clasped her shoulders and held her in front of him firmly. "I'm here because I love you," he said hoarsely. "I have for a long time now, and I always will." Giving her no chance to respond, he rushed on. "I want what my parents had—a relationship that will last the test of time. And the best way to ensure that is for us to make it official."

"Official," Susan murmured, feeling stunned and happy all at once.

"Yeah, official." Jake grinned. He tugged her close, so they were touching everywhere. He tangled his fingers in her hair and tilted her head back beneath his. He was grinning still as he continued, "To put it in legal terms, I think we should enter into a binding contract that not only stipulates the mundane aspects of our daily lives, but also encompasses our hearts and souls."

Susan started to smile as Jake spoke. "If that is the kind of proposal I think it is, I've never heard a more convoluted version of it in my life," she complained wryly.

"I thought you'd appreciate it. After all, the usual 'Will you marry me' has been done to death. Don't you think?"

"I do." Susan paused. Joy filled her soul, until she was so light and buoyant she could almost float. She studied his face. "You mean it, don't you?" she whispered in a voice filled with wonder. "*You really are* asking me to marry you."

"I really am." Jake swept her into his arms and held her close, until they were touching in one long, electricity-filled line. They kissed, until Susan felt all her dreams were finally coming true.

Finally, Jake lifted his head. "I love you, Susan. For now and forever, and that will never change. And if you agree to be my wife, as I hope you will, I swear I'll be the best husband you could ever want. Although—'' he grinned mischievously and finished in a lazy Texas drawl, as he traced the curve of her mouth with the soft pad of his thumb ''—like any bronc,'' he warned, ''I probably will need some breaking in.''

''Breaking you in will be my pleasure,'' she said with a laugh.

''Is that a yes?''

''That's a yes, Counselor.'' Susan touched her mouth to Jake's. They kissed lingeringly. When she was tingling all over, she drew back slightly. ''But before we go any further, I want to fine-tune our agreement, seeing as it's going to be legal and binding. About babies . . .'' she began cautiously.

Jake grinned. He looked as though he had just won the lottery. ''As many as you want.''

''Well, one to start.''

''Agreed.''

''I keep my job.''

Jake nodded. ''I wouldn't have it any other way.''

''And you keep yours.''

''Absolutely,'' he concurred.

Susan couldn't stop smiling. ''I even promise to campaign for you.''

''Then I certainly ought to win,'' he murmured, pressing a kiss on her brow. ''Anything else?''

Susan trembled with a mixture of pleasure and anticipation. ''Just one more thing.''

''Fire away.''

Susan wreathed her arms about his neck. ''Just for the record, Jake Lockhart—''

''Yes?''

Susan smiled at him and said softly, ''I love you, too, with all my heart and soul.''

## COMING NEXT MONTH

**#301 FLIGHT OF THE RAVEN by Rebecca York**
*Peregrine Connection #2*
Julie McLean was a rank amateur on the trail of the Raven, the most notorious spy in the Western world. Was he Aleksei Rozonov, the smooth Russian whose kisses made her as hot as Madrid in summer...
and made her forget she was a woman on a mission?

**#302 I'LL BE HOME FOR CHRISTMAS by Dawn Stewardson**
When Ali Weyden's dead husband called, it was to say he had their son and was holding him for ransom. Ali had no place to turn—except to crime writer Logan Reed. She knew he could handle the situation, but she hadn't expected him to offer her tender loving care....

**#303 THE KID WHO STOLE CHRISTMAS by Linda Stevens**
To Shannon O'Shaughnessy, little Joey, heir to the Lyon Department Store fortune, was like the son she never had. But then a week before Christmas, he was abducted—and the only suspect was the new store Santa, a sexy but secretive man she hired—and loved...

**#304 BEARING GIFTS by Aimée Thurlo**
There was nothing like attempted murder to chill all Christmas cheer. Relations between softy Mari Sanchez and cynic J. D. Hawken were already icy—until their sudden joint custody of a gutsy, endangered little girl landed the duo in perilously hot water....

## AVAILABLE THIS MONTH:

**#297 EDGE OF ETERNITY**
Jasmine Cresswell

**#298 TALONS OF THE FALCON**
Rebecca York

**#299 PRIVATE EYES**
Madeline St. Claire

**#300 GUILTY AS SIN**
Cathy Gillen Thacker

## HARLEQUIN®

# I N T R I G U E®

Into a world where danger lurks around
every corner, and there's a fine line between trust
and betrayal, comes a tall, dark and handsome
man. Intuition draws you to him...but instinct
keeps you away. Is he really one of those

Don't miss even one of the twelve sexy but secretive
men, coming to you one per month, starting in
January 1995.

**Take a walk on the wild side...with our
"DANGEROUS MEN"!**

If you enjoyed this book by

**JANICE KAISER**

Here's your chance to order more stories by one of
Harlequin's favorite authors:

### *Harlequin Superromance®*

| | | | |
|---|---|---|---|
| #70403 | BODY AND SOUL | $2.95 | ☐ |
| #70494 | THE BIG SECRET | $3.39 | ☐ |

### *Harlequin Temptation®*

| | | | |
|---|---|---|---|
| #25517 | THE MAVERICK | $2.99 | ☐ |
| #25529 | WILDE AT HEART | $2.99 | ☐ |
| #25544 | FLYBOY | $2.99 | ☐ |

(limited quantities available on certain titles)

| | |
|---|---|
| **TOTAL AMOUNT** | $ |
| **POSTAGE & HANDLING** | $ _____ |
| ($1.00 for one book, 50¢ for each additional) | _____ |
| **APPLICABLE TAXES\*** | $ |
| **TOTAL PAYABLE** | $ |
| (check or money order—please do not send cash) | |

To order, complete this form and send it, along with a check or money order for the
total above, payable to Harlequin Books, to: *In the U.S.:* 3010 Walden Avenue,
P.O. Box 9047, Buffalo, NY 14269-9047; *In Canada:* P.O. Box 613, Fort Erie, Ontario,
L2A 5X3.

Name: _____

Address: _____ City: _____

State/Prov.: _____ Zip/Postal Code: _____

\*New York residents remit applicable sales taxes.
 Canadian residents remit applicable GST and provincial taxes.

HCGTBACK1

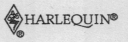 HARLEQUIN®

# HARLEQUIN®

# I N T R I G U E®

*A Decade of Danger & Desire*

**Harlequin Intrigue invites you to celebrate
a decade of danger and desire....**

It's a year of celebration for Harlequin Intrigue, as we
commemorate ten years of bringing you the best in romantic
suspense. Stories in which you can expect the unexpected...
Stories with heart-stopping suspense and heart-stirring
romance... Stories that walk the fine line between danger
and desire...

Throughout the coming months, you can expect some special
surprises by some of your favorite Intrigue authors. Look for
the specially marked "Decade of Danger and Desire" books
for valuable proofs-of-purchase to redeem for a free gift!

### HARLEQUIN INTRIGUE
### Not the same old story!

DDD

# *"HOORAY FOR HOLLYWOOD"* SWEEPSTAKES

## HERE'S HOW THE SWEEPSTAKES WORKS

### OFFICIAL RULES — NO PURCHASE NECESSARY

To enter, complete an Official Entry Form or hand print on a 3" x 5" card the words "HOORAY FOR HOLLYWOOD", your name and address and mail your entry in the pre-addressed envelope (if provided) or to: "Hooray for Hollywood" Sweepstakes, P.O. Box 9076, Buffalo, NY 14269-9076 or "Hooray for Hollywood" Sweepstakes, P.O. Box 637, Fort Erie, Ontario L2A 5X3. Entries must be sent via First Class Mail and be received no later than 12/31/94. No liability is assumed for lost, late or misdirected mail.

Winners will be selected in random drawings to be conducted no later than January 31, 1995 from all eligible entries received.

Grand Prize: A 7-day/6-night trip for 2 to Los Angeles, CA including round trip air transportation from commercial airport nearest winner's residence, accommodations at the Regent Beverly Wilshire Hotel, free rental car, and $1,000 spending money. (Approximate prize value which will vary dependent upon winner's residence: $5,400.00 U.S.); 500 Second Prizes: A pair of "Hollywood Star" sunglasses (prize value: $9.95 U.S. each). Winner selection is under the supervision of D.L. Blair, Inc., an independent judging organization, whose decisions are final. Grand Prize travelers must sign and return a release of liability prior to traveling. Trip must be taken by 2/1/96 and is subject to airline schedules and accommodations availability.

Sweepstakes offer is open to residents of the U.S. (except Puerto Rico) and Canada who are 18 years of age or older, except employees and immediate family members of Harlequin Enterprises, Ltd., its affiliates, subsidiaries, and all agencies, entities or persons connected with the use, marketing or conduct of this sweepstakes. All federal, state, provincial, municipal and local laws apply. Offer void wherever prohibited by law. Taxes and/or duties are the sole responsibility of the winners. Any litigation within the province of Quebec respecting the conduct and awarding of prizes may be submitted to the Regie des loteries et courses du Quebec. All prizes will be awarded; winners will be notified by mail. No substitution of prizes are permitted. Odds of winning are dependent upon the number of eligible entries received.

Potential grand prize winner must sign and return an Affidavit of Eligibility within 30 days of notification. In the event of non-compliance within this time period, prize may be awarded to an alternate winner. Prize notification returned as undeliverable may result in the awarding of prize to an alternate winner. By acceptance of their prize, winners consent to use of their names, photographs, or likenesses for purpose of advertising, trade and promotion on behalf of Harlequin Enterprises, Ltd., without further compensation unless prohibited by law. A Canadian winner must correctly answer an arithmetical skill-testing question in order to be awarded the prize.

For a list of winners (available after 2/28/95), send a separate stamped, self-addressed envelope to: Hooray for Hollywood Sweepstakes 3252 Winners, P.O. Box 4200, Blair, NE 68009.

CBSRLS

| OFFICIAL ENTRY COUPON |

# "Hooray for Hollywood"
## SWEEPSTAKES!

Yes, I'd love to win the Grand Prize — a vacation in Hollywood —
or one of 500 pairs of "sunglasses of the stars"! Please enter me
in the sweepstakes!

This entry must be received by December 31, 1994.
Winners will be notified by January 31, 1995.

Name _____

Address _____ Apt. _____

City _____

State/Prov. _____ Zip/Postal Code _____

Daytime phone number _____
(area code)

Account # _____

Return entries with invoice in envelope provided. Each book
in this shipment has two entry coupons — and the more
coupons you enter, the better your chances of winning!

DIRCBS

allance dripped to her throat, angered by the interruption.
They were alone, and she hadn't time to take back her answer.

"I'll wait out there for you," he said slowly.